√ P9-DGH-505

it must be

Christmas

it must be Christmas

Jennifer Crusie
Donna Alward
Mandy Baxter

St. Martin's Paperbacks

10/10

This is a work of fiction. All of the characters, organizations, and events portrayed in this novel are either products of the author's imagination or are used fictitiously.

"Hot Toy" previously appeared in *Santa, Baby* in 2006.

IT MUST BE CHRISTMAS

"Hot Toy" copyright © 2006 by Argh Ink.
"Christmas at Seashell Cottage" copyright © 2014 by Donna Alward.
"Christmas with the Billionaire Rancher" copyright © 2015 by Mandy Baxter.

All rights reserved.

For information address St. Martin's Press, 175 Fifth Avenue, New York, NY 10010.

ISBN: 978-1-250-10637-7

Our books may be purchased in bulk for promotional, educational, or business use. Please contact your local bookseller or the Macmillan Corporate and Premium Sales Department at 1-800-221-7945, ext. 5442, or by e-mail at MacmillanSpecialMarkets@macmillan.com.

Printed in the United States of America

St. Martin's Paperbacks edition / October 2016

St. Martin's Paperbacks are published by St. Martin's Press, 175 Fifth Avenue, New York, NY 10010.

10 9 8 7 6 5 4 3 2 1

Contents

❄ ❄ ❄

Hot Toy

✻ ✻ ✻

by Jennifer Crusie

Chapter 1

Trudy Maxwell pushed her way through the crowded old toy store, fed up with Christmas shopping, Christmas carols, Christmas in general, and toy stores in particular. Especially this toy store. For the worst one in town, it had an awful lot of people in it. *Probably only on Christmas Eve,* she thought, and stopped a harried-looking teenager wearing an apron and a name tag, accidentally smacking him with her lone shopping bag as she caught his arm. "Oh. Sorry. Listen, I need a Major MacGuffin."

The kid pulled his arm away. "You and everybody else, lady."

"Just tell me where they are," Trudy said, not caring she was being dissed by somebody who probably couldn't drive yet. Anything to get a homicidal doll that spit toxic waste.

"When we had them, they were in the back, row four, to the right. But those things have been gone since before Thanksgiving." The kid shrugged. "You shoulda tried eBay."

"And I would have, if I hadn't just found out I needed

it today," Trudy said with savage cheerfulness. "So, row four, to the right? Thank you."

She threaded her way through the crowd, heading for the back of the store. Above her, Madonna cooed "Santa Baby," the ancient store speakers making the carol to sex and greed sound a little tinny. Whatever had happened to "The Little Drummer Boy"? That had been annoying, too, but in a traditional way, like fruitcake. She'd be happy to hear a "rum-pa-pum-pum" again, anything that didn't make Christmas sound like it was about getting stuff.

Especially since she was desperate to get some stuff.

The crowd thinned out as she got to the back of the store. Halfway down the last section of the fourth row, she found the dusty, splintered wood shelf marked with a card that said: *Major MacGuffin, the Tough One Two.* It was, of course, empty.

"Damn," she said, and turned to look at the shelf next to it, hoping a careless stock boy might have—

Six feet two of broad-shouldered, dark-haired grave disappointment stood there, looking as startled as she was, and her treacherous heart lurched sideways at the sight.

"Uh, merry Christmas, Trudy," Nolan Mitchell said, clearly wishing he were somewhere else.

Yes, this makes my evening, she thought, and turned away.

"Trudy?"

"I don't talk to strangers," Trudy said over her shoulder, and tried to ignore her pounding heart to concentrate on the lack of MacGuffins in front of her. She'd been polite and well behaved with Nolan Mitchell for three dates, and he'd still dumped her, so the hell with him.

"Look, I'm sorry I didn't call—"

"I really don't care," Trudy said, keeping her back to him. "In October, I cared. In November, I decided you were a thoughtless, inconsiderate loser. And in December, I forgot all about you."

Madonna sang, "Been an awful good girl," and Trudy thought, *Like I had a choice.* The least he could have done was seduce her before he abandoned her.

"It's not like I seduced and abandoned you," he said, and when she turned and glared at him, he added, "Okay, wrong thing to say. I really am sorry I didn't call. Work got crazy—"

"You're a literature professor," Trudy said. "*Chinese* literature. How can that get craz—" She shook her head. "Never mind. You didn't like me, you didn't call, I don't care." She turned back to the shelf, concentrating on not concentrating on Nolan. So it was empty. That didn't necessarily mean there were no MacGuffins. Maybe—

"Okay, I'm the rat here," Nolan said, with the gravelly good humor in his voice that had made her weaken and agree to go out the fourth time he'd asked her even though he was a lit professor, even though she'd known better.

The silence stretched out and he added, "It was rude and inconsiderate of me."

She thought, *So he has a nice voice, so he's sorry, big deal,* and tried hard to ignore him, and then he said, "Come on. It's Christmas. Peace on earth. Goodwill to men. I'm a man."

You certainly are, her id said.

We've been through this, she told her baser self. *He's no good. We don't like him. He's bad for us.*

"Okay, so you've forgotten I exist. That means we can start over." He came around her and stuck his hand out. "Hi. I'm Nolan Mitchell and I—"

"No," Trudy said, annoyed with herself for wanting

to take his hand. "We can't start over. You were a grave disappointment. Grave disappointments do not get do-overs."

She turned away again and put her mind back on the MacGuffin. Okay, this was the worst toy store in the city, so the inventory control had to be lousy. If somebody had shoved a box to one side . . .

She dropped her shopping bag and began to method-ically take down the faded boxes of toys to the right of the empty MacGuffin shelf. They were ancient but evi-dently not valuable *Star Wars* figures, a blast from her past. There was a little Han Solo in Nolan, she thought. Maybe that was why she'd fallen for him. It wasn't him at all, it was George Lucas and that damn light saber. She put Nolan out of her mind and kept taking down boxes until she reached the last layer. None of them were MacGuffins.

"Trudy, look, I—"

"Go *away*; I have problems."

"You have *Star Wars* problems?"

"No. I have Major MacGuffin problems. If you know where to get one, I will talk to you. Otherwise, leave."

"I can't." Nolan smiled at her sheepishly. "I'm look-ing for a MacGuffin, too."

"I figured you more for the Barbie type." Trudy started to stack the boxes back on the shelf again.

"No, no, I'm a collector." Nolan picked up a box and put it back for her, and she thought about telling him to go away again, but she really didn't want to put all the boxes back by herself. "It's important to get the toys mint in the box." He held up a box with a crumpled corner. "See, this is no good."

"Thank you for sharing." Trudy put another box back. When he continued to help, she decided he could put them back by himself and moved to the dusty boxes to the left of the empty MacGuffin shelf. Action figures from *The Fantastic Four.* The store really did have an inventory problem; those were completely out-of-date. Well, if there wasn't a Mac to the right, there would be one to the left. Life could not be so cruel as to send her a Nolan but not a MacGuffin.

She began to methodically remove every *Fantastic Four* box on the shelf, while Nolan restocked the *Star Wars* figures and tried to make small talk about the MacGuffin, asking her if she'd bought one there before, if she shopped in the store often, if she knew anybody who'd bought one there. She ignored him until she'd pulled out the last box and there was still no Mac-Guffin, and then she took a deep breath. Okay, Plan B. Maybe on the other side of the shelf . . .

"Trudy, I—"

"Unless you have a MacGuffin, I'm not interested."

"Okay," he said. "I understand." He put the last of the *Star Wars* boxes back and smiled at her. "Have a great Christmas and a happy new year, Trudy."

He turned to go and she turned back to the shelf, irrationally depressed that he was going. She *wanted* him to go, that was the *point*—

She heard him say, "Hello, Reese," and then somebody else said, "Hey, I heard you guys talking about the MacGuffins. You found any?" and Trudy looked up to see the kind of guy who looked like he'd say "dude" a lot: early twenty-something, clueless face, muscled shoulders, tousled hair. The only non-surfer thing about him was his shopping bag with a pink confetti-printed box sticking out of the top. Both the box and the guy looked vaguely familiar, but Trudy couldn't place either one.

He grinned at her. "Hey, Miss Maxwell, you're lookin' good."

Trudy looked closer but still didn't recognize him.

"You don't remember me." His grin widened with forgiveness, and he added, "I sure remember you," and Trudy thought, *What a shame he's too young for me. I could seduce him in front of Nolan.*

He stepped closer. "I'm Reese Daniels, your father's research assistant last year. You helped me find that book on the Ming Dynasty your father wanted. You know, in the library."

"Good place to find books," Nolan said, his voice considerably cooler than it had been when he'd talked to her.

"Right. Reese. Got it," Trudy said, placing him now as the guy her father had called the most inept RA of his career.

Reese smiled at her. "I sure have missed your dad since he went to London."

"Oh, we all have," Trudy lied, and stuck out her hand. "Call me Trudy." She looked at Nolan. "You can call me Miss Maxwell," she said to him. "No, wait, you're not going to call me at all. Weren't you leaving?" Reese still held on to her hand, so she took it back.

He nodded to Nolan. "So you and Professor Mitchell found a MacGuffin?"

"Professor Mitchell and I are not together." Trudy picked up her shopping bag and moved around both of them. "And I haven't found a MacGuffin yet. But I will."

Reese followed her around to the next row and the other side of the empty MacGuffin shelf. "Well, I'm not sorry you're not with Professor Mitchell, Trudy," he said when they'd rounded the corner. "I never got the chance to get to know you better. Your dad worked me pretty hard. But the best part about being his RA was always seeing you."

"Thank you." Okay, for some reason this infant was trying to pick her up. Whatever. She had problems, so later for him.

Trudy zeroed in on the boxes that backed up against the MacGuffin shelf. Dolls this time, with big heads and miniskirts and too much eye makeup. Too bad Leroy wasn't a girl; she could have loaded him up with pop-tarts. But no, he had to have a violent, antisocial 'Guffin.

"Men." She put her shopping bag down again and began to take the dolls off the shelf. Over the tops she could see Nolan restocking *Fantastic Four*s. He shook his head at her, probably disgusted she was flirting with an infant like Reese, and she turned away to see the infant looking at her, confused.

"Men?" he said. "Did I say something wrong?"

"What?" Trudy said, stacking doll boxes on the floor. "Oh, not you. My nephew, Leroy. He's five and he wants a Major MacGuffin doll, and of course, I can't find one."

"Yeah, you had to shop early for those," Reese said, sounding sympathetic. "So I guess you haven't seen one here?"

"I would have shopped early if I'd known his father wasn't going to get him one," Trudy said, exasperated. "But since his father told me he was going to, I didn't."

"So what are you doing over here?" Reese frowned, looking at the dolls she was taking down.

"I'm looking for a misplaced MacGuffin. This place is pretty sloppy, and I'm hoping there's one stuck at the back of a shelf someplace because if there isn't, I'm screwed." She took the last box down and faced another empty shelf.

On the other side, Nolan looked serious as he put back the last of the Fantastic Four boxes. He couldn't possibly care that she was talking to Reese. Unless he was one of those guys who didn't want something until somebody else wanted it. He hadn't seemed like that kind of guy.

He'd seemed pretty much perfect: smart, funny, kind, thoughtful . . .

Ignore him, she told herself, and started to put the boxes back. *Okay, suppose I was hiding a toy so I could come back and get it later, maybe when I had more money. I found the last MacGuffin, but I didn't have enough to pay for it, so I needed to hide it. The first thing I'd do is go to another row of shelves so nobody who wanted one would trip over it accidentally.*

Nolan came around the end of the shelf and started to say something and then saw all the doll boxes on the floor. "Great."

Trudy ignored him to smile at Reese and then picked up her bag to go look in a different aisle.

"So no MacGuffin," Reese said. "Really sorry about that."

"Yep," Trudy said, and then stopped when she caught another glimpse of the pink confetti-patterned box sticking out of Reese's shopping bag. "What is that?"

He looked down. "This? It's some nail polish doll my niece wanted."

Nail polish doll? Trudy reached down and pulled the box out of the bag. "Oh, my God," she said, looking closer at the Pepto-Bismol pink box that said: *Twinkletoes!* in silver sparkly paint. "This doll is twenty-five years old!"

"I think it's a reissue," Reese said, sounding confused as he tried to take it back.

"Is the box mint?" Nolan said, and Reese frowned at him and tugged on the box again.

"A reissue." Trudy held on to the box. Her sister would have a heart attack if she knew they were making these again. She brought the box closer to see through the clear plastic. Yep, it was the same pouting blonde bimbo, Princess Twinkletoes, and there at the bottom next to Twinkletoes' fat little feet was the same pink plastic manicure set with three heart-shaped bottles of polish—pink, silver, and purple—that had made Courtney's six-year-old heart beat faster, the Hot Toy of 1981. "Where did you get this?"

Reese yanked the box from her hands and nodded to the next row. "Over there," he said, sliding the box back into his bag. "There are a lot of them."

Trudy rounded the corner to see the Twinkletoes shelf, crammed full of hot pink boxes. Evidently lightning did not strike twice; Twink was clearly not the Hot Toy of 2006. *You get a little age on you and nobody wants you*, Trudy thought. Well, unless you were Barbie. That bitch lasted forever. Trudy picked up a Twinkletoes box.

Reese came to stand beside her. "Your nephew wants a doll?"

"This is the doll my little sister never got," Trudy said. *And she could use some payback this Christmas.*

"How old's your little sister?"

"Thirty-one."

"Oh."

Trudy looked up at the confusion in his voice. "Courtney was supposed to get this the Christmas she was six, but my dad forgot. He told her it fell off Santa's sleigh."

"Uh huh," Reese said, probably trying to picture her academic father talking about Santa.

"That was his line for whenever he forgot the Christmas presents," Trudy said, thinking of Leroy, waiting at home for his MacGuffin. If she didn't find a MacGuffin, would she be reduced to the "fell off the sleigh" line?

Never.

"Did he forget a lot?" Reese said, sympathy in his voice.

"Pretty much every year. You know professors. Absentminded." Trudy shook her head. "Never mind. I'm rambling. My mind's on my sister and my nephew."

"Well, hey, it's Christmas. That's where your mind is supposed to be. Family." Reese smiled at her, gripping his own Twinkletoes box. "Listen, I have to get going, but maybe we can have coffee sometime?"

"Sure." Trudy smiled back at him automatically, her mind on the Twinkletoes. Would a gift that was a couple of decades late distract Courtney from her divorce?

Hell, it couldn't hurt.

Reese walked away, and she looked closer at the Twinkletoes box in her hands. It had a crumpled corner and she remembered what Nolan had said. The box should be mint. She put her shopping bag down and began to take the Twinkletoes boxes off the shelf. Courtney was going to get a perfect Twinkletoes, pink box and all.

Nolan came around the end of the row and sighed when he saw the boxes on the floor.

"Go away." Trudy took down the next pink box.

"Listen, is there anything I can do to make you not so mad?"

"Mad? I'm not mad." Trudy studied the Twinkletoes box. Smudge on the top. She dropped it on Nolan's foot. "Why would I be mad?"

He picked it up. "That's what I asked."

She pulled another Twinkletoes box off the shelf and

shoved it at him. "Okay, here's why I'm mad. I didn't want to go out with you because you were a professor, and I grew up with a professor, and it was no fun because you get forgotten a lot because your dad is thinking about something that happened four millennia ago, so I said no, four times I said no, but you kept at me and I weakened and went out and *I really liked you, you bastard*, and you were smart and you were funny"—she shoved another box at him—"and I thought, gee, maybe this will work out, maybe this is a professor who won't forget, but evidently it was just the thrill of the chase or something because you dropped me"—she threw the next box at him and he caught it, balancing it with the first two—"and I never knew why since you never bothered to tell me; you just fell right off the sleigh—"

"Sleigh?" Nolan said.

". . . so *I'm a little upset with you.*"

Nolan sighed. "Look, you changed."

"Of course I changed," Trudy snapped. "It's been three months. I've grown. I've matured. I'm in a new and better place now. A place without you. Go away." She went back to the Twinkletoes shelf, pulling boxes off at random and dropping them on the floor, appalled to realize that she was close to tears. He did not matter to her; the fact that she'd thought he was darling was immaterial; the fact that she'd told her sister he might be The One was immaterial; the fact that her father had said, *Nolan Mitchell, that's a little out of your league, isn't it?* was . . . Well, her father was a jerk, so that didn't count.

"No, you changed from the library," Nolan was saying. "You were funny in the library. You talked fast and made weird jokes and surprised me. I liked that. And then I took you out and you, well, you kind of went dull on me."

Trudy stopped dropping boxes on the floor. "You took me to a faculty party. If I hadn't gone dull on you, you'd have lost points. You'd have been Nolan who brought that weird-ass librarian to the October gin fling. I was *helping you*."

"Did I ask for help?" Nolan said, exasperated.

"And you took me to dinner at the department head's house. You wanted me weird there?"

"I couldn't get out of that," Nolan said.

"And then the Chinese film festival." Trudy dropped another box to the floor. "I thought I was going to see *Crouching Tiger Two,* but it was some horrible depressing thing about people weeping in dark rooms."

"It was?" Nolan said, confused.

"Not that you'd know, since you *left right after it started*," Trudy snarled, flinging a box at him. "You got a call and walked out of the theater, and I was left with people weeping in Chinese—"

She stopped to stare at the shelf, the next box in her hand, her heart thudding harder than it had when she'd first seen Nolan.

There was a camouflage-colored box at the back.

She dropped the Twinkletoes box and pulled out the camo box and read the label: *Major MacGuffin, the Tough One*! "Oh, my God." Trudy held on to it with both hands, almost shaking.

The box was not mint—the cellophane was torn over the opening, a corner was squashed in with a black *X* marked on it, and there were white scuff marks on the bottom—but the MacGuffin scowled out at her through the plastic, looking like a homicidal Cabbage Patch doll dressed in camouflage, a grenade in one hand and a gun in the other, violent and disgusting and the only thing Leroy wanted for Christmas.

"I do believe in Santa," Trudy said as Nolan came closer.

"That's a Major MacGuffin." He sounded stunned.

"Can you believe it?" Trudy was so amazed she forgot to be mad.

"No," Nolan said. "I can't. I knew you were an amazing woman, but this puts you in a whole new league."

"What?" Trudy said.

"I'll give you two hundred bucks for it," Nolan said.

"*No*." Trudy stepped away from him, holding on to the MacGuffin box.

Nolan smiled at her, radiating sincerity. "I know, your nephew wants a Major MacGuffin, but he doesn't want that one. He wants the Mac Two. The one that spits toxic waste and packs a tac nuke, right?"

Trudy thought of Leroy, waxing rhapsodic about how the 'Guffin spit green stuff when you squeezed him. "Yes."

"What you have there is a MacGuffin One," Nolan said, sounding sympathetic and entirely too reasonable. "Last year's model. No toxic waste."

Trudy looked back at the box. It did look different from the picture Leroy had shown her. "What does this one do?"

"It has a gun. Basically, it shoots the other dolls."

"And the hand grenade?"

"Just a plastic ball. Doesn't do anything." He shrugged, unimpressed.

"Damn." Trudy looked down at the doll's ugly face.

"Two fifty," Nolan said.

Trudy glared at him. "No. This is for my nephew. And I have to go now. Thanks for putting the boxes back."

"Trudy, *wait*," Nolan said, but she picked up a perfect

Twinkletoes box, stepped over the rest of the pink boxes, and headed for the checkout counter, her belief in Santa restored if not her belief in the rest of male humanity.

❄ ❄ ❄

Trudy got in the long line to the register, clutching both the Mac and the Twinkletoes boxes, stepping back as a woman in a red and green bobble hat slid in front of her at the last minute. Then Nolan got in line behind her and said, "Three hundred. It only costs forty-nine fifty new. That's six times—"

Trudy jerked her head up. "*No.* I'll never find another one of these tonight."

Nolan nodded, not arguing. "Okay. Five hundred."

"Are you nuts?" Trudy said.

"No, I told you, I'm a collector." He stepped closer, and she remembered how nice it had been having him step closer on the three lousy dates they'd had.

She stepped away.

Nolan nodded to the Mac. "You are holding a doll that is actually rarer than the Mac Two. They didn't make many Ones."

"It's not rarer from where I'm standing," Trudy said. "I actually *have* this one, and there are no Mac Twos in sight."

"That looks like an original box," Nolan said. "May I?"

"No," Trudy said, holding on to it and the Twinkletoes box, trying to put her shopping bag between them to block him, but he'd already opened the top and was reaching in. "Hey." She elbowed his hand away as he pulled out the instruction sheet. "*Give me that,*" she said,

and he opened it so that she could see the drawing of
the MacGuffin showing how to detach the silencer from
the gun.

"No toxic waste," Nolan said. "It's a Mac One."

He slid the instructions back in the box. "Two thousand," he said, and then Trudy heard somebody say, "I'll
be damned," and turned to see Reese staring at her from
the front of the checkout line.

"You found it," he said.

"Yes." She turned back to Nolan as he closed the box
again. "No. I'm not selling it. This one is Leroy's." She
checked to make sure the MacGuffin was still in the box,
complete with hand grenade and gun, and then her cell
phone rang.

She fumbled the boxes until she could hold both of
them with one arm, looked at the caller ID, clicked the
phone on, and said, "Hello, Courtney."

"Did you get it?" Courtney said, and Trudy pictured
her, sitting on the edge of her Pottery Barn couch, her
thin fingers gripping her Restoration Hardware forties
black dial phone, every auburn Pre-Raphaelite ringlet on
her head wired with tension.

"Sort of." Trudy looked through the plastic window
on the front of the Mac box at the fat little homicidal
doll. "Damn, he's ugly."

"What do you mean, *sort of*? Did you *get him*?"

The line moved and Trudy stepped forward, bumping her shopping bag into the woman in the bobble hat.

"I'm so sorry," she said as the woman turned. "Really sorry."

The woman smiled at her, motherly in a knitted cap
with red and green bobbles, her arms full of teddy bears.
"Isn't it just awful, this Christmas rush? . . ."

Her eyes narrowed as she saw the MacGuffin.

Animals in the bush probably looked like that when they sighted their prey. Trudy clutched the MacGuffin box tighter.

The woman jerked her face up to Trudy's. "Where did you get that?"

"In the back, shoved behind some other boxes." Trudy tried to sound cheerful and open. "Boy, did I get lucky."

The woman's chin went up. "That's not this year's."

"No toxic waste." Trudy nodded. "Well, you can't have everything."

"I'll give you a hundred dollars for it," the woman said, her eyes avid.

Piker. "No, thank you."

"Who are you talking to?" Courtney said, her voice crackling with phone static.

"A lovely woman who just tried to buy the Mac-Guffin from me."

"No!"

"Of course not, but listen, I've got last year's model. The Mac One. I don't think—"

"Evil Nemesis Brandon is getting this year's model. The Mac Two. With extra toxic waste."

Trudy shifted her weight to her other foot. "Okay, this 'Evil Nemesis Brandon' stuff? You have to stop that. Do you want Leroy thrown out of kindergarten for calling names?"

"Evil Nemesis Brandon's mother knows we don't have a Mac," Courtney said. "I saw her today at Stanford Trudeau's Christmas party. She said if we hadn't found one, Brandon would let Leroy borrow his last year's doll."

"Okay, she's a terrible person, but you have to stop calling her kid names."

Trudy shifted the boxes, trying not to drop either one, and the eyes of the woman in front of her followed the

Mac box. A man with a cap with earflaps, standing in front of the woman in front of Trudy, looked back idly and then froze and said, "Is that a Major MacGuffin?"

"Last year's model," Trudy said to him, and shifted the boxes again. *It's like being on the veldt. Gazelle vs. lions.*

The woman in front of her stepped closer, and Trudy backed up and bumped into Nolan.

Lots of lions.

"Do you have any idea *how humiliating that was*?" Courtney was saying. "Do you have any idea—"

"Well, that's what you get for going to a cocktail party while I'm busting my butt searching for a nonexistent war toy." The line moved up and Trudy followed, praying she wouldn't drop the Mac box. There'd be a bloodbath if she did. "I'm all for you getting out and playing well with others, but it's Christmas Eve and you should be home with your family, baking something, not looking for your second husband. I'm sure Stanford Trudeau is a lovely man with an excellent retirement portfolio, but—"

"I'm baking gingerbread men *and* a gingerbread house right now, and Stanford Trudeau is five. It was Leroy's playgroup's Christmas party. And that woman *mocked* me."

Trudy took a deep breath and reminded herself that Courtney had troubles. "Okay, so now you can tell her he has his own last year's doll. I'm getting ready to buy it right now."

"Last year's is not good enough!" Courtney said, her voice rising.

"Oh, get a grip. This one is a collector's item. It has a hand grenade."

"And a gun," Nolan said from too close behind her, obviously listening in.

"And a gun," Trudy told Courtney as she ignored Nolan.

"Who said that?" Courtney said. "Who's with you?"

"Nolan."

"Nolan." Courtney sounded confused and then she said, "*Nolan Mitchell*. The Chinese lit prof with the swivel hips you thought was going to be The One?"

"Yes," Trudy said, cursing her sister's excellent memory.

"Whoa," Courtney said. "He's the only guy you ever wore sensible shoes for."

"I just ran into him," Trudy said repressively. "It was an accident. It will not happen again."

"It could happen again," Nolan said.

"I don't believe in The One anymore," Trudy told Courtney, ignoring him. "But he is right that this Mac has a gun. Very convenient. It can shoot the other dolls."

"That's not funny."

"Well, I don't think so, either." Trudy shifted the boxes again, making the woman in front of her twitch. "This is a really horrible toy, Court."

"I mean it's not funny that it's not this year's. Leroy has been talking about toxic waste for weeks."

"See, that's not a good thing."

"Two hundred," the woman in front of her said.

"No." Trudy shifted the box again. "Listen—"

"Leroy says that Evil Nemesis Brandon—"

"Will you stop calling him that? I don't believe for one moment that Leroy came up with 'Evil Nemesis Brandon' on his own. That was you."

"That was Prescott," Courtney said, loathing in her voice for her AWOL husband. "But Leroy cares. A lot. He . . . Wait a minute. Talk to him."

"Court, no—"

Trudy heard the phone clunk as the line moved up a

couple of feet. She stepped forward, thinking, *At least Courtney will have the Twinkletoes this year.* Courtney had been waiting to polish those toes for twenty-five years.

And now poor little Leroy would probably be waiting another twenty-five years for his toxic waste. She had a vision of herself many years in the future, handing the Mac Two to a sad-eyed thirty-year-old hopeless wreck of a nephew.

"Three hundred," the woman in the cap said.

"No." Trudy heard the phone clank again and then she heard her nephew's voice, bright as ever.

"Aunt Trudy?"

"Hey, bad, bad Leroy," she said, smiling as she pictured his happy little face under his shock of little-boy-blond hair. "Isn't it time you were in bed?"

"Yes. And then Santa will bring me a 'Guffin. Hurry up and come home so you can see."

"You know, Leroy," Trudy said, looking at the box in her arms. "There are several kinds of MacGuffins and they're all good—"

"I want the one with toxic waste," Leroy said clearly. "It's okay. I told Daddy, and he told Santa, and Santa said he'd bring one. And Nanny Babs said Santa never lies."

I'm going to kill that fucking son of a bitch. And then I'm going to kill that fucking nanny. Assuming they ever come back from Cancún. "Well, we'll just have to see, won't we? Now you go to bed—"

"I know, and when I wake up, Daddy will be on vacation, but he loves me, and Santa will be here with my 'Guffin." He breathed heavily into the phone for a moment and then said, "Brandon said there isn't any Santa Claus."

Rot in hell, Evil Nemesis Brandon. "What do you think?"

"I think there is," Leroy said, not sounding too sure. "And I think he's going to bring me a 'Guffin tomorrow."

"Right," Trudy said, holding on to the box tighter.

"With toxic waste," Leroy said.

Oh, just hell. "Merry Christmas Eve, baby. Go to bed."

"Aunt Trudy?"

"Five hundred," the woman in front of her said. "And that's my final offer."

"For the love of God, *no*," Trudy said to her, and then said, "Yes, Leroy?"

"Do you believe in Santa?"

What is this, a movie of the week? "Well . . ."

"Mommy says Evil Nemesis Brandon is wrong."

"Don't call him that, sweetie."

"Is he wrong?" Leroy's voice slowed. "It's okay if there isn't a Santa." His voice said it wasn't okay.

Nolan nudged her gently, and she realized the line had moved again. "Well, Leroy, I don't really know if there's a Santa. I've never seen him."

"Oh."

Trudy swallowed. "But that doesn't mean there isn't one. I've never seen SpongeBob, either."

"SpongeBob?" Nolan said from behind her.

"SpongeBob is real. He's on TV." Leroy sounded relieved. "So is Santa."

"Well, there you go," Trudy said, feeling like a rat.

"That's the best you've got, SpongeBob?" Nolan said.

Trudy turned and snarled, "He loves SpongeBob. Shut up."

"I know there's a SpongeBob," Leroy said, happy again.

"As do we all," Trudy said.

The woman in front of her let her breath out between her teeth, clearly frustrated. "It's the old MacGuffin; it's not worth more than three hundred."

"I'm sure you're right," Trudy said to her. "Leroy? Honey, it's time for you to go to bed."

"And when I wake up, I'll get a 'Guffin," Leroy said. "Good night, Aunt Trudy."

"Good night, baby," Trudy said, and the phone clunked again as he dropped it.

"Your nephew's name is Leroy?" Nolan said.

"It's a nickname," Trudy said, not turning around. "His real name is Prescott Thurston Brown II."

"Oh." He paused. "Good call getting a nickname."

She heard the phone clunk again as Courtney picked it up.

"That little bastard Brandon," Courtney said.

"I think I prefer 'Evil Nemesis,'" Trudy said. "He's just a kid, Courtney."

"His mother is a hag," Courtney said. "After she offered Leroy a hand-me-down MacGuffin, she asked me if I'd found another nanny."

"Bitch," Trudy said, and then smiled when the woman in front of her finally turned away, offended.

"He's counting on that toxic waste." Courtney's voice was still teary, but now she sounded a little slack.

"Court? You haven't been hitting the eggnog, have you?"

"No, the gin. I'm a terrible mother, Tru."

"No, you're not." Trudy shifted the boxes again.

"I can't even get my baby toxic waste for Christmas."

Trudy heard her sob. "Okay, step away from the gin. You're getting sloppy drunk in front of your kid. Do something proactive. Wrap some presents. Ice your gingerbread."

"I'm out of Christmas paper. And I tried to ice those little bastard gingerbread men, but their arms kept breaking off."

"Were you twisting them?"

Above Trudy's head, the ancient speakers blared Madonna singing in baby talk again.

"Sing 'The Little Drummer Boy,' " Trudy said to the speakers. "Anything but 'Santa Baby.' God, Madonna is annoying."

"She's a good mother," Courtney said. "I'm a *terrible mother.*"

"No, you just have terrible taste in husbands and nannies."

"I wasn't the one who picked out the nanny," Courtney said, her voice rising.

"Right." Trudy moved up another step. "Sorry. She came highly recommended." *I'm pretty sure yours is the first husband she ran off with.*

"I wasn't the one who brought home the husband, either," Courtney cried.

"Okay," Trudy said, tempted to fight back on that one.

"I'm being punished, aren't I?" Courtney said. "I stole my sister's boyfriend—"

"Ten years ago," Trudy said. "I'm over it. I was over it before you stole him. You're not being punished. I didn't want him, which I told you at the time. He's a jerk, I have an affinity for jerks—"

"Hey," Nolan said.

"—and you're better off without him."

"But not without the MacGuffin!"

"I'm *working on that.*" Trudy looked around the last toy store in town. *How the hell am I going to get this year's MacGuffin?* "I'll get it, Court."

"And two toxic wastes," Courtney said, gulping.

"Two toxic wastes. Got it." Maybe if she just stuck

the toxic-waste packets in the MacGuffin box, Leroy wouldn't notice the doll didn't actually spit it.

"And wrapping paper," Courtney said, sounding less frantic.

"Right." Trudy grabbed a package of red-and-white paper off the rack that came before the checkout counter and snagged a roll of Scotch tape while she was at it. "Got it. I gotta go. Go do something besides drink."

"*This year's* MacGuffin," Courtney said.

"Your gingerbread is burning," Trudy said, and clicked off the phone.

"Trouble at home?" Nolan said, sounding sympathetic.

"Absolutely not. Everything is *fine*."

He reached past her, nudging her gently with his shoulder as he pulled two bright green foil packages off the counter rack. "You'll need these."

He dropped them on top of the MacGuffin box and she saw the words *Toxic Waste!* emblazoned on them in neon red.

"Thank you," she said, and then the woman in the bobble cap picked up her bags and left, and Trudy dumped everything onto the counter.

The cashier looked at the MacGuffin box with something approaching awe. "Where'd you find this?"

"On a shelf behind some other boxes," Trudy said for what she sincerely hoped was the last time.

"Man, did you ever get lucky," the cashier said, and began to ring it up.

"That's me," Trudy said, trying to forget that Nolan was about to leave her again, that the wrong MacGuffin was in front of her, and that Madonna was still lisping about greed overhead. "Nothing but luck, twenty-four-seven."

"A thousand," Nolan said from behind her when she'd

handed over her credit card and seen the MacGuffin go
in one shopping bag and the Twinkletoes in another.
"Come on; that's a damn good offer."

"No," Trudy said, picked up her bags, and left.

❈   ❈   ❈

Fifteen minutes later, Trudy stood on the street corner,
juggling her three shopping bags and signaling awkwardly for a cab. There was one around the corner that
was stubbornly off duty, and every other one that went by
had people in the backseat. They were probably just circling the block to annoy her. She shifted the bags again,
her feet aching as the cold from the concrete permeated
the thin soles of her boots, trying to think of a way to get
a Mac Two short of breaking into Evil Nemesis Brandon's house and stealing his.

It started to snow.

*If I had some matches, I could strike them all and
bask in the glow,* Trudy thought, and then a cab pulled
up in front of her and Reese opened the door.

"I got a lead on this year's MacGuffins," he said as
he got out to stand in front of her. "Get in and we'll go
get them."

Trudy gaped at him. "You're kidding."

"No. I know this guy."

Trudy frowned at him in disbelief. "You know this
guy. I've been to every toy store in town, but you know
this guy."

"Not a toy store. A warehouse."

"A warehouse. No, thank you." Trudy reached around
him to signal for another cab, which passed her by, its
tires crunching in the snow. She craned her neck to see
around the corner, but the cab that had been there was

gone. The streets were emptying out, stores starting to close. *I am so screwed,* she thought.

"Oh, come on." Reese held the cab door open for her and gestured her in. "This guy called around and found out about this warehouse where they got a shipment in, but the delivery people didn't come back for them. He says there are dozens of them there." Reese smiled at her, surfer cute. "So the warehouse guys are selling them out the back door. We're gonna pay through the nose, but hey, they've got Mac Twos."

Trudy put her hand down and tried to be practical—getting in a cab and going to a warehouse with a virtual stranger would be stupid even if he had been her father's research assistant—but the snow was falling faster, and the bags weren't getting any lighter, and the stores were closing, and Leroy still didn't have a MacGuffin. "My feet hurt."

Reese gestured to the cab again. "Sit."

Trudy sat down sideways on the backseat with her feet on the curb, balancing her three bags on her lap. "A warehouse."

"With a big shipment of Mac Twos." Reese looked down at her, his patience obviously wearing thin. "And I'm betting we're not the only ones who know about it, so we should get a move on."

Trudy put her forehead on her bags. The cab radio was playing some cheerful rap lite that Trudy liked until she heard the singer say, "Santa Baby."

Reese stepped closer, looming over her. "Scoot over so I can get in."

Trudy lifted her head. "For all I know you're a rapist and a murderer."

"Hey." Reese sounded wounded although he looked as clueless as ever.

"It's nothing personal. Ted Bundy was a very attractive man."

"Oh, *come on*. I worked for your dad. You're in a *cab*. You can tell the driver to wait while we go inside."

A Mac Two. It was too good to be true. Much like Reese the surfer boy hitting on an older college librarian was too good to be true. And he had a cab, too. It strained belief, something she was pretty weak in to begin with. "How did you get a cab?"

"I held out my hand and it pulled up." Reese sounded exasperated. "Look, if you don't want to go, I do. In or out."

"Oh, just hell," Trudy said.

Reese shook his head and went around to the street side of the cab and got in. "Make up your mind, Trudy," he said from behind her as he closed his door. "It's Christmas Eve and it's getting later every minute."

Okay, he'd worked with her dad, and Nolan seemed to know him from the department, and he was probably not a psychotic killer, and he said he knew where there were Mac Twos. Did she really have a choice?

She put one foot into the cab, dragging her packages with her, keeping the other foot on the curb.

"So this warehouse," she began, and then stopped, getting a good look at the inside of the cab. It was festooned with LED Christmas lights blinking red and green in time to the music, the song's refrain whispering, "Gimme, gimme, gimme, Santa Baby." She saw Reese look up at the ceiling and followed his eyes to a shriveled piece of mistletoe safety-pinned to the sagging fabric. "My God."

"Mistletoe," Reese said.

"Pretty limp," Trudy said, squinting at it.

"I'm not."

"I have Mace."

He ducked his head and kissed her, bumping her

nose, and it was nice, being kissed in a warm cab by a younger man, even if there was snow drifting in through the open door and the foot she still had on the curb was freezing. *Gimme, gimme, gimme,* Trudy thought, and wished he were Nolan.

Reese pulled back a little. "Thank you for not Macing me."

"I was thinking about it," Trudy said, and he kissed her again, putting his arms around her and pulling her close, and this time she kissed him back, because it was Christmas Eve and he might be getting her a Mac II. And because he was a pretty good kisser even if he wasn't Nolan, who was a grave disappointment anyway.

Then Nolan leaned into the cab and scared the hell out of her.

"So, where are we going?" he asked cheerfully.

"Where did you come from?" she said, her heart hammering.

"Looking for a cab." Nolan smiled at her. "Can't find one." He nudged the leg she had stretched out to the curb. "Can I share yours?"

"No," Reese said, evidently not planning on taking any classes from Nolan in the future.

"It's polite to share a cab on Christmas Eve, Mr. Daniels," Nolan said.

"I'm not polite, Professor Mitchell." Reese tightened his grip on her.

Trudy looked from one to the other. They were glaring at each other, which was sort of flattering until she remembered that they probably both wanted the Mac Two more than they wanted her. Well, there had to be safety in numbers. What were the chances they were both serial killers?

"I'm polite." Trudy pulled her foot into the cab and scooted over, stopping when her hip touched Reese's.

Nolan slid in until his hip touched hers, and shut the door.

The cab grew warmer.

"Where are we going?" he said. "Tell me it's a place with MacGuffins."

Trudy nodded. "A warehouse. With MacGuffins mint in their boxes."

"Way to go, dude," Nolan said to Reese.

"Out," Reese said, still hanging on to Trudy.

"Oh no." Trudy pulled away, leaning into Nolan in the process. "I'm only going if he goes."

"I'm touched," Nolan said.

"No, you're not," Trudy said, moving back from him again. "Safety in numbers. Any number. Not you specifically." She smiled at Reese. "We'll all go together."

Reese looked as though he might argue and then sighed. "Go," he said to the cabbie, and gave an address that Trudy knew was in the warehouse district, probably now dark and deserted and half an hour away.

Well, at least she knew Nolan wouldn't attack her. The dumbass had no interest in her body at all.

"Gimme, gimme, gimme," the radio sang.

"I hate Christmas," Trudy said, and settled back as the cab jerked into motion.

Chapter 2

"So," Nolan said as the cab moved through the falling snow and the brightly lit streets. "This is really nice."

"No, it isn't," Reese said.

Actually, it was. Nolan was pressed warm against her, and if she forgot everything that had happened and repressed all her common sense, it was almost like they were together again, and that felt good. *Pathetic,* she thought, but she didn't move away from him.

"What's in the other bag?" Nolan said, looking into her first shopping bag. "Is that a cow?"

"Yes," Trudy said. "It says, 'Eat chicken,' when you pull its string." He looked at her in disbelief, and she said, "Well, earlier in the evening that was hysterically funny."

"It *is* funny," Reese said, tightening his arm around her. "It's very funny."

Nolan frowned. "I hadn't figured you for the stuffed-animal-giving type," he said, taking the lanky spotted cow out of the bag.

"Really," Trudy said coolly. *I hadn't figured you for the grave-disappointment type.*

"More the educational-toy-giving type. You seem so . . . practical."

It was embarrassing to think what she had figured him for. *He's smart, he's funny, and he's got swivel hips,* she'd told Courtney. *Just imagine.* Yeah, that was the kind of statement that came back to haunt you.

"You know. You seem pretty . . . straight," Nolan said. "Being a librarian and all."

"I'm the assistant director of library sciences," she told him, trying to crush him with disdain.

"Right." Nolan nodded. "A librarian."

"Yes," Trudy said, giving up. "I'm a librarian."

Reese tightened his arm around her. "I never thought of you as a librarian. I think that's a terrible thing to call you."

Well, yeah, except I am *a librarian,* Trudy thought, and then her cell phone rang and she answered it.

"*Three* toxic wastes," Courtney said, her voice much looser now. "I want to bury Evil Nemesis Brandon in the stuff."

"There's no need to be unpleasant," Nolan said to Reese over her head. "It's Christmas Eve. Goodwill to men."

"Not to you," Reese said.

"Here's the situation," Trudy said to Courtney, putting one hand over her ear to shut out the cab radio—*gimme gimme gimme*—and the two guys bickering over her head. "I met one of Dad's old research assistants in the toy store, and he says he knows where they have this year's MacGuffin, but it's out in some dangerous deserted warehouse on the edge of town."

"He can get one of this year's? *Yes.* Go!"

"Good to know you'll sacrifice me for a homicidal

toy," Trudy said. "But that's okay; I'm already on my way."

"What's this guy's name?"

"Reese Daniels."

"Did you check his ID?"

"No, Courtney, I did not check his ID."

"Always a good idea," Nolan said. "You never know with research assistants. They can turn on you like that."

"Who's that?" Courtney said.

"Nolan."

"Still?"

"Yes," Trudy said repressively.

Reese took his wallet from his jacket, flipped it open, and showed her his driver's license.

Trudy squinted at it. "His driver's license says 'Reese Lee Daniels.' Born 1982."

"A younger man," Courtney said, distracted. "Is he cute?"

"Sort of," Trudy said. *If you like surfers. Dude.*

"I really think you and I should go out again," Nolan said. "Let's give us another chance."

Trudy closed her eyes in the dark and thought, *No, it will not work out, he'll just forget you again.*

"Do you mind?" Reese said. "She's with me."

"Forget cute," Courtney was saying on the phone. "Does he have a job? Does he look like he'll be faithful?"

"No," Trudy said to Nolan. "No more faculty, no more film."

"Okay, we'll go to the Aquarium." Nolan put the cow back in the bag. "It'll make you calm. You can taunt the sharks."

"I bet he won't be faithful," Courtney said.

"What kind of person taunts sharks?" Trudy said to Nolan. "They're trapped in a tank."

"Okay," Nolan said, the voice of reason. "Where do you want to go? Your choice."

"Do you *mind*?" Reese said to him again. "This is my cab. Stop putting on the moves."

"I'm not asking you," Nolan said to him.

"He'll betray you," Courtney was saying gloomily. "Younger, older, they're all rats."

Trudy ignored the two guys to answer her. "That's the gin talking, honey. I thought you were going to ice gingerbread."

"I swear," Nolan said to Trudy. "No more film festivals."

Trudy waved her hand at him to get him to shut up so she could hear Courtney.

"I *am* icing gingerbread." Courtney sounded more depressed than ever. "But I broke more arms off. So I switched to the gingerbread house, and I got it together, but now the gumdrops won't stick." She sounded ready to weep.

"Why don't you wait until I get home and I can help you," Trudy said, trying to make her voice cheerful. "You probably just need thicker icing."

"Damn."

"What?"

"A gumdrop fell into my drink. Wait a minute."

Trudy listened for a moment.

"You know, they're not half bad in gin."

"Court, put the gin away and go lie down. I'll be home as soon as we get done at this warehouse, and then we'll finish the gingerbread house together."

"No more faculty parties, either," Nolan said.

Reese leaned forward, smushing Trudy between them. "She doesn't want to go out with you, *okay*?"

"That warehouse sounds dangerous," Courtney said. "Get the cab number and the cabbie's name."

Nolan shook his head at Reese. "We don't know that she doesn't want to go out with me. She never really got to know me."

"And whose fault is that?" Trudy said, turning on him. "Three dates and then you don't call, you don't write. But hey, it's not the end of the world." *And you never kissed me, either. Han Solo would have kissed me.*

"Trudy?" Courtney said.

"In a minute," Trudy said to her.

"I know, I know, that was bad of me; I'm really sorry," Nolan was saying. "But you didn't seem like you were having a good time."

"A good time? I was on my best behavior, you jerk. What else did you need? Cries of delight at the faculty party? Moans of appreciation for the movie popcorn? Which, I might point out, I ate alone. Did you think—" She stopped, realizing that arguing made it sound like she cared. "Never mind. I'm sure you had a good reason for disappearing out of my life without a reason. Forget it."

"Forget what?" Courtney said. "The name of the cabbie? You never gave it to me."

Trudy leaned over to look at the cab license for her, and Reese tightened his arm across her shoulders. "Alexander Kuroff," she said into the phone as she straightened.

"Write it down," Courtney said.

"I don't have any paper," Trudy said, and Nolan rummaged in her shopping bags and pulled out the Christmas paper she'd bought.

Trudy tore the cellophane off the corner of it and said, "No pen."

Both men offered her pens, Reese a beat behind Nolan. Trudy took Reese's and wrote the cabbie's name on the white space around the red printed words on the paper.

"And the cab number."

"Court—"

"Read it to me so I can write it down, too."

Trudy read it off. "I don't see what good my writing it down is going to do. If I die, the wrapping paper goes with me."

"You're not going to die," Nolan said. "I'm here."

"Oh, give it a rest," Reese said.

"What cab company?" Courtney said.

"Yellow Checker," Trudy said. "And I'm stopping this conversation now."

"Call me every hour," Courtney said. "If you don't call me, I'll call you. Every hour until you come home with the MacGuffin."

"What are you going to do if I don't call and I don't answer?"

"Call nine-one-one. But you're going, right?"

"I'm on my way," Trudy said, sitting back.

"Every hour," Courtney said.

"Every hour."

"I'll watch out for her," Nolan said, close to the phone.

"Who's that?" Courtney said on the phone.

"Nolan again," Trudy said. "He wants a MacGuffin, too."

"Well, at least he's the devil we know."

"We don't know him that well."

"Hey," Nolan said. "Your dad can vouch for me. We've been in the same department for two years."

"That is not a recommendation."

"What?" Courtney said.

"Dad can vouch for him."

"Push him out of the cab."

"Her dad can vouch for me, too," Reese said, sounding about twelve.

"I have to go, Court," Trudy said, before they started punching each other on the arm. "It's going to be a while." She handed Reese his pen back and started to put the wrapping paper back in the bag one-handed and then looked at it more closely in the lights from the street. "Oh, *hell*."

"What?" Courtney said.

"I got *birthday paper*," Trudy said. "I need Christmas paper, and this is *birthday*—"

"*Trudy,*" Courtney wailed.

"Maybe you can fake it," Reese said, with badly concealed exasperation. "If it's just a bunch of animals, it could be anything."

Trudy held up the paper. It said *Happy Birthday* over and over and over. "No animals. Just 'Happy Birthday' in red."

"Well, then you're screwed," Reese said, sounding bored with the whole thing.

"No, she's not." Nolan held out his hand. "Give it here."

"You're going to fix this?" Trudy said. "How are you going to fix this?"

Nolan wiggled his fingers. "Gimme."

She handed the paper over and watched while he took out his pen again and wrote *Jesus* under every *Happy Birthday*.

"You're a grave disappointment, but you're also a genius," Trudy said, giving credit where it was due.

"Did he fix it?" Courtney said.

"Yes," Trudy told her.

"Make him help you get the Mac."

"*Goodbye*, Courtney," Trudy said, and hung up.

"So you'll go out with me again?" Nolan said, handing the paper back.

"Not a chance in hell." Trudy put the paper in the bag with the cow.

"Okay, lunch," Nolan said. "Lunch isn't really a date."

"Oh, give it up," Reese said, and let his head fall back against the top of the seat. "I have lost my patience with you."

"Well, look for it," Nolan said. "Maybe it fell off the sleigh."

"Man, I don't know about you," Reese said.

"I'm a man of mystery," Nolan agreed. "Another reason Trudy should see me again." He smiled at her in the dim light as the cab sped toward the warehouses. "So, meet me for coffee?"

"She doesn't want to meet you for anything," Reese said.

Yes, I do, Trudy thought.

"So, coffee," Nolan said, warm and solid beside her.

"Gimme, gimme, gimme," the voice on the radio said.

Kill me now, Trudy thought, and put her head on her shopping bags.

❀   ❀   ❀

The streets grew dark as the cab left the city proper and turned into the warehouse district, and ten minutes later they stopped outside a deserted building, the parking lot lit by one lamp, high over its main door.

Reese opened the door and got out, holding the door for Trudy, who slid over on the seat and peered out at the darkness.

"There aren't a lot of people here buying MacGuffins," she said, staring at the empty lot.

"They probably sold out of them while you were trying to decide if I was a rapist," Reese said, sounding peeved.

"We could turn around and go back," Nolan said. "I'll buy the coffee."

Trudy took a deep breath and got out, her three shopping bags bumping against her knees.

"Want me to take those for you?" Reese said.

"No," Trudy said as Nolan got out behind her.

"You are not a trusting woman," Reese said.

"I don't think they make those anymore," Nolan said to him. "Tell you what, since you found the warehouse, I'll pay for the cab."

"Keep the cab," Trudy said, and turned back to Reese.

"The Macs are in here," Reese said, and opened the door to the warehouse.

There was light inside, but Trudy stopped at the door to wait for Nolan. He talked to the cabbie, and then he turned and came toward her and the cab drove away.

"Hey, I told you to keep the cab," she said, and Nolan took her arm.

"He's coming back," he said, and his voice sounded different as he looked over her head into the warehouse.

"Why is he leaving at all?"

Reese came back to the door. "Come on in. You're letting the heat out."

Trudy took a deep breath and stepped over the threshold into the warehouse, dragging Nolan with her since he wouldn't let go of her arm.

The place was a cavern filled with rows of shelving crammed with boxes, a giant version of the old toy store. High above, industrial lighting made the center space by the door bright, but the rest of the place was dark. It wasn't silent, though. There was a radio somewhere blaring "The Little Drummer Boy."

"Rum-pa-pum-pum," Trudy said, not at all reassured.

"Over here," Reese said, and led them away from the door, Trudy pulling Nolan along, since he still wouldn't let go. "You can leave your Mac here." He dropped his bag with the Twinkletoes in it. "I'm leaving my bag here."

"Where are the MacGuffins?" Trudy said, keeping a tight hold on her own bags.

"And who are *they*?" Nolan said, and Trudy looked back to see three men now standing in front of the door. They looked a lot like Reese, young and dudelike in denim jackets, but they weren't smiling.

Uh-oh, Trudy thought.

"Wait here," Reese said, and went over to confer with the men.

"You know, I don't feel good about this," she said to Nolan.

"Good instincts," Nolan said, not taking his eyes off the men. "Come here."

He tugged on her arm, and she let him pull her over to the closest row of shelves.

"Be with you in a minute," Reese called back, and Trudy nodded to him, and then Nolan jerked her arm and she tripped after him between two rows of shelves and into the darkness.

"What are you doing?" she said.

"Shhhh." He kept going, tugging her deeper into the gloom of the unlit shelving.

"What do you mean, 'Shhhh'? What's going on?"

"Quiet." Nolan pulled her down another side row and then across another one, effectively losing them both in the darkness.

"Stop shushing me. I don't like—"

He stopped and cupped her face with his hands and whispered, "Trudy, please shut up."

"Why?" Trudy whispered back.

He leaned closer and whispered in her ear. "Because I think Reese is a bad guy. And I think he wants your MacGuffin. And I think those guys out there are his minions. So we should—"

"Minions?" Trudy said, so startled she spoke out loud.

Nolan put his hand over her mouth. "And we don't want them to find us," he whispered. "Not unless you're prepared to give up that MacGuffin."

Trudy shook her head, and he took his hand away and bent to her ear again. "Then we should hide it here. They're going to find us, and we can tell them the box is here and let them spend the rest of their lives looking for it—"

Trudy shook her head again. *"No."*

He slapped his hand over her mouth and whispered, *"Listen.* I'm not a toy collector, I'm an undercover cop."

Trudy pulled back, trying to see him in the dark. "I don't believe it," she whispered back. "An undercover cop who teaches Chinese lit?"

"I'm a well-educated undercover cop."

"This is your explanation." She shook her head and started to move away, and he pulled her back.

"Look," he whispered in her ear, "we knew the bad guys were operating from the university lit department, and I really do have a degree in Chinese. And some literature. Hey, I'm a good teacher."

Actually, he was, Trudy remembered. That was another thing that had made her want to go out with him, competence. And now he was telling her that there was a toy-theft ring operating out of the lit department. " 'The bad guys.' Is that really cop talk?"

"It's too dark to show you my ID. Want to feel my badge?"

"You have to be kidding me."

"Your buddy Reese—"

"He's not my buddy," Trudy said, and then she heard Reese call her name from the center space of the warehouse and stepped closer to Nolan.

"Listen to me," Nolan said. "They're toy hijackers and they want that doll. If things get bad, *give it to them*."

Toy hijackers? "No."

She heard him draw in his breath in exasperation, but she didn't care.

"This is for Leroy," she whispered. "His rat daddy ran off with the rat nanny, and his mother is in meltdown, but he knows Santa is bringing him a MacGuffin. He's getting it."

"Oh, Christ," Nolan said under his breath. "I'll get him another one, I swear. Just give them that one so we can walk out of here alive."

"That's not very heroic."

"I'll be heroic when you're not here," Nolan whispered. "Now I just want you out in one piece."

"I'm not giving up Leroy's Mac. What's your Plan B?"

Nolan sighed his exasperation and then took her arm and drew her deeper into the shelves. "We hide."

"Hide?" Trudy whispered back. "How—"

"Shut up," he whispered, and she did, following him deeper into the darkness until they came to a wall. He took her hand and led her along the wall until he found a staircase, and then he took her slowly up the stairs, testing each tread to make sure it didn't creak, which wasn't really necessary since "The Little Drummer Boy" had given way to Brenda Lee singing "Rockin' Around the Christmas Tree," making her usual Christmas fortune in residuals.

When they reached the top, they were on a walkway, looking out over the warehouse beneath the windows of a darkened office. Nolan tugged her arm and she sank down with him on the metal platform as silently as possible, her shopping bags rustling.

"Now what?" she whispered.

"Now we wait for backup."

"What backup?"

"The backup I sent the cabbie for. Shhhh."

He was peering over the rail, but they were too far away to see into the lighted part of the warehouse.

"You're really a cop?" Trudy whispered. "Why do I find that hard to believe?"

"I don't know," Nolan whispered back. "Why are you holding on to that damn doll when that could get us out of here?"

"What if you're not a cop? What if Reese is your accomplice and you're working together to get the Mac from me?"

"For our mutual nephew?" Nolan's whisper sounded a lot tougher now, but that might just have been the exasperation in his voice. "Has it occurred to you that you're trapped in a deserted warehouse with a bunch of thugs?"

"Yes," Trudy whispered back. "Well, no. For all I know, that's Reese's glee club out there. Maybe it's his bowling night. They're all wearing the same jacket."

"Be serious, Trudy. You're risking your life for a doll so your nephew won't be disappointed on Christmas Day in spite of the fact that his father is gone and his mother is in a gin coma."

"Hey."

"Shhhh. He's already disappointed, Tru. His family's gone. Give Reese the doll. When he makes a run for it, we'll arrest him. He won't get away with it."

Trudy pushed him away. "First, my sister is not in a gin coma. Second, his family is not gone; he has me and his mother when she sobers up. Third, if I give Reese this doll and you arrest him, the doll becomes evidence and I never see it again. So no. Leroy is going to get this doll tomorrow morning. He is going to believe in Santa, since he can't believe in men or nannies. When does your backup get here?"

"I don't think you can indict all men because of one rat daddy."

"Yeah? How many times have you lied to me tonight?"

Nolan leaned back against the wall. "Too many to count. But I'm still here trying to save your cantankerous butt. That should mean something."

"I have only your word for that and as we know, you lie."

"Okay. We'll sit here and wait and hope Reese doesn't find us."

"That's your plan? Hope he doesn't find us?"

"You always this cranky?"

"Only when I'm cold, I'm tired, I'm scared, and men keep lying to me while I'm trying to get a kid the Christmas present he deserves."

"Okay, *fine*." Nolan shifted on the platform, his whisper savage in the darkness. "We'll take the doll if we can get out of here with it. Just promise me that if he says, 'The doll or your life,' you'll give him the doll."

"No."

"Trudy—"

"I can't." Trudy swallowed hard. "Leroy believes. Do you know how long it's been since I believed in anything? In anybody? But Leroy believes that when he comes downstairs tomorrow morning, there'll be a Mac-Guffin under his tree. He *knows* there will be because he believes in Santa Claus; he believes the world is a good place. And he's going to keep on believing that because I'm taking this doll home no matter what." She shifted against the cold wall. "Besides, nobody shoots anybody over a doll."

Nolan sighed. "I suppose it has occurred to you that you've lost your grip."

"No," Trudy said. "I've lost my faith. My grip is *just fine*." She pulled the shopping bags closer. "Leroy gets the Mac and Courtney gets the Twinkle, and then we'll put our lives back together."

"Their lives," Nolan said.

"Mine, too. My resolution for 2007 is to start believing in people again." She leaned closer to him. "I might start with you if you help me get this doll home."

He was quiet for a while. "Okay. I'll try to help you."

She pulled back. "I'll try to believe in you, then. No guarantees, of course."

"Okay, fine, I will help you," Nolan said.

"Promise me," Trudy said, gripping his coat. "Promise me that Leroy will have this Mac tomorrow morning."

"Trudy—"

"Fine." Trudy stood up, trying to keep her bags from rustling. "I'll do it myself. Could you move? I need to get past you to the stairs."

"I promise," Nolan said.

She looked down at him in the dark. "Easy to say."

"I promise," he said grimly, getting to his feet. "But now you have to do what I say."

"And why would I do that?" she said.

"Because you trust me."

"Ha."

"Then why are you listening to me?"

Trudy bit her lip. "I might trust you a little."

"All the way, Tru," Nolan said. "If I'm going to get you out of here, you have to do exactly what I say."

Trudy felt him close, his body warm next to hers

in the darkness. If she was going to start trusting people, he might be the place to start. "You never even kissed me," she whispered. "What was that about? You never—"

He bent and kissed her, not gently, and she clutched at his jacket, wanting something to hold on to, putting her forehead against his shoulder when he broke the kiss because it had felt so right, everything about him felt so right.

The radio changed to "Grandma Got Run Over by a Reindeer."

Our song, Trudy thought. "Okay. I trust you. What do we do next?"

"Pray," Nolan said, sounding a little breathless. "Because we're in a world of hurt here."

"Well, then—"

Something moved behind him and Trudy saw one of the minions, just his face, for a second before Nolan jerked his elbow back and caught the guy across the nose. He turned and hit him again before he fell, catching him before he rolled off the platform. Trudy fumbled in her purse for her miniflash, but by the time she found it and turned it on, the guy was at Nolan's feet, his arms tied behind his back with a belt, and Nolan was putting on the guy's blue jacket.

"*Turn that off,*" Nolan whispered, and Trudy did.

"So you're a cop," she whispered back.

"Here's the plan."

"How did you know where to hit him?" Trudy said. "It's dark as hell in here. How did you know?"

"You were looking at him," Nolan whispered back. "I hit what you were looking at. We have to move now; this guy found us and the others will, too. So I'm going down there to distract them. You're going out the door. If there's nobody out there yet, run for the street."

"I'm not leaving you," Trudy said, holding on to his sleeve.

"Trudy, I'm safer with you out of here than I am with you in here. You're a distraction. Now follow me until I get out into the light and they see me. Then run like hell for the door. Got it?"

She didn't want to leave him, that was wrong. But he was probably right, she wasn't going to be any help at all. "Okay."

"One more thing," Nolan said, and kissed her, and this time it hit her hard, he was going out there to save her, and she kissed him back with everything she had.

When she came up for air, she was dizzy. "Maybe we should stay here," she whispered. "Hiding is good. We could do this until the backup shows."

"They'll come looking for this guy," Nolan whispered back, nodding to the minion at his feet. "We'll do this later." He looked at her, shook his head, and kissed her again, and she relaxed into him, irrationally happy about the whole mess.

Then he stepped back and she sighed.

"Right. Later," she said, and followed him down the stairs toward the light.

❀   ❀   ❀

Nolan left her in the first row of shelves nearest the door, just steps away from the lighted part of the warehouse and the way out. "Watch until their backs are turned," he said. "Then run like hell."

She nodded, and he disappeared down the row again as her heart pounded.

He would be okay. Nobody killed over toys, even Major MacGuffins. They wouldn't do anything to him. She was almost sure. She bit her lip and waited, and then her cell phone rang, and she grabbed it and answered it before it could ring again.

"*Don't do that*," she whispered into the phone.

"You didn't call me," Courtney said. "You're fifteen minutes late."

"Yeah, well there are guys after us," Trudy whispered.

"*What guys?*" Courtney said. "*What us?*"

"Nolan and me. Reese's got a ring of toy thieves here—"

"Toy thieves? What are you talking about?"

"Call nine-one-one," Trudy said, and then realized Courtney didn't know where they were. "We're—"

Somebody took her cell phone out of her hand, and she screamed and turned.

"Let's talk," Reese said, and shut off her phone.

"I'm not giving you the Mac," Trudy said, holding her bags behind her.

Reese sighed. "Trudy, I don't know what Nolan's told you, but I'm positive it's not the truth."

"He's a cop." Trudy took a step back. "And boy, are you in trouble."

"He's a double agent for the Chinese government," Reese said.

Trudy tightened her grip on her bags. "Whoa. You've got a better imagination than he does. He said you were a toy thief."

Reese looked taken aback. "A toy thief? Who the hell steals toys?"

"The Grinch," Trudy said. "I don't know. It sounded plausible when he said it. It still sounds plausible compared to the Chinese-double-agent bit."

"I am not a toy thief," Reese said.

"But you don't have a nephew, either. Because we're

in this warehouse and there are no Mac Twos, which means you had to get me here for some reason."

"The Chinese spy codes." Reese nodded toward her bags. "They're in that MacGuffin box. I'm with the CIA and I need them."

"Fat chance." Trudy stepped back again. "I don't care what alphabet you flash at me, you are not taking this Mac from me."

"Look on the box, Trudy," Reese said patiently. "In the lower right-hand corner, there should be a black X."

"There isn't," Trudy said, holding the bag tighter.

"It's small," Reese said. "Look for it."

Trudy hesitated, but he met her eyes without flinching. *He's telling the truth,* she thought, and put her bags down. She took the Mac box out of the bag and stepped into the light to look at it.

Sure enough, in the lower right-hand corner on the back was a small black X.

"You put it there," Trudy said, not wanting to believe Nolan was the bad guy.

"When?" Reese said. "You haven't let that box out of your hands since you got it."

"Oh, hell." Trudy swallowed. "I need this doll, Reese."

"It's okay," Reese said. "I don't need the doll. I just need the instruction sheet. That's where the codes are. Deal?"

Trudy bit her lip. Leroy didn't need the instructions; he probably knew more about the toy by now than the designers did. Toy hijackers and Chinese double agents were both ridiculous; Leroy was real. "Okay."

Reese held out his hand for the box, and she tightened her grip.

"Just the instructions." She opened the lid and felt

down the back of the box for the paper, but there was nothing there. "Damn." She held the box into the pool of light cast by the fixture far above her and looked in. "It must have fallen under the doll." She carefully pulled the doll out, still wired into the cardboard backing that showed explosions, and shook the box upside down.

"Trudy," Reese said, his voice grim.

"I'm looking." Trudy dropped the empty box to un-wire the MacGuffin to see if the instructions had lodged behind it.

Reese picked up the box and began to dissemble it, checking in all the folds. "It's not here."

"It's not here, either." Trudy pulled the cardboard background away from the doll and handed it over, holding on to the Mac tightly. "And it was earlier."

"How do you know?"

"Because Nolan checked—" She stopped, appalled.

"Nolan opened the box and took out the instructions," Reese said, sounding grim.

"But he put them back, I saw him," Trudy said. "He slipped them behind the cardboard and closed up the box."

"He palmed them, Trudy. He got the codes."

Trudy thought back. "He couldn't have. I was watching him, right up to . . ."

Reese looked at her patiently.

"Right up to when you called to me in the checkout line," Trudy said, clutching the Mac closer and feeling miserable. "I looked away to talk to you. Did you see him take them?"

"No," Reese said. "I was looking at you."

Trudy felt ill. "Can I have the box back? At least I can give the doll to Leroy for Christmas." She bent, keeping the doll in one hand, and picked up the shopping bags with the cow and the Twinkletoes in them.

"Look," Reese said. "I need your help. Nolan's a bad guy, and he's somewhere in this warehouse with those codes, and he trusts you. You call to him, get him to come out to us, and we'll take it from there."

Trudy stepped back. "You'll hurt him."

Reese shook his head, moving closer. "You watch too many movies. Spies don't hurt people, they just swap information. And that's all we're going to do. Take back the codes." He smiled at her, his baby face reassuring. "Just call out for him, Trudy. He'll come to you. He likes you. Then you can take the doll and go home, and you'll have done a good thing for your country, too." She hesitated and he said, "Of course, I'll have to check the doll before you go to make sure there's nothing else there." He held out his hand for the MacGuffin.

Of course you will, Trudy thought, and looked around him at the door. Could she shove him out of the way and get out?

"Come on," Reese said. "Who are you going to trust, me or the guy who lied to you and stole the instruction sheet?"

Good question.

She stuck the Mac under her arm, looped the two remaining shopping bags over her wrist, and opened her purse.

"Trudy?" Reese said.

"I'm gonna go with the guy who lied," Trudy said, and Maced him.

❄　　　❄　　　❄

Reese had stopped screaming by the time Trudy found the staircase again, which comforted her some. If he was really a CIA agent, she'd just Maced a good guy, but on the other hand . . .

Actually, there wasn't an other hand. She'd just Maced a good guy.

"What the hell did you do to him?" Nolan whispered, and she jerked back, almost dropping her last two bags.

The Mac she kept her grip on.

"I Maced him. How'd you know I'd be here?"

"I figured this is where you'd run to once the other guys blocked the door. You were supposed to get out."

"Yeah, well, you were supposed to be the good guy," Trudy whispered back. "You took the instructions, you bastard."

"Yeah," Nolan said. "So?"

"So you're not a cop," Trudy said. "You're a double agent for the Chinese, you rat—"

"He *told* you that?"

Trudy stopped. "That is pretty far-fetched."

"Trudy, he's the double agent for the Chinese."

Trudy glared at where she thought he was in the darkness. "Do you guys just make this stuff up as you go?"

"MacGuffins are made in China," Nolan whispered. "They marked one box last year and sent it over to that toy store. We just found out that it went missing and never got picked up, which is why we had the toy store staked out."

"We who?" Trudy whispered back. "No, wait, I know this part. You're the CIA. And I'm pissed off. Do you really think I'm going to believe this crap? That the Chinese secret service puts codes in dolls? Why don't they just *e-mail* them?"

"Computers can be hacked."

"And Major MacGuffins can't?" Trudy looked at the doll in her arms.

"One sheet of paper, all the codes," Nolan said. "On microdot. Very efficient. Except they lost them last year."

"So this is about last year's codes?" Trudy shook her

head. "Why would you want last year's codes? This story needs work."

"Because with last year's codes we can decipher all of last year's transmissions that we intercepted. Which is what's going on right now."

"Right now."

"I took them out of the box and passed them on," Nolan said. "If you'll give the doll to Reese, he'll realize it's over and hit the road."

"Evidently not," Trudy said. "He knows you've got the instruction sheet and he doesn't seem to be leaving. I'm not buying any of this, you know. But I also don't care about any of it. As long as Leroy—"

"I know, I know, he gets the doll." Nolan sighed. "I can't believe I promised you that. I'm going to end up getting shot for some stupid doll."

"Yes, but you're saving a little boy's Christmas," Trudy said. "That's very heroic."

"I'm still gonna get shot," Nolan said. "So here's what we're going to do. You're going to take your Mace—"

"I dropped it," Trudy said.

"Great," Nolan said.

"Well, I never Maced anybody before. He scared the hell out of me when he screamed. But I'll be better now. And I don't need the Mace. I've seen *Miss Congeniality* twenty times, it's Courtney's favorite movie."

"What are you talking about?"

"That SING thing. Solar plexus, Instep, Nose, Groin."

"No." Nolan's whisper was flat in the darkness. "Do not think you're Rambo. Just run for the damn door."

"Okay." Trudy shifted the Mac to her other arm as she tried to remember what other weapons she might have in her purse. No Mace. No knife. No gun. She clearly hadn't come out prepared for Christmas Eve. Not even a nail file. . . . "Wait a minute." She reached in one of the bags, pulled out Courtney's Twinkletoes box, and pried the top open.

"What are you doing?" Nolan whispered.

"Arming myself." Trudy opened the manicure set wired next to Twink's feet. There was a nail file in there, just as she'd remembered. "Got it."

"Do not fight with anybody," Nolan whispered, the order clear. "Just run for the damn door."

"Okay." Trudy put the nail file in her coat pocket.

"We need something to create a disturbance. Too bad that grenade in the Mac doesn't work. I could use a grenade."

"There's a gun," Trudy brought up the Mac's hand so she could look down the barrel of the Mac's revolver. "What's this thing stuck on the end?"

"A silencer," Nolan whispered. "If only I had one for you."

"So is the gun louder with it off?"

"*Don't* fire that thing, we don't know what it'll do." Nolan peered over the edge of the stairs.

Trudy leaned back against the staircase and looked at the gun. It was a horrible thing to give a kid. What were people thinking? Evil Nemesis Brandon's mother must have had a politically correct meltdown when she realized what was in the box, but she got it for him anyway. Well, good for ENB's mom. Trudy resisted the urge to pull the trigger and pulled on the silencer instead, which popped right off. "Whoops."

"Shhhh."

The silencer felt a little heavy for something that was basically a plastic cap. Trudy stuck her hand in her purse and found her miniflash. Hunching over to shield the light from the warehouse, she looked inside the cylinder. There was something rectangular stuck in there, about half an inch wide, with a slice of something white in it.

"Oh, hell," Trudy said out loud.

"Shhhh." Nolan turned on her. "You—"

"It's a thumb drive," Trudy whispered.

"What?"

"The silencer. It's a USB key, a thumb drive, you know, a mini hard drive. It wasn't just the code in the instructions—"

Nolan leaned in to look, and Trudy felt him press warm against her as he took the silencer, his weight a comfort, especially since she knew she was holding something that Reese probably would shoot her for.

"This is not good," she whispered.

"Oh, honey, this is great," Nolan said in her ear. "Oh, babe, do you have any idea what you just found?"

"The thing Reese is going to kill me for?" Trudy said.

"He's not going to kill you," Nolan said, but he didn't sound as though he were giving the thought his full attention. "Give me that doll."

"No," Trudy said. "You can have the silencer, but you can't have—"

She heard something and shut up as Nolan froze.

Then he leaned forward and whispered in her ear, "I need your tape."

She frowned at him, and he began to go silently through her bags until he held up the Scotch tape she'd bought to wrap Leroy's Mac a million years ago. Then he put the gray plastic silencer on the underside of the gray railing along the wall and began to wrap tape around it.

Good thing I got the invisible kind, she thought, and wondered if she was ever going to get home.

"Okay," Nolan whispered when he was done. "We're

going out there again. And I will distract them and this time you will run for the door even if your phone rings."

"How are you going to distract them?"

"Give me that cow."

"The cow?" Trudy handed over the bag with the cow and hugged the Mac to her.

"You pull the string and it talks, right?"

"It says, 'Eat chicken.' "

"Right. Come on."

"Aren't you going to kiss me good-bye again?"

"No. I'm going with you this time."

"That's good, I like that better," Trudy said, and followed him down the stairs again, clutching the Mac and the Twinkletoes bag.

When they were back at the end of the row by the door, Nolan pulled the string and wrapped it around the cow's body. "Door's there," he whispered, nodding toward it.

She nodded back and gripped the nail file in her pocket while he drew his arm back.

"With your shield or on it, cow," he said, and tossed it over the shelves.

The string unwound itself before the cow cleared the top, and it mooed, "Eat chicken" as a fusillade rang out. Nolan shoved her toward the door, and she ran for it, hitting Reese, who was running around the end of the shelves, his eyes still red and streaming from the Mace as he raised his gun. He grabbed for her, and she stabbed him in the gun arm, dropping her Twinkletoes bag but still clutching the Mac as he screamed, and then she kicked him in the knee and ran like hell for the door, wrenching it open as Reese fired, hearing the bullet ping on the metal as she dove for the darkness.

❋ ❋ ❋

Trudy ran for the edge of the parking lot, clutching the Mac, adrenaline pumping, not stopping when she heard, *"Hold it!"*

Somebody grabbed Trudy's arm and swung her around and she saw it was the cabdriver. *"Give me that doll,"* he said.

"No." She smacked him with the bag and as he raised one hand to protect his head, she saw the gun in the shoulder holster under his leather jacket.

"Damn it," she said, and swung her elbow sharply into his solar plexus, stamped down on his instep, punched him in the nose, and then tried to kick him in the groin and missed and got his thigh instead, collapsing him onto the pavement.

Good enough, she thought, and took off for the street, only to have somebody else grab her arm just as she reached the chain-link fence.

"No," she said, and tried to turn, but whoever it was wrapped his other arm around her waist and pulled her back against him.

"Stop it!" Nolan said. "It's me. Give me the Mac."

"No," Trudy said, furious, and smacked her head back into his nose. She heard him swear and knew she'd gotten him, but he didn't let go, so she tried for his instep, but he jerked her off her feet.

"Trudy, stop it."

She swung her elbow back again and missed, and he kicked her feet out from under her and dumped her onto the grimy, wet pavement, yanking her arms behind her.

"You couldn't make this easy, could you?" he said as her cheek scraped on the ground. "You had to be a hardass."

"You bastard, you promised me I'd keep the doll," she said, and then she felt him yank her wrists together

as he slapped handcuffs on her and took the Mac away from her.

"Trudy Maxwell. You've been taken into custody for criminal obstinacy."

"Fuck you," Trudy said into the pavement. "And you have to be an actual cop to take me into custody, which you are not, so don't think I'm not going to sue your ass for kidnapping."

He put his arm under her and lifted her gently back onto her feet. "I'm not kidnapping you."

"Yeah?" Her hair fell in her eyes and she couldn't brush it out, which made her madder. "You and Reese, this was all a setup. He didn't even shoot at you back there, he shot at me. You were working together."

Nolan swung her around and gave her a gentle push back toward the warehouse. There were more cars there now and a van, and while she watched, somebody shoved Reese into the back of one of the cars. He was hand-cuffed.

"Not working with Reese," Nolan said.

"I don't see any police department insignia on these cars," Trudy said, shrugging off his hand as he prodded her forward. "In fact, I don't see any insignia at all."

Nolan stopped her in the pool of light from one of the warehouse lamps and showed her his ID.

" 'NSA,' " Trudy read. "Very cute. Got one for the CIA and the FBI, too? How about FEMA, I hear they're really tough. Not as tough as double agents for the Chinese, of course. How dumb do you think I am?"

"Trudy, I am NSA, Reese was a double agent for the Chinese, and I really did try to help you."

"Yeah," Trudy said bitterly. "That's why I'm in hand-cuffs now."

"You're in handcuffs because you're resisting,"

Nolan said. "I'm trying to get a promotion here, and you're beating me up. It makes me look bad."

"Great. That's what this is about, some damn promotion? Knock a helpless woman to the ground and steal her little nephew's Christmas present?"

"The 'helpless' is debatable," Nolan said as they went past the cabbie, who was dabbing at his bleeding nose and glaring at her. "You owe Alex an apology."

"He attacked me."

"He was trying to get you into the cab so he could get you away from here," Nolan said. "He's one of ours."

"He was trying to take the doll, so he's not one of mine," Trudy said, and then she saw the woman they were moving toward. She was wearing a red and green bobble hat, but she didn't look like a Christmas shopper anymore. "Who the hell is she?"

"My boss," Nolan said.

Trudy waited until they were in front of the woman, and then she said, "Is this guy really an NSA agent?"

"Yes." The woman spoke without any expression whatsoever, which only made Trudy madder.

"Well, he groped me in that warehouse," Trudy said.

"I'm not at all surprised," the woman said, and held her hand out for the Mac.

Nolan gave it to her.

"You *bastard*," Trudy said.

"Trudy, it's national security."

"No, it isn't," Trudy snapped. "You got the codes when you got the instruction sheet, and then you got the USB key when you got the silencer. You don't need the doll. You don't care that a little kid is going to wake up tomorrow and know that everything in his world is a lie, that doesn't bother you—"

"Trudy," Nolan said, misery in his voice.

"—as long as your *work* gets done." She wrenched away from him, her hands still cuffed behind her. "You guys, guys like you and Reese and Prescott, you don't care about anything as long as you get what you want. Well, *fine,* you got it. Now take these handcuffs off me, because you know damn well you're not going to arrest me for anything."

"You have to promise to stop hitting people," Nolan said.

"Fine," Trudy said. "I promise."

He unlocked the cuffs and she kicked him in the shin. He said, "Ouch," and grabbed at his leg.

"You promised me," Trudy said. "You said I could trust you, and I was as dumb as Courtney, I believed you." She turned back to his boss. "You need me for anything else or can I go home to my devastated family?"

"We have questions," the woman said, and gestured to the car. "We'll have you home in a couple of hours."

"Fine," Trudy said, refusing to look back at Nolan. "I'll tell you anything you want as long as you give me back the Mac."

"Unfortunately not," the woman said.

"Here's your Twinkletoes," Nolan said, holding out a shopping bag. "I found it in the warehouse."

Trudy took the bag. "Rot and die," she said, and walked toward the car.

"Trudy, be reasonable," he said, following her. "This is *national security*—"

She turned around and he almost bumped into her. "You didn't have to kiss me and tell me I could trust you. You didn't have to make me believe in you again. You had the NSA out here, you were always going to get that damn doll. You could have left me my dignity, but no, you had to sucker me in."

"That's not fair."

She stepped closer. "That's why I hate you. That's why Leroy's going to hate his dad and his mom and me tomorrow, because he knew there was no Santa, but we all said, 'Trust us, Santa's gonna come through for you.' We hung that kid out to dry. He's going to be right to hate us. And I'm right to hate you."

She turned to get into the car, and he caught her arm and said, "Trudy, I'm sorry," and she shook him off and got into the backseat without looking back at him.

Chapter 3

Trudy borrowed a cell phone and called Courtney to tell her she was all right. Then she faced Nolan's boss, who ditched the hat with the green and red bobbles and became tough, efficient, thorough, and polite, none of which made Trudy feel better. She answered everything the woman asked, and when she was finally released, it was well after midnight. She took her purse and the battered bag with the Twinkletoes and rode home through the snow in the back of a black car, too tired and too defeated to argue anymore.

I couldn't do it alone, she thought. *I really needed that bastard's help; nobody could have done it alone.* But she still felt like a failure. If only she hadn't trusted him, hadn't trusted Reese, hadn't gotten in that cab in the first place, hadn't ever talked to Nolan at all, they'd never have known she'd found the MacGuffin and Leroy would have it now. Her throat swelled and she stared at the back of the driver's head and willed herself not to cry. Not in front of the NSA, anyway.

She tiptoed into the house, but Courtney called out

from the dimly lit living room. Trudy went in and found her on the couch, glass in hand, her feet propped up on the coffee table that held a bowl of white icing, a lopsided gingerbread house, and a stack of gingerbread men with a knife stuck through them. She was staring into the gas fire, and the glow reflected off the tinsel on the tree while Christmas music played low and slow in the background.

"Do you have it?" Courtney said, her voice dull.

"No." Trudy went around the mess on the coffee table and sat down beside her, dropping her bags on the floor. "The Feds took it from me. For national security reasons. Nice gingerbread house."

"It's crooked," Courtney said, clearly not caring. "The Feds?"

"Turns out Nolan works for the NSA. I know. Unbelievable."

"I believe it." Courtney sat unmoving, her eyes on the fire. "That's just my luck. Even the government is out to get me."

"Two governments. Reese the Surfer turned out to be a double agent for the Chinese." Trudy leaned forward, pulled the knife out of the gingerbread, and scooped up a glop of white icing.

"Well, at least you're meeting men." Courtney picked up her glass to drink and then made a face when she realized it was empty. "So why did they want the Mac?"

"It had the codes to the Chinese spy network on the instruction sheet and then something else was on this thumb drive disguised as a silencer for the gun." Trudy smeared the icing on the roof. The white mass hung there for a moment and then began to slump its way to the edge. Not enough powdered sugar. The icing plopped off onto the cardboard base, looking like a snowbank.

"Chinese spy codes?" Courtney said.

"I wouldn't have believed it, except that I saw the thumb drive. That and there were so many guys in bad black suits there at the end." She glopped more icing on the other side of the roof. It slumped and became a snowbank, too. Definitely too thin. "Where's the sugar, Court?"

Courtney gestured to the kitchen with her glass.

The kitchen looked like a war zone, bodies of mutilated gingerbread men everywhere, red and green gumdrops stuck to the island like body parts, and a drip of icing pooled on the floor like thick white blood.

"Christmas didn't used to be this violent," Trudy called back to Courtney, and then picked up the powdered-sugar box, the half-filled bag of gumdrops, and some toothpicks. Toothpicks were good. She could probably have done more damage in the warehouse if she'd had toothpicks. She could have stuck several of them into Reese.

And more into Nolan. *Nolan,* she thought, and blinked back tears. *Damn.*

She went back to the living room. Courtney hadn't moved.

Trudy dumped her armload on the coffee table and sat down beside Courtney. "Forget about rotten men. There was one good thing that happened tonight. I got you a present."

Courtney turned her head a millimeter. "Does it have gin in it?"

"No, but you want it anyway." Trudy pulled the Twinkletoes box out of her last shopping bag and handed it to Courtney, who stared at it for a moment, her eyes unfocused.

Then she sat up slowly, her forehead smoothing out, her lips parting. "Where—"

"They're making them again. Like a reissue. Second chance. Do-over."

"Oh, please," Courtney said, but she said it while she was ripping the cellophane off the package. She pried open the top and pulled out the cardboard shell with the Twinkletoes doll and her manicure set wired to it. "These aren't the same colors of polish as the old one."

"I'm sorry—"

"These are better." Courtney began to unwire the doll. "She has really big feet."

"Well, she needs really big toenails if little kids are going to paint them." Trudy watched her for a minute and then went back to the gingerbread house as Courtney set up her play station. One thing had gone right that evening, she thought as she beat sugar into the thickening icing. Now if she could get the icing and the gumdrop shingles to stay on the iced roof, that would be two. It was tomorrow morning that was going to be bad.

Poor Leroy.

Damn it.

She began to spackle the roof with the thicker icing, thinking vicious thoughts about government agents who took toys from little kids on Christmas. She picked up a red gumdrop and shoved it into the icing with more force than necessary and almost cracked the roof.

Easy, she told herself and looked back at Courtney, who was studying the Twinkletoes doll with an odd expression on her face.

Well, she was drunk.

Trudy shoved another gumdrop into the icing and dared it to fall off. It didn't.

At least Leroy would have a gingerbread house in the morning. That might help calm things down. She filled in rows of red gumdrop shingles, trying to think of things to say to him.

"Sorry about your Mac, Leroy, but Santa sent you this nice toy cow instead."

No, they'd shot the cow. Jesus.

"Santa got delayed over Pittsburgh but he's going to put your Mac on backorder."

No, Santa was not a mail-order house.

"Maybe it fell off the sleigh."

Trudy shoved another gumdrop in. *Bastards.*

Not that Leroy would throw a fit. He wasn't a fit-throwing kind of kid. But he'd be disappointed; that stillness would be on his face, like the stillness that had been there when his father left.

Men, she thought, and shoved in another gumdrop, but that wasn't fair, she knew it wasn't fair. Nolan had risked his life for her at the end. Maybe even before the end, maybe that was why he'd gotten in the cab, because he cared. Trudy sat up a little. "You know, I think he came along in the cab to save me."

Courtney had the doll out now and her shoes off. "Who?"

"Nolan." Trudy watched Courtney pry open the bottle of silver nail polish, awake and alert, if still a little unsteady from the booze. "He took the Mac away from me at the end after he'd sworn to me he wouldn't, but when he got in the cab at the toy store, he thought he already had the codes. He didn't need me anymore. Maybe he got in to protect me from Reese." She put the last gumdrop on the roof gently. Maybe Nolan cared about her, at least as much as he cared about the Mac.

She looked closer at the roof. The gumdrops seemed to be sliding down.

Beside her, Courtney painted the first Twinkle toe, her face concentrating on the job. Court didn't look particularly happy, but she did look alert. That was something. Trudy picked up a green gumdrop and flattened it and then threaded it onto a toothpick, the first set of branches for a gumdrop tree.

Okay, so Nolan worked for the NSA. Well, good for him, protecting his country. And of course he had to lie to her about his name, he was undercover.

And if he'd gotten into that cab without needing to, if he'd gotten in with her to save her, then maybe he was a good guy. She flattened another gumdrop onto the toothpick and then paid attention for the first time to the music in the background, a slow growly voice singing, "Hurry down the chimney tonight."

She looked at Courtney, jolted out of her fairy tale. "Is that 'Santa Baby'?"

Courtney nodded as she finished Twinkle's last toe. "Yeah. I couldn't get it out of my head after you talked about it."

Trudy listened to the slow, jazzy version on Court's stereo. "That is not Madonna."

"Etta James," Courtney said. "The only good thing I know about Pres is his taste in music. And his kid." She screwed the top back on the polish and looked at the doll, her pretty face puzzled.

"What's wrong?"

"This is a dumb toy." Courtney turned Twinkle around so Trudy could see her vapid plastic face.

Trudy sighed and stuck the last green gumdrop on the top of the toothpick. "I always thought so, but then I wasn't the manicure type. You probably would have loved it when you were six." *Timing is everything. If Nolan already knew all he needed to about the codes when he got in my cab—*

"No, it would have been a huge letdown then, too." Courtney set the doll on the table, where its pink party dress flopped into the icing. "I'm sure there's a lesson in this, but I'll be damned if I know what it is."

"I know what you mean." Trudy stuck her gumdrop tree into the gingerbread beside the door. The red gumdrop shingles had moved another millimeter. "I'd love to find a meaning for what happened tonight besides 'Don't trust men,' but I don't think there is one." *Except maybe Nolan came with me to keep me safe.*

"You don't know that yet." Courtney picked up the manicure set and unzipped it. "The doll was a letdown, but this could be a really great manicure set. You have to believe."

"Do you really think so?" Trudy said, trying not to sound hopeful.

"No. But I think that's what I'm supposed to say." Courtney opened the pink plastic manicure set. "And this is not a great manicure set."

"Oh, sorry," Trudy said. "I used the nail file to stab somebody, so it's gone."

"No, it's in here." Courtney held the case so she could see in. "It looks like it's in pretty good shape. No blood."

Trudy straightened. "It shouldn't be in there at all. The last time I saw it, it was stuck in Reese."

"Must have been a different box." Courtney took the file out. "This box was kind of mushed in the back. Did you—"

Trudy took the box and turned it over. The bottom corner was smashed, as if somebody had driven it into a counter, and over the creases was marked a tiny black *X*.

Oh no, she thought as her hope deflated. This was why Reese had been in the toy store; he'd been picking up this year's codes. And that was why Nolan had gotten in the cab: he hadn't been trying to save her, he'd been following Reese and the Twinkletoes. More Chinese codes, not her. *You're so dumb,* she told herself. *He betrays you and you still want to believe.*

"What?" Courtney said.

"Nolan picked up the wrong Twinkletoes box in the warehouse. He got Reese's instead of mine." Trudy pulled out the instruction sheet. "He wanted this." She stared at the flimsy paper with its bad illustration of Twinkle and its warning not to drink the nail polish in both Chinese and English. "I bet this is this year's codes." She looked over at Courtney holding the neon pink nail file. "Let me see that, please."

Courtney handed over the file, its thick pink plastic handle first. Trudy grabbed the file end and yanked on the handle until it came apart.

"What are you doing?"

"It's a thumb drive," Trudy said when she was sure it was. She showed the end to Courtney. "More espionage stuff. Nolan saw Reese leave the store with a Twinkle, but I had one, too. He got the two bags mixed up in the warehouse and gave me the one with the codes by mistake."

"What does that mean?" Courtney said.

Trudy felt like throwing up. "It means that he's going to show up here and take your Twinkletoes away."

Courtney sat back. "That's okay. It's lousy nail polish, too."

"Another dream shattered," Trudy said, trying to make it sound like a joke.

"Twinkle or Nolan?"

"Both." Trudy packed up the box, feeling sick and stupid.

"Gin?" Courtney picked up her glass.

Trudy shook her head. "You know how dumb I am? I'm so dumb, I believed in that bastard even though I knew he'd lied to me. I even believed he got in that cab to save me. That's how much I wanted to believe."

"He did save you at the end."

"To get the doll," Trudy said, miserable. "And now I'm alone and Leroy is not getting a MacGuffin. So how dumb am I?"

"You're not dumb."

Trudy sank back into the couch as Etta began to sing "Have Yourself a Merry Little Christmas." "Because you know what? I still want to see him. He took my MacGuffin and I still want to see him. I want to *kill* him, but I want to see him."

Courtney nodded in sympathy. "I know. I hate Pres but I'd take him back. That's so sad."

"Prescott will come back," Trudy said tiredly. "When the novelty wears off, he'll want his nice home and his cute kid and his pretty wife again." *And I hope you slam the door in his face because that's what I'm going to do when Nolan comes after this doll.*

Courtney shook her head. "Forget Pres. Tell me about Nolan. Did he say, 'I'll call you'? What was the last thing he said?"

"He said, 'I'm really sorry'," Trudy said, remembering the miserable look on his face at the end. That had been something: he knew he'd screwed her over.

"And what did you say?"

"I think it was, 'Rot and die.'"

"You think you might have been overreacting there?"

"No." Trudy sat up again and stuck another red gumdrop on the roof of the gingerbread house. "I think I just told him the truth. Which was the best thing I could have done. I don't care if he thinks I'm nuts or irrational or anything else, I told him the truth. He did the worst possible thing he could do to me, so don't bother show-

ing up with flowers, making cute apologies and bad
jokes. And yes, I know it's not all about him. I know he's
cashing Daddy's emotional checks, but right now? It's
about him."

"He sounded like a nice guy when you were dating
him."

"He is. He's great. Hell, Dad's a nice guy most of the
time. That's why we believed in him for so long. He
loved us, he was a good guy, how could he keep forget-
ting us like that? Jesus, Courtney, I could have ended up
in a relationship like that. 'Nolan's a nice guy, he loves
me, why am I bleeding from the ears all the time?' "

Courtney nodded. "Yeah. I know. It was almost a relief when Pres left because I could finally stop aching
with disappointment." She sighed. "Except there's
Leroy. Now I ache for Leroy. Especially tomorrow
morning."

"We did it to him, you know." Trudy blinked back
tears. "We should have said, 'Leroy, there is no Santa,
and there's not going to be a Mac Two under the tree on
Christmas Day, although we will do whatever we have
to do to get you one as soon as possible because we love
you and always will.' We should have told him the truth.
Hell, Evil Nemesis Brandon told him the truth. Pretty
damn bad when the only person you can trust is your
Evil Nemesis." *You and me, Leroy.*

"I hate the truth. Except this part." Courtney gestured
to the Twinkletoes box. "The part where you almost got
yourself killed trying to get him that MacGuffin. The
part where you brought me a Twinkletoes to make up
for twenty years ago. The part where you're fixing my
gingerbread house. The part where we'll take care of
Leroy together tomorrow. I like that part of the truth."

Trudy dropped the gumdrops and sat back next to her

sister, and Courtney snuggled closer and put her head on Trudy's shoulder.

"Yeah," Trudy said, patting her arm. "I like the part where you waited up for me. And did the boring part of the gingerbread house. And didn't tell me I'm an idiot for still wanting a lying bastard."

"So it's not so bad," Courtney said as the first gumdrop slid off the roof of the gingerbread house.

They watched for a minute while another slowly followed the first one.

Trudy thought about putting them back again and decided to let them slide. "What are we going to tell Leroy tomorrow?"

"How about, 'Maybe it fell off the sleigh'?" Courtney said.

Trudy sighed. "Well, it beats, 'Aunt Trudy had a Mac for you, but the United States government lied to her and took it away.'"

"Yeah," Courtney said. "He's mature for his age, but we'd never be able to explain that one. I'm still not sure I get it."

"That's okay." Trudy straightened. "I get it. Let's go to bed."

She stood up and pulled Courtney to her feet and steered her in the direction of the stairs, and when her sister was gone, she walked around shutting off lights and turning off the fire, stopping when she came to the stereo where the CD had changed. Judy Garland was singing "Have Yourself a Merry Little Christmas," the carol that most made Trudy want to kill herself every holiday. She stood in the darkness and listened to Judy break her heart and let the tears drip as she thought of Leroy in the morning and of Nolan that night. *I really did believe in you,* she thought. *For about five minutes, I believed, and it felt really good.*

Then Judy finished her song and Trudy turned the stereo off and went to bed.

❄   ❄   ❄

The next morning, Trudy curled up in an armchair in her flannel robe and mainlined coffee while Leroy opened his presents. When he was done, he turned and looked at them, standing straight in his Lilo and Stitch footie PJs, and said, "'Guffin?'"

Courtney swallowed. "It wasn't in there? Gee, baby, maybe it fell off the sleigh."

Leroy looked at her with the five-year-old version of, *How dumb do you think I am?*

Trudy put her coffee cup down and took a deep breath. "Leroy, here's the thing. There really isn't a—"

The doorbell rang, and she stopped, grateful for any interruption. "I'll get it." She went to the front door and looked through the square windows at the top, through the gold wreath Courtney had hung on the outside.

Nolan was standing there, looking like three kinds of hell.

Good, she thought, *you're as miserable as I am,* and opened the door. "Oh, look, it's a Christmas miracle."

He was holding two Christmas gift bags, slumping with exhaustion as the snow started to settle on his thick, dark hair. "Merry Christmas, Trudy."

"Ho ho ho," Trudy said. "I was just about to explain to my five-year-old nephew that there is no Santa. Can you come back at another time? Never would be good for me."

He held out one of the bags. "Chill on the Santa. I got you covered."

"Uh huh," Trudy said.

"Go ahead. Look."

She took the bag and looked inside at the top of a camo-colored box that said, *New! Now with Toxic Waste!* "You are kidding me." She pulled out the box and saw the Mac Two, its pudgy little face uglier than ever now that its lips were pursed to spit goop. "How—"

"Top-secret," Nolan said, trying an exhausted smile on her. "I'd tell you, but then I'd have to kill you."

"That's lame." She put the Mac Two back in the bag, hope beginning to rise that maybe he wasn't a rat until she remembered that what he'd really come for was the Twinkletoes. She handed the bag back to him. "You're too late. And your patter is falling off."

"It's six A.M., I've had no sleep, and I'm freezing." Nolan held the bag out to her again. "Everything I have is falling off. Will you take this, please?" Then he looked past her, toward the floor, and said, "Hi."

Trudy turned to see Leroy, blinking up at them, looking absurdly small in his footie pajamas.

"What's that?" Leroy said, pointing to the Christmas bag.

"I found it out on the front lawn," Nolan said. "I think it fell off the sleigh." He handed it to Leroy.

Leroy looked into the top of it and his face lit up. *"Mom!"* he yelled. "You were *right!*" He took off for the living room and then stopped and came back. "Thank you very much for finding my 'Guffin," he said to Nolan, and then took off for the living room again, so happy that Trudy felt her throat close.

"Cute kid," Nolan said, and looked back at Trudy.

"Thank you," she said, feeling absurdly relieved. *Don't get suckered by this guy again.* "Well, I'd invite you in, but I'm still mad at you. So thanks. Merry Christmas. Have a good life. Somewhere else." She shut the door in his face.

"If you don't sleep with him, I will," Courtney said

from behind her. "He got my kid a *MacGuffin*. He forgot the extra toxic waste, but what the hell."

"He's not leaving," Trudy said as the doorbell rang again. "Go get your Twinkletoes, he's going to ask for it next." She opened the door.

"Forgot this." Nolan handed her three packages of toxic waste.

"How do you feel about dating women with children?" Courtney said.

"Get the Twinkletoes," Trudy said, and Courtney went back to the living room.

Nolan leaned in the doorway, looking too tired to stand. "Look, I know you're mad, and I don't blame you, but I want to see you again. We got off to a bad start because we were lying to each other—"

"I never lied to you," Trudy said, outraged.

"You like faculty cocktail parties? And you really wanted to see that foreign film I took you to?"

"I was trying to help you," Trudy said. "I was trying to fit into your world."

"You were boring as hell," Nolan said.

"Hey!"

"But not last night. Last night you were somebody I want to see again. Without the violence."

Trudy leaned in the other side of the doorway, watching the snow swirl behind him. "You know, if I didn't know what I do know, I'd be pretty happy with that speech. But I know what you came for. Tell me the truth and you can have it. And then you can go away forever."

"If I'm going away forever, I'm not getting what I want," Nolan said.

"Funny," Trudy said. "Okay, play your stupid game. Courtney's getting the doll."

"What doll?" Nolan said.

"The one with the smashed-in corner and the *X*. Like

the MacGuffin. Only this year it's the Twinkletoe—"
She stopped as Nolan's face changed from exhausted to
alert.

"Let me see it," he said, and stepped inside, pushing
her in front of him and closing the door behind him as
Courtney came into the hall with the box.

"Hi. I'm Courtney, Trudy's sister." Courtney handed
him the Twinkletoes.

"Nice to meet you, Courtney." Nolan took the box.

"The instructions are in there," Trudy said, a little un-
certain now. "The USB key is in the nail file this time."

"You are kidding me." Nolan opened the box and
took out the manicure set. Then he tucked the box under one arm, took out the nail file, and yanked the handle off. "You're not kidding me," he said, looking at the
end of the USB key. "I will be damned." He put the file
back in the case and the case back in the box. "I have to
make a call. You stay here." He went back out onto the
porch, shutting the door behind him.

"Thanks, I will," Trudy said to the door.

He hadn't known about the Twinkletoes.

Courtney went up on tiptoe to see out the little windows. "He's on his cell phone."

"Yeah?" Trudy said.

He really hadn't known about the Twinkletoes.

Courtney sank back on her heels. "He didn't know
about the Twinkletoes, Tru. I think he's a good one. Plus
he's hot."

"Maybe," Trudy said, and then the doorbell rang
again.

"I'll just go see what my son is doing with his new
tac nuke," Courtney said, and went back into the living
room.

Trudy took a deep breath and opened the door.

"The thanks of a grateful nation are yours," Nolan

said, meeting her eyes and taking her breath away. "Now about us."

"Us?" Trudy said, her voice cracking.

"Yeah, us. I know I really screwed you over last night."

"Well, national security and all," Trudy said.

He really hadn't known about the codes in the Twinkletoes.

"But I keep my promises," Nolan said, his eyes steady on hers.

"Good for you," Trudy said.

He hadn't known.

"I said you'd have this on Christmas morning." Nolan held out the other bag. "I know it's a mess, but . . ."

Trudy took the bag and looked inside. "What the . . ." She pulled out the Mac One. The box was gone, and the doll was battered and mangled, but it was her Mac. She squeezed it, and it made a crackly sound. "What did you do to it?"

"They had to take a code machine out of it," Nolan said. "So I got some paper from the paper shredder and restuffed it."

Trudy pulled up the Mac's jacket to see a broad band of duct tape wound around its belly. "Duct tape."

"I don't sew," Nolan said. "Besides, duct tape is better. It's a guy thing."

Trudy smoothed the little camo shirt back down and tried to rub the smudge of dirt off the Mac's nose. He looked nicer now, she thought, all ripped up and eviscerated and dirty. More vulnerable. Plus one of his eyebrows had come off, so now he just looked half-mad. *Kind of like me.*

"Reese threw the box away in the warehouse," Nolan went on. "I looked but couldn't find it. The silencer was the thumb drive, so that has to stay with NSA. They think the ammo belt may have something in it, too. And his boots—"

"How did you ever talk them into letting you take the doll?" Trudy said, amazed.

"I didn't give them much choice," Nolan said. "My future was riding on it."

Trudy blinked up at him.

"You know. Assuming you're ever going to talk to me again."

"You got in the cab thinking you already had the codes, didn't you?" Trudy said. "Did the NSA tell you to do that?"

"No, they told me to stay put since they had the cab under control."

"Why'd you get in?"

Nolan shrugged. "I wasn't that sure they had it under control."

"You came along to protect me," Trudy said.

"Yeah," Nolan said. "But don't go giving me any medals because that turned out great for me. We ended up with everything we needed because I got in that cab. Following you around made me look like a genius to my boss." He shook his head. "And now we have this year's codes. You're good for me, Gertrude."

Trudy wrapped her arms around the Mac, feeling the crunch of its duct tape against her stomach. "You turned out pretty good for me, too, Nolan."

He nodded and met her eyes for a long moment.

Kiss me, she thought.

Then he said, "I have to go."

"Of course," Trudy said, deflating.

"But I would like to come back," he said, as if he were choosing his words very carefully. "Can I have you, uh"—he shook his head—"see you later tonight?"

Under the Christmas tree with all the lights on.

"Yes," Trudy said primly. "That would be very nice." *Kiss me.*

"Okay then." Nolan looked at a loss for words. "About seven?"

"Seven is good," Trudy said. *Kiss me.*

"I'll see you at seven then," Nolan said. "I really will, I promise."

"I believe you," Trudy said. "Thank you for the Mac-Guffin." *Kiss me, you idiot.*

"Uh, you're welcome. Thank you for the Chinese spy codes." He turned to go.

"Wait," Trudy said, and when he turned back, she grabbed the lapel of his coat and pulled him down to her and kissed him good, and he dropped the Twinkletoes and pulled her close, squashing the Mac One between them.

"I'm crazy about you," he whispered when he broke the kiss.

"I'm crazy about you, too," she said, dizzy with happiness. "Hurry back."

"I will," he said fervently, and then he was gone, off into the snow, but he'd be back. He'd promised, and she believed him.

She closed the door and went back into the living room just in time to see Leroy squeeze the Mac Two so that green toxic waste shot across the room as Madonna sang "Santa Baby" on the radio and Courtney dipped a broken gingerbread arm into her gin.

"I love Christmas," Trudy said, and went to join her family.

Christmas at
Seashell Cottage

❄ ❄ ❄

by Donna Alward

Chapter One

Charlie Yang had never considered herself much of a joiner. So it went without saying that she was surprised to find herself in the middle of setting up a nativity scene in front of the Jewell Cove church, stuffing scratchy straw into a crudely constructed manger. They'd had an early snow, and the layer of white covering the ground and the branches of trees and shrubbery added to the feeling of holiday spirit that had taken over since Thanksgiving.

Like a well-oiled machine, Gloria Henderson and her army of church ladies had taken charge of the volunteers and had assigned jobs to everyone. The men were tasked with anything requiring a ladder and heavy lifting—including lugging three wise men, Mary and Joseph, the shepherds and sheep, and every last bit of the nativity to the front yard. Right now Bill—Charlie had forgotten his last name—from the service station was positioning the figures in the proper places, which were the exact same spots they occupied each and every year, apparently. Charlie gave a dry chuckle. You could always count on small towns, and Jewell Cove, Maine, was no different. It was practically steeped in saltwater traditions.

Still, it stung a little that the committee had taken one look at Charlie's attempt at the red-and-green velvet bows and suggested she might be better suited to helping with something else. She was a doctor, for heaven's sake. She could suture a wound and leave barely a trace of a scar. Surely her bows weren't that bad . . .

She'd been sent off to the front of the church with specific instructions: set up the manger, uncoil and string the lights, and put Baby Jesus in place. Charlie huffed. She'd been number three in her graduating class from med school. She could set up a nativity scene with one hand tied behind her back. She shivered against the cold, zipped her puffy jacket up the last three inches, and wished she'd thought to wear a hat to keep her ears warm.

"Manger, check." She wrestled the wooden structure into position by inches until it was in the middle of the nativity. "Straw, check." She took off her gloves for a minute and padded the bottom of the manger with a small brick of synthetic straw, pulling the pieces apart and fluffing them up. As soon as it was done, she hurried to put her gloves back on. "Now for Baby Jesus." Charlie looked around at the boxes of Christmas decorations that surrounded her. "Aha! Baby Jesus, check!" She retrieved a doll from a box, already wrapped and safety-pinned into swaddling clothes, and stared down at the straw padding the bottom of the crude manger. "This doesn't feel right," she murmured to the doll. She looked in the box for a blanket or fabric of some sort. "I can't just put you down on the prickly straw. Surely the new Messiah deserves something softer to lie on."

After a few minutes of digging through the boxes for

something that might suit, Charlie sighed. "Well, Baby Jesus, we'll just have to wait to put you in your manger until I can think of something to use to cover the straw. Until then, I need to get these lights untangled."

She sat down on the cold, wooden platform the church had set up to house the nativity scene. It was a lonely, solitary task and she found herself carrying on a one-way conversation with the doll just to break the silence. "I have skills, Baby Jesus. Specific skills. Skills that I should be using right now with my patients. Not sitting in the cold unraveling tangled lights." She sighed in frustration.

God, she was talking to a doll. A doll who was, at this moment, staring at her with unseeing, unblinking eyes. It was a little bit creepy, so she turned her attention back to the task at hand, working away at a stubborn knot, muttering to herself. Once again the gloves came off; there was no way she could straighten the knotted wires with the material in the way. She blew on her fingers and started again.

"You know," she continued, "when I agreed to help out, I'd thought it would be a good chance to be a part of the community. Outside of work, I mean. And . . . here I am alone. As usual."

Charlie cursed under her breath as the knot let go only to reveal another. A burst of laughter drew her attention away for a moment, and she watched as a couple strolled along the sidewalk holding hands.

"Wanna hear something stupid, Baby Jesus? The closest thing to a romantic relationship I have right now is an infatuation with the man who works on the docks. You know?" She paused, studying the glassy eyes of the doll next to her. "Of course you don't know. You're a doll. And the Savior of all mankind, right? You have bigger fish to fry than my nonexistent love life." She laughed to herself. "I'm pathetic. But let me tell you, that man is hot. Tall, dark, and rugged." In her mind she could picture the look of him, long legs and broad shoulders, his strength evident even beneath work pants and the navy jacket he typically wore. She sighed. "I don't even know his name. How dumb is that?"

"Um, excuse me, but who are you talking to?"

She jumped at the sound of a deep voice behind her, a muted squeak bursting from her mouth, then spun around to find a giant of a man standing there, feet planted, arms crossed, and an amused expression on his face. Not just any man. *The* man.

Her cheeks flamed with embarrassment. "Baby Jesus?" she suggested weakly. Busted talking to a doll. She felt about three years old.

He chuckled. "Really?" He nodded at the bundle in her arms. "What were you going to do? Brain me with him?"

What? It took a few seconds before she realized that she'd grabbed the doll like a weapon and was currently holding it like she was a quarterback ready to go long. Charlie looked down at the doll's face and then tucked it more securely in her arms. "You startled me, that's all," she replied, emitting a breathy laugh. Holy crap. From afar he'd looked big, but her dream guy was over six feet for sure, probably closer to six four, big feet in big boots, faded jeans, and one of those plaid quilted jackets she'd seen a lot of the men around here wear when the weather was cold but not downright frigid. His arms were crossed, and the stance accentuated the muscles in her arms and shoulders. His hair was thick and dark, highlighting a face that sported a stunning set of brown eyes with long lashes, a strong jaw, and good cheekbones.

"I'm Charlene," she offered, only stammering a little, holding the doll in one arm and extending her other hand. "Charlie, actually."

"Dave," he replied, stepping forward to shake her hand. The contact sent a ripple of pleasure down her arm. "Do you always talk to dolls?" He grinned openly now, a slight dimple popping in one cheek.

"Only when I'm trying not to freeze to death." She smiled back, her pulse hammering. *Don't say something dumb,* she warned herself. Like blurting out that she'd watched him working each day from the wide windows at Breezes Café. The last thing she needed was to seem all . . . stalkerish.

"You're one of the doctors in town, aren't you?" he asked, dropping her hand. "I've seen you around."

He had? And if he knew she was the doctor, he had to have asked about her, right? As she wrapped her mind around that astounding fact, she tried to remain cool. "That's me."

"I'm working down at the boatyard for the time being."

"I know."

Damn it. Why couldn't she bite her tongue?

His eyebrows went up, and she offered a smile that she hoped wasn't too goofy-looking. "Small town," she reminded him, and he chuckled, sending a warm shiver over her. It seemed her rugged mystery man was just as attractive up close. Lucky for her. Perhaps she'd been neglecting her love life for a little too long.

Dave smiled at her. "I'm pretty new around here. The guy I work for is helping out today and mentioned they needed some help. I thought I'd lend a hand. Maybe meet some people." His eyes were warm. "Looks like I'm off to a good start."

She hoped she wasn't blushing, because she got the feeling he was flirting. She blinked, then smiled back. "I think you're off to a very good start."

Their gazes held for a few moments and Charlie held her breath. This was something she wasn't exactly used to. To have her mystery man standing before her, in the flesh, making conversation . . . surreal. To say the least.

"Anyway, sorry about the manger," he apologized, breaking the spell. "It's kind of crude, but I didn't have much time to put it together."

She looked down at the rough wood. It wasn't fancy, but it was solidly constructed. "You built this?"

"Apparently the one they had was falling apart. Time to replace it." He shrugged. "I'm more used to working with boats and engines than carpentry, but I borrowed some tools, got some scrap wood from my landlord, and gave it my best shot."

"Aren't we lucky that you're so . . . handy." And hot. And friendly.

"I'm not sure about that. Anyway, you seemed to be standing around the manger for a long time and I wondered if something needed fixing."

Charlie looked up at him, feeling her cheeks heat again beneath his honest gaze. Good heavens, where was her confidence? "There's nothing wrong with the manger. It's silly, really. I . . ."

"You?" he prompted.

She swallowed. "I put in the straw but I was wondering if there was anything to put over top of it before I put down the, uh, baby."

"Over top?"

"You know." She gestured with her free hand. "Like a blanket or something. Because the straw is so scratchy and rough."

His gaze softened and she felt a little bit embarrassed and a little bit melty.

"I don't think it's going to matter to the doll, Charlie."

He finally said her name and it sounded so nice in his deep, smooth voice she wondered if she was really looking at Dave, the Christmas angel.

She let her eyes meet his, felt the connection to her toes. "It's not *just* a doll," she said softly. "It's Baby Jesus."

And there was that smile again, and a hint of perfectly white teeth. "You're right," he responded, taking a step forward. Charlie held her breath as he came closer, peering over her shoulder at the wood and straw. He smelled good too. A little like lumber, but more like man. The kind of scent that made a woman want to burrow her face into the soft fabric of his shirt and just breathe deeply . . .

He took a step back and she let out her breath. Okay. Granted, her time in Jewell Cove had been a significant dry spell, but this was getting ridiculous.

"I might have something in my car that would work. I'll be back in a minute."

"Okay," she replied, feeling dumb, but enjoying the view as he walked away toward the church parking lot.

❄   ❄   ❄

Dave strode away toward the parking lot feeling a little bit off balance after the encounter with the good doctor. The men on the dock called her Dr. Pit Bull, and Dave thought they must be thinking about two different people. Charlene—Charlie—seemed quiet, and, well, cute. She'd blushed when they'd talked and stammered a little too. In fact, she'd looked adorable, standing there with the doll and surrounded by tangles of Christmas lights.

He reached his SUV and opened the trunk. Inside the plastic tub containing extra windshield washer, oil, and jumper cables was a crumpled pile of rags, mostly comprised of old T-shirts. He grabbed a beige one, closed the tailgate again, and headed back toward the nativity scene where Charlie waited. She was a tiny little thing, maybe five foot four or five, her build slight. She rather reminded him of a ballerina, with a dainty strength about her. Her black hair was braided precisely, highlighting porcelain smoothness of her skin, and a set of exotic brown eyes that a man could lose himself in. She was absolutely stunning.

The doll was still in her arms when he reached the nativity again, and he grinned at the strange sight. He held out the shirt. "This is clean, and nice and soft. Will it work?"

The smile on her face made the day worthwhile. "That's perfect! Plus, it's almost the same color as the straw. It'll blend in really well."

It was cute how she was worried about authenticity. And the comfort and welfare of a plastic doll.

Dave folded the cotton and draped it over the bumpy straw. He watched as Charlie lay the doll down as carefully as if it were a real baby, then stood back. "That definitely looks better," she said, hands on her hips.

He considered pointing out the cold Maine weather and paltry covering on the doll, but was afraid she'd take that to heart too and insist on covering the manger with heavy blankets, which he was sure wouldn't have been found in Bethlehem.

"Much better," he replied, but he couldn't take his eyes off of her. Petite and pretty, pit bull doctor, sentimentalist. Which was she, or was she all those things? It had been a long time since he'd been this intrigued by a woman. It wasn't exactly an unwelcome feeling.

"Hey, are you all right?"

Charlie's voice interrupted his less-than-pure thoughts. "Yeah, sure. Sorry."

He got the feeling Charlie was going to say something more, but one of the church ladies came bearing down on them like a woman on a mission. "Charlene, we could use your help in the sanctuary. We're putting together the caroling booklets for the tree lighting tomorrow night."

Ah yes. Dave looked at Charlie's face and saw it transform into a polite, welcoming mask, and he nearly laughed. He'd bet ten bucks that she adopted the same expression when she walked into an exam room and greeted a new patient.

"Sure thing, Mrs. Henderson. I think the nativity is all done. I'm still working on the lights . . ."

The older woman's lips pursed a bit in disapproval. "Well, maybe Bill can finish that up. He knows how we display them."

Mrs. Henderson moved on to fuss about the figures, muscling a shepherd and staff about two inches to the right before declaring herself satisfied. "There. That's wonderful. We're nearly done inside as well. The ladies' group has provided lunch for the volunteers. Soup and sandwiches, which should be on in exactly . . ." She checked her watch. "Thirty-six minutes."

Heaven forbid the lunch be a minute early or late.

"Mr . . . ?" Mrs. Henderson looked up at him suddenly, and he got the strange feeling that she was taking stock of him.

"Ricker," he supplied with a nod.

"Yes, you just moved here, didn't you?"

Nosy. Bossy and nosy. She had a way of talking that reminded him of the military. Sharp and precise. "Yes, ma'am. From Virginia." He tried another one of his smiles on her, thinking that perhaps he and Dr. Yang really weren't that different after all. "I built the manger."

"Right." She eyed him curiously. "You're working for George Adams down on the docks. Hope he's got enough work to keep you busy."

Now it was his turn to be embarrassed and he hoped the raw bite to the air covered any flush in his cheeks. He wasn't rolling in it but he could make ends meet. Besides, this was just a temporary job until he figured out exactly where he wanted to settle.

"I don't know about you, but I think I can smell that soup all the way out here. Are you coming in with us, Dave?" Charlie jumped in with the attempted save.

As much as he might enjoy spending more time with the pretty doctor, he wasn't sure he was up to the sheer volume of hen clucking that was likely to happen over lunch. "No, but thanks for the invite. I've got to get back home. I'm running low on wood and should probably split a bunch to tide me over for a few days."

He waited for lightning to strike through the leaden sky. He'd just flat-out lied, in front of the church with the steeple and cross directly in front of him.

"Well, thank you for all your help," Mrs. Henderson said. "You be sure to come to the tree lighting tomorrow night in the square. The choir's leading the caroling and there's free hot chocolate for everyone."

"Sounds great," he responded, giving that automatic smile again.

He looked down at Charlie. She was watching him curiously, as if trying to puzzle him out. Her gaze burned into his, and he thought for a moment he saw a devilish twinkle in their depths. "Oh yes. Everyone comes out for it," Charlie said. "It's one of the highlights of the season." Her voice sounded exactly like an advertisement and he had a hard time not laughing at what he was certain was false enthusiasm.

"Everyone?" he asked.

Mrs. Henderson didn't miss the skeptical tone in his voice. "Oh, the whole town shows up," she insisted. "You'll be there, won't you, Charlene?"

"Of course. I wouldn't miss it." Again with the too-bright enthusiasm. Was Charlie also a bit of a wallflower?

"Maybe I'll know someone, then," he offered. Had he really just agreed to go? He had to be off his rocker. Christmas carols? He couldn't carry a tune in a bucket. And hot chocolate? He'd much prefer a couple fingers of whiskey in front of the fire back at the cottage.

"Right. Well, Charlene, we really need those booklets done up. Thanks for your help, Mr. Ricker." Mrs. Henderson got right back to business and began stomping her way to the front steps of the church.

"I'd better go," Charlie said quietly, looking up at him. "That woman means business."

"She'd be a great drill sergeant," he remarked.

Charlie laughed lightly, the sound dancing in the crisp air.

"So will I see you tomorrow night?" she asked, a hopeful note to her voice. "I get the feeling we're both kind of like the new people in town. Welcome to join in, but still a little on the outside. Sometimes I think everyone in Jewell Cove has known each other forever."

"I'll probably make it," he answered. "Not much else to do but sit out at the cabin and stare at the fire."

She laughed again. "That sounds pretty nice to me."

And just like that he imagined her sitting there with

him, perhaps a glass of wine in her hand, and that silken black hair loosened from its braid while the fire snapped and crackled behind them . . .

Get ahold of yourself, man. Dave swallowed and shoved his hands into his pockets. "Aw, it won't kill us to show up, will it?"

"So I guess I'll see you then."

"Guess so." He pulled a hand out of his coat. "Nice to meet you, Charlie."

She took his hand again, but there was more holding than shaking happening and he felt the pull to her through the innocent contact.

"You too." She pulled her hand away. "See you around."

He watched her walk away. She didn't look back at him, just made a straight line through the snow to the church doors. He let out a breath. He'd come to Jewell Cove to start over, to be closer to his daughter, Nora.

Meeting the pretty doctor hadn't been on his agenda, but he wasn't about to complain. After all, he'd learned long ago that sometimes the best things happened when you least expected them.

Chapter Two

Charlie tugged her hat down over her ears a little farther and inwardly agreed that her prediction had been bang on. The whole town did come out to the tree lighting—at least it looked that way. Memorial Square was full of people, the scent of fresh snow, evergreen, and chocolate heavy in the air. There was laughter and conversation and happy greetings, but Charlie hung back. She found it awkward, being overly friendly with the townspeople and then having them in her exam room the next week. She tended to isolate herself, maintain that little bit of personal distance. She wasn't sure how her boss, Josh Collins, managed to separate personal from professional, but he did. Brilliantly. Just like he did everything.

She snagged herself a cup of hot chocolate, both for the comforting heat and to give her something to do with her hands. There was an unoccupied corner by the gazebo, and she made her way there, smiling at people as she went along. There were lots of "Hi, Dr. Yang," and

"Merry Christmas, Dr. Yang," greetings but none to Charlene or Charlie.

This was how she'd wanted it when she first moved here, but now she wasn't so sure. Wouldn't it be nice to be a part of something? To belong and fit in? She leaned back against the gazebo wall and watched the gathering with a bit of longing. Sure, it would be nice, but she had no idea how to go about it. She should call Lizzie, she realized. Her best friend and college roommate did much better with interpersonal relationships. Heck, if it hadn't been for her, Charlie wouldn't have had any social life in college at all.

She sipped at her chocolate. Lizzie had come into their dorm room that first year of med school and had made life bearable. Lizzie had gone to med school because it was all she'd ever wanted to do. Charlie had gone because it was expected. Study. Succeed. For her parents, it had been about prestige and money and being able to say their only child was a hotshot doctor. One did not merely get by. One strived to be *the best*. Otherwise, what was the point?

It really choked them now that she was a simple GP in a small town. She felt the disapproval every time she saw them, which was always at the family home on Beacon Hill. Not once had they driven up to Jewell Cove to see where she was living.

"Hey, is there room for one more to hide over here?"

A delicious shiver ran up her spine. She looked over her shoulder and saw Dave, cradling his own cup of chocolate, a thick knitted hat on his head and a heavy winter jacket making him look even bigger than he had yesterday. She vowed that she would not be as awkward as she'd felt in front of the church.

She smiled. "You realize you're ginormous, right? Good luck hiding anywhere."

He chuckled. "It's in my genes. My dad's six three and my mom's five eleven. I was bound to be big."

"Brothers and sisters?"

He raised his eyebrows. "Two of each. I'm smack in the middle of the birth order."

Good heavens. Five of them? "You must be intimidating when you're all together. Any big plans to get together for the holidays?"

"We're all grown. My older brother and sister are both married and have kids. My younger brother, Jason, is engaged and my baby sister, Samantha, is just finishing college. We're spread out too, so having us all together doesn't really happen very often, though we try. This year Mom and Dad are spending Christmas in Texas at my brother's, spoiling grandkids." He took a sip of his chocolate and then looked down at her. "What about you? Siblings?"

She turned her gaze to the very tall Christmas tree in the center of the square. His family sounded wonderful, even if they were spread out across the country. She focused on the huge star at the top of the tree as she answered. "There's just me. My parents live in Boston."

"So close enough you can all be together for Christmas. Lucky."

He'd think so, wouldn't he? Because that's what families did. But not hers. She forced her voice to be light, nonchalant. "Oh, they're traveling over the holidays. A cruise or something."

She knew how it sounded. The problem was, the situation was exactly how it appeared. They weren't a warm and fuzzy family. Being together felt like work. She supposed it had been nice of them to invite her along for the trip, but the idea of being stuck on a cruise ship for Christmas, playing third wheel to her parents wasn't Charlie's idea of a perfect holiday.

They stopped chatting as the mayor, Luke Pratt, got up to make a short speech. The elementary school choir then performed three verses of "O Christmas Tree," their sweet, youthful voices filling the air as a few errant flakes of snow drifted through the darkness. As the last note faded into the night, there was a breathless pause and then the tree came to life, multicolored bulbs lighting up the square and causing a chorus of ooohs and aaahs to wave through the gathering, and then clapping broke out, the sound muffled by heavy mittens and gloves.

"That's pretty impressive," Dave remarked from behind her.

She nodded, staring at the tree, the beautiful colored lights sparkling in the chilly evening. "I've always liked the lights with all the colors." She looked over her shoulder and smiled at him. "White ones are elegant, and I know some people like all red, or green, or whatever. But I think the variety is so cheerful, don't you?"

"Oh, absolutely." He was grinning, and she knew he was teasing her a little bit. She liked it. It was far better than the formal "Dr. Yang" she got when she crossed the square.

They were interrupted by someone from the church, thrusting a caroling booklet in Charlie's hand. "We've got a bigger crowd than we expected," the woman explained. "Would you mind sharing?"

"Of course," Dave answered. He stayed where he was, a few steps behind her, even as the church choir led the first carol, easing into the evening with a familiar and rousing rendition of "Jingle Bells."

Charlie turned around and stared at him. "Either you're incredibly farsighted, or you're not singing."

He squinted at her—and then laughed.

"Nuh-uh," she chided. "If I'm expected to sing, so are you."

"Believe me, you don't want me to."

"Then fake it." She smiled at him sweetly. "Aren't we supposed to be suffering together here?"

"You'll only suffer if I sing. We could demonstrate our solidarity by abstaining."

They were talking during the singing and a few dirty looks were aimed their way.

She shoved the booklet in his hands. "Just mouth the words," she commanded. "And smile."

He held the booklet but had to hold his arm straight down so it was low enough for her to see. Not that they needed the words to "Jingle Bells." Charlie joined in, feeling awkward and singing softly. Just enough so she could hear herself, but not loudly enough that anyone nearby could discern her voice from the others.

And then she heard it, a deep rumble an octave below hers, slightly off-key, slightly mumbled, as Dave started jingling all the way. She hid a smirk behind a sip of hot chocolate, then joined in for the last chorus.

As the next carol was announced, he leaned over, his mouth ridiculously close to her ear. "I saw you laughing."

She put on an innocent expression. "I swear I didn't."

"I told you I couldn't sing."

"Yes, you can. What you should have said was you can't sing well." And then she did giggle.

And he gave her shoulder a nudge as if to say, *Brat*.

The next song was more somber, and the crowd started singing "O Little Town of Bethlehem." That was followed by several others, both religious and secular until Charlie's hot chocolate was long gone and her fingers and toes were starting to get cold. She shivered and wrapped her arms around her middle, shifting her feet to get warm. How long did these things go, anyway?

And then Dave moved closer behind her, blocking her from the cold with his broad body, putting his left arm around her and pulling her back against his puffy coat while the right one encircled her, holding the lyrics booklet so they could both see.

She should pull away. She should simply say she was getting cold and leave. But she didn't. It felt too good, having the bulk of his body close to hers, barely touching and yet sheltering her just the same. He was near enough she could feel the gentle vibration of his voice through his chest as the crowd started singing "Silent Night." The mood had turned soft and reverent, the voices blending beautifully as the earlier cloud cover shifted away and left a sky full of twinkling stars. Something stole through Charlie then, a lovely yet wistful sense of contentment. Maybe she wasn't perfect. Maybe she didn't quite fit in here. But right now, the heart of Jewell Cove wasn't such a bad place to be.

Her eyes stung a little and she blinked quickly, picking up the words of the second verse. It had always been her favorite carol, so calm and peaceful and beautiful. A few voices sang in harmony, and Charlie realized that this was the happiest she'd been in a long time.

The song faded into the night and there was a pause while everyone, by tacit agreement, let the last note linger on the air.

❄   ❄   ❄

Dave looked down at the warm woman in his arms. Her head didn't quite reach his chin, and she felt tiny and petite as she leaned against his chest. He didn't want to let her go, not yet. And he didn't think she wanted to leave either, because she stayed where she was as Gloria Henderson got up and reminded everyone about the Evergreen Festival coming up. The evening ended with a cheerful version of "We Wish You a Merry Christmas" and then the crowd began to disperse.

She started forward but his arm tightened, pulling her back against his chest. "Hurrying away so soon?" he asked quietly, putting his lips close to her ear. Close enough he could kiss the soft skin just behind her earlobe. He didn't, but he was tempted.

"I should go. It's cold out." Her voice was breathy. She was feeling it too. But she stopped pushing against his arm and settled back against him once more, in the fleeting moments where they were in the tenuous limbo of the event being over but not yet attracting any attention.

He definitely didn't want the night to end yet.

"I thought you might be interested in that drink. And the fire."

❋   ❋   ❋

Nerves and anticipation coiled in Charlie's stomach, a delicious blend of "I shouldn't" and "I really want to." Wasn't this what she'd been fantasizing about since she'd first seen him? That he'd show up and proposition her in that smooth, velvety voice?

Charlie slowly turned around and lifted her chin so she could meet his eyes. Just as she suspected, they were serious with a glint of teasing . . . or was that challenge? She was an achiever. Challenges were her personal kryptonite. It was almost impossible to turn one down. Add into that the fact that she knew exactly what she was looking for in a man, and his invitation became tempting in the extreme. He had a good sense of humor. He was nice, and gentlemanly. Not a bad start, really.

"I'm not looking for a hookup," she said, casting a quick look around to make sure she couldn't be heard. "Just so you know. It's not really my style." As much as she disliked the rigid structure of her childhood, the end result was that she was constantly weighing pros and cons and making decisions based on logic and not impulse.

Saying yes would definitely be an impulse move.

"Charlie, look at me."

She met his eyes again. The challenge was gone, replaced by something deeper. Something she couldn't help but respond to.

"It's just one drink. I've spent the last few weeks working my butt off. I liked you yesterday. Other than the guys down at the dock, you're the only person I've really met in town." He gave her a little wink. "And you're definitely better looking than they are."

She wasn't beating social engagements off with a stick either. The clinic was small, just her, Josh, and their receptionist-slash-nurse, Robin. There was no office Christmas party, no family, no tight circle of friends. She understood the kind of isolation he was talking about. More than that, she was really attracted to him.

She wavered. "One drink, nothing more." She wanted to sound firm but her voice had a husky, soft tone she didn't quite recognize.

They'd stepped away from each other, preparing to leave the square when Josh came up behind them. "Charlie, you came to the tree lighting. I wasn't sure you would."

Charlie blinked. So much for slipping away unnoticed.

"And you've got a date." Josh grinned at her and she felt like a little sister at the mercy of a big brother's teasing.

"You're being transparent, Josh."

He actually had the temerity to look innocent and offended. "Me? Transparent? Right." He held out his hand to Dave. "Josh Collins. I'm the other doctor in the Jewell Cove practice."

"Dave Ricker." Dave shook Josh's hand and smiled. "I'm working at the boatyard."

Josh tilted his head and wrinkled his brow. "Hey, are you the guy renting Tom's cottage out at Fiddler's Rock?"

Dave nodded. "Yeah, that's me. You know Tom?"

Josh grinned. "He's my cousin. Welcome to town. Listen, a bunch of us are going to the Rusty Fern for a bite to eat. Come along and I'll buy you a drink," he offered. "You too, Charlie," he added as an afterthought.

"I think we already have plans," Dave replied, his gaze leaving Josh and falling on Charlie.

Charlie looked from Josh to Dave. "You did say you didn't know many people in town," she said, surprisingly grateful for the invitation. "And you mentioned something about a drink. This way you kill two birds with one stone." She let the words hang in the air. It was a chance to spend more time with him without it getting too intimate too fast. Fantasies were one thing. But Charlie was a little more reserved when it came to the actual execution. This might be a chance to get to know him better, rather than being swept away by her mystery guy.

Dave sighed. "Sure, why not?" he agreed. He leaned down and whispered in her ear. "But you still owe me a date."

She shivered with anticipation. She had to admit, it felt great being pursued. It had been ages since that had happened.

"Great!" Josh said. "I'll go round up the others."

Before they could answer, he was gone again, melting into the departing crowd.

"Do you get the feeling we were just bulldozed?" Dave asked.

She laughed. "I've learned to pick my battles where Josh Collins is concerned."

"And tonight wasn't one of them?"

She smiled, feeling a little cheeky. "It saved me from having to turn you down later," she explained, and started walking away. "When you would have propositioned me. You coming or not?"

He caught up to her, laughing a little as he looped his arm through hers. "I'd say you assume too much, but you probably don't. Just so you're aware, I haven't given up."

His persistence sent a wave of warmth through her. Their steps slowed and Charlie left her arm linked with his as they ambled down the block. Little flakes of snow were drifting lazily down, settling on the sidewalk with a soft shush. Evergreen wreaths with huge red bows hung from each lamppost, and the businesses that had remained open for late shopping were lit up with Christmas lights. Last Christmas she'd just moved here and hadn't taken the time to really enjoy the holiday season and the sense of community that pervaded the town. This year was different, though. She couldn't help but be swept along in the festive spirit.

"You're awfully quiet," Dave remarked, pulling her arm closer to his side.

She tilted her head and glanced up at him. "Sorry. I'm just enjoying the walk. It's so pretty out tonight."

"It is, isn't it?" He angled a look down at her. "It's been a while since I've seen snow at Christmas."

"Really?"

He nodded. "Yeah. I was deployed a few times, and there's not exactly a lot of Christmas spirit in the Middle East."

Deployed. So he was military—or ex, since he was

working on the docks. Now that Charlie thought about it, it fit. There was something in his bearing, the way he carried himself. Confident but not cocky. Respectful and with intent.

He paused, taking a deep breath of cold air as if savoring it. "Before that I was stationed in California. Not much snow there."

"I guess not. How long have you been out, then? I mean, did you resign or get medically discharged or something?"

He stopped in the middle of the sidewalk. "Hmm. A lot of questions."

"I guess I figured if we're going to get that nightcap at some point, I might want to know a little bit about the man behind the invitation."

His dark eyes searched hers for a moment. A group of teenagers went past them, talking loudly, half of them with their heads buried in their phones.

He shrugged. "I was a SEAL. I'm thirty. I was already older than most of the guys on my team. Besides, it was time to come home. Stop running around the world being Rambo." He smiled. "And now I'm back to where I started. Working on boats and being by the ocean. It suits me."

A SEAL. She couldn't deny the little shiver of excitement that rippled up her spine. Not just a soldier but an elite one. She tried to lighten the mood a little. "I didn't realize SEALs had a best-before date."

"Only with some things." His gaze burrowed into hers again, surprising her with its intensity. "I promise, with just about everything else, I'm nowhere near approaching my shelf life."

Oh. My.

They were nearly to the churchyard when Dave stopped suddenly, looking over at the nativity. There was a thin film of snow on the tops of the statues, but it really did look lovely, especially with the single small floodlight casting a glow on the scene. She looked up at him and saw a frown marring his face, his brows pulled together in the middle.

"What's the matter?" she asked.

"Stay here. I thought I saw something."

She waited as he stomped through the snow on the church lawn. Down the block, she noticed as a person jogged to a parked car, got in, and wasted no time driving away. She looked back at Dave, whose body blocked her view of the manger. More perplexing was the way he stared at it, his body utterly still.

"What on earth are you doing?" she called out.

A thin, plaintive sound traveled on the cold air, and she looked around to see if anyone was passing close by with a stroller or baby in their arms. But the crowd had dispersed and there was barely anyone on the street now. Her gaze turned back to Dave and her heart thumped against her ribs at the same time as her stomach seemed to drop to her feet.

He was standing in front of the manger. And instead of a T-shirt and plastic doll, he appeared to be holding a baby, wrapped in a red blanket.

Chapter Three

Awake now, the baby cried a bit, a helpless little wail that made Dave hold him or her a little closer to his jacket, tucking the blanket more firmly around the tiny form.

"Dave?"

He stepped forward. "I think we have a big problem, Charlie."

She rushed forward, stirring up snow until she reached him and pulled back a corner of the blanket. "Oh my God. This baby can't be more than a few weeks old. We need to get inside where it's warm."

"The pub?"

She frowned. "I guess. No, wait. My office is only a few blocks over. He . . . she . . . needs to be examined. Did you see anyone? What about that car that rushed away?" Without waiting for an answer, she whipped out her cell phone, walking as she talked. Dave followed right at her heels.

"Hi. It's Dr. Yang from the clinic. Who's on duty to-night?"

There was a momentary pause as the person on the other end answered.

"Can you have him meet me at the clinic right away? I'm on my way now." She ended the call and then automatically dialed again.

"Josh? It's Charlie. I have to take a rain check on tonight. Something's come up." There was another pause and Dave watched as Charlie's face wrinkled with annoyance. "No, not *that*. We just found . . . something . . . at the nativity. I'll explain it all later. I don't have time right now."

She hung up and nodded at him, all business. "Let's hurry. The police are on their way and we have to get this little one inside and out of the cold."

The wind had picked up a bit and Dave unzipped his coat partway, then tucked the bundle inside, cozy between his body and the protective nylon shell. Charlie smiled and said, "Great idea" as she led him to the corner and left, going up the street, turning left again at the next corner until they were standing outside a house that had a floodlit signing announcing JEWELL COVE MEDICAL CLINIC.

She dug in her purse for keys, went to the back door and opened up, then quickly disarmed the security system.

"Come on in," she invited, flicking on a light.

The reception area was bathed in a welcoming glow. The office was warmer than outside, but still chilly, and Dave stood by feeling helpless as Charlie bustled around, turning up the heat and flicking on lights. She'd gone from sweet, blushing Charlie to super-efficient Dr. Yang in the blink of an eye. Now he understood a little better why she might have earned the nickname Dr. Pit Bull.

"Okay," she finally said. "Let's have a look at this little one."

Dave looked down inside his coat. He must have thrown off some good heat because the baby was sleeping, little tiny lips moving in and out as it breathed. As gently as he possibly could, he slid his opposite hand inside and cradled the baby's bottom in his wide palm, using his shoulder and upper arm to assist him in shifting the baby out of his coat.

"You're good with babies," she offered. She reached for the bundle and took it into her hands. They were good hands, he realized. Despite her small size, her hands were strong and capable. Ordinary—no polish, just smooth, rounded nails, and as their fingertips brushed, her skin was soft against his. Yesterday they'd had the thickness of gloves between them. Now, as their hands touched while shifting the baby, the contact felt somehow intimate. It was the damnedest thing.

Cradling the infant in the crook of her elbow, Charlie peeled back the blanket. The baby was dressed in a blue fuzzy sleeper and a thin stretchy hat.

She smiled up at Dave. "I'm guessing it's a boy."

There was no note tucked in with the baby as far as Dave could see. Instead he followed Charlie to an exam room with better lighting. She lay the sleeping baby carefully on the exam table and began looking him over. First, checking what she could with the sleeper on, and then she began unsnapping the pajamas. The baby woke then, disturbed by the feeling of being undressed and exposed. At the same time there was a knock at the outer door.

Charlie never looked up from her examination. "Could you get that? It'll be the police."

Dave went to the door and flipped the lock, letting in the other man, who was dressed in his uniform and was big enough that Dave figured most men in town would think twice before picking a fight. "Officer," he greeted, holding open the door. "I'm Dave Ricker."

"Is Dr. Yang in trouble?" The cop pushed into the reception area, his eyes sharp.

"No, no, of course not." Dave shook his head. "Follow me. She's in here."

The officer followed Dave back to the exam room and brushed by him at the doorway. "Dr. Yang? Are you okay?"

She looked up, keeping one hand on the baby's belly, as if anchoring him in place. "Hello, Todd."

Dave watched as the burly officer's hard gaze softened as he looked at the baby. "Well. Who have we here?"

"I wish I could tell you." She met Dave's gaze across the room. "Dave, this is Todd Smith. Come on in and tell him what happened, Dave, and I can finish up my exam. This little guy would probably like to be bundled up again."

Dave stepped a little outside the door, the urge to cuddle the infant, to quiet his crying surprisingly strong. He watched as Charlie felt the little one's tummy gently, her concentration focused solely on the baby. "It might be quieter out here," he suggested.

He felt strange now that his arms were empty. He'd gotten used to holding the baby so quickly.

"You said your name's Dave?"

He turned away from the sight. "That's right. David Ricker. I'm renting a cottage in the area and work on the docks. Charlie and I were at the tree lighting tonight."

"Together?"

There was an edge to Todd Smith's voice that Dave recognized. That was another thing he was learning about small towns. People looked out for each other. He was actually really glad that someone had Charlie's back. He got the feeling she felt she was mostly on her own.

"Not *together together,* if that's what you're getting at." Though they would have been if Dave had had any say about it.

"Go on."

"We were walking to the pub—we were going to meet some people there for a bite to eat. I thought I saw someone hanging around the manger, and then they went running off."

Smith's gaze sharpened as he looked up from his notepad. "You saw who left him?"

"Not exactly. I mean I did, but I just saw a person. I couldn't tell you what they looked like. Young, maybe? Slight. Probably a woman. A girl." He let out a breath.

"So you checked it out."

"I did. When I looked in the manger, I couldn't believe it. Who the hell would leave a baby outside, in a nativity scene, on a December night?" His jaw tightened. "What if we hadn't been there? That baby might have frozen to death."

Smith nodded. "Lucky for him you did see. Why didn't you wait there? I would have looked the scene over."

"It was cold. Considering the baby, Charlie wanted to come here where it was warm, and make sure he was okay."

"That's all right. I'll call this in and go back over and see what I can find."

Charlie came back to the reception room, the baby dressed again in his sleeper and wrapped in the blanket. "He's a bit on the small side, but otherwise he looks well enough," she decreed with a smile. The baby was burrowed into her neck, sucking on his fingers. "But he's going to be hungry really soon."

It looked disturbingly right, the way she was holding the child.

"I have to contact child services," Smith said quietly. "He'll have to go into foster care until this is sorted out."

"Of course," Charlie answered, while Dave's gut churned. This poor little thing. Abandoned and then pawned off into foster care. It didn't seem right.

Charlie's hand was on the baby's head now, stroking the fine, blond hair. "Listen," she said to Smith, "why don't we leave him under my medical care until morning? That's soon enough, don't you think? We've got a stock of diapers and emergency formula here. I can care for him until then, make sure there aren't any other medical issues that weren't immediately apparent. You'll have a better idea of the situation by then too."

"You're up to it? Because this baby's pretty little. There'll be no sleeping through the night or anything."

Charlie smiled softly. "I'll be fine. I did my neonatal and pediatric rotations and everything." She bounced the baby a little bit. "We'll be fine, won't we, buddy?"

Dave jumped in, even though he questioned whether or not he should. "I can help too."

Smith raised an eyebrow. "What sort of experience do you have with babies?" he asked, laughing a little. "Because believe me, it's harder than it looks. My sister has two. I volunteered to babysit for a weekend once." He shuddered, and Charlie laughed.

Dave paused, annoyed at how easily Charlie seemed charmed by the young officer, annoyed at how he was made to feel left out of their little club. "I have a daughter," he said quietly, his gaze shifting to Charlie, watching as her smile slipped from her lips and her eyes registered confusion.

He probably should have mentioned that before inviting her back to his place. But it wasn't exactly icebreaker sort of conversation. It was the kind of thing he'd rather ease into.

"A daughter?" she whispered, and he felt like an absolute heel for springing it on her and for letting himself be baited by his own stupid male pride.

"Yes," he replied. "She lives with her mother in Kennebunkport."

"Oh."

He hated the disappointment he saw in Charlie's face. But now wasn't the time to explain. Instead he turned his attention to the police officer. "I'll help Charlie get settled, give a statement at the station, whatever you need."

"I appreciate your help, Mr. Ricker." He wrote a phone number on a slip of paper and handed it over to Charlie. "This is my cell number. You call if you need anything or think of something you might have missed." Smith gave her a stern look. "You should program that into your phone too, so you can avoid calling dispatch."

"I don't think that's necess—"

"You do it. You're part of this town and around here we look out for each other. You'll be getting a call from us too, I expect. I'm sure there will be more questions."

He was gone in a gust of cold air, leaving them alone in the clinic again, the silence loud between them.

❆   ❆   ❆

Charlie hadn't thought she'd ever be glad to hear a baby cry, but the moment the infant sent up an impatient squall, she finally let out her breath.

She could focus on the baby and not on Dave. Dave with his soulful eyes, helpful nature . . . and his kid.

He had a child. It seemed to her that was pretty important information.

"I need to fix some formula," she murmured. "Here. You hold him. It'll be faster that way." Without sparing him another glance, Charlie turned away and headed down the hall to a cupboard, where she removed a can of baby formula. Then she marched to the kitchen in the back, putting a kettle on to boil and then taking a bottle and nipple out of the cabinet. She wasn't sure how she felt about this new tidbit of knowledge. Wasn't sure she even had the right to be out of sorts about it.

Dave had followed her down the hall and now stood in the doorway. The baby wasn't soothed at all, even as he jostled his arms up and down a bit. The cries only increased in pitch.

"Do you have everything you need?" he asked, over top of the racket. "He's a hungry little guy."

Charlie nodded, pouring the formula into a bottle and screwing on the top, then immersing the bottle in a cup of hot water to warm the formula. They stood in the small kitchen, the shrill cries rubbing on the edge of Charlie's nerves.

She looked up at Dave. "So. You have a daughter."

He nodded, staring her straight in the eyes. "Yes. And an ex to go with her, of course. You might as well get a complete picture."

He was edgy. Well, too bad. "It might have been nice information to have."

He switched the baby to his other shoulder. "I met you yesterday. Asked you out tonight. I wasn't really sure of the when-to-bring-up-the-ex-and-kid protocol."

"I'm not sure either. It just feels weird."

"Why? Because you said yes?"

He started patting the baby on the back as the tension in the small kitchen ratcheted up some more. "So you and Officer Todd. Is there some history there?"

She frowned at the abrupt change in subject. "What?"

"You know. You guys seemed pretty friendly. He was awfully protective of you."

She burst out laughing then, turned back to the sink, and took the bottle out of the water. "You think Todd and I have a thing?" It was ludicrous. Todd was a good five years younger than she was, and she was pretty sure he had a girlfriend. "First of all, I wouldn't have . . . flirted with you if I were with Todd. And in case you didn't notice, he was nothing but professional earlier."

His voice was quieter now. "You're right. I guess I just got a little jealous."

Jealous? The idea sent a swirl of something delicious through her tummy. She turned back around and rested her hips on the edge of the counter, determined to keep her composure. The baby's cries had subsided to whimpers now. "Believe me, there's nothing romantic between Todd and me."

"Just so you know, I wouldn't make a move on someone else's girl," he stated, and it made her want to smile. He sounded about sixteen years old. But she supposed it was a good thing. Honor and all that.

"Poor thing," she murmured, taking the baby from his arms so she could offer the bottle. "Can we put a pin in this and talk about it later? Right now I just want to focus on one thing at a time." She laughed a little as the baby began drinking lustily. "And getting this guy fed and comfortable is top priority, don't you agree?"

Dave nodded, and let the matter drop. "I just can't believe it," he said quietly. "Who would leave a baby out in the elements like that? It's barbaric."

Charlie regarded him sadly. "Things like this happen more than you'd think. People can't cope. They get to the end of their ropes, and they do uncharacteristic and terrible things. As a doctor, I can't let myself judge."

"You've seen something like this before?"

She felt her heart constrict. She tried not to dwell on past cases. Still there were always a few that she couldn't forget. Ones that haunted her long after they were over. "Once," she said quietly, "when I was working backshift in New York, the ambulance brought in a preemie. She'd been left in a garbage can. The mother just . . . didn't know what else to do and she panicked. The baby only lived a few hours after coming in."

One of the hardest things she'd ever done as a doctor was call that time of death.

But then she shook off the heavy feeling of failure. "There are reasons why I chose to be a family doctor in a small town." She didn't want to get into all the reasons why, or how she'd found herself struggling to deal with the traumatic cases she saw on a day-to-day basis. She'd chosen Jewell Cove because it seemed idyllic. Like an East Coast Mayberry, where bad things simply didn't happen. A place where she might find the life she wanted rather than the one that was expected.

Of course bad things did happen, no matter where a person lived. Tonight was a prime example, though at least this one had the potential for a happy ending.

"Anyway," she continued, smiling a little, "thanks to you, we got to this little boy in time. He looks to be full term and hungry as a horse. You saved him tonight, Dave." She smiled up at him. "Let's go to the reception area where it's more comfortable."

There was a beanbag chair in the kids' area, and she held the baby against her shoulder while she lowered herself into it carefully. The form settled around her and she crossed her legs yoga-style. She took the opportunity to burp him and then reintroduced the bottle. The baby took it eagerly, little lips fastening about the tip with a ferocity that made her laugh. "Okay, okay," she soothed, adjusting the angle of her arm for better comfort.

Dave sat in a chair across from the play area and watched her. She couldn't tell what he was thinking, but from the way his mouth was set and the troubled look in his eyes, she guessed it wasn't good.

"You don't have to stay, you know," she said, letting out a breath. "Formula, diapers . . . I have all I need."

"You're going to stay here all night?"

"It wouldn't be the first time," she said easily. "Seriously, there are worse places to spend a night."

He smiled tightly. "I know. I've stayed in a few myself. But why don't you go home?"

She pulled the bottle away for a minute and wiped a dribble of milk off the baby's chin before letting him have some more. "It's just easier. My car's still down on the waterfront, and I don't have a car seat either. It's really okay, Dave. It's warm in here, there's a fold-out cot in the back, and there's even some food in the fridge if I get hungry." She tried to stifle a yawn but failed. The truth was she was dead tired tonight, though she didn't really know why. Maybe it was all the fresh air. Or maybe it was the brief surge of adrenaline from finding the baby. Now that she'd slowed down, relaxation was setting in. Not to mention how warm the baby felt in her arms. He really could throw some decent body heat for an infant.

"You're sure? I could stay if you wanted. So you don't have to stay alone."

It was sweet of him to offer. Charlie was starting to think that despite surprises tonight, Dave was a really decent guy. But she was a big girl and she didn't need to be rescued. Once more she removed the bottle from the baby's mouth, and then put him on her shoulder and be-

gan patting his back, trying to relieve any gas that had
built up from his gulping most of his supper.

"I spend every night alone," she answered, blushing
a little. "The only difference is I'm here and not at my
house."

"I suppose," he answered, and she would have sworn
he looked disappointed.

The sharp crack of a burp echoed through the office
and they both laughed.

"There," she said softly, shifting the baby to the crook
of her arm again. "That must feel better!"

This time when she put the nipple by his lips, he
latched on and his eyes started to drift closed. Her heart
shifted a little as one tiny little hand moved to rest along
the side of the plastic bottle, willing it to stay in place.
What a sweet little treasure he was.

"I guess I'll take off, then," Dave said, rather reluctantly, she thought.

"Thank you for all your help tonight. I mean it. This
little guy is so lucky you came along."

To her surprise, Dave got up from his chair and knelt
in front of her. "I think he's lucky you came along," he
said softly. "You're a real natural with him, you know
that?"

"A baby's needs are pretty simple." She brushed off
the compliment, disturbed by how touched she was by
it. They'd just met. But it was the perfect thing to say.

"Still." He reached out and brushed a little piece of
hair away from her face. "I was deployed when my
daughter was born. I only got to see her at this age a few
times."

Charlie looked away and bit her lip. "Do you see her
now?"

He smiled then, and it lit up his face. "Yeah. Janice
and her new husband moved to Kennebunkport and

opened a little inn. I came here so I could see my baby girl more often. I don't want to miss out on all those important moments, you know? Jewell Cove isn't permanent for me, but this job does let me be close while I figure out what happens next."

If he'd been attractive before, the knowledge that he was trying to be a good father definitely tipped the scales even more in his favor.

He stepped back. "Call me if you need anything, okay?"

"I will," she answered, but she knew she wouldn't. She didn't have his cell number, and she didn't know the number for his rental cottage either. Which was okay. She'd be fine here tonight.

He reached the door, but before he opened it he turned one last time. "Please lock this behind me," he ordered.

"Yes, boss."

He smiled at her once more before slipping out into the cold night, leaving her alone with the baby and the silence. And perhaps what surprised her the most was how, after he was gone, she really wished he'd stayed after all.

Chapter Four

The sky was overcast when Dave crawled out from beneath the covers. He hadn't slept much, though that wasn't entirely surprising after his exciting evening. He might as well get up and get on with his day rather than lie in bed.

The shower was hot and he dressed quickly in the cold air of the cottage, pulling on jeans and a thick sweater. God, he'd forgotten how raw and unforgiving an East Coast winter could be. There wasn't any work today to keep him busy, so he bundled up, scraped the windshield of his SUV, and headed into town.

The only thing open this early on Sunday morning was the café, so Dave stopped and bought two large coffees and a selection of pastries before heading up a street to the clinic. Maybe Charlie wasn't even there anymore, but he felt uncomfortable with how they'd left things last night. He hadn't exactly kept his interest in her a secret. Looking at it now, in hindsight, he could understand why she'd backpedaled when she found out about his kid.

Lights were on inside when he arrived, so he cradled the tray holding the food in one hand and tapped lightly on the door with the other. Moments later Charlie came out of an exam room, the baby on her shoulder and a bottle in her hand. Her usually neat-as-a-pin hair was disheveled and sticking out of a frayed braid, and she had bags under her eyes. Clearly it hadn't been a good night for her either.

She shifted the bottle, turned the dead bolt, and stood back so he could open the door.

The office was warm, and he hurried in and shut the door behind him before he let in too much icy air. "Good morning," he said softly, peering over her shoulder at the baby. His tiny eyes were closed and his fingers pinched the soft fabric of her sweater. "Rough night?"

"He's asleep now, isn't he?"

At his nod, she sighed. "Little bugger. Kept me up most of the night and now he's out. Typical."

Dave let out a soft laugh. "Can't blame a man for wanting your attention all night," he joked, delighted when her cheeks colored a bit. "Here. I brought coffee. And very-bad-for-you white flour and sugary things."

"I take back all the bad things I thought about you last night," she said solemnly, reaching for the bag. "Let's go to the kitchen. I'm not sure if I dare put this guy down or not."

Once in the kitchen, Dave put down the tray and stripped off his jacket. Charlie looked up at him with naked yearning in her eyes. "Can you take him while I have something to eat? I feel like I'm going to keel over, and he can stay nice and cozy. And quiet."

She slid the baby into his arms without waiting for an answer and immediately moved to the counter, grabbing one of the coffees and opening the paper bag, peering down inside before selecting a rather large apple

Danish. Her first bite was huge, and glaze clung to the corners of her mouth.

Dave had a lot of thoughts about kissing that glaze from her lips. And if he hadn't been holding a baby in his arms, he might have. But if—when—he kissed Charlie, he wanted to have his hands free so he could put his arms around her and hold her close.

He looked away, taking a deep breath. She wasn't the kind of woman a man played with. He should probably just let well enough alone. Still, thinking about her was better than thinking about the baby in his arms and how the weight felt foreign and familiar at the same time. At least the little guy wasn't crying. Dave figured he'd be okay as long as the baby slept on.

"Let's go into my office," she suggested. "I have my desk chair and there's a decent armchair there too. I'll bring the stuff and you can have some coffee. It doesn't look like you got much sleep either."

He frowned, following her down the hall. "It doesn't?"

She shook her head, and he watched the ratty braid move back and forth. "It's in the wrinkles around your eyes. And you showered this morning but you didn't bother to shave."

He hadn't. He knew a day's growth of stubble was on his cheeks. More than that, she'd noticed. Despite how exhausted she was, she'd noticed all that about him in the space of a few seconds. It was flattering as hell.

Her office was extraordinarily tidy, just as he would have expected, and she pulled the padded chair closer so they could use her desk as a table. He eased himself into the upholstery, careful not to wake the baby, and reached for the thick paper cup.

Charlie sat in her chair, took another healthy bite of Danish, and watched him with keen eyes.

"What?" he asked, after several seconds had ticked by.

"I'm trying to puzzle you out."

"Never a good idea. I'm a complicated man." He grinned at her, trying to dispel her solemn gaze, but it was no good. She was focused now.

"You're good with babies."

"Why is it so important to you?"

She paused then, furrowing her brow a bit. "You mean, your personal life is none of my business."

"I wouldn't put it that bluntly . . ."

"But that's what you mean."

Awkward silence settled over the room. Finally he spoke again. "No, I don't mean that at all. It's not an easy thing to talk about. I get that you're curious given that we . . . that I . . . started something."

"That's part of it," she agreed.

He wasn't immune to the lovely feeling of warm baby curled up against his sweater. "You're a tough woman, Charlene Yang."

"Thank you." She smiled and took a satisfied sip of her coffee.

"You want the truth? All right. Here it is. Anyone I go on a date with wants to know who Dave Ricker is. Coming right out and admitting I have an ex and a daughter . . . that can be intimidating. I'm not just a guy. I'm a dad."

"And women are turned off by that?"

He was saved from answering by another tap at the front door.

Thanks to the coffee, pastry, or a bit of both, Charlie looked slightly revived as she said, "That'll be the social worker. Hang tight."

She was back moments later with a middle-aged woman who identified herself as Marissa Longfellow. She looked kind, like a schoolteacher, and smiled at the sight of Dave holding the baby in his arms.

"He certainly looks contented," she noted.

"He likes Dave," Charlie replied. "He fell asleep right away last night when Dave held him inside his jacket. Then Dave went home and it seemed like he cried for hours."

Marissa laughed. "Sounds about right. All of mine went through a stage at this age. For three or four weeks they'd be up in the middle of the night and just wouldn't settle. And then poof. One day they got their days and nights the right way around and I'd start getting good sleep. Or at least a good chunk of sleep at a time. Well, let's see to the official paperwork, shall we? I have those papers for you I mentioned, Dr. Yang, and then we'll be good to go."

"Dave, are you okay here for a few minutes? He's so contented at the moment."

"No problem. I'll just drink my coffee and we'll have some male bonding time." He smiled up at her.

They left the office, and he took a sip of coffee then put the cup back on the desk. The baby in his arms took a deep breath and let out a sigh. Dave adjusted his hold so the little guy was cradled just right, then slid down in the chair a little so that his head rested against the padded back and his legs stretched out comfortably. He closed his eyes. He'd missed these first moments with his daughter and he could never get them back. But he didn't regret the choices he'd made since. It had meant giving up being a SEAL, but it also meant being part of his daughter's life as she grew up, and that was more important.

❄   ❄   ❄

Charlie came back for the baby and stopped in the door-way to her office, her heart catching at the sight before her.

The baby was lying on Dave's wide chest, still sound asleep, while Dave's rough hands held him snug and safe. A soft snore broke the silence. Dave had fallen asleep too, and it was as sweet a picture as she'd ever seen.

"Dave," she said softly, stepping into the room. He never moved, not a muscle, and she smiled to herself. He was really out. "Dave," she repeated, louder this time, and he snuffled before opening his eyes slowly.

"I fell asleep."

"You did."

"He's quite the little furnace, isn't he?"

She shrugged. "He didn't exactly settle that well for me."

And there it was. The slow, sexy, slightly smug smile.

"Is it time?"

She nodded, wondering if she was crazy to be taking on this new responsibility. She'd been up all night, been at her wit's end trying to soothe the child, been peed on when she didn't get the diaper on fast enough, and was tired and still hungry. And yet the thought of the tiny bundle going somewhere else felt so wrong. Most of the time she was able to put her desire for a family of her own on the back-burner. Whether it was her ticking clock or what, that talent was getting more and more difficult lately. To her surprise, she'd found herself offering to care for the infant while the police investigated the case.

"Yeah, it's time to get this little man settled." Charlie moved closer.

"If the parents are local, it shouldn't be too hard to find out if he has family. How many baby boys could have been born in the last few weeks, anyway?" Dave asked on a yawn, shifting the baby as he sat up.

Of course, if the family wasn't local, that was a whole other thing. Still, it was a good starting place.

"Here, let me take him." She slid her hands under the warm little body and lifted. His eyes opened as she moved him into her arms, staring at her without really seeing, not crying, but just taking a few moments to wake up from his comfortable nap.

Marissa was waiting with a car seat and warm blanket and strapped him in securely with competent hands. Charlie went forward and put the little cap back on his head. "He needs to keep warm," she murmured. "It's cold out today."

"Are you sure you have everything you need?" Marissa smiled at her. "It's a big thing you're doing."

"I'll go right from here to the drugstore."

"If there's any problem, anything at all, you'll call, won't you? There's lots of support available. And I'm here day or night."

Dave stepped forward. "What? I thought you were taking the baby with you?"

Marissa slid a file into her case. "Dr. Yang is going to watch our little one for a few days. Just temporarily, of course." She smiled. "She's done such great work with our foster care support group. I have complete confidence in her."

Charlie looked over at him, wishing she had the same confidence in herself but determined to do the right thing. "His weight's a little low, and monitoring his health makes sense right now. Hopefully it's just a case of nutrition and we can get him back on track."

"And we have fewer foster families available every day," Marissa added. "Ideally, we'll find a family member quickly who can be awarded temporary custody, and if not, then once his weight is up, this little guy will be settled with a good family. Well, I'll be on my way, and let you get home and settled. I'll talk to you soon, Charlie."

She was gone in a gust of wind and left the two of them standing there. Charlie took a deep breath. There was no turning back now. For better or worse, she was temporarily in charge of an infant boy.

Dave came closer and put his hands on her upper arms. She looked up, surprised to find his eyes filled with understanding.

"Feeling overwhelmed?" he asked simply.

"A little," she admitted. "I'm probably just tired. And even though he was fussy, he really is a sweetie. I'm sure we'll be fine."

Dave grinned and squeezed her arms. "Well, he's your little Baby Jesus, after all. Kind of difficult to harden your heart to that."

She laughed a little. Come to think of it, she'd had more of those silly little chuckles in the last few days than she'd had in a very long time.

"I couldn't bear the thought of him going to strangers this morning. How silly is that? But oh my. I've kind of leaped in with both feet."

"If it makes you feel any better, every parent in the world leaps in with both feet. One minute you're alone, the next you're a parent. It's a big shock."

"Is that how it was with you?"

He chuckled. "Definitely. I'd never changed a diaper or given a bottle or any of those things. You at least know what you're doing. You've got a head start."

His pep talk made her feel better. "Thanks. So why *did* you come back this morning anyway?" she asked, pulling away. She picked up the carrier and together they headed back to her office where the cold coffee and sweets waited. "I figured you'd be sleeping in after your exciting evening."

"Couldn't sleep, and I was worried about you. This isn't the coziest place to spend the night."

"Clearly you've never tried to sleep in an inner-city emergency room," she called out, as she poured the now-cold coffee down the sink.

He came up behind her, balling up a sticky napkin. "No, but I've slept in some nasty places just the same. Like in the desert where you sweat your balls off during the day and then freeze at night and you and your buddies huddle together because you're out of fuel."

She burst out laughing.

"Good times," he confirmed, with a twitch of his lips. "Very . . . cozy. And you know what? I think that's the first time I've really heard you laugh."

She found that hard to believe. He made her smile a lot. But perhaps she hadn't laughed. It felt good.

"Look," he suggested, "your cottage is on the way to mine. You're dog-tired. Why don't I take you both home and you can pick up your car later?"

Her stomach took that swirly dip again. "That's not necessary. A drop-off at the waterfront would be fine . . ."

"We had some snow last night and the roads are a little slick. Maybe I didn't sleep well but I bet I got more than you plus I just had a nice little catnap. We can stop by the drugstore for whatever you need first."

It was tempting. She was exhausted. Gosh, how did new parents do it night after night? Lord, she was about to find out, wasn't she?

He reached for his coat. "Come on. You know you're dying for a hot shower and a pair of sweats and some sleep."

Oh God, that sounded heavenly.

"All right."

"Get your coat. I'll warm up the truck."

Several minutes later they were loaded down with diapers and formula and back on the road toward

Fiddler's Rock. Charlie had her purse and the bag of pastries on her lap as Dave negotiated the winding turns, and hard flakes of snow bit through the air as they left town behind for the relative peace of the seaside road. The baby slept on, comfortable in the car seat, lulled by the motion of the car.

"Which place is yours?" he asked, as they passed the Blackberry Hill intersection.

"About a mile past the curve, on the left."

As they got closer, the flakes started coming down heavier. She motioned for him to turn as they approached the driveway to her place. Even in the gloomy weather, she loved it. The gray shingle siding and white trim were old-fashioned and cozy, and she'd put a big evergreen wreath on her door, complete with a gigantic red bow.

"Nice spot," he remarked, putting the truck in park.

"Isn't it?" She looked over at him and smiled. "The trees make it so cozy, but then you go on the back deck and the bay is spread out for miles. It's even nicer in the summer. I'm not much of a gardener, but I'm trying to expand a few perennial beds."

He'd left the truck running and she asked a little hesitantly, "Do you want to come in?"

His gaze met hers evenly. "Is that what you want? Or are you just being polite?"

"You're very direct, you know."

"Is that a problem?"

"Not really. Takes some getting used to, I think." She bit down on her lip. "I can't eat all these pastries alone. Come in. We'll get this little guy settled and I'll make a decent cup of coffee. It's the least I can do after all your help."

She wasn't as direct as Dave. Her words made it sound like a thank you when it was really an "I'd like to spend more time with you" thing.

He shut off the ignition and pocketed the keys. "I suppose I could do that. You take this stuff in, and I'll bring the baby."

Once inside Charlie immediately went to the thermostat and turned up the heat. "Gosh, it's cold in here." She slid off her boots and hung up her coat. "Make yourself at home. I'm going to start on the coffee."

He came in behind her and shut the door, put down the carrier, took off his boots, and placed them precisely beside hers before hanging his jacket on the coatrack. "Are you sure you don't want a hot shower first?"

She wondered if she still smelled of baby spit-up. Plus the idea of a shower and comfy, fuzzy clothes was incredibly tempting. "I wouldn't be much of a hostess if I did that." Dave picked up the car seat once more and they walked through to the kitchen.

But Dave stopped at the living room. "Hey, you've got a fireplace. Seriously, go shower. I'll watch the baby and start a fire. When you come out, it'll be warmer in here."

Apparently he was taking her "make yourself at home" comments seriously. She put the bakery bag on the butcher block. "It does sound good . . ."

"Go. We'll be here when you get back."

"I won't be long."

She left them there and headed to the bedroom, gathered a pair of yoga pants and a bulky Harvard hoodie, and scooted into the bathroom. The shower felt glorious and she nearly didn't want to get out, except she knew he was waiting. Her heartbeat quickened as she thought of it. She'd invited him in for pastry and coffee, but she was in a steaming shower and he was building a fire and there was clearly an attraction at work here. Was something more going to happen? Did she want it to?

The hot water ran in rivulets over her breasts. God, she did. It had been a very long time since she'd felt like this. The bigger question was, would she let something happen? Because they barely knew each other. Attraction, desire . . . were all well and good. But it felt weird, knowing that the mystery man she'd been fantasizing about was flesh and blood, in her house, and unless her radar was way off, interested in her. Despite the fact that she looked like death warmed over this morning.

"Oh, stop analyzing and get out of the shower already," she muttered to herself, shutting off the spray. There was no rush for anything. They could totally take it one step at a time. Get to know each other better. She *did* have some self-control, after all.

The air in the bathroom was still cold and she hurried to dry herself and get into her clothes. It would take too long to blow-dry her hair, so she simply squeezed out the water with a towel, brushed it, and held it back off her face with a thin black headband. She smoothed on some moisturizer, swiped a bit of lip balm over her lips, and decided that was enough—she didn't want to appear too obvious.

She pressed a hand to her stomach, took a deep breath, and opened the bathroom door.

The cottage was already warming up, thanks to the thermostat and the fire she could hear crackling behind the grate. Entering the living room, she saw Dave squatting before the fireplace, adding some small sticks to the dancing flames. She hadn't actually had a man back to her place since moving to Jewell Cove. Her little living room was changed just by having him in it. It felt smaller. More alive. Over by the sofa, the baby slept on, his head at a slight angle, one of Charlie's throw blankets draped over him.

"You're very good at building a fire," she said quietly from the doorway.

He looked over his shoulder. "I could claim it was my

military training, but the truth is, I was in the outdoors a lot as a kid. My dad's a fisherman on the Chesapeake."

She went to his side and squatted too, holding her hands out to the warmth of the fire. "Is that where you learned to fix boats?"

He nodded. "Yep."

"But you didn't go back there when you left the army?"

"I did for a while." He threw two thicker logs on the fire and closed the screen.

Talk about basic answers. Charlie frowned. "And then you moved here to be closer to your daughter?"

He rested his forearms on his knees. "Yes. I did my time, but it's so hard to be a SEAL and a dad at the same time. George Adams is actually an old friend of my dad's. He offered me a job, and that lets me support myself and be close to her."

Charlie was curious about how his ex fit into all of this, but didn't want to ask. Instead she focused on his daughter, who he clearly doted on. "What's her name?"

"Nora. Nora Emily Christensen."

Christensen. Not Ricker. Bit by bit Charlie was beginning to realize that the situation between Dave and his ex was complicated.

"That's a beautiful name," Charlie replied, standing up. "Now, the fire's going, I'm warmed up, and I promised you good coffee."

She left him in front of the fire and went to the kitchen to put on the kettle. While it was heating she got out coffee beans, her grinder, press, and frother. She put the remaining pastries on a pretty plate and ground the beans, and then when the water boiled, she warmed the press and mugs and put the milk in the microwave to heat.

It was a slightly more finicky process than using a

regular coffeemaker, but it was worth it, in Charlie's opinion. Within a few minutes she had freshly pressed coffee with a rich swirl of frothed milk added. She put both cups and the pastries on a small tray and carried it all into the living room.

Dave was still sitting on the floor in front of the fire, staring at the flames.

"Hey," she said, putting the tray down on a small coffee table. "You don't have to sit on the floor, you know."

He looked over at her and smiled, some of the tension gone from his face. "Just watching the fire. You've got a nice place here, Charlie. It suits you."

She liked the light colors—white, with bits of creamy beige and blue and greens. It reminded her of the ocean and sand, very soothing and relaxing. "Thanks. It's the first place I've ever decorated myself, for myself." She'd liked the cottage so much that after her first six months of renting, she'd bought it from the owner.

He laughed. "I'm not much of a decorator. Then again, I didn't need to be. The Navy had it covered. And now I'm renting, which suits me fine."

"Have some coffee while it's hot," she suggested. She nearly sat on the sofa but decided the rug in front of the fire was fine for her too. She sat, cross-legged, handed Dave his mug, and grabbed her own, then put the plate of pastries between them.

"This is good," he complimented, taking a sip. "Damn. Really good."

"Fresh beans and a press. Makes all the difference," she replied, taking a sip of her own. She reached for a pain au chocolat and a paper napkin. The flaky pastry sent wisps of crumbs flying at her first bite, but she didn't care. Butter and chocolate together was heavenly.

Dave snagged a sugared doughnut from the assortment and bit into it. For a few minutes they munched happily, in comfortable silence. What was amazing was that they didn't feel the need to make small talk or break the stillness.

Her coffee was half gone when Dave finally restarted the conversation. "So," he said, wiping his sugary fingers on a napkin, "you know a bit about me. How about you? Where did you grow up? Why did you become a doctor?"

The buttery croissant went papery in her mouth. She didn't like talking about herself much. "Oh, my story's pretty boring."

"I doubt that. Especially since you're avoiding the topic." He leaned back on his hands. It made his shoulders look incredibly muscled, she noticed.

"Okay, so here's the short version. I grew up in Boston. My mother teaches at the Berklee College of Music and my father works in clinical research for a pharmaceutical company. My dad is second-generation Chinese, and my mom's family probably came over on the *Mayflower*." She rolled her eyes at him and continued on. "They have very busy careers and very high expectations of their one and only child."

"So you became a doctor."

"Sure. After several years of violin and piano lessons, courtesy of my mother, and a lot of pressure to major in biochem." She let out a breath. "There were good points to that too, though. They were so busy with their own careers and social lives that I stayed under the radar quite often. And I did want to become a doctor." Eventually, anyway. Lucky for her. She couldn't imagine what might have happened if she'd hated medicine.

He looked at her steadily. "It sounds lonely."

Her heart gave a little thump. "It was, actually. And I know they're disappointed that I'm a family doctor in a small town and not doing important research like my dad or being a top trauma doctor like my best friend, Lizzie. But I'm happy with my choices. I like my job and I like it here."

And maybe she was still lonely at times. But she'd work on it. After all, she'd taken the step of volunteering for the church Christmas decorating, and look what had come from that. Sunday morning coffee and sweets in front of a fire with a gorgeous man. Progress.

She smiled to herself.

"What's so funny?"

"If I told you, you'd get a big fat head, so never mind." She pushed away the plate, her sweet tooth finally satisfied. "You make me laugh, Dave, and that's kind of nice."

He put down his coffee cup, then took hers and put it down too, on the brick hearth in front of the fireplace. Her pulse hammered frantically, beating at the base of her wrists. It was the kind of move she expected a person made before they made a bigger move. When he turned back to her, she swallowed thickly, nervous and excited all at once.

He put his hands on the sides of her thighs and pulled her forward, so she was sitting beside him but facing him, close enough that she could see gold-and-chocolate flecks in his dark eyes. Her breath shortened, her chest cramped as he lifted his hand and cupped her jaw. His thumb grazed the corner of her mouth and her breath stopped altogether. He removed his hand and put his thumb to his lips, tasting the buttery crumb he'd taken from her mouth.

Oh my.

Charlie was certain her eyes widened as he leaned closer, taking his time, making sure. Half of her was a jittery mess of nerves and the other half wished he'd hurry the hell up already, but she made herself be patient.

To wait, to let him take the lead. If things hadn't gone hinky last night, this was where they might have ended up, after all.

He closed the final distance between them and her eyelids drifted closed as his mouth touched hers for the first time.

His lips were soft, warm, and tasted like coffee and nutmeg and something that was just him. He nudged subtly, prompting her to deepen the kiss, and she did, somewhat shyly but enjoying the slow sweetness of it. One of his hands reached around to cup the back of her head, controlling the contact in a way she wholly approved of. She liked how he took charge of the kiss without forcing anything. Hesitantly she reached out and placed her palm on his chest in silent approval.

"Mmm," he murmured against her lips, the vibration of the sound sending ripples of desire through her. "You're good at that, Charlie."

"So are you," she replied, a little bit breathless.

"Should we try it again?" he asked.

There was no way she could say no. The combination of suggestion and teasing was impossible to resist.

This time she leaned forward and slid into the kiss, hungering for more. She put her hands on his shoulders and shifted until she was sitting across his lap, her fingers sliding through his hair as the contact deepened and quickened with urgency.

Chapter Five

God, she was sweet, soft and pliant beneath his hands.

Dave forced himself to go slowly, even though his blood was raging and his desire for her was burning hot. There was something about Charlie that was fragile. Something that made him want to take his time. For the first time in years, he worried about being careful with a woman.

She was so beautiful today, so approachable in her soft yoga pants and fleecy hoodie. Testing, he slid his hand beneath the waistband of the sweatshirt and touched the silky skin of her belly, gliding upward until he encountered the satin fabric of her bra. He cupped her small breast in his hand, the point of it pressing against his palm and he reminded himself to not hurry. Even if he did want to. Desperately.

Instead he focused on kissing her, thoroughly, until his mind was clouded with only her.

"We probably shouldn't do this," she murmured.

"I know," he answered, closing his eyes and letting the sensations fill him completely. He kissed her again.

She tasted so good. Like rich butter and smooth chocolate and woman.

Panting, she broke the kiss and leaned away a little. "I need to stop."

He did as she asked, even though it damn near killed him. He pulled the hoodie back down and rested his forehead on her shoulder, working on regaining his senses.

Her breath came hard and fast. That and the crackling of the fire were the only sounds in the room for several seconds.

"Wow," she finally breathed. He took it as a good sign she didn't pull away from him. Their legs were still entangled on the rug, though their hands and clothing were all in the right places.

"Wow is right. That's some good coffee, missus."

She giggled, and he loved it. It had been too long since he'd made a woman laugh, and the sound warmed him from the inside out.

"I don't know if it was the caffeine, the sugar rush, or just you," she said softly. Her hand stroked at his hair and he kept his eyes closed, loving the feel of it. "But that was . . . unexpected."

"Not for me," he admitted. "I've wanted to do that since you nearly threw that doll at me the other day."

She did slide away then, sitting all the way up. He rested his elbows on his knees and grinned up at her surprised face.

"You did?" she asked.

"Do you honestly think I would have gone to that caroling nonsense otherwise?"

The look on her face was priceless. She looked so . . . pleased with herself. Dave had the sneaking suspicion she had no idea how attractive she was right at this moment. Even in an oversized hoodie with her lip gloss thoroughly kissed off. Especially then.

"You are very good for my self-esteem," she admitted.

"And you're good for my self-control," he replied, and then chuckled. "Don't mind me if I don't thank you for it."

She tugged at the hem of her hoodie. "I, uh . . . help me out here. Is there a way to transition from this gracefully?"

And then he laughed. He couldn't help it. Neither one of them was particularly smooth, were they? And he liked that about her. A lot. She seemed incapable of playing games. That was damned refreshing.

"I'm no good at this either," he admitted. "It's probably really bad form to talk about exes at this particular moment, but it's been a while since I had to navigate . . ." He paused, scrambling for the right word. "Dating," he finished, not sure if that was the right choice or not, but *relationships* seemed premature.

"You guys were together a long time?"

"Not too long. We were friends." He felt his cheeks heat. "Friends with, uh . . . well, anyway, Nora was a surprise. I haven't dated much since then. I was away, then figuring out what was next, and being a dad . . ." He raised an eyebrow. "You?"

She laughed. "Are you kidding? I had med school and then crazy, crazy hours. Hard on relationships."

"And there's been no one here in Jewell Cove? I find that hard to believe."

She shrugged. "It's a small town. There's not always a huge selection on the dating market. And then there's the fact that everyone is a potential patient. Awkward . . ."

She looked at him earnestly. "I spent most of my

childhood studying or practicing violin. I had friends, sure, but social skills didn't come naturally to me. I swear, if it wasn't for my college roommate, I'd be a hermit."

"You're no hermit," he confirmed, and he slid over closer to her. "Hermits are old and wrinkly and hairy."

"I think you're confusing them with trolls."

He laughed, then kissed her quickly. "Maybe."

"So if I make a confession, you won't laugh at me?"

"Cross my heart." He made the motion across his chest and she smiled sweetly.

"I'm not good at the fling thing. I'm more of a slow mover. Just so you know . . ."

"Hey," he offered gently, realizing that the more he got to know her, the more he liked her. "We only just met. There's no hurry. Besides, last night was the most unusual first date I've ever had. There's something different about you, Charlie."

"Um, is that a good thing or a bad thing?"

It took all his willpower not to kiss her again. "I like being with you," he said. "And I'd like to see you again. Let's start there."

"Like living in the moment? Keeping it simple?"

"Yeah. Like that." He halted, considered before he spoke again. "I'm not really the jump-in-headfirst kind of guy when it comes to relationships either."

She looked up and her lips curved the slightest bit. "I wouldn't be opposed to getting to know you a little better too."

The attraction hummed between them again and Dave considered whether or not he wanted to start over . . . or pick up where they'd left off. He looked over his shoulder, saw the baby still sleeping, and debated. Finally he decided to wait. Charlie needed to nap when she could, and he shouldn't get in the way of that. "I should probably go," he decided. "You really do need some sleep. I'll call you?"

"I'd like that."

She walked him to the door and waited while he shoved on his boots and put on his jacket. "Drive safe," she advised, and he nodded.

"I'm only a couple more miles up the road. But I will. Don't worry."

"And thanks for the drive home."

"You're welcome."

There was an awkward pause where he had his hand on the doorknob, not quite out the door, but almost. He wanted to kiss her. Finally he leaned in a bit and dropped a small kiss on her lips. Not too much. Just enough to let her know that he was interested.

"I'll call you," he repeated, and went out the door into the snow and ice.

❄   ❄   ❄

Charlie was already at work the next morning when her cell phone vibrated with a new text. Her heart gave a little thump when she saw the short message.

It's Dave. Do you need a lift to pick up your car? I can pick you up on my way to work.

She'd deliberately set the alarm for a half hour earlier than normal and called one of the two taxis that Jewell Cove offered. With the added time required to get the baby ready, the last thing she wanted was to be late to work. She knew everything would take her longer and was still trying to figure out how she was going to manage appointments. By seven fifteen she'd been on her way to the waterfront where she'd warmed up her car and scraped the ice and snow from the windows, and by seven thirty she was in her office tackling her e-mail as best she could.

She'd had a lot of time to think since yesterday morning and had decided to take a step back from whatever had been developing between her and Dave. Looking back at the last few days, she realized she'd been dealing with two different situations, neither of which was conducive to clear thinking. First, there'd been the whole fantasy-in-the-flesh thing when he'd shown up at the church and then at the tree lighting. She'd been, as Thumper said in *Bambi,* "twitterpated."

And then there was the whole baby-in-the-manger thing. It had been an extreme situation, and at the end of it she'd been exhausted.

She put down her coffee and quickly tapped a reply.

I'm already here. But thanks for the offer. I appreciate it.

There was a long pause before he answered again.

Okay. Talk soon.

That was it. Short and sweet. No suggestion of when they might get together next. She was relieved. Wasn't she? She should be. She'd given herself a firm talking-to after she'd gotten some sleep. Put things in perspective. Did she even have time for dating right now? She looked down at the carrier which doubled as a seat. The baby was awake and staring up at her with big blue eyes. She'd been up twice during the night to feed him. Babies took up a lot of time.

The truth was, she was nearly thirty. She figured that any man she got involved with pretty much had to come with keeper potential. It was simply the way she was wired. She'd never wasted time on things that were going nowhere. Sometimes she wondered what that would be like. Pointless? Or liberating? Either way, she had her laundry list of attributes for her future partner. Top of it were marriage and father material. Dave certainly seemed devoted to his daughter, but how long would he stay in Jewell Cove?

She enlisted Robin's help in caring for the baby, putting his seat in the reception area, taking turns changing him or carrying him around when he was fussy. Midmorning, two cups of coffee and four patients later, Robin came back and let her know that Todd Smith was in the waiting room and wanted to talk to her. Figuring it could only be about the baby, she checked her watch and nodded. "Bring him back here, Robin. If it's about the investigation, we won't want to talk where everyone can hear."

"Sure thing, Charlie." Robin smiled and scooted out, returning only seconds later with Officer Smith trailing behind her.

Next to the petite receptionist, Todd Smith looked big and imposing, especially in his uniform. He'd removed his hat and had it tucked under his arm, and she realized some of his bulk came from the impressive array of gear on his belt as well as the probability of a flak jacket beneath his clothing.

"Morning, Dr. Yang," he greeted.

She smiled. "You can call me Charlie," she offered. "Unless you prefer the title for official business."

He smiled back. "Too bad I am on official business." Before she could dissect that particular comment, he motioned toward a chair. "May I?"

"Oh, of course. Do you want a coffee or anything?"

There was a tap on the door frame and Robin came in, carrying a steaming mug. "Here you go, Todd. Heavy on the cream, no sugar."

"Thanks, Robin." He smiled at the receptionist and then grinned at Charlie. "Robin already asked when I arrived. Thanks for the offer, though." He took a sip and sighed. "That's way better than what Bryce makes up at the station."

Charlie sat in her chair and crossed her ankles. "So. I take it you have news?"

He took another drink of coffee and then put the cup down on the corner of her desk. "Well, yes. But not the kind we hoped for." His gaze met hers. "We did a records check. Couldn't find any unaccounted-for babies from any of the nearby hospitals. We went back over three weeks."

She frowned. "Huh. I really thought that would work, you know?" She thought for a second and then voiced an idea. "What if the baby had been born at home? It happens. Not often, but it happens."

"You mean with a midwife or something?"

"Sure, that too. Couldn't you cross-check birth-certificate registrations against the hospital records?"

He nodded and smiled. "Actually, we've already started on that."

Charlie sat back in her chair and pondered. It was hard to hide a pregnancy, or any record of it if the mom had been receiving regular prenatal care. Surely it would only be a matter of time until they found the baby's mother. "Well, something will hopefully turn up."

"It takes time. The wheels of bureaucracy and all that. I just wanted to give you an update, seeing as how you've got a stake in this too. I was surprised to see him with you today."

She gave a little laugh. "I couldn't resist. He's sweet. Even though he kept me up all night."

Smith shuddered. "Yuck. Been there done that. During a few of my Uncle of the Year moments." He laughed. "I like my sister's kids much better now that they're mobile. It'll be even better when they hit Little League."

She looked at the officer closely, took quick stock of him. Tall, handsome, stable job, liked kids, settled . . . he ticked all the right boxes. But she didn't get that tummy-lifting, butterfly sensation that she did when she saw Dave. How inconvenient.

"Charlie, would you mind stopping by the station, maybe tomorrow? It might be good to go over your statement from Saturday night. See if you remember anything else that might help us out."

"I don't work until one. I can probably pop in tomorrow morning."

"That'd be great. Well, I'd better be going." He hesitated for a minute, then caught her gaze and held it. "This Ricker guy that was here on Saturday. Are you . . ."

"No." It wasn't exactly a lie. But she couldn't deny that Todd looked relieved at her answer.

"Oh. It seemed like you were."

"We were merely walking to meet Josh and some others at the pub. He didn't want me to be alone is all."

Liar.

She checked her watch. "Listen, thanks for stopping by. I do have another patient waiting, though."

He stood and nodded. "And I've got to get back to work. Take care, Charlie." His smile was warm enough to melt icicles.

"Thanks, Todd. You too."

When he was gone, she took a minute to sit and recover. Unless she was greatly mistaken, and she could be—her romantic radar wasn't the best—Officer Smith had been sending out some signals. On Saturday night he'd been rather protective of her too, she remembered. She didn't know him well, but they'd met on several occasions . . .

"Charlie? Exam room one is waiting." Robin appeared in the doorway with a smile. "Can't blame you for needing to sit down, though. Todd Smith in uniform is . . ." She stopped talking and merely made the motion of fanning herself.

Charlie couldn't help but laugh. "Don't let Josh hear you talking like that."

"I suppose we shouldn't let on that we call him Dr. Hottie then?"

Charlie nearly choked. "Oh my God. He'd die."

With a cheeky grin, Robin disappeared and Charlie made her way to the exam room, grabbing the chart off the door. Enough fun—it was time to get back to work.

Chapter Six

Charlie wished this wasn't the first time she'd had to give a police statement, but she'd done her share during her ER rotation. Then there was the time she'd stopped at a gas station for a pint of ice cream and had found herself in the middle of a domestic dispute. As the boyfriend had come charging across the parking lot, the cashier had locked the outside door. Charlie hadn't thought twice. She'd taken the girl into the storage closet and locked them in until police arrived, spending several minutes trying to calm the girl down.

Her parents had been livid that she'd inserted herself into a potentially dangerous situation. That had been the day that she'd realized that she simply did not think the same way as her mother and father did and she'd known exactly what she was going to do. She asked herself why she'd become a doctor and the answer had been clear—she'd done it to help people. That was the marker of her success—not acclaim or status or money. She didn't give a rat's ass about becoming chief of anything or top of her field. Prestige meant nothing to her. She'd been around it her whole life and found it to be an empty ambition. And so she'd stood up for herself for the first time ever, put her foot down, and found herself part of a small practice here in Jewell Cove. No regrets. Not one.

Now here she was again, in the middle of a situation that wasn't her doing, sitting, waiting. Drinking terrible police station coffee while the baby sat in his car seat, his bright eyes open and staring at a colorful toy bar she'd bought during a very necessary trip to shop for the necessities like clothing and a proper snowsuit. An additional surprise had been Josh's sister, Sarah, who had arrived at the office with baby items from when she'd had her children, like a playpen with a thick pad at the bottom that Charlie could use as a makeshift crib.

Absently she checked her e-mail on her phone—nothing major other than a couple of e-bills that required payment and a few newsletters she'd read later. She picked up a magazine and flipped through it, but nothing really grabbed her interest. She was about to resort to a game of spider solitaire when the office door opened and she looked up.

And saw Dave.

She was immediately transported to two days earlier, sitting on her floor and kissing him. Her face had to be turning red even as she tried a friendly smile. The look he gave her was sweet, as if they shared a secret, and she melted a little bit. Why was it he could turn her to mush with just an expression?

"Good morning, Dr. Yang," he said easily. "I guess you're here for the same reason I am."

"I guess so." She pushed on the arms of the chair and stood. Her heels increased her height by a few inches, but she was still a good five inches or more shorter than he was. She tugged at her black skirt, brushed her hands over the fabric.

"Dr. Yang? Come on in." The officer on duty called her into the office and she picked up the car seat. She was starting to get used to the weight of it.

"It's good to see you, Dave."

She moved to pass him and he caught her arm. "How about an early lunch when you're done?" He leaned close, his words soft. "I don't have to be at work until one."

"Me either," she confessed, and then wondered why she'd been so quick to answer. Hadn't she decided yesterday that it was better to just let things go? Besides, he'd been the one to say *talk soon* and then hadn't texted again . . . Clearly it was much easier to put him off with a text message than it was face-to-face.

"So we're on? You can fill me in on how this little guy is doing." He peered down into the seat, a goofy smile on his face.

She hesitated. It was just lunch, after all. Perfectly platonic and public, right? And she did have to eat before doing her stint as the walk-in doctor this afternoon.

"The Tuesday special at Breezes is meatloaf and mashed potatoes," he urged.

"That sounds fine to me. I'll see you when you're done."

She didn't want to keep the officer waiting, so she slipped inside the office and took a chair to answer any lingering questions about Saturday night.

It didn't take as long as she expected, and she was out thirty minutes later. Dave was sitting in the chair she'd vacated, flipping through the same magazine. "Ready?" he asked, standing.

"I guess." She put her scarf around her neck and then went to put on her coat. In an instant, Dave was there, helping her slip her arms into the sleeves and balance the baby. "Thanks," she murmured, buttoning the buttons and taking her gloves from the pockets.

"It's a cold one," he observed as he held the door and they stepped outside into the police station parking lot. "Did you walk over from the clinic?"

"No, I drove here straight from home." She looked around and didn't see his truck. "You walked up, didn't you?"

"I did."

"Guess you're riding with me, then."

He took the carrier from her hands and they started across the parking lot. Dave was right, it was bitterly cold; the kind of aching cold that seeped through clothing right into the bones. She hadn't worn boots today either, and her heels and nylons gave no protection against the weather. Halfway across the lot, her shoe slipped on a sheet of ice and she felt herself careening backward.

"Oopsie daisies!" The funny expression slipped from Dave's lips as his hand caught her elbow, keeping her upright. "Careful there."

She could feel the strength of his fingers through the thick wool coat. "Thanks. I should have worn boots today."

"No kidding. Don't get me wrong, your legs look great. But those shoes are not made for ice and snow."

She got out her keys, feeling a bit fluttery from the compliment. "I know. I figured with just four hours at the office today, I'd skip the boots."

The heater took a minute or two to kick in, and the drive was so short that Charlie's toes had barely started to thaw when they parked on the street outside the café. It was only eleven thirty; they'd arrived before the lunch rush. This time, when Charlie got out of the car, Dave took her arm securely so she wouldn't slip on any black ice on the sidewalk, and carried the baby with his other hand.

Breezes was toasty warm and smelled heavenly when they walked in. A local radio station played over the speakers and despite the cold outside, it was cheery and bright on the inside. It had already been decorated for Christmas, with gaudy tinsel draped along the lunch counter and silk poinsettias on every table. Above the wide window overlooking the harbor, a gold and red and green shiny sign said MERRY CHRISTMAS and in the corner, an artificial tree was up and lit with colorful lights and red and green ornaments.

"Lunch for two today, Charlie?" the waitress, Linda, called out from the kitchen. "I'll be right out. Just putting up a takeout order. Sit where you like."

Charlie chose her usual table without thinking; a table for two with comfortable wood captain's chairs and an unimpeded view of the docks. "Hey," Dave said as he hung his coat on the back of his chair and then sat down. "I can see the boatyard from here. Cool." He pulled a spare chair over and put the car seat on it. "There you go," he said softly, smiling down at the tiny face staring up at him. "You get a chair like everyone else."

She was very aware that the boatyard was visible, and instead of meeting his gaze or responding, she kept her eyes down and reached for the menu tucked in a wire holder on the table.

Linda didn't waste any time bustling over with two glasses of ice water. "You beat the rush today, folks. And oh my soul, who is this adorable boy?" Linda peered into the car seat and smiled. "Aren't you handsome," she cooed, and Charlie couldn't help but smile.

"I'm watching him for a few days. He's our baby in the manger." Charlie knew the grapevine would spread the news anyway, so she filled Linda in on the details. "Dave and I were just at the station, answering a few final questions, and thought we'd grab lunch before going to work."

"Oh, of course. What can I get you? The special's meatloaf and your choice of potato with carrots, and we've got a holiday special happening all month long. Stuffed turkey breast with mashed potatoes and gravy, peas and carrots, cranberry sauce, and dessert."

"I'll have that," Dave said quickly. "Sounds perfect."

"And you, Charlie?"

Dave's meal sounded like an awful lot of food. Usually she went for a salad or a bowl of soup, but today she was starving. Besides, she could go home after work and have something light, right?

"I'll have the meatloaf with mashed," she answered, smiling. "Thanks, Linda."

"It'll be right up," she answered. "I'll bring you some coffee while you wait. It's wicked cold today."

The radio station was interspersing holiday songs with their regular playlist, and Charlie caught herself tapping her toe to a country version of "Santa Claus Is Coming to Town." "Not to be corny," she suggested, "but it's beginning to look a lot like Christmas around here."

He nodded. "I know. Now that the tree's up in the square, every single window is lit up and decorated. I mean, a lot of stuff went up right after Thanksgiving, but it's a full-court press now."

She smiled, waited while Linda poured their coffee, and then replied as she added milk to her cup. "So, are you a Santa or a Scrooge?" she asked.

He grinned. "Maybe a little of both. Sometimes it can get to be a bit much. The hoopla and the crowds and how it can all seem like a competition. But then there are other things I like about it too. We always had good Christmases growing up. There wasn't always a lot of money to go around, but with the five of us there was always something fun. There was always a new board game every Christmas, and sports equipment. One year the three of us boys all got new baseball gloves. We took them outside to play and I swear I couldn't feel my fingers when I came back in, they were so cold. We used to have New Year's Eve movie nights too, with all of us crowded around the TV and my mom would make popcorn and Kool-Aid. It was the only time we were ever allowed to stay up past midnight."

"That sounds so fun. It was only me at home, so the only time anything like that happened was if I had a friend over, or went to their house."

"And that didn't happen very often?"

She shook her head. "Not really. My parents always threw a Christmas Eve cocktail party. It was not really . . . kid friendly. And they went out for New Year's, and I had a sitter until I was old enough to stay alone." She shrugged.

"Wow. You missed out on a lot."

She shrugged again. "It was what it was."

Linda came back bearing two huge plates of food. "Oh my word," Charlie exclaimed, but the aroma was so good that her mouth was already watering. "That smells so good, Linda."

"You just holler if you need anything else. I'll be back with dessert and more coffee in a bit."

The café was starting to fill up now, the lunch regulars filtering in, rubbing their hands together to keep warm. The tunes on the radio were drowned out by conversation as Charlie and Dave dipped into their meals. Gus, the main cook at the café, hadn't let them down. Charlie's meatloaf was moist and flavorful, the potatoes smooth, the carrots sweetened with just a hint of something.

"If I could cook like Gus, I'd never eat out," Charlie

admitted. "I do okay in the kitchen, but the guy is a master of comfort food."

"I agree. His crab cakes are almost as good as my mother's." Dave dipped a piece of turkey in cranberry sauce and popped it in his mouth. "And this sauce is not from a can."

"I think Gus would rather die than cook anything that wasn't from scratch." Charlie laughed. "So, what are your plans for this Christmas?"

It was a simple, harmless question but it dampened the good mood considerably. "I haven't decided. I need to talk to Janice about that. I'm sure they have plans. "

"Plans that don't include you?"

He smiled. "That might be awkward. I'm just, well, at loose ends a bit. Missing my family. So." He lightened his voice and smiled down at the baby, who was surprisingly content. "Our Baby Jesus. Still no sign of the Virgin Mary."

"Or Joseph," Charlie added, letting the matter of Christmas drop. "I honestly thought someone would have come forward by now."

"I'm thinking someone would have to be in a pretty bad situation to abandon their kid."

"Well, I'm sure we'll hear something soon." She met his gaze. "I think he's very lucky we happened by at that moment. It couldn't have been planned any better. I mean, the night of the tree lighting. Everyone in the square for a good hour or more, and then tons of foot traffic. It was almost as if whoever left him wanted him to be found."

What she said sank in and they stared at each other. Maybe the manger wasn't that random after all. "I'm sure the police have thought of that." Dave nodded at her. "But you're right. I mean . . . remember what you said about that case you handled? Someone trying to . . ." his voice tightened, ". . . dispose of a baby wouldn't put him in a church manger on the busiest night of the season. Know what I mean?"

Charlie swirled the last bite of meatloaf in rich gravy. "Right. They'd put him somewhere he wouldn't be found."

"Still," he argued, "it's winter. What if we hadn't come along? In these temperatures he wouldn't have survived very long. Even if the intention was to have him found, there would always be a chance he wouldn't be." Dave's face darkened. "Hell of a big gamble to take with your baby's life."

"I agree." She looked up at him and asked the question that had been bothering her for the last two days. "Dave, I can't go on calling him 'the baby.' Is it wrong to want to give him a name?"

Dave chuckled. "Not at all. It's been getting kind of awkward, actually." They both looked down at the baby, whose lids were drooping sleepily.

"He looks like an angel," Charlie whispered. "Even if he does keep me up most of the night. I can't resist that little face."

"Then name him after an angel."

"Gabriel?"

Dave grimaced. "Too predictable."

"Raphael?"

"The painter or the Ninja Turtle?"

She made a face, then pulled out her phone and Googled angel names. "Maybe this wasn't such a good idea. Most of the names have *i-e-l* at the end. Jophiel. Hesediel."

Dave laughed and ate a forkful of mashed potatoes and gravy. "Yuck."

"Wait. There are gospels here though. Paul. John. And . . . ooh. Daniel."

"I like that."

"Me too." She looked up at Dave with surprise. "Hey, did we just name a baby together?"

"Well, temporarily. His birth certificate probably says something else. "

Right. Reality. Not her baby. Not her life. She had to be careful she didn't start pretending it was. She put her fork and knife on her plate and wiped her lips with her napkin. "I should get back, I suppose. It'll give me time to feed Daniel . . ." She tested the name on for size, ". . . before I start my appointments."

Dave frowned at her. "You're going now? Without pie? Is it possible to have a meal here without pie?"

Charlie laughed. "Oh, it's possible, otherwise I'd be the size of a house. I eat here most noon hours."

She realized what she'd just said and hoped he didn't pick up on it. But then, why would he? It was her own embarrassment speaking, that was all.

"Your loss," he said easily. "Pie comes with my meal and I'm going to take full advantage."

She opened up her purse to grab her wallet but Dave reached across the table and put his fingers on her wrist.

"Lunch is on me," he said quietly. "I invited you, re-member?"

"I don't mind paying my share," she replied, still star-tled by the intimate touch. It was made worse when she looked up and into his dark, chocolaty eyes. They were so beautiful. The kind of eyes a girl could get lost in if she wasn't careful.

"Would that make you feel better? So you wouldn't have to call this a date?"

Her lips fell open, and she tried to respond but didn't know what to say.

"It's just lunch," he finally said, slipping his fingers off her wrist. "Falls under the getting-to-know-you-better category. No biggie, okay? You can get the next one."

Assuming there would be a next one.

"Then . . . thank you for lunch."

"Anytime."

Why was this so easy for him and so hard for her?

With a parting smile, she hefted the car seat and made her way to the doors, out into the wintery air. If anything, it had only gotten colder outside.

Keeping her distance from Dave was proving to be a challenge. As she started the car and felt the cold blast of air as the fan kicked in, she sighed. It would be easier to avoid him if her heart was really in it . . .

❄   ❄   ❄

By Thursday night Charlie was going a little crazy. The last text from Dave sat on her phone, mocking her. Thanks for lunch and talk soon, it said. But there was no talking. He'd gotten her message loud and clear.

Charlie plumped the pillow she held in her lap and stared, unseeing, at the evening news. She couldn't make up her mind what she wanted to do. She'd always been a planner, with the future mapped out in front of her. Things fit into tidy little boxes and that was comforting. Reassuring. And Dave Ricker didn't fit in a tidy box. He was a nice guy and he liked her and she liked him. Which, if she were being honest, was frustrating as hell. He was definitely a more go-with-the-flow kind of guy, unsure of what came next or where he'd go. He wasn't a long-term thinker. His relaxed attitude drove type-A people like her a little crazy.

She reached for the glass of merlot she'd poured and took a restorative sip. If Lizzie were here, she'd have some definite opinions . . .

Charlie snagged the cordless phone from the base and

hit the speed dial. It only rang twice when Lizzie answered. "Dr. Howard."

"Hello, Dr. Howard."

"Charlie! Hey, girl!"

Charlie laughed. This was so what she'd needed. Lizzie was driven and borderline workaholic, but she was Charlie's best friend and always knew how to make her laugh, even with a simple greeting. "Hey yourself. Where are you?"

"Driving home."

"I'll call you back."

"Don't be silly. Bluetooth, baby."

Charlie chuckled. "You're in a good mood."

"I guess. I'm off shift for three days. That works for me."

Charlie sank down into the cushions and sipped her wine again. "What? You haven't taken on extra shifts?" She raised her eyebrows. "There must be a man involved."

There was a beat of silence.

"Liiiizzziiieeee!"

The warm laughter on the other end made Charlie feel so much better. "Okay. But I'm not spilling because I don't want to jinx it. Soon."

"Killjoy."

"How's the mystery man? Still watching him from the café?"

"Funny you should mention that." Charlie stared into the crackling fire, swirled the wine in the glass. "We, uh, actually met."

"Oooh, do tell!"

Charlie heard the blare of a horn through the phone. "You sure you don't want to talk later?"

"I'm sure. I'm on my way to pick up my dad and go see my mom. I could use the distraction."

Charlie got a lump in her throat. Mrs. Howard had always been good to her, and her early onset Alzheimer's had hit the family hard. If Lizzie wanted distraction, Charlie would give it to her.

"We met when I was decorating the churchyard for the holidays."

Lizzie let out a hoot that made Charlie grin. "Wait, you were decorating the church?"

"I know. Do you want to hear the story or not?"

Lizzie's laughter mellowed and Charlie grinned to herself. "Anyway, the next night we hung out at the tree lighting ceremony and we were going to go get a drink when we found a baby."

The line went quiet for several seconds. "You found a baby? Did I hear that right?"

"Yep. An abandoned baby. So our date turned into calling the cops and dealing with social workers."

"Well, that'll be a story to tell the grandkids." Lizzie's good humor was back.

"I'm not so sure, Liz." Charlie put down the glass and sighed. "I was so stupid, having this crush on someone I'd never met. It's totally different now that I know him in person."

"Different good or different bad?"

"Both?" She picked at a thread on the pillow. "You know me, Liz. I see men as candidates with potential."

"Yeah. You do. Which is no fun at all."

Charlie giggled a little. "Right. And this guy? I don't know if he's a candidate. He's got a kid and just moved to town, and I'm not sure he's even staying or if he even wants to be a father again . . ."

The sharp bark of laughter on the other end cut Charlie off. "You already talked about that stuff? Honey, you're more involved than you realize."

That's what she was afraid of.

"Crappy thing is, Liz, that I want to spend more time with him. He . . . he floats my boat, if you know what I mean."

Lizzie laughed again. "Yeah, I know what you mean." Charlie wondered what the heck her friend was being so close-lipped about. Maybe this developing romance of hers was serious. If Charlie had learned anything, it was that Liz would tell her when she was ready. She always did.

"Charlie?"

"Hmm?"

"I think you should have a torrid affair. I mean, you never have. A no-strings, great sex, live in the moment affair. That's assuming this guy is torrid affair material?"

She thought back to Sunday morning on the living room floor and how badly she'd wanted to rip his clothes off even though they'd kept it strictly to kissing. "He is." The words came out slightly strangled.

"Sister, you are leaving out some pertinent details."

"You could always come for a visit. Maybe over the holidays."

There was a beat of silence. "Tempting, but I think I'll be kind of occupied over Christmas. It's Dad's first one without Mom at home and Ian will be around . . ."

"Ian. So that's his name."

"Long story."

"Whenever you're ready."

Lizzie chuckled. "Damn, I'm glad you called. Really glad."

"Me too."

"Listen. You do what you're comfortable with as far as things go with the mystery man. I'm just saying . . . not every guy needs to have a wedding registry above his head and tick all the right boxes, know what I mean?

Sometimes you can just go with it. In fact, this might be better because you could go into it without any expectations from each other. For Pete's sake, have a fling, Charlie. You've never done anything spontaneous in your life, other than moving to Jewell Cove. And look how that's turned out for you. It's a little slow for my speed, but I know you love it there."

She did, and she was glad Lizzie recognized it. Her family certainly didn't.

"The torrid affair might have to take a backseat. I'm looking after the baby temporarily. He's a bit small, and it's not for very long."

"You're looking after a baby?" Liz's voice came across the line loud and clear. "Are you crazy?"

Charlie laughed. "I'm exhausted. But it's good practice."

"Better you than me, sister."

"I'll think about what you said," Charlie promised. "Thanks for the pep talk. I needed it."

"Next time I want better details. But I'm here at Dad's, so I'd better go."

"Love you," Charlie said, missing her friend desperately.

"Love you back. Text me a pic of the mystery man. I want visuals."

Charlie was laughing as she clicked off the phone.

Lizzie had certainly given her something to think about. She was right. Charlie had never done anything spontaneous. Plus they were attracted to each other. It could work.

Or . . . not. Things were rarely that straightforward, were they? Besides, as alluring as the idea was, Charlie wasn't sure she knew how to go about having a "torrid affair," as Lizzie put it.

Chapter Seven

It was all going fine until Friday at eleven o'clock. Routinely she and Josh closed up shop on Friday afternoons, with one of them remaining reachable during the afternoon through the answering service in case of a patient emergency. That rarely happened, since anything urgent automatically went to the closest hospital or the nearby walk-in clinics. Today their last appointment was at eleven thirty, which meant they might actually wrap things up by twelve thirty or one. She'd thought to do some Christmas shopping at the town shops, maybe grab some decorations for the cottage. Instead Josh poked his head inside her door when she was between patients.

"Hey. It's Robin's birthday today. I said we'd take her to lunch once we wrap up here."

Charlie liked Robin. She was even impressed that Josh knew it was her birthday and was making an effort. But she really, really didn't feel like going to lunch and having to make small talk.

"Where?" she asked, knowing she couldn't really say no.

"Breezes?"

Right. And she'd find herself watching the waterfront, looking for Dave. He hadn't called or texted again this week. Whatever interest he'd had, it had clearly waned.

"We always go there. If we're knocking off for the week, what about the pub?" At this time of day, the pub catered to the lunch crowd, and she could take Daniel along with her.

"I'll ask. There's something to be said for Friday-night nachos and wings." He smiled at her. "So you're in?"

How could she say no? "Yeah, I'm in." She'd just go do the dutiful lunch thing and then her shopping. On Fridays the stores remained open until nine. She'd have lots of time, even if she had to stop and give the baby a bottle somewhere. Truthfully, she could really use some sleep, but she could stand to get out a little too. How did new moms manage?

But fate stepped in once more, with a last-minute appointment that Josh felt he couldn't put off. And indeed he couldn't. The patient was all of five years old, and her mother didn't have a car for driving to a hospital. While Josh waited for them to arrive and then treated the child for bronchitis, Robin got out the small box of holiday decorations and spruced up the waiting area a bit, adding a small rope of lights along the front of the reception desk, putting a tiny bottle-brush tree on the magazine table in the corner, and hanging a battered synthetic evergreen wreath on the door. Meanwhile, Charlie supervised from the comfy chair in the waiting area, feeding Daniel his bottle and sitting with her feet up for a few minutes. It put them behind schedule, but it was relaxing just the same.

By the time Josh had sent the patient's prescription to the pharmacy, Charlie and Robin were waiting, stomachs growling. It was nearly two o'clock.

The weather had been cold the last few days, but today it had turned sunny and milder, a welcome reprieve from the bitter, raw wind that seemed to seep through the bones. Charlie parked the car in the lot next to the pub, in one of the last available spots. She put Daniel in a borrowed stroller before they all made their way inside, into the welcoming warmth of the bar.

Their food had just been served when the door swung open on a gust of wind and a group of five blew in with it. Five big, burly men in heavy jackets and thick knitted hats, one with a particular set of dark eyes that immediately found Charlie and made her traitorous body respond with a jolt of pure electricity. What was with the crazy physical attraction, anyway? All Dave had to do was show up and she got this jacked-up, excited feeling racing through her veins. She had to get a grip.

It had been easier to put off the impact of her attraction when he was out of sight, to pretend it was all in her head. Not so easy when he was standing there, larger than life, reminding her of exactly what it was like to be in his arms. He kissed like a freaking angel, that's what. Made her forget all her good intentions.

"Charlie, you okay?" Robin nudged her arm. "I just asked you to pass the ketchup."

"Oh. Sorry." She offered a weak smile and reached for the squeeze bottle. Her wrap and sweet potato fries smelled delicious but she wasn't sure she could eat.

For heaven's sake. He was just a man. Mortal. Imperfect.

She looked up. Caught his eye. Held her breath.

Josh nudged her elbow. "What's going on?"

She hadn't realized she was biting her lip until Josh spoke to her. She released it and pasted on a bright smile. "What do you mean?" She picked up a fry, dipped it in sauce, and took a definitive bite.

"Last time I saw you with that guy, you were at the tree lighting. Then the whole thing with the mystery baby happened. Now he walks in and you're wound tighter than a watch. What am I missing?"

"Nothing." She deliberately ignored looking over at the corner where Dave and his buddies had taken their seats. "Once the cops left, Dave went home. He came back to the office the next morning and gave me a lift back to my place. That's all."

Josh was so quiet she stopped dipping her fry and put it on her plate before turning to face him. "What?"

"Did he do something he shouldn't have?"

There was a protective note in Josh's voice that grated on her nerves. She frowned at him. "What is it with the men in this town, anyway? You sound as bad as Todd Smith."

But her sharp reply and frown did nothing to deter Josh. "I work with you. I care about you. You're a single woman. I just like to protect my friends, that's all. And if this guy is bothering you, I've got your back."

"Me too," Robin piped up from across the table.

"It's not like that," she answered, laughing tightly. "Besides, I can handle myself, I promise. Right now I just need something to eat. Like my sweet potato fries that are getting cold."

The topic was set aside as they finished their meal, even though Charlie was always aware of Dave back in the far corner, talking and laughing with his pals. Charlie actually thought she might be able to scoot out of the pub and tackle her shopping, and when Josh paid their bill for lunch, she stood and reached for her coat and scarf while Robin excused herself to go to the bathroom.

Charlie's hand was nearly in the second sleeve when the weight of her coat disappeared and the hole of her sleeve shifted into a more accessible position. Her tummy flipped over as she realized it had to be Dave, standing close behind her. She shrugged the coat over her shoulders and took a breath. She could do this. She could have a conversation with him without wanting to rip his clothes off.

She turned around and realized she was wrong. He was just so . . . everything.

"Hey," he said quietly, and her tongue felt thick in her mouth as she struggled to find something cool to say.

"Hi."

It could have been worse. What was it about him that turned her into an idiot?

"How've you been?"

"Fine. You?"

"Not so great, as it happens."

"Oh?" She relaxed a little. "Did you get the cold that's going around? I've been seeing people in the office all week."

"No," he said quietly, his gaze locked on hers. "I've been wanting to call you since Tuesday, and keep convincing myself I shouldn't."

Boom. Forget relaxed. All her senses went on high alert again.

"Dave, I . . ."

"And that's why. I didn't want to hear you turn me down or scramble to find an excuse to say no."

She wanted to explain, but it would sound so terribly juvenile to admit to him that she'd watched him for weeks during her lunch hour. That he'd been her guilty little pleasure, a kind of escape from the day-to-day real world. It would sound creepy. Neither was it possible to bring up the other reason—that she was looking for a husband and father to her as-yet unborn children and didn't think he was that guy. Talk about putting the cart before the horse . . . That would be enough to send any man running for the hills.

"Anyway, have a nice weekend, Charlie. It was good to see you." He peeked into the stroller and a soft smile curved his lips. "You too, sprout," he said quietly, and she melted all over again.

And that should have been the end of it. Except she didn't want him to walk away. What she wanted to do was break free for once from the only kind of existence she'd ever known. One based on pros and cons and logic and safety and security. The one that never took risks. She'd bought the requisite dollhouse cottage on the sea in an idyllic small town with the perfect job, putting all the pieces of the puzzle together to find the life she craved.

Which, she was quickly realizing, was simply setting herself up for failure.

"Dave?"

He turned back.

"Look, uh . . ." Wow, she sounded so eloquent and composed. She tried a weak smile. "Do you want to take a walk or something?"

His gaze warmed. "I thought you'd never ask. Let me ditch the guys and grab my jacket."

Robin came from the bathroom. "Oh, you're ready. Shall we go?"

"You go ahead," Charlie said. "Daniel and I are going to catch up on some shopping."

Which might have been a good excuse if Dave hadn't returned in record time. "I'm back."

Robin's grin was wide and her eyes twinkled. "Yes,

you are. Well, Charlie, you have fun *shopping.*" To make matters worse, she winked at them. "I'll see you Monday morning."

"I hate small towns," Charlie muttered, and Dave chuckled behind her.

"Oh, come on. They have a certain charm."

Charlie pulled on her gloves as they made their way to the door. She wasn't quite prepared for the blast of cold air that smacked her in the face as they stepped outside, though, and she adjusted the blanket tucked around the baby. "It's funny," she said, huddling into her coat. "This is considered a mild day. And it really is so much better than earlier in the week. But you know what? It's still damned cold."

Dave laughed beside her. "There's a lot of winter left. You should get used to it. Personally, I can handle the cold if we still get sun, you know?"

She did know. There was something about dull, gray, dreary days that made her want to sleep and eat carbs all day long. She was always glad when the time changed in spring.

"So, was that a late lunch or early dinner?" she asked, as they started to stroll along the boardwalk.

"We decided to knock off early today," Dave said in reply. "Friday afternoon, and we had a good week. We brought Jim Williams's boat into dock this afternoon, but there wasn't much sense in starting anything until Monday morning." His big body sheltered her from a bit of the wind. "Know what always amazes me? Lobstermen this time of year. What a thankless, cold job. You think it's cold here, imagine being out on the water, checking traps. Brrr."

They wandered along the boardwalk for a minute. Finally Dave spoke again, his voice deeper than it had been only moments before. More private, intimate.

"You've been avoiding me, haven't you?"

"No!" The answer came out before she could consider what best to say. "I mean . . . damn. I just did some thinking after our lunch the other day."

"Did you sit down and make a checklist?"

Her cheeks flamed, despite the cold. "Look, Dave, I've had relationships before. And they were . . ."

She broke off the sentence and considered. What made this different? "They were people I already knew. That I had something in common with."

"Doctors and med students, then."

She nodded. "Well, yes." She looked over at him and tried being as transparent as she could. "We already had something in common, so no shortage of things to talk about. We ran in the same circles, knew the same people."

"Wow, Charlie," he said, shaking his head a little. "I totally didn't have you pegged as a snob. I'm just a guy who works on the docks, right?"

She stopped walking, shocked by his assumption, be-latedly realizing how it sounded. "God no! That's not it. It's more . . ." She struggled to explain. "I guess it was more that we all had similar lives. Crazy schedules, goals, expectations for the future."

"Safe," he supplied.

"I suppose so," she agreed, though she'd never con-sidered that before. It made complete sense now that he'd said it, though. She'd dated within that sphere because it was comfortable. Expectations were managed. There was little ambiguity.

"The thing you have to understand about me is that I don't really know how to be . . . I don't know, spontane-ous. I've always based decisions on logic, common sense. There's always a plan and a goal."

"Good God, that sounds terrible."

She couldn't help it, she laughed, and he chuckled too. Their boots made scuffing noises on the boardwalk and gulls wheeled and cried above the harbor. The tension between her shoulders began to let go. Maybe this was what she'd needed too. Some fresh air and relaxation.

"It isn't as terrible as it sounds." Not always, anyway. "It probably comes from having two very driven parents. We didn't do anything on a whim or for sheer pleasure. It had to have a purpose. I don't even remember them going out just for fun. Dinner dates and social events were for networking. Course selection was based on advancement. Medical school provided me with security . . ."

"I'm getting the picture. Sounds like you had a very . . . productive upbringing."

That was it exactly.

"I don't really know how to do anything else. And I don't mean to scare you, but I've never looked at relationships as simply a way to pass the time. I know I said we should enjoy the now but honestly I don't know how to do that. Everything fits into a bigger plan, you see."

He stopped walking and faced her. "Like a house with a white picket fence and a husband and dog and two-point-five kids?"

Nailed it. She was afraid to admit it but she nodded anyway. "Yeah. Like that."

"And I'm not keeper material."

She let her silence answer. And yet there was this stupid, crazy physical attraction thing she felt whenever he was near. What the heck was that about, anyway?

They were now standing in the middle of the sidewalk on Main Street. It wasn't the best place to be having this kind of conversation. Her hands were shoved into her pockets, and his nose was red from the cold and she said what was on her mind anyway. "If I hadn't taken a taxi to work that morning, would this have gone differently?"

His gaze held hers. "I certainly hope so."

He had a way of saying things that sent a delicious shiver rippling through her body. She recognized it for what it was: anticipation. Pure, simple, in-the-moment desire and possibility.

"Nothing's changed for me, Charlie." His gaze dropped to her lips. "I enjoy your company. I'd like to enjoy it more, but I can't put a label on it or make it part of a bigger plan. Hell, I don't even know if I'm going to be staying in Jewell Cove, you know that. But that doesn't mean we can't try."

The ball was clearly in her court. She knew the rules, and the only question was if she could abide by them. Part of her balked and said to listen to reason. It cautioned her not to waste her time on something that was probably going nowhere. But a bigger part of her was tired of being reasonable, and safe, and predictable. Not once in her life had she done anything wild or risky. She never threw caution to the wind or acted in a way that was less than sensible. Daniel started to fuss a little, so she started walking again, Dave taking his cue and joining her. She hoped the movement of the stroller would soothe the baby for a little while longer.

"By enjoy my company, you mean . . ." she asked the leading question, not sure how she wanted him to answer.

"I don't know. I'd be lying if I didn't say I was crazy attracted to you."

Zing went the arousal meter.

"But I can see you're not a 'leap into it headfirst and deal with the consequences later' kind of person."

No, she wasn't.

"A date," he suggested. "A real date. Something

casual that we can do together. No commitments, no pressure. Just a single date on a Saturday. What do you say?"

A date. What would be the harm? Besides, with a date things were planned. There wasn't as much chance of getting caught off guard, was there? A date had a basic itinerary. Dinner. A movie, something. "What did you have in mind?"

He thought for a moment. "You said you had shopping to do," he finally said, looking down at her. "But I think I kept you from it. The Evergreen Festival is tomorrow and I've never experienced one. We could go together, take Daniel too, of course. That's pretty low-key and casual."

It certainly was. In fact, it didn't sound very date-ish at all. She should be relieved, so why was she slightly disappointed?

"You want to spend your day shopping?"

He shrugged. "Why not? Besides, I was thinking about getting something for Nora for Christmas. I'm clueless when it comes to little girls. Maybe you could help me."

Oh, that was playing dirty.

"We could have lunch and finish our shopping. The weather's supposed to be fine. It'll be a great day for it."

Wow. When he said low-key, he meant it. How on earth could she refuse? Never mind she was planning on attending the festival anyway.

"It sounds like a nice day," she agreed.

"Then it's a date." He dropped his shoulders and looked supremely pleased with himself. "I can stop by your place and pick you up."

They'd wandered back along the dock now, nearly to the public lot where her car waited. Dave lifted a hand to George Adams at the boat works, then shoved his hands back in his coat. "He's a good boss," Dave said. "Fair. Good sense of humor."

"Do you think he'll keep you on?"

"I don't know. I guess I'll cross that bridge when I come to it. I spent a lot of years being told where I was going and what I was doing. It was all about the mission and my orders. Now that I'm a civilian, I get to figure all that out for myself. I don't see any point in rushing into anything."

Charlie couldn't imagine not having a firm plan. But she was starting to realize that maybe that wasn't such a bad thing. People could become slaves to plans. And then what happened when they didn't work out?

❋　❋　❋

Dave stared up at the ceiling, resisting the urge to flip and flop around in the bed. He'd awakened early and his thoughts ran to Charlie and what he was doing with her. He honestly hadn't planned on staying in Jewell Cove that long—it was a temporary fix until he could make some decisions, a way to stay close to Nora in the meantime. But something about the good doctor had knocked him for a bit of a loop. Enough that he was losing sleep over it.

He knew he was up for good now. Rather than toss and turn, he slipped out of bed, grabbed some clothes and his phone, and went out to revive the fire in the stove that had died overnight.

He added a couple birch logs, hoping the papery bark would ignite from the coals and get things going again. He'd just checked the weather on his phone when it vibrated in his hand, indicating an incoming message.

He exited and went to look, and his heart jumped up in his throat as the latest picture of Nora showed in a little block in the conversation. Janice had sent through another picture.

He touched the image with his finger and his daughter's face filled the screen, all light curls and brown eyes and bewitching smile. Lord, she was beautiful. The eyes were his, but everything else was her mother. It was disconcerting.

His throat tightened.

He closed the pic and went back to the conversation. Janice had typed something with the attachment.

`Latest of Nora, when we put up the Christmas tree. She's asleep but looking forward to next weekend.`

His thumbs hovered over the keyboard. Finally, he typed in a reply.

`Me too. What are you doing up so early?`

The answer came back immediately.

`Nora has a cold. I've been up to give her medication and cuddles. Now I can't sleep.`

You and me both, he thought, but in his case it was thinking about the woman he'd be spending the day with and there was no way in hell he'd type that message to his ex.

There were days—a lot of them—that he felt badly he hadn't given Nora a two-parent home. The truth was, he hadn't really, truly been in love with Janice. He'd been trying to make a romance out of a friendship, and that just didn't work. He thanked God that they were able to maintain an amicable relationship.

`I was thinking of getting Nora a Christmas present. Any suggestions?`

He didn't even know his own kid well enough to shop for a Christmas gift.

A few minutes later a reply came.

She's going through a puppy stage.
DO NOT GET HER A PUPPY. The stuffed
kind would be nice though.

He gave a huff of laughter at the all-caps. Oh, wouldn't that leave Janice fit to be tied, if he got a real dog? But he wouldn't pull that kind of trick.

Good to know, he typed. Do you need
anything?

This time the answer was quick to come back. Brian and I are managing fine, Dave. Don't worry.

Better go. See ya.

He got out of the conversation and put the phone on the coffee table. He was glad she'd sent the picture. Glad they'd chatted—even if it was just texting back and forth.

Then he thought about Charlie, and the way that she kissed, and his pulse leapt. That was all it took. Just a thought and his body reacted. He wondered why. Wondered if it was just a symptom of his long dry spell, or if it was something more. Something that was distinctly Charlie that caused him to get the automatic sense of urgency and protectiveness. And how much he should act on it.

Maybe first he should figure out if it was really real.

He sat in the corner of the sofa until daylight began to filter through the windows, and then he got up and started making coffee.

❄   ❄   ❄

The sun was out and the air was crisp and cool as they made their way down the hill to where the main shops were. Already crowds of people were milling about, carrying shopping bags, bundled up in winter clothes and sipping from paper cups of coffee or hot cider. Charlie nudged Dave's elbow and grinned. "Every store has a themed Christmas tree, see?"

They were at the far end of Main, where the shops began, and the first store was the bakery. A fat pine tree sat in the corner of the veranda, and it was decorated with ornaments shaped like cupcakes, cookies, loaves of bread, and kitchen utensils. Today, instead of wheeling the stroller through the crowds and packed stores, she had Daniel tucked into a Snugli carrier where he stayed warm and secure against her chest. The weight felt foreign but somehow nice too, and it left both hands free for shopping bags and browsing. Not to mention the baby seemed to love being snuggled as she carried him around.

"Shortbread," Charlie announced. "I'm fueling this shopping trip with shortbread." She grabbed Dave's hand and dragged him along, into the full shop that was noisy and squished and smelled like vanilla and fresh bread and cinnamon.

Decisively she approached the counter and ordered a plastic container of two dozen shortbread nuggets. "We can share," she said, paying for the cookies and tucking them into a cloth shopping bag. The cashier gave her a pamphlet and put a cookie-shaped stamp on a square next to the shop name. "Get all the stamps and you can enter to win a shopping spree," the chirpy cashier said, and Charlie called out her thanks and tucked the paper into her purse.

They stopped next door at the Shear Bliss salon, where the tree was decorated with sample bottles of hair products. Charlie was really getting into the spirit now, especially when people she recognized lifted a hand in a wave or stopped to say hello. Maybe she hadn't realized it until lately, but she was finally starting to feel like a part of this community. But as she went outside and rejoined Dave, she held back a little too, not holding his hand or walking too closely. A part of her wanted to keep that part of her life private. She'd never much been into PDAs.

Charlie's shopping bag was starting to fill up, with a tin of hibiscus tea from The Leaf and Grind added to her purchases as well as a box set of bubble bath and lotion from Bubbles. Dave, though, was still empty-handed. "Come on," Charlie chided. "There must be something you need to buy. You have sisters and stuff, right? Plus you said you wanted to find something for Nora."

He smiled down at her. "I think you're shopping enough for the both of us."

"Oh, this is hardly anything." She pulled him along to the bookstore, past a sparkly artificial tree adorned with paper ornaments. On closer examination, she realized that each round ball was constructed of strips of paper . . . strips of book pages . . . overlapping each other. It was a clever idea, and she paused briefly before the tree, reaching out to touch one of the fragile balls.

"Oh, look at this one," she said wistfully. "It's all Shakespeare." There were random lines from several plays, and as she turned the ornament in her fingers a line jumped out at her. *Whoever loved that loved not at first sight?* She couldn't name the play, but it gave her a little shiver just the same. Of course, she and Dave weren't in love. But still. She'd been the one to look down over the docks and get that silly swirly feeling whenever she saw him.

Dave peered over her shoulder. "I didn't know you were a fan."

She nodded, scanning the strips for more familiar words. "My parents used to assign reading to me. It was no big deal. I read the first one and I was hooked. Though some plays I enjoy more than others."

"Like *Romeo and Juliet*?"

"Are you kidding?" She turned her head and laughed up at him. "Young love meets tragic ending. Not my favorite. But it did provide some great romantic lines." She let the ornament fall back among the boughs and turned all the way around so that she faced him completely. *"My bounty is as boundless as the sea, My love as deep; the more I give to thee, The more I have, for both are infinite."*

She hadn't meant for it to be so serious, but the way he was looking down at her made her shift and slide away toward the door. "Anyway, let's go inside."

The store was crammed full of people, filling the narrow aisles. "Go browse," she instructed him, moving away. She hadn't shopped in a while, and she knew there were several titles she was waiting to add to her shelf.

He disappeared into the nonfiction section.

It took no time at all for Charlie to pick out a couple of the latest thrillers for Lizzie for Christmas. She hadn't mentioned it to Dave, but half the stuff she'd already bought today was for Lizzie. Buying for her parents was like buying for the people who had everything, so Charlie had already sent gift certificates for her parents to do some shopping before their holiday cruise. Other than token gifts for Robin and Josh at the clinic, she had no one else to buy for.

She found Dave in the kids section, a frown on his face. "Find anything you like?" she asked, holding her volumes in her arms.

"I don't know what's good. What's popular?" His dark eyes pleaded with her for help. "I mean I've read to her, but I'm overwhelmed by bunnies and ducks and princesses. She's almost three. Is that too young to really appreciate a book for Christmas?"

Charlie took pity on him. "It's never too early for books," she decreed.

Holding her books tightly against her chest, Charlie leaned forward and pulled a good-sized hardcover from the shelf. "I'd get her something she can have as a keepsake. When I was little, my grandmother gave me a copy of *The Night Before Christmas*, and I read it every Christmas Eve." She didn't mention that she read it alone in her room, while her parents entertained downstairs, or that it was still packed away in her things. "How about *The Polar Express*? The illustrations are beautiful and it's a classic." She handed him the book.

He ran his hand over the glossy cover. "That's a good idea."

"I do have them occasionally. Are you ready to go? I'd like to hit Treasures before we make our way down to the gallery."

"Sure. I'm ready."

At the checkout Charlie got her "passport" stamped and collected a free bookmark on the way out the door. She was waiting outside, talking to someone who'd stopped to admire a very cute sleeping Daniel, when Dave finally came out.

"That took a while," she said, waving good-bye to the woman who'd stopped.

He shrugged. "They had to change the register tape."

They made their way one street up to Treasures, a beautiful old house on the corner of Lilac Lane. Once in the door, they were assaulted by sounds and colors and activity. A middle-aged woman worked the register while someone else bagged and wrapped, and Charlie saw two children disappear into a back room where a sign said WORKSHOP IN PROGRESS.

"This place is crazy."

Charlie laughed. "Josh's sister owns it. She runs classes here sometimes too. I've been meaning to take one, but somehow I never sign up."

He looked over at her as they moved out of the way of some browsing women. "Afraid of looking silly? That maybe there's something you're not good at?"

She thought about that for a moment, then shook her head. "No, that's not it. It's more . . . I'm not sure how useful it would be. I'd end up making candles or a pair of earrings or something, and it seems a bit . . ."

"Frivolous," he finished. "And maybe fun. Charlie, you think everything has to have a purpose or fit into a bigger picture. But sometimes fun really is enough. It's a purpose all on its own. To enjoy life just for the sake of enjoyment."

"I'm learning," she said, leaning closer to him.

His eyes delved into hers and she felt a delicious shiver run down her spine.

"I'm always willing to help. I'm a very good teacher."

She just bet he was and it sent a thrill rippling over her. She changed the subject, particularly since the crowd was growing larger in the store and she didn't want to be overheard. "Come on, let's browse around. Maybe you can find something for your mom and sisters, hmm?"

They shopped for several minutes. Though she'd already sent the gift cards, Charlie found a gorgeous hand-painted candle-and-holder set for her mother and bought another hand-painted glass ornament for Lizzie. She treated herself to a new knitted infinity scarf, and on impulse grabbed a thick wool hat-and-mitten set for Dave, just in case they ended up exchanging presents. She was admiring a rack of sterling silver and crystal earrings when Dave came over, a huge smile on his face.

"What did you find?" she asked.

He held out a large plastic case. She looked at the cardboard insert. "It's a puppet show. Oh, how sweet!"

He beamed. "Finger puppets, which should be easier for little fingers, right? There's one set up over there. The wings fold out so it stands on its own, and the puppets get stored in little pockets on the back. There are little curtains with Velcro and everything."

"You're excited."

"I'm happy I found something that I'm certain about, I think. I mean, little girls would love something like this, right?"

"I think so. And no little parts to worry about. It's really lovely, Dave."

He looked down at her and she got that swirly feeling again.

"Are you ready? We can hit the last few shops and then get lunch."

"I'm ready. If I buy anything more I won't have arms to carry it." She kept the mittens and hat beneath the thick infinity scarf, out of sight.

Their parcels were bagged and wrapped and paid for, and they stepped outside into the bright winter sunlight. They decided to walk back to the clinic and stow their parcels in his truck before grabbing lunch at Gino's. Gino was doing a brisk business selling pizza by the slice with a can of soda as a festival lunch special.

The sun chased some of the chill out of the day, and they found an empty bench along the dock where they could eat. Daniel was awake but content, and Charlie lifted her pizza slice high and took a bite, sighing with pleasure as the flavors exploded on her tongue. "It's been a good morning."

"Yes, it has. Thanks, Charlie."

"For what?" She squinted in the sunlight as she looked over at him. He had a little piece of cheese stuck to the corner of his mouth and she reached over and wiped it off with the side of her thumb.

"For taking me shopping."

"You asked me, remember?" She popped the last piece of tender crust into her mouth and took a gulp of soda.

"Well, I wouldn't have if we hadn't . . ." He reached over and took her hand. "If we hadn't talked yesterday."

Fling, she reminded herself. This would be a fling and nothing more. She would not get her hopes up. She would not read more into this than there was. Dave was a live-life-as-it-comes kind of guy, not someone to plan a future with. Live in the moment. Be spontaneous. Why was she finding it so difficult? For heaven's sake, it was a simple date.

"It was fun," she answered, trying to adopt a flirtatious tone.

"How fun?" he asked, and he wiggled his eyebrows, making her laugh. She leaned sideways and jostled him with her shoulder.

"So," he said, when the last crumb of pizza was eaten, "are there any more stores you'd like to visit?"

She shook her head. "I think we made it through most of Jewell Cove already."

"That's too bad."

"It is?" She turned on the seat and looked at him. His gaze caught hers and she was momentarily spellbound as the seconds drew out.

"Charlie," he whispered, leaning forward.

She caught herself leaning in too, her heart pounding like crazy as he kissed her, the baby between them. Nothing major, just a soft, sweet, mingling of lips before he sat back again. She was sure there must be stars in her eyes when she looked at him, but she couldn't help it. That was possibly the sweetest, nicest thing to happen to her, maybe ever.

"I don't want the day to end so soon," he said quietly, "and I'm trying to come up with something to do."

She was feeling the same way. There'd been no pressure in that last kiss, just a really nice moment between two people who were enjoying each other and their date. The whole day had put her in the holiday spirit, far more than she'd expected. "Well, you do have the SUV. There is one thing we could do this afternoon."

"What's that?"

"Have you bought a Christmas tree yet?"

He leaned against the back of the bench. "I wasn't actually going to put one up."

"You have to." She put her hand on his knee. "It's not Christmas without a tree. I wasn't going to either, but I changed my mind. It seemed pointless if I were going to be by myself, but if I have Daniel much longer . . . it's his first Christmas. All kids should have a Christmas tree, no matter how old they are."

He laughed. "You're sentimental. Go figure."

She smiled at him. "Maybe I am."

Daniel started to squirm and she knew she'd been lucky for him to stay this quiet for this long. "Someone's selling trees in the gas station lot. Do you want to check it out? I need to change the baby too. Give him a bottle before he turns into Mr. Crankypants." In some ways this was the strangest date she'd ever been on. How many people took a newborn on a first date?

"Okay, but there might be another problem you haven't thought of."

"Oh?"

He tilted his head and regarded her lazily. "Sugar, if I wasn't going to put up a tree, chances are I don't have any decorations to put on it."

Right.

She looked at her watch. "We could hit the department stores in Rockland first. Stock up on lights and ornaments and pick up the trees on the way back."

"I dunno. That seems like quite a commitment."

She laughed. "The afternoon, or the tree?"

"Both. You sure you're both up to it?"

She raised an eyebrow. "Seriously. What else are we going to do this weekend? A pit stop for some hot water to heat a bottle and we'll be good to go. Consider this me, learning to do something on a whim."

He grinned. "I'm game if you are."

"Let's hit the road then. I'm betting the tree guy packs up by five."

Chapter Eight

As a rule, any big chain department store was a cacophony of Christmas music, impatient children, and intercom announcements this close to the holidays. Today was no exception. Charlie stepped inside and immediately felt overwhelmed. There was a reason she did most of her shopping in small specialty stores or before the Christmas rush. Right now it felt like everyone on the midcoast was crammed into this one store, hungry for bargains and frantic for deals and short on patience and goodwill toward men.

"It's Saturday," Dave remarked, grabbing them a metal cart. "And you thought the crowds at the festival were bad."

"Then we need to be strategic." Charlie adjusted the straps of the Snugli and looked down into Daniel's face to be sure he was okay. His eyes were alert but he was content after his bottle and changing. They started down the widest aisle as Charlie began ticking items off on her fingers. "You need a tree stand, skirt, lights, and ornaments at the very least."

"That sounds like a lot."

"Just think how much money you'll save next year." She smiled up at him. "Anyway, if we head to the seasonal section, we should be able to find everything we need there."

She led the way while Dave wheeled the cart behind them. Before long they found themselves in the middle of a Christmas wonderland, full of lights and tinsel and ornaments that sparkled. Charlie ignored the crush of people and simply enjoyed the bright colors. Truthfully, she loved the idea of Christmas. Maybe growing up she hadn't had the warm, intimate, down-home family holiday that she saw on all those Christmas specials, but she still liked the schmaltz. It had been better too, when she'd started visiting Lizzie at the holidays. Her family really knew how to do it up right.

She turned around to say something to Dave and burst out laughing. He'd put a Santa hat on his head, one of the plushier ones with the big white pom-pom on the end. With his dark eyes and slight shadow of stubble, he looked both adorable and mischievous and very, very dangerous to her willpower.

"Very nice," she complimented.

He held out his hand. In it was a green-striped hat with white fluff around the edge. "Here. You can be my elf," he suggested.

She put it on her head and felt ridiculous. They were actually in the middle of a department store wearing the childish things and while she tugged hers off, Dave left his on. He grabbed her discarded hat and tossed it into the cart. "You never know," he said, wheeling along the aisle.

She wasn't sure what she'd never know, but she followed him anyway, marveling at how he just took things in stride. He was perfectly okay being silly, wasn't afraid to look a little foolish. Not so damn serious all the time . . .

She stopped in the middle of the aisle as what she'd just thought truly sank in. She'd been describing herself, hadn't she? Was she really that uptight and boring? She didn't try to be.

Dave stopped to pick out a tree stand and she caught up to him, reached into the cart, and took out the hat. When he turned around, she had it on with the peak of it flopped over at a jaunty angle, the tiny bell at the end making a faint tinkling noise.

"What are you doing?" he asked.

"Trying to remove the stick from my butt," she replied. "Is it working?"

He burst out laughing so suddenly that she couldn't help but grin. The smile was wiped clean off her face though as he took a step forward and planted a smacking kiss on her lips. "I dunno," he answered. "But it's a good start." He let his fingers graze the top of Daniel's head in a little caress before stepping back.

They moved along the aisle and then Charlie asked the question that had been on her mind for quite some time. "Do I really have a stick up my bum? Am I really that boring?"

Dave had his hand on a soft, velvety tree skirt, but he put it back on the shelf and faced her. "What? No! What made you ask that? You are not boring. You're smart and you have a great sense of humor—when you let it out to play. Listen," he said, coming forward so he was only a few inches away from her. She looked up at him and saw he was dead serious. "I like that you're focused and driven. I like that you're smart and you're quick in a tight spot, like you were the first night with the baby. There's nothing wrong with you, Charlie. I think once *you* figure that out, you'll loosen up more and worry about things less."

Her throat had tightened painfully during that little speech. His insight was so bang on she didn't quite know how to respond.

"Now," he commanded, "help me decide on this thing. This red fuzzy stuff or the green shiny stuff?"

Charlie huffed out a little laugh at his descriptors for velour and sateen, and put her hand on the red. As they continued through the section, picking up strings of lights and packs of ornaments, Charlie realized that she could really get to like Dave. A lot. So much that it was starting to get harder to remember why she was so opposed to being with him in the first place.

❆   ❆   ❆

By the time they started the downhill slope into Jewell Cove, Charlie was asleep. Dave looked over at her and felt a warm sort of protectiveness steal over him. She'd definitely enchanted him in the store today, wearing the goofy elf hat right up to the cash register, where she'd taken it off so that the cashier could ring it in. He liked that she had a bit of a silly side and that she'd felt safe enough with him to let it show, even for just a little while. Truth was, there wasn't much he didn't like about Charlene Yang and that was equally pleasant and disconcerting. Pleasant because he liked being with her. She made him smile, laugh. Made him think and didn't let him off the hook easily. But it scared him a bit too, because he'd enjoyed kissing her a lot.

She woke as they rolled to a stop just before the service station. "Oh my gosh! I slept the whole way back!"

He nodded. "You must have had a long week. I didn't want to wake you."

She pointed to the station. "Well, pull in. We haven't bought trees yet. They're still open."

It must be the doctor in her, he thought, the way she could go from being asleep to fully alert in such a short amount of time. He was the same way, had been that way since he started soldiering. You slept during sleep time, and when it was time to get up, you hit the ground running. Old habits were hard to break.

The lot was just about to close up for the night, but they each managed to get a tree and strapped them onto the top of Dave's SUV with the help of the lot owner. It was dark by the time they left town limits and headed toward her cottage. When he turned in, his headlights swept across the front yard. With no lights on, inside or out, the place felt lonely.

"I didn't think we'd be gone so long," she explained. "I'll go turn on some lights and then we can get the tree down."

She took Daniel inside, along with the first of her bags, and Dave followed with the rest of the decorations. He left her settling the baby in a playpen, then went to work on the straps holding the trees in place, making sure to release hers but leaving his securely fastened. The outside lights came on, casting a circle of light around her front step, and he saw a glow come from the front windows as she turned on a few lamps. By the time she managed to get outside again, he had the tree standing up and was waiting for instructions on where to put it.

"Wow, that was fast." Charlie grabbed the final bag and slammed the tailgate. "Bring it in. I'll get the stand ready."

"You know where you want it?"

"Of course." She shrugged. "I made room in the living room. I took so long because I was settling Daniel in the bedroom. I'm not sure how long he's going to hold out. It's been a long day and he's been really good. It can't last forever."

He followed her inside, got her to hold the tree as he took off his boots, then carried it through to the living room. She hustled ahead of him carrying the tree stand, and then put it down before shrugging out of her coat. As he waited, she deftly set it up and loosened the bolts that would hold the tree in place. "Okay," she said, looking up as she stood on her knees. "Bring that sucker over and we'll get it in place."

He lifted, she guided, and within seconds the trunk slid into the hole. "Keep it straight!" Charlie called out, her voice muffled from beneath the branches. She was lying on her stomach now, reaching in under the tree to tighten all the wing nuts. "Okay! Let it go!"

He cautiously let go of the top of the tree and it stayed steady. Charlie scooted backward on her belly and then popped up, her shirt mussed and spruce needles decorating her hair. "So? What do you think?" she asked.

"Perfect. Just the right size."

"I think so too." Her eyes dancing, she disappeared into another room and came back with a box. She plunked it on the sofa and started rooting around. "Aha. Here it is." She withdrew her own tree skirt, a cute felt thing with sewn-on reindeer faces and antlers that were puffed out from the base fabric.

She was back down on her stomach again, sliding forward until she could put the skirt around the base. When she appeared again, he noticed a smudge of dust down the side of her breast.

He had to get out of here. The last time he spent any time in her living room they'd started kissing. It was about to go that way again if he wasn't careful. He thought spending the day together would be easy and fun. And it had been. A little too easy and a little too fun. Silence settled around them, heavy with potential. Waiting. Waiting for one of them to make a first move. Or not.

"Well," Dave said, "I should be going. I have to unload my tree and get my stuff inside."

"Oh, right. Of course." His words seemed to have broken the spell and Charlie smiled at him. "It turned out to be a longer day than we planned, but a fun one. I think I have my Christmas shopping all done!"

Her voice was a little too bright: was she disappointed, or relieved?

"I got a start on mine, for sure," he admitted. He still hadn't purchased anything for his parents, or his siblings and nieces and nephews.

She walked him to the door, their steps meandering a little as he waited for an invitation. Which was stupid since he'd been the one to suggest leaving. It was for the best, right? And yet the day had been so nice, so fun and easy, that he was disappointed it was over. All that waited at home was whatever he could throw together for a meal and a hockey game on TV.

"Thanks for everything," Charlie said quietly as they reached the tiny foyer. "It was a really great date."

"Even though our plans changed?"

She smiled up at him. "I think, especially because our plans changed," she answered.

"Are you going to decorate your tree tonight?" Dave asked, his hand on the doorknob, putting off leaving for just a few moments longer.

"I don't think so. I'm too tired. Besides, it'll give me something to do tomorrow."

Right. Normally the idea of a quiet Sunday afternoon

was alluring, but the idea of putting his tree up alone seemed rather depressing. And yet the ebullient Charlie seemed excited about the prospect.

"Sure." He knew it was a lackluster reply. He really should go. But then there was the fact that this marked the official end of their date and he had to decide how exactly he wanted to leave things. With a simple good night? A hug?

A kiss?

She was standing close enough he only had to reach out a little to put his arm along her back and pull her close. She put up her hands and they stopped her progress into his arms, pressed against his chest as her chin tilted up . . .

There was no way he could *not* kiss that pert little mouth. He didn't want to come on too strong so he tempered the heat that flared in him simply from holding her close, and took his time, sweetly exploring her lips as he held her body against his.

He let it end after a single kiss. He'd promised a date and nothing more, and he tried to keep his promises. Which was why he rarely made them.

"Thank you for the wonderful day," he murmured, his voice husky in the silence of the foyer. "I hope we can do it again, Charlie."

He nearly reconsidered as she ran her tongue over her lower lip, and he wondered if she could taste him there. "I hope so too, Dave. I had a good time."

He was moving in for a second kiss when the baby started crying. They both froze in mid-move, and he was gratified to hear Charlie sigh. Did that mean she was as disappointed as he was?

"I'd better go," she said quietly, stepping away. "Somebody's not very happy."

He got out of there while he still could, with the picture of her dark eyes and soft, kissable lips still in his mind. The whole drive home he wasn't sure if he was happy for the first time in months or if he'd just made a huge mistake and if Daniel hadn't just done him a huge favor. Despite Dave's best intentions, he was falling for her.

❄️   ❄️   ❄️

Charlie stared at her decorated tree and frowned. The lights were fine, the garland looped perfectly, the ornaments sparkling in the sun that filtered through the windows. She should be happy with it, but she wasn't.

She couldn't stop thinking about Dave, the way he'd looked at her yesterday, how he'd kissed her good night, all soft and swoony. He was over at his place now, with his own tree and brand-new decorations. Was he feeling as lonely as she was?

It was the first Christmas she didn't have any plans of any sort. Up until this morning she thought she was okay with it. But now, staring at the tree, she knew she wasn't. There would be a present from her parents and one from Lizzie. She'd open them all by herself. And then she'd heat up a takeout turkey dinner from Breezes.

Tears stung her eyes.

"Enough of feeling sorry for yourself!" She said the words out loud and reminded herself that she was cozy and comfortable in a snug little cottage while there were others out there far worse off. She looked over at Daniel, on his back on a blanket, waving his little arms and legs and smiled. Well, maybe she wasn't completely alone. She was falling for this little baby head over heels, and she had to remind herself that this was only a temporary situation. She couldn't let herself get too attached . . . and yet she couldn't seem to help it either.

She knelt on the blanket and played with the tiny fingers and toes, cooing to him in nonsensical syllables. He was still too little to laugh, and she kept looking for a smile. It wouldn't be long. Days, maybe a week or two, and he'd show her that first smile. She'd looked it up . . .

Definitely getting too attached, but she couldn't find it in herself to be sorry.

It was a beautiful afternoon, so after they'd both had lunch she decided they'd take a walk. The sun was out, and it made the snow and trees glitter like a fairyland. There was no self-delusion at work. As she pulled on her heavy boots and retrieved a hat and scarf from the tiny entry closet, she knew she was heading toward Dave, probably with an idea of giving him a hand with his tree if he hadn't finished it already.

The road to her cottage and on to Fiddler's Rock was a side road that ran mostly parallel to the main highway and hugged the shoreline of the cove. As such, most of the traffic was local traffic, and Charlie only met maybe a dozen cars on the half-hour walk to Dave's place, the stroller wheels making gritty noises on the asphalt. Chickadees had taken up residence on the snow-covered branches and alternated their chirpy calls with the throatier "dee dee dee" sounds. Charlie took deep breaths of the crisp air. By the time she reached Dave's, she was warmed up from the exercise and the sun that had seeped through her winter clothing. The motion and fresh air had lulled Daniel back to sleep. With a soft laugh, she wished he dropped off to sleep this easily at night.

She knocked on his door and waited, but there was no answer. Surprising, because his truck was in the yard. She hopped down the steps and peered around the corner into the backyard. It didn't take long to find him. The lot sloped down to the beach, and she caught sight of his plaid jacket through the shrubs. He was sitting on a boulder, tossing rocks into the water, the lapping of the gentle waves soothing and rhythmic.

She often found it too cold on her deck, but she understood the allure. In warmer weather she spent a lot of time looking out over the bay, listening to the waves and the gulls, letting the sounds ease her mind.

She took Daniel from the stroller and snuggled him against her shoulder. "Hey, stranger," she called, announcing her arrival. She sauntered closer, taking her time as she picked her way down the rocky path to the beach. "Is this a bad time? I got my tree up. It was feeling a little empty at my place. I thought a walk in the sun would do us good. And . . . I wondered how you were getting on with your tree."

"It's in the stand."

"I see."

They sat for a few minutes in silence.

"Sorry," he apologized. "I'm in a cranky mood and not the best company, I guess."

"It's okay." She smiled softly. "Everyone's entitled to a bad day. Anything I can do to help?"

He huffed out a humorless chuckle. "The doctor is in?"

"I figure if you want me to know anything more, you'll tell me. If not, I'll mind my own business."

He sighed. "I was supposed to have Nora next weekend. But Janice called and said her husband's family has invited them all to Boston for some big holiday event. I feel like an ogre saying no, but I missed my last weekend because she was down with the flu."

"That's rough." Charlie covered his gloved hand with hers, repositioning Daniel on her shoulder. "But Nora knows you're a good father, and so does Janice."

"I guess it just bugs me to think that I'm letting my

family down. And I know it doesn't make sense. I'm not the one changing plans. But still." He met her gaze. "This is the first Christmas I get to spend with her and I feel like I'm missing out."

There was no reason why Charlie should feel jealous, but she did. She had no claim on Dave, and she wasn't sure she wanted to have one either. All they'd shared were a few kisses, a lunch, and a first date. But hearing him talk about his family was like a shot to her irrational heart. He already had what she wanted so badly.

"She's bringing Nora by later this afternoon," he added, and Charlie swallowed thickly. "Kind of a consolation for me losing my visitation time."

"I see." It was the only response she could come up with. She knew she was being petty, but she wondered if Dave wanted to see his ex. If he still had feelings for her. And there was no way on earth Charlie would ask those questions.

"Okay," she said, taking a breath and scrabbling off the rock. "I'll get out of your way." It seemed Daniel had had enough too, because he squirmed against her chest, fussing. She patted his back with her mittened hand.

"You're not in my way."

"Are you sure?" He definitely hadn't invited her in, or to stay, or anything else. She was feeling worse and worse, just when she'd thought maybe she should put her misgivings aside and take a chance on them.

"I get it, Dave. You would rather we weren't around when your daughter visits."

He ran his hands over his hair as she turned to go. She'd only taken a few steps when his voice stopped her again.

"Charlie, when Janice and I parted ways . . ."

She turned back. Faced him head-on.

". . . I think both of us were relieved. We'd always

been better friends than lovers. We tried for Nora's sake, but there was no point."

"You're telling me this why?"

"Because you seem to think I don't want you around. It's not that. It's just . . . I only have a few hours. I want to talk to Janice about visitation and it's probably better if I do that without an audience."

"It's fine, really. I should get Daniel home anyway."

He took his hands out of his pockets again and reached for her, pulling her into a warm hug. Daniel squirmed in the close quarters but they both ignored him, focusing on each other instead.

"Are you jealous?" he whispered.

She smelled the clean, woodsy smell she was getting used to, the softness of the flannel of his quilted jacket. "Of course not," she lied.

"Charlie?"

"Hmm?" Why was she getting so lost in his eyes? Daniel whimpered, the sound muffled in his plushy snowsuit.

"Are we starting something here? Because it feels like we are."

"Do you want to be?" she asked, and held her breath. The more she got to know him, the more her misgivings melted away. He had potential. He was a good man making his way through a complicated situation. Surely that was reason enough to curb her usual need to define and categorize and just chill. Take it one step at a time.

"How can you ask that? Ever since we met, I've been trying to find ways to spend time with you. You make me laugh, which is something I haven't done much of recently. You're kind and a little bit shy and . . ." He paused and framed her face with his other hand too. "And you're beautiful. I'd be crazy not to want to see you again."

She pushed away the little voice that insisted that *nowhere* was a possible destination for the two of them. Charlie was getting thoroughly sick of hearing that voice, and she was starting to understand why. It was because every time she'd tried to make a decision for herself, her parents had insisted that it would take her nowhere. That their way was better. Safer. They knew best way more than she did.

She swallowed. Told herself this wasn't about rebellion but about finally, finally trusting herself to make good decisions. To know what was best for herself.

"Me too," she whispered.

His lips were cold as they kissed, but she didn't mind in the least. With a slight groan of pleasure, she twined one arm around his neck and he squeezed his around her waist, their bodies angled so they fit together without crushing the baby. The wind made a shushing sound in the fir trees around them, cocooning them from the outside world.

When they finally broke apart and Charlie's heels were back on solid ground, Dave gave a little chuckle. "Phew," he said.

"Phew is right. But I'd better go, let you get ready. I'll talk to you later?"

"I'll call. Let you know how it went."

She gave him a final peck on the lips and then stepped back, lifting a mittened hand in a wave. "Good luck."

"Thanks." He nodded at her. "And thanks for understanding, Charlie."

"Of course."

It only took a few moments to fasten Daniel back into the stroller and start home to the cottage, her thoughts whirling with Dave, his kiss, their conversation.

Chapter Nine

When Charlie didn't hear from Dave on Sunday night, she pretty much reconciled herself to the fact that she'd been constructing sand castles in the sky where he was concerned. A few dates and a few kisses did not a relationship make. Even if he had said it was something more. Obviously, it wasn't enough to get him to pick up the phone.

Reality check, Yang, she reminded herself early Monday morning as she cradled Daniel in one arm and poured herself a cup of Josh's high-test sludge from the office pot with her opposite hand. It had been a rough night. Daniel had fussed and she'd been up every two hours trying to get him to settle.

It was Josh who finally stepped into her office between patients and told her to sit for five minutes.

"You look like death warmed over. You need some time off?"

"Of course not." She was managing okay. It was just a bad day was all. "We had a rough night. Nothing serious."

He crossed his ankle over his knee. "Charlie, it's a big thing taking on a newborn. There's a reason why women take maternity leave."

"Is his being here a problem?"

Josh's face softened. "Of course not. The practice isn't that busy, and I don't mind covering a little bit. It's a good thing you're doing."

"Thanks, Josh." She let out a breath of relief. "I appreciate the support. You've been really understanding."

Josh smiled. "Hey, I'm not a scrooge. Besides, I know it's only temporary."

The words left a gaping hole in her heart. "I don't want to give him back," she confessed. Every maternal instinct she'd tamped down for the last few days came roaring back. She did want this. She wanted a family of her own, to love and to be loved. To be needed. She swallowed as she rubbed her hand over Daniel's tiny back.

Boy, Dave was right about one thing. Life didn't come with a perfect blueprint for happiness.

"Are you planning on adopting him?"

She swallowed. Was she? "I don't know. I want a family, but one thing I've learned is that being a single parent is really hard. I'm just enjoying him while I have him and trying not to worry too much about the future."

She sat back, surprised at the words that came out of her mouth. Her, the super planner, who had everything mapped out and on schedule. She was living in the here and now. Wouldn't Dave have something to say about that?

She wished she hadn't thought of Dave at this moment . . . Dave, who already had a child of his own. She wanted him to have a relationship with Nora, but she wondered how much room there was for her in that scenario. It had been nice spending time with him over the weekend. Wonderful, in fact. She wasn't a fast mover but she'd definitely let her mind wander to certain places, wondering if they were headed in that direction.

But the reality was that the weekend was a little like a vacation. They'd shopped and ate pizza and kissed and flirted, but it was an anomaly. A nice memory. This, right here, was who she was. Anything else was just . . .

Vacation.

Josh tapped his chin, and she could tell he was considering his next words. Her stomach twisted with nerves. He was her boss, after all. And she knew she'd been juggling trying to care for Daniel and still see all her patients. She didn't want to let him down. And this morning she was just so *tired* . . .

"I was thinking," he said, his voice soft but firm, letting her know what was coming next wasn't exactly a suggestion. "Maybe you could find someone to help with Daniel while you're working, if you're so determined to not take time off."

Leave him home? With a sitter? At his age?

"He's bottle fed, which makes things much more convenient. You could use your office, set up a playpen, bring in a comfy chair. I even have the perfect candidate."

"You do?"

He nodded. "My mom. She's going crazy, waiting for more grandkids."

"Josh, I don't know what to say. You've asked her already, haven't you?"

He smiled. "I might have put a bug in her ear. You're not superwoman, Charlie. Just think about it and let me know. And after your last appointment this morning, go home. I'll cover walk-ins today."

"But it's my shift . . ."

"Consider it a Christmas present. Or an order from your boss, if that doesn't work."

She was touched. Josh wasn't always touchy-feely but his gesture was so thoughtful. After he left her office, Charlie grabbed the chart for her next patient.

She found herself wondering about Daniel's mother. In her job, she tried to keep an open mind, because she was generally shown time and again that unless you walked in someone else's shoes, you just didn't know what they had been through. But still, even if leaving him in the manger had been planned as they suspected, it was dangerous. Desperate.

Clearly, she wasn't entirely objective about this situation. But that was what she loved about this job too. When she'd first moved here, she'd been so professional, able to distance herself from her patients. But slowly she'd started caring about them in more than just an empathetic way. They weren't family, but they *were* community.

The thought was comforting somehow. Maybe Josh was so good at it because he'd been here all his life. Maybe, just maybe, this was starting to be her home too.

Shortly after eleven Dave texted to ask if she wanted to meet for lunch. She waited until her current appointment was finished, and then considered. Did she want to see him again? Hell yes. She was dying to know what had happened between him and Janice.

When she caught her next break, she called him instead of texting, and asked if he was busy for dinner. When he said he wasn't, she offered to bring dinner to his place after work. She'd grab some takeout Chinese and meet him at the cottage.

She was afraid she might be falling for him, and how stupid was that? He wasn't even sure if he was staying in Jewell Cove, and she called herself ten times the fool for letting her imagination get the best of her.

Chapter Ten

Charlie sat back in her chair and put her hand on her stomach. "Oh my God. I'm so stuffed I think I'm going to blow up." Dave was still polishing off his mountain of cashew chicken and fried rice, but Charlie was so full of lo mein that she couldn't think of eating another bite. "That was good."

It was extra nice to have a night out without the baby . . . in some ways, this felt like more of a date than their official date had. Tonight Meggie Collins was at Charlie's house, getting to know Daniel and crocheting something pretty out of pink yarn. Josh's idea had been a good one. Charlie loved looking after Daniel, but the break was lovely too.

Dave nodded. "I haven't had takeout like that in ages. When I was stationed at Little Creek, there was this place we used to go to that had the best hot-and-spicy beef thing. It was perfect with a cold beer." He grinned at her. "Or two."

"Do you miss that life?" she asked. "Being in the Navy?"

"I wasn't just in the Navy, Charlie. I was a SEAL."

His smile had faded. "I know," she answered quietly. Just as she knew there was a difference. She'd never asked him what he'd done or seen or anything more about his job. She figured a man couldn't do a job like that without facing a few ugly truths about the world.

They sat in silence for a few more moments and then Charlie couldn't stand it. She got up and started clearing away the mess. Maybe this hadn't been such a good idea after all. Dave didn't seem his usual happy-go-lucky self. He was . . . broody.

She rinsed the plates and started running water in the sink to wash the few dishes they'd dirtied. His chair scraped against the floor as he pushed it back and stood, and her heartbeat quickened a little when he came up behind her and reached around for the drying cloth.

"You didn't ask me about yesterday," he said. "It must be killing you."

Annoyance flared. "Don't flatter yourself."

He gave a little laugh at her sharp reply. "Easy, tiger. I just meant that you aren't always patient when it comes to wanting answers. I figure you're either not interested in what happened or you're too afraid to ask."

She hoped her expression portrayed calm and perhaps a touch of ennui. "Why on earth would I be afraid?"

"Charlie," he said quietly, and her heart knocked against her ribs.

"Don't say my name in that kind of voice. I've been an idiot, okay? We can just go back to being friends, like we said."

She scrubbed at a plate and put it in the drying rack. He instantly picked it up and dried it. "Whoever said we were just friends?"

She didn't reply. Damn, he was patient. More patient than she was. They continued washing the dishes until there was nothing left to wash, and then Charlie finally said what had been on the tip of her tongue ever since she walked in the door.

"You promised you'd call."

He put down the towel. "Okay . . ."

"When I left. You promised to call to let me know how it went. And then you didn't." She looked up at him.

"Charlie . . ."

She waved the rest of whatever he was going to say away.

"I know I'm being stupid. But you were right, I was jealous. You were talking about your family, and I kept thinking about you and Janice talking, bonding. And it's stupid, but when you didn't call . . ."

His lips curved the slightest bit. "Charlie, sweetheart." There was such warmth in his voice that it cut into Charlie. "Janice is pregnant again."

The words made Charlie look up at him quickly. To her surprise, he didn't look upset by the information. "She and her husband?" Charlie asked, then realized it was a stupid question. Dave and Janice had been over for a long time, right?

He nodded. "Yep. She's happy. Far happier than she was with me."

"And that bothers you?"

"That she's happy? Of course not. I'm happy for her, and happy for them. I guess if I was looking for a sign that Janice and I were wrong for each other, this is really it."

Charlie didn't even realize she'd been holding her breath until she let it out again in a long, measured exhale.

"I'm going to take a few days before Christmas and drive down. Take Nora her gifts and spend some time with her. That's what Janice wanted to talk about."

"Are you thinking of moving closer? It's not a huge drive from here to there, but it's long enough."

"Would it bother you if I did?" he asked, and silence fell in the room. What was he asking?

"Why would it bother me?" Why couldn't she come right out and ask what she wanted to ask? Say what she wanted to say? She didn't usually have a hard time speaking her mind. Maybe it was because she was afraid to hear the answer. "I've seen you with Daniel." She met his gaze. "I would never want to do anything to stand in the way of your relationship with your daughter."

She smiled up at him, feeling completely false. She wasn't cheerful. Wasn't happy. She was let down. Mad at herself for getting her hopes up. For pretending that it didn't matter that he wasn't looking for a relationship. "Anyway, I should go."

"So soon?" He came closer, close enough she had trouble breathing. "But I haven't decorated the tree yet. I thought we could do that together. It looks so naked, sitting in the stand with nothing on it."

She took a step back. "And then what? I don't think I can do this." Her insides trembled. Why was it so hard to say the truth? To verbalize her own needs? She would do it this time. She would.

"Do what?"

"This!" She gestured with her finger, moving it between the two of them. "I know what you said from the beginning. About seeing where all this goes, no pressure or anything. I know all this in my head, Dave. My head is not the problem."

"Then what the hell is?" he asked, his voice brittle. "I thought we were just going to enjoy being together, no strings, no demands."

"The problem," she said, her throat tight, "is that I'm not built that way. I want to be. I want to be that

carefree, easy kind of person who can accept something at face value, who can live in the moment and enjoy it. And I've tried but it doesn't work, because that's
not who I am. When you smile at me . . . when you kiss
me . . ."

"You want more?"

"I want more. I want all of you and I know all of you
isn't available."

He cursed. His dark gaze heated as they stared at
each other, both breathing heavily as the tension closed
in on them.

"You know I want you, right?"

God, how could he make his voice so smooth, so deep
and sexy and filled with promise? This was what she was
fighting against. Fighting and losing. When they were
apart, she could be rational. But when he was close, the
moment he said or did something like this, she lost all
perspective.

"Don't," she whispered. And wished the word had
come out stronger.

"We've been doing this dance," he said, ignoring her
plea. "Keeping things easy. You think your voice of reason is giving you trouble?" He was so close now she
could almost feel the heat of his body against hers. "I
find myself calling or texting and wanting to be with you
and then when I'm with you, I just want to touch you.
Damn it, Charlie, it's been killing me to leave it at a few
kisses and then walking away."

She swallowed. Hard. He was right before her now.
Big, strong, former SEAL confessing to wanting her.
Her, little Charlene Yang who always stayed in the
background and never caused any trouble. Charlene
Yang, who had found it so difficult to make friends
here that up until a few weeks ago she'd made do with
watching him from a restaurant window and the most

illuminating conversation she'd had was with a doll at the church nativity scene.

He wanted her. And she wanted him so badly she was nearly dying with it. The only thing holding her back was knowing that she would be giving him the power to really and truly hurt her. If she took one step in his direction, she'd be taking responsibility for that.

"Charlie," he murmured. "Look at me."

His eyes were so intense she stopped breathing for a second.

The anticipation was so strong that she would swear she could already feel him touching her even though they were inches apart.

"I used to see you working on the docks and wondered who you were," she admitted, her voice soft. She swallowed against a lump of nervousness in her throat. "I would imagine that you would show up somewhere and . . . and . . . and sweep me off my feet."

It should have sounded stupid but instead the words fanned the flames of attraction, ramping up the tension between them. "I just . . ." She bit down on her lip, realizing she was probably doing this badly, but stumbling along anyway. "I just want you to sweep me away. Can you do that?"

His breath came out in a rush and he reached down and clasped her hand, gripping it tightly. "You're sure? I'm asking because you'd better be damned sure you know what you're doing."

"Yes," she answered meekly. "Please."

He muttered something incomprehensible, stared at her for a long moment. The air snapped and sizzled between them and she licked her lips, watched his pupils widen, felt her muscles tighten with delicious anticipation. No one had ever looked at her that way. Not ever.

Not with such desire and intent and all it did was fuel her own longings.

For once in her life she was not going to think or dissect or weigh the ramifications. She was going to feel and she'd let the cards fall where they may.

He reached over and pulled her straight into his arms. His mouth fused to hers, fierce in its intent, all-consuming and wonderful, his tongue sweeping into her mouth as his strong arms lifted her against his body, hard in all the right places. She loved his sheer physicality, and she wrapped her arms around his shoulders and held him tight.

His hands circled around and cupped her bottom, and she wrapped her legs around his waist. Dave made a raw sound in his throat and took a single step backward, which put her hips up against the kitchen counter, and she pressed her core against him, letting the pleasure of the moment soak in.

He backed off, breaking the kiss, running his tongue over his lower lip as if tasting her there. Her body was feeling jacked up and liquidy all at once. He reached for the neck of his T-shirt and pulled it over his head, revealing a muscled body that up to this moment, she'd only seen in pictures. For the first time in her life, any thoughts of anything beyond the next few minutes didn't exist. He'd succeeded in wiping them all away.

This time he took a little more time with her. He dropped the shirt on the floor and stepped back into the V of her legs, kissing her again, slowly and persuasively. She slid her hands over the hard curves of his shoulders, loving the feel of his warm skin beneath her fingertips. Encouraged, she reached down and slid her hand along the curve of his ass, pulling him closer against her.

His breathing grew ragged, all from her simple touch.

It amazed her that she had that sort of effect on him, and it fed her female vanity.

"You drive me crazy," he said, sliding his lips over her cheek and pulling her earlobe into his mouth. When making out in the kitchen was no longer enough, he wrenched his mouth from hers and picked her up in his arms as if she weighed nothing.

Swoon-worthy. The guy had gone into total alpha mode and she loved it. She linked her arms around his neck and let him carry her down the hall to his bedroom.

"You took the 'sweep me away' thing seriously," she said softly, looking up at him as he laid her gently on the bed.

"I'm just getting started," he answered, flicking on the bedside lamp, reaching into the night table drawer for a condom.

Oh God. They were really doing this. And she was going to get to enjoy that body, have it all to herself. What a giddy thought.

Dave sat on the edge of the bed and reached for her. She sat up and moved into his arms, losing herself in the feeling of having him surround her. He gently pulled the elastic from her hair and sank his hands into the heavy mass of it, pulling her head back as he undid the braid, the weight of it falling over her shoulders. With her head tipped back, he took full advantage and dipped his head, running his tongue over the sensitive flesh of her neck. When his fingers slid from her hair and traced a gentle path down the side of her face, goose bumps broke out over her skin.

"You're sure?" he asked, and she loved the way his gaze searched her face. Hungry, but not reckless. She was hungry too. Hungry for him.

"I'm sure." Slowly, she reached for the buttons of her shirt. One by one she undid them, slipping them from the buttonholes, pulling the tails out of her trousers. Dave took over then, pushing the soft fabric off her shoulders until she was sitting before him in her bra. She was doubly glad she'd worn the black one today, with the scalloped lace around the edges. Right now she realized the push-up padding wasn't necessary. Her breasts strained against the material, the peaks hard and pointed in anticipation of his touch.

"Wow." His grin slipped sideways, teasing her. "You drive me crazy, you know that?"

"Likewise," she answered, and this time he pushed her back into the comforter and she got to feel the heat of his skin pressed against hers. She was pretty sure it was the most erotic feeling on earth, this skin-to-skin thing.

He reached behind her and undid the clasp of her bra with one hand, then pulled it down her arms and dropped it on the floor. "It's pretty," he murmured. "But not as pretty as this." He cupped a breast in his hand and then let his mouth follow.

She was going to die, she was sure of it. But if this is what it felt like, she was totally okay with it. When he licked her nipple, a moan slid from her throat.

After that everything seemed to speed up. Hands hurried, stripping off the last of the clothing, scattering it on the floor until they were both naked on the bed. His hands and mouth seemed to be everywhere, igniting her senses until her whole body was on fire. Charlie reached out and took him in her fingers and he groaned. "We need to slow down," he said, his breath hot in her ear. "Or I swear to God it's going to be over before it gets started."

She giggled with the sheer elation of pure feminine power.

He reached for the condom. "You're prepared." Her

heart hammered against her ribs. This was where all the foreplay was leading. To him. Inside her. She didn't want to wait. She wanted to grab the packet, rip the foil, and get on with it. Never in her life had she felt this pounding need for fulfillment.

"After what happened at your place . . . I wasn't going to take any chances. I knew this day was coming."

She watched, intrigued, as he took care of putting it on. Then all she could do was lose herself in the overwhelming sensations of being completely and thoroughly pleasured by a lover, once, twice, and a third time that left her so weak and sated she could barely move. Then, and only then, did he release the hold on his control, growling her name as he pushed her up the bed until she felt the headboard against her skull.

Moments later, the harsh sounds of their breathing began to temper and the sweat on their bodies cooled. Charlie lay on her side, looking over at him, marveling that they'd just done everything they'd done.

There'd been no choice to make once he'd touched her. She'd been incapable of stopping. They had simply lost themselves in each other. He'd possessed every square inch of her body and now she felt gloriously limp in the afterglow.

Then she heard it . . . a low, satisfied chuckle that reached in and warmed her from the inside out.

"What's so funny?" she asked, unable to keep the smile from her face.

"Nothing's funny." He rolled over to his side and opened his eyes. "That was just . . . spectacular." He grinned at her. "Who knew you were so bendy, Chuckles?"

She should take him to task for calling her Chuckles right now. And she would, except . . . well, she liked it. From him, anyway. "I've done a lot of yoga."

"I hear it's supposed to be good for stress."

If he only knew.

She raised an eyebrow. "Anytime you want to try. Naked yoga is liberating." His eyes widened and she laughed as she teased him. "Nothing like getting in touch with your spirituality when it's just you and the mat."

"Eeeew."

Her lips twitched.

"You're teasing."

"I am."

He reached over and grazed his fingers over her hip. "I like it."

She did too. He was the most comfortable-in-his-own-skin man she'd ever met. It was more than the boneless bliss she was feeling after a thorough lovemaking. It was a freedom, a lightness that she suspected came from living in the moment rather than from an agenda.

She shivered and Dave reached toward the bottom of the bed, pulling up a blanket to cover them. Then he lay on his back and opened his arms wide. "Come here," he said quietly. "We can huddle up to keep warm."

She was still naked. She suspected she should be feeling if not bashful, at least a little self-conscious. But she wasn't. She slid over next to him and rested her head along the curve of his shoulder, draped one arm over his ribs, and lifted her knee, settling it along the length of his leg.

"God, you're a cuddler," he murmured, squeezing her close.

She never used to be.

"Is that okay?"

"Yeah." There was this texture to his voice that she would never tire of. A bit deep, a bit husky, 100 percent masculine and sexy. She closed her eyes and let out a breath.

"You know, I'm kind of sorry I stopped things that first morning. If I'd known this was waiting for me . . ."

He chuckled and the vibration rippled through her. "I'll take that as a compliment."

"You should."

"You're not so bad yourself."

Her hand ran up his back and encountered smooth scar tissue. It reminded her of what he'd been through . . . the parts she knew about and the parts she didn't. She traced her finger along its path. "What is this from?"

He shrugged. "Oh, one of my many badges of honor. No big deal."

"It doesn't hurt?"

"Not anymore." Then he smiled wickedly. "Wait. If I said it did, would you kiss it better?"

She swatted his shoulder.

"You want to talk about it?"

"I've just had mind-blowing sex and a gorgeous woman is naked in my arms. What do you think?"

She smiled in the darkness. "Obvious distraction, but I still have to ask. You think I'm gorgeous?"

"Are you kidding?" His wide palm curved over her hip. "Have you looked in a mirror lately?"

She relaxed further, sinking into his embrace, twining her legs with his and running her toes up one of his calves. "Hey, Dave?"

"Hmm?"

"I needed that." After she said it she realized it was a bit ambiguous. She could have been talking about the sex or the compliment. Truthfully, she thought she rather needed them both.

He kissed her forehead. "I know."

She wasn't quite sure what he meant, but she was too

mellow to ask. He felt so good. Warm and strong. The blanket was soft on her skin and he'd turned off the light, so the room was gray and dim. The woodstove in the next room had been stoked and the heat of it made her feel lazy. She was going to doze off and she was completely okay with it.

She curled into his embrace. "It's so warm and toasty in here. I never realized how great wood heat was. So much nicer than a furnace or radiator."

He nodded against her hair. "A stove can really crank it out. Plus, if the power goes out, I can stay warm. Cook. It's a bit rudimentary, but convenient."

She imagined being snowbound here with him and the idea held some merit. The stove meant he had to split wood, she thought. She took a moment to appreciate the image in her mind of him with an axe, his muscles bulging and shifting as he split logs. When had she started going for the physical labor kind of guy?

She snuggled in closer. She supposed that happened when she'd first seen him on the docks in the fall, all work boots and broad shoulders and a ball cap.

"Charlie?" His voice was soft in her ear, sending ripples of pleasure down her spine.

"Mmm?" She answered lazily.

"Stay a while?"

She turned in his arms so she could look up at him. His hair, just a touch on the shaggy side, was ruffled and mussed, and his jaw held a hint of stubble after the long day. He was so attractive. So . . . virile.

"I wish I could. But Daniel's staying with Josh's mom and I should get back soon."

"Right. Damn." His fingers slid along the soft skin of her arm. "Maybe just a little while longer?"

"A little while," she agreed.

She hadn't realized he was tense until his shoulders

relaxed. "Cool." His fingers ran up and down her arm, an absentminded gesture that Charlie reveled in.

Good heavens, what would her mother say? Her mom had always pushed her to "guard her sexuality like a priceless treasure." Charlie rolled her eyes. Mother probably expected Charlie to have remained a virgin too. She sobered. Well, it had been long enough that she wondered if she could reclaim virgin status. Up until tonight, that is.

Dave's fingers traced a slow, gentle line up the outside of her arm and she gave in, letting out one last deep breath before sliding into sleep.

Chapter Eleven

Her breathing was deep and even.

Her skin was soft, and a scent like vanilla and flowers filled his nostrils: soft and light and mingled with the scent of sex.

He hadn't expected it to be so . . . consuming. So possessive. But from the moment he'd put her on the bed and stripped her of her jeans, something had clicked. A proprietary sense that said *Mine*.

He'd never been a dominating man and it wasn't like that now either. But there'd been a crushing need to possess her and, conversely, to be possessed. To know that he was capable of bringing her to ecstasy over and over again and to hear his name on her lips as she shuddered around him. And then . . . not to take her but to lose himself inside her.

And that scared the shit out of him. Big time. Despite the spontaneity of the moment, being with her hadn't been thoughtless or fun or careless. It had been fast and sometimes rough and other times inspired, but he'd made sure to protect her and when their eyes had met

as he climaxed, something had shifted painfully inside
him. A connection he hadn't been prepared for. If he
wasn't careful, he might fall in love with her.

A delicate snuffle came from beside him. She was
really and truly asleep in his arms and it filled him with
a sweetness he'd forgotten existed. There was trust in
making love, but it was fueled by desire and lust and
need. The real trust was now, afterward. And clearly
Charlie trusted him.

The idea made him panic just a little bit. He hadn't
planned on staying in Jewell Cove. His dad had hooked
him up with the job at George's, something to keep him
going until he found a permanent situation. Except, he
admitted to himself, he hadn't been looking for a different situation. Charlie made staying seem . . . possible.
Perfect, maybe.

Charlie wasn't the kind of woman a man fooled
around with. He'd understood that from the start. So he
either had to break it off with her and let her go, or really
be involved. They'd been fooling themselves, thinking
they could keep things casual.

But being open to the possibility of "them" meant
opening himself up to the chance of loving . . . or being
hurt. Or worse—hurting her. Because deep down he
knew they were two very different people. She loved
plans and charts and lists, and he knew life involved a
certain measure of improvisation. She had a day planner and he went with the flow. Wouldn't they end up
driving each other crazy?

Her arm tightened and his eyes slammed closed, loving the feel of her wrapped around him so damn much
it scared him. He'd forgotten what it was like to be the
center of someone's world, even for five minutes.

She was the center of his too. At least for a little while.
So he left his eyes closed and let his muscles relax, shift-

ing a little so they were entwined together. He'd wake her soon, but not yet. He wanted to hold on to the perfection of this moment as long as he could. Then he'd do what he had to do.

❄   ❄   ❄

Charlie woke slowly, then lifted her arms and executed a long, limber stretch. She couldn't remember a time when she felt this relaxed. The soft fleece blanket slid over her skin and she realized she was still naked.

Her cheeks heated and her stomach did a little flip. Oh my. They'd done it. Charlie, who planned everything, who examined every angle of a situation before making a decision, had taken a huge leap and had sex with Dave Ricker.

It had been amazing. Stupendous.

And she was alone in the bed.

She crawled out from beneath the blankets and shivered in the cool air. Draped over a chair was a flannel shirt, and she picked it up and put her arms in the big sleeves, buttoning it up the front. It was huge. The cuffs came down over her hands and the tails covered her to mid-thigh. Charlie lifted a handful of the fabric and drew a long breath, her head filling with the masculine scent of him. As an afterthought, she snagged her panties from the floor and stepped into them. Barefoot, she left the bedroom and went in search of him.

He was in the kitchen. Dressed in plaid pajama pants and a T-shirt, he looked both adorably cuddly and casually sexy. He was whisking something in a pan on the stove, and there was a hint of chocolate in the air.

"That smells good," she said softly, and he spun around.

"You sure are quiet," he said, smiling at her. "I didn't hear you get up."

She went forward to see what he was concocting. "Oooh, hot cocoa. Yum."

"Made with real milk, none of that powdered stuff." He smiled at her but she got the slippery feeling that something was wrong. He was too nice. Too polite. "I was going to wake you soon. It's nearly ten. I thought some hot cocoa before you had to relieve your sitter."

"At least it's a bit warmer out here," she said, wrapping her arms around her middle.

"I brought in some wood for the fire too." His gaze dropped to her improvised nightshirt. "Nice," he added.

Not that she'd say it out loud, but she'd watched lots of movies where the confident, sexy woman wore her lover's shirt after sex, and wondered what it would be like to be that girl. It felt fantastic, if she were being honest. Who knew she could be that woman, anyway? It's not like she had a history of hookups, and men certainly hadn't been beating down her door. She suspected, however, if she said anything of the sort she'd sound silly and awkward, so she met his gaze evenly. "You don't mind?"

"Of course not."

But there was no innuendo, no shared intimate look or smile. Unless she was totally off base, Dave was backing off. Big time. Why? Maybe tonight hadn't been as good for him as it had been for her . . .

"Dave, did I do something wrong?"

He spared her a glance. "Of course not." It seemed to be his stock answer. His gaze slipped back to the pan and he grabbed a ladle. "Hand me a mug, will you?"

Mechanically she took a cup from the cupboard and handed it to him. He poured the rich cocoa into the mug and handed it to her, then repeated the process with his own cup.

She perched on a chair at the table, unsettled, and sipped. "What's wrong?" she asked.

She knew whatever he was about to say was a lie because his face took on an expression of innocent denial. "Nothing. Why would something be wrong?"

"Because you're acting strangely. Because I woke up and you weren't there and you've brought in wood and made cocoa. Something's on your mind, I can tell."

He sighed. Stared into his cup. "We can talk about it later. You need to get home soon."

Classic avoidance. Charlie tried taking a drink to simply be doing something but the moment it touched her tongue her stomach twisted.

There were times Charlie deeply resented her upbringing, but today she totally understood what her mother had meant when she said that sex had the power to change everything. In this case, it hadn't changed in a fairy-tale-come-true way, had it?

She didn't trust herself to speak. Thought back to that first moment that they'd met, how unsettled and awkward she'd been. The man before her wasn't some fantasy guy from the docks anymore. That seemed like another time and place. He was real, flesh and blood, and currently pulling away from her.

And then she looked across the table at Dave and knew that she couldn't pretend forever. She was tired of feeling like she always had to please people. That if she was just quiet and went along with everyone else's plans for her everything would be fine.

She'd come to Jewell Cove to get away from that. Trouble was, she was still accepting it in her personal relationships and that wasn't okay.

"I have a few minutes. If something's wrong, I want to know."

He shifted in his chair. Charlie frowned. Difficult conversations were so not her strength.

"It's fine."

"No, it's not. Dave, we made love. You asked me to stay. Now you're treating me like nothing happened." Encouraged by the steadiness of her voice, she lifted her chin. "Honestly, I don't think I did anything wrong. Which means you're running scared. What I want to know is why."

He pushed back his chair and took his mug—his cocoa unfinished—to the counter.

"Hey," she said. "Avoidance is my party trick. For God's sake, Dave, just be honest with me. If you think we made a mistake, just say so."

He turned around and met her gaze. "Being with you was great," he answered, his voice rough. "But yeah, it was probably a mistake. My mistake, Charlie, not yours. I got involved with you when I knew I shouldn't have."

She gave a quiet snort. "That makes two of us."

"See? That's what I mean. We were both pretty honest from the beginning about what we did and didn't want. Then we ignored it. Convinced ourselves it didn't matter. I told myself it was nothing serious. That we were just enjoying each other's company."

"Until tonight. Because sex changes things."

He nodded slowly. "Yeah, it does. And all the things I'd been ignoring were suddenly there in front of me again. I'm not sure I can be the perfect man for your perfect plan."

Her body felt strangely heavy. Perhaps it was the weight of disappointment. She thought it was more likely that it was inevitability, because she knew, deep down, that he was right. She'd always thought so.

He ran his hand through his hair. "I told you from the beginning that I wasn't staying in Jewell Cove. That I'm not sure what the future holds. Shit, Charlie. I've tried a serious relationship and I'm terrible at it. The idea of marriage . . ."

"Who said anything about marriage?" she interrupted, turning in her chair so she was facing him, and crossed her left knee over her right. "Aren't you getting a little ahead of yourself?"

"Am I?" He stared at her. "Come on, Charlie. You're not a fling sort of person. You're a lifer. You want the whole enchilada. The husband and the kids and the little house in the 'burbs. You're a liar if you say otherwise."

"I never asked any of that from you."

He paced through the tiny kitchen. "I know that. That's what I'm saying. We knew this about each other but we pretended not to notice. I told myself it would be okay. That you knew what you were getting into. That it was only a few dates and a handful of kisses and it was no big deal. Until . . ."

Silence fell over the kitchen.

"Until?" she finally prompted.

He let out a breath. "Until tonight. Tonight was a big deal. It wasn't just a kiss good night. It was . . ."

Again he paused and she met his gaze evenly. She knew what he wasn't saying. There'd been a connection between them that had been far more potent than either of them had expected.

"It was too much for you," she said quietly. "You're right, you know. I do want those things. I always have. And I told myself I didn't and I conveniently forgot I did when we were together because I like being with you. I like kissing you and I loved making love with you. You're absolutely right, Dave. I want the whole enchilada."

She deserved better. "I spent my whole childhood feeling like I was in the way. I took what attention I could get. Dressed in what I was supposed to, showed up at events when it was requested, got good marks. Tried to please them, anything to get a smidgen of genuine affection. To mean as much to them as their precious jobs and precious itineraries. And you know what? It never worked. And you know what that made me? Afraid. Timid. Unable to stand up for myself. Do you know what happened when I took this job? I had already signed the contract and rental agreement before I told my parents. I didn't even tell them until I was already here in Jewell Cove. Even when I was rebelling, I was afraid to confront them. Afraid to disappoint them."

"Jesus, Charlie."

"Yeah. And I was afraid to disappoint you too, so I told myself I'd just go along with whatever you wanted. Not interested in a relationship or a family? That was okay. We'd just have fun. But you are so right. I'm not built that way. I want a man who loves me, and a family of my own and children who can be whatever the hell they want when they grow up as long as they're happy. I want them to feel love and acceptance and I want smiles and laughter. I want it all, Dave. And tonight, for about five minutes, I caught a glimpse of what it could be like if you gave us half a chance."

"I told you . . ."

"I know. I didn't listen. I heard what I wanted to and ignored the rest."

She was slightly out of breath, amazed that she'd said all that, wondering how she'd kept it inside all these years.

Dave was staring at her in shock.

"What the hell are you so scared of?" she asked. "Or is it that you don't have the capacity to care at all? Is that it?"

"Maybe I don't. Maybe I'm just a selfish prick who only thinks about himself. Maybe I've got a huge ego and the world revolves around me. That's what you're saying, isn't it? Or is it that I'm a coward? Which option is most appealing to you?" His words were hard, brittle. The heat in his eyes had cooled, dulled. "We both pretended for a while but I'd just hurt you in the end, Charlie."

Once again silence fell over the room. There was something he wasn't saying. Something more than his marriage. He'd been pretty forthcoming about that, so she guessed whatever it was had to be important. Hurtful.

"Shit," he said, quieter now. "It wasn't supposed to be this way. I thought I could handle it. Tonight was amazing. You need to understand that. But this has to stop now, before someone gets hurt. Before I hurt you."

She blinked a couple of times. She would not babble, or cry, or be an emotional wreck. She would also be honest, because wrong or right, she'd started to believe they had a chance. "Don't you get it? You already hurt me."

"Don't say that."

"What, and lie?" She went to him, put her hand flat on his chest. "You're a good man, you know. Somehow, somewhere, I think someone made you feel like you weren't. And I think that's not because you let someone down but because someone let you down. Until you figure that out, you're never going to be happy."

"You'd better get home to Daniel."

There was no emotion in his words, just dismissal and finality. She retreated to the bedroom and pulled on her clothes, braided her hair, and went back to the kitchen, where Dave was sitting at the table, staring into his cup of cold cocoa.

Wordlessly she put on her boots and her jacket and picked up her handbag. She went out and shut the door behind her, latching it with a quiet click, wondering how she could have been so stupid as to let herself fall in love with the wrong man.

Chapter Twelve

Charlie ended up putting in extra hours at the clinic. A flu outbreak swept through the schools, and she and Josh doubled up their hours so that whenever one was taking appointments, the other was working walk-in or administering flu shots. The lead up to Christmas was anything but relaxing, and it was only Meggie's help with babysitting that kept her afloat. She managed to package Lizzie's presents and ship them off, with a promise to visit for a weekend in the new year. As the virus spread, Josh and Charlie saw increased numbers of senior citizens presenting with the same symptoms that often progressed to bronchitis or pneumonia, both of which required more than simple rest and fluids.

By December 18, it hit Charlie and laid her flat for three days of fever, chills, and a hoarse cough. She spent her downtime on the sofa with a soft blanket, drinking hot lemon and honey and sleeping whenever Daniel saw fit to nap too. Because he was so small, she took particular care with hand washing, praying he didn't come down with it too. And during her waking hours she spent way too much time thinking. Thinking about Dave, and how everything had gone wrong, and how for the first time in several years she'd fancied herself in love.

How could that be? She'd always believed a big component of being in love was being loved in return. That it wasn't one-sided. But he certainly hadn't loved her. Liked her, yes. Enjoyed her company, yes.

But he hadn't been a fool like her. She replayed moments in her mind: how they'd look into each other's eyes, the way he kissed, how he'd laugh at something and tilt his head back just a little bit. The way he raised one eyebrow just a little before he said something sarcastic, and the way only one dimple popped when he smiled.

She'd been smitten. No doubt about it. And she missed him. She could tell herself she didn't, but what purpose did that serve? No sense lying to herself. He was up the road at his cottage or working in town and going about his day completely and absolutely without her. Like she didn't even matter.

Charlie's bout of self-pity was interrupted by a knock on the door. It was Josh, and he carried a box in his arms.

She tugged her blanket closer around herself, blinked at him blearily, and held open the door. "What on earth is that?"

"Word got around town that you came down with this bug. It's a care package."

She stepped aside as he came in and stomped his boots. "A care package?"

He nodded. "Today I'm your delivery boy. Can you take this?"

She took the box from his arms, shocked at how weak she felt. Once he'd removed his boots he took the box back. "Let's put this in your kitchen."

She followed behind him, her slippers scuffing

against the floor as she sniffled and then reached for a tissue from the box on the counter. Josh put everything down on her table and started taking things out.

An ice cream container, which he handed over. "My mom's chicken soup. Her not-so-secret ingredient is a dash of curry powder. You look like hell. I recommend a bowl of it, stat."

She laughed a little, which started her coughing. Without saying a word, Josh found a glass and got her some water. Then he took a bowl from the cupboard, poured some of the soup into it, and shoved it in the microwave.

"Right. Next . . . Shirley at The Leaf and Grind sent over some tea." He put the little tin on the table. "She recommends honey to sweeten it. Jess sent eucalyptus candles to help with congestion." Those went beside the tea. "Mary at the bakery brought in a dozen cinnamon rolls, which annoys the hell out of me because no one ever gives me cinnamon rolls and they're my favorite." The rolls were added to the assortment on the tabletop.

Josh handed over a small plastic bottle. "Robin says to take a hot bath with some of this in it and you'll feel lots better."

Charlie was overwhelmed. Good heavens, homemade soup and tea and aromatherapy . . . just for coming down with the flu? "What about you, Josh?" she joked, as the microwave beeped, indicating her soup was done. "What did you bring me?" She opened the door and caught a little of the scent, even through her plugged nose. Her stomach rumbled and she realized she couldn't remember when she'd put anything other than fluids in her tummy.

Josh held up a bottle. "I'm not much of a cook. But codeine cough syrup will do. You should at least get some sleep." He grinned at her. "You really do look like hell, Charlie. Do you need someone to take Daniel for a day or two?"

"Thanks for this," she grumbled, but then she looked up at him and smiled a bit. "Thank you, Josh. And Dan and I will be fine. He's been sleeping better lately, only up once in the night. I just put him down. I should be good until about one in the morning." She took a sip of water. "This is pretty amazing and a real surprise."

He gave a shrug. "That's what happens in a place like Jewell Cove. People help each other out. Sometimes it's suffocating, but everyone means well. Almost everyone, anyway," he amended with a crooked smile.

She sat down at the table with her soup. "You want to join me? There's lots here."

"I'm good. I'll sit for a minute though, if you don't mind."

"Okay." It seemed odd that he'd hang around, but her head was pretty fuzzy. She might not be the best judge of what was weird and normal at the moment. The first taste of soup made her close her eyes in gratitude. The broth was hot and rich and filled with vegetables and chicken and soft noodles. "Oh, tell Meggie that this is delicious and just what I needed."

"I will." He hesitated for a minute and then leaned on the table on his elbows. "Charlie, are you okay?"

"It's just the flu, Josh."

"That's not what I mean." He looked slightly uncomfortable. "Look, I don't like to pry into people's private lives, but you've been burning the candle at both ends for the last week, and now you're sick and it looked like things were heating up with that Dave guy. Did something happen there?"

"There's nothing happening there, don't worry," she replied, scooping up more soup to keep busy, to keep her from thinking too much.

"Do I need to have a talk with him?"

She swallowed and looked up in surprise. "What?"

"You're my business partner now. And my friend. And if you need help, I hope you know you can ask me."

A silly grin broke out over her face. "Are you saying you'd beat up Dave Ricker if he hurt my feelings, Josh?"

Josh looked at her evenly. "He's a big boy. Not sure I'd beat him up, but I'd give it a good try."

Her eye stung with unexpected tears. "That's sweet. I never had a big brother, you know. But this feels like something a big brother would say."

He smiled at her. "Look around you, Charlie. You're part of this community. People care about you. I know it's hard at first, coming to a place where it seems everyone has known each other forever, and have all this shared past stuff. It's hard to come back to that too, you know. I didn't find it easy last year. People get in your business. But they're also there when you need them. I guess what I'm saying is, don't let this get you down. There are people who care about you."

"Wow, Josh, this is pretty touchy-feely for you."

He chuckled. "Don't I know it. My sisters are much better at this kind of thing, but since you and I share an office, I put on my big-girl panties."

Josh could be really businesslike, or so charismatic that Charlie often felt outmatched. But he was really approachable today, relaxed and cracking jokes.

"I'll be fine. Dave and I just want different things. We kind of ignored it for a while, but there it is. It wouldn't have worked out anyway."

"Bummer," Josh replied.

She laughed, coughed, and then sighed. "Yeah. Bummer."

"Well, listen, I should go and let you get your rest.

We miss you back at the office. I was run off my feet today."

"Slave driver. Now I know why you brought this stuff over. So you can get me back in the office and go back to your cushy hours."

He laughed. She saw him to the door, and when he was ready to go, she thanked him again. Once he was gone she returned to the kitchen, finished her soup, and decided to run a bath using some of Robin's bubbles.

It wasn't until she sank into the hot water that she let the emotions in. She'd been holding them back for days now, but the virus, added to her long work hours and then the unexpected generosity of friends had her protective shields down. The steam made a peppermint and eucalyptus scented cloud in the bathroom as she finally cried.

She'd trusted him. She'd believed in him. Wrong or right, foolish or not, she had. And for a brief, wonderful moment, she'd lain in his arms and believed in the possibility of forever.

But that moment was gone. It was time she let it all out and then moved on.

❄   ❄   ❄

December 23 rolled around. Charlie had received a huge parcel from Lizzie and placed it beside the Christmas tree since it was too big to fit underneath. She'd mostly recovered from her flu, though by the time she got home at night she was exhausted. Honestly, she was looking forward to having the two extra days off for the Christmas holiday. With nothing planned, she'd eat her takeout, talk to Lizzie, watch a few movies, and drink hot cocoa. To her surprise, several other packages made an appearance. Not so much for her, but for Daniel. There was something from Meggie, which wasn't a huge surprise, but also packages from Josh's sisters with Daniel's name on them. Robin gave her a care package for pampering herself and there was a little gift bag with something for Daniel. She sat in front of the tree with him, watching the curiosity in his eyes as the colorful lights lit up the room, and kissed his soft, downy head. She wasn't alone. And maybe he wouldn't understand what was going on or remember a thing, but she was determined to have a real Christmas for his sake.

Even though the outbreak was winding down, the clinic was still busy. Between regular appointments and walk-ins, both Josh and Charlie were run off their feet. It was midafternoon when Charlie stepped into the exam room to meet a new patient. The chart said she was a walk-in and her name was Michelle Green.

"Hi, Michelle." She smiled at the young girl sitting next to the bed. "I'm Dr. Yang. What can I help you with today?"

The girl didn't look particularly sick, though her color was a bit pale and her hair was limp. Mostly she looked tired. No, not tired. Worn. Charlie smiled reassuringly.

"I, uh . . ." The girl suddenly looked down. Lifted her hand and started chewing on a fingernail.

Charlie's heart softened. She couldn't be more than eighteen, maybe nineteen, and something was clearly bothering her. Charlie sat on her rolling stool and edged her way closer to Michelle, so they were sitting facing each other at equal heights.

"Are you ill? Or is there a problem I can help you with?" Charlie touched Michelle's knee lightly. "I'm here to help. Everything is confidential."

Michelle looked up, her blue eyes swimming with tears. "Are you the Dr. Yang who found that baby a few weeks ago?"

It was a strange question to ask, and Charlie's heart started beating faster. Oh my. She was going to have to tread very, very carefully. Could this be Daniel's mother?

"I am."

Michelle looked down again and Charlie saw a tear streak down the girl's cheek. "Is he okay?" she whispered.

Charlie nodded, a lump in her throat. She was sure now. No one else would come into her office, asking these questions, their emotions so raw. "He's doing just fine."

She nodded again. "Okay. Thanks. I should go . . ." Awkwardly, the girl got up and reached for an old winter jacket hanging on the back of her chair.

"Don't go yet," Charlie said, alarmed but trying to adopt a soothing tone. "Michelle, have you seen a doctor since you delivered? You're a little pale. It wouldn't hurt to have a checkup, make sure everything's okay."

"I don't know what you mean." She gripped the jacket tightly, and her face took on a belligerent expression. But Charlie could see beyond it to the fear. This poor kid.

Charlie reached out and rubbed Michelle's arm reassuringly. "It's okay. I promise you it'll be okay."

"I just . . . Oh God." She sank back down into the chair and covered her face with her hands.

Charlie kept her voice soft. "You put him in the manger on purpose, didn't you?"

Michelle nodded, moved her hands so they were in her lap, twisting together nervously. "I knew everyone would be at the tree lighting and I saw you and your husband walking by. I waited to make sure . . ."

At that point she dissolved into tears. Charlie squatted in front of her and held her hands. "You waited to make sure . . ."

Michelle hiccupped. "That you noticed. I wouldn't

have left him there alone. If no one had come, I would have gone back for him. I wouldn't have let him die." She sobbed again. "I wouldn't have done that. I just didn't know what else to do. I couldn't look after him . . . I didn't want anyone to know . . ."

"Of course. It's all right. We're going to make everything all right, okay?"

"I just wanted to know he was okay."

"And he is. Michelle, can you tell me where and when you had your baby? Were you in a hospital?"

She nodded. "Yes, in Dover, on November nineteenth."

Across the state line in New Hampshire. Which was why nothing had turned up when they checked Maine hospitals.

"And everything went all right?"

She nodded again. "I was discharged the next morning. A friend came to pick me up and take me . . . home."

"No complications since?"

The pale pallor of her skin made way for a slight blush. "Um, I bled a lot."

"Are you still bleeding?"

She shook her head. "Not for the past couple of days."

That was a relief, then. She really did need a thorough exam, but Charlie wanted to keep her talking as much as she could. "Michelle? Do you want to tell me why you left your baby here in Jewell Cove?"

Charlie could see Michelle swallow. The girl wouldn't meet her eyes again and Charlie could understand why. Michelle was fighting a battle within herself . . . wanting to know about the welfare of her child while at the same time probably feeling ashamed and embarrassed and scared.

"It's okay. I'm not here to judge you."

Another pause, and then Michelle spoke. "I couldn't

look after him. When I got pregnant, my parents kicked me out. I was working at the mall and living on my own, but I could barely make the rent. I didn't qualify for any maternity leave and I couldn't go back to work because I couldn't afford day care. All he did was cry. All *I* did was cry. I couldn't think of what else to do. A friend of mine lent me her car and I just . . . drove. When I was in Portland, I heard some people in the store talking about driving up to Jewell Cove for the weekend, that there was some big tree lighting event every year. I thought it would be pretty. I didn't even think about what I was going to do until I drove by the church and saw the manger there, all lit up."

Her tears had stopped and she finally met Charlie's gaze again. "I was stupid. I know that now. I'm not equipped to be a mom, Dr. Yang. And Jewell Cove . . . it's nice here. It seemed like a place where a kid could be happy, you know?" Her voice caught. "I thought it was just better if I . . . disappeared."

"But it wasn't better, was it?"

She shook her head. "I wanted him to have a better life than I could give him. I let him down. So I parked behind the church. And then you guys came along and I knew he'd be okay."

Michelle broke down again, and Charlie let her cry it out. She snagged the stool again and sat down, staying close to the overwrought girl. "Are you feeling a little better now? What do you say we give you that exam?"

Michelle screwed up her face and Charlie laughed a little, trying to lighten the mood. "I know. Not your favorite thing in the world. But making sure you're healthy is number one right now, okay?"

She nodded. "Okay."

Charlie went to the cupboard and took a gown out of the drawer, a real cotton one rather than the paper they normally used. She would treat this girl with kid gloves. It was a sensitive situation that was going to get worse before it got better. "I'll leave you for a minute to change."

"Dr. Yang?"

Charlie had her hand on the doorknob, and turned back.

"What's going to happen to me now?"

Charlie smiled reassuringly. "Let's get this exam over with first. Then we'll worry about the rest, okay?"

She slid out of the room and shut the door behind her, then rested her head against the wall for a moment.

"Charlie?"

Josh's worried voice came from his office across the hall. She opened her eyes and let out a sigh.

"Make sure she doesn't leave, okay?" Charlie poked her head into his office. "Daniel's mom is in there."

"Holy shit."

"I know. She's scared to death. I'm going to give her an exam."

"Do you want me to call Bryce?"

She thought for a moment. If Michelle had left the baby at a hospital, or a police station, it would have been better for her. But she hadn't. She'd abandoned the baby in a churchyard.

"I've got her talking. Give me some time. I may be able to get her to come around to turning herself in. It would be the right thing to do. She needs help. She's just a kid, Josh."

Josh nodded. "You've got a good heart, Charlie. I'll hang around a bit, though, in case you need me to make that call."

"Thanks."

She took a moment to go to the reception desk and quietly asked Robin to cancel the rest of her afternoon appointments. The whole time she fought against the sinking feeling that she might lose Daniel. What had initially been a situation lasting a few days had been weeks and she couldn't imagine the cottage without him. But he wasn't hers, and she had to remember that. Steeling her spine, she gathered what she needed and re-entered the exam room, pasting on a new smile.

While the exam was uncomfortable, Charlie was reassured that Michelle was doing fine. Rather than give her a requisition for blood work that would never get done, Charlie did it right then and there. She expected they'd find some slight anemia, and figured what Michelle really needed was a few good meals, some rest, and counseling sessions. Michelle had gotten dressed again and Charlie pulled a chair over next to the girl's.

"So. What do you want to do now?"

"I don't know. I could go back to Dover . . ."

Charlie was relieved that going home didn't seem too appealing. "What do you really want?" she prodded gently.

"I want to see him." Michelle looked up at her and she seemed so young, too young, to be dealing with something this huge.

"In order to see him, you're going to have to tell people who you are. And even then, I can't promise it'll happen."

"Can't you just . . . I don't know, help me see him somehow? I promise I won't even say who I am. I just want to see him."

Charlie closed her eyes and prayed for the right words. "I can't do that, Michelle. I can't lie for you. I can help you, absolutely, but not by lying." She thanked God that today Meggie had offered to look after Daniel at the cottage. How awkward it would be if he were here, like he normally was, and started crying.

She saw Michelle's hands start to shake. "You mean I have to turn myself into the police?"

"Yes." Charlie nodded. "But I'll help you with that. And the officers here are very nice. You don't have to be afraid of them."

"But what if they put me in jail?" Michelle's eyes were wild now. "I made a mistake. I don't want to go to jail. I just want to see my baby. Be sure he's okay. I never meant for any of this to happen!"

Charlie reached out and rubbed Michelle's knee, hoping it was calming and reassuring. "I know." She'd seen people with no remorse before, with no conscience. This wasn't like that. Michelle was as much in need of a social worker as her baby. Her records said she was only nineteen. Barely out of high school and alone and pregnant with no support. Desperation could drive people to do strange things. "I promise I'll help you. And I know for sure that coming forward will make things easier on you. You need to do this, Michelle. For yourself and for your son."

Michelle nodded a little, and a few tears trembled on her lashes. "I'm just scared."

"I know. But you don't have to do this alone now. We can help you get some support, okay?"

"Dr. Yang?"

"Yes?"

"You're a very kind person."

Charlie's heart softened even further. She was nearly tempted to explain that she knew he was doing well because she was looking after the baby, but that might cause more trouble than solutions, so she held her tongue. The situation was complicated enough as it was.

Michelle took a deep breath and let it out, almost as if fortifying herself for what was to come. "Do you think

I could talk to them here instead of having to walk into the police station? I'd feel like such a . . . a criminal." Her cheeks flushed.

"You're welcome to use the room here, no problem," Charlie replied, hugely relieved.

Michelle nodded.

"Okay. I'll be back in a bit, once I make a few calls. You'll wait here?"

She nodded again. "I promise."

Charlie left and went straight to her office to make the necessary calls, and then grabbed a juice box and a couple of granola bars from the kitchen. Michelle looked like she could use something to eat, and while it wasn't much, it might put some color back in her cheeks. She delivered the snack and gave Josh an update, then met with Todd Smith and a female officer who had come along on the call and filled them in on what she knew. By that time the social worker had arrived and it was time to get the ball rolling.

Charlie entered the exam room once more. "Michelle, this is Marissa Longfellow. She's the case worker."

"Hi, Michelle. It's very good to meet you."

"I don't want to go to jail," Michelle stated quickly. "I just wanted to know he was okay, you know?"

"He's perfectly fine, so you don't have to worry about that. Right now I'm here to help you. Together we're going to sort everything out, okay?"

Charlie put her hand on Michelle's shoulder. "The two of you can use the room for as long as you want. I'll be in my office if you need anything."

She left, took a precious few minutes to pour herself a cup of coffee, and then retreated to her office to make sense of the afternoon's events.

❄   ❄   ❄

In some ways, Dave wished he could have stayed in Kennebunkport longer. He'd taken three days off work and stayed in a room at Janice and Brian's small inn. It had been awkward at times, but the truly odd thing was that Dave liked Brian. He was good for Janice, and he was also a great dad to Dave's daughter. Dave wanted Nora to be raised in a happy home. That was the most important thing, and thankfully everyone was willing to work together. Nora's next visit would be to Jewell Cove, for New Year's, and Dave couldn't wait. He wiped his hands on a rag, trying to rub off the grease on his knuckles. He didn't have much time coming to him, but he'd ask George for a few extra days, particularly as they'd talked about him staying on indefinitely. It was time to stop running and make a home.

And so while that part of his life was great, his romantic life had ground to a complete halt. He'd ruined things between him and Charlie, probably for good. She'd walked out and never called, not once. Not a text message, not a peep. He'd known from the beginning she was a strong woman. Stubborn. It was part of what he loved about her.

He was just punching out for the day when Josh pulled into the parking lot next to the boatyard. Which perhaps wasn't that noteworthy except Josh hopped out of his truck and made straight for George's small office. Dave's stomach twisted. He hoped nothing had happened to Charlie . . .

He pulled on his gloves and greeted Josh cordially, if not cautiously. "Hey, Josh. What're you doing here?"

"Probably pissing my partner off. She didn't call you, did she?"

"No." The nagging feeling of dread persisted. "Is she okay?"

"If you mean is she physically okay, I'd have to say

yes, although I think she's still beat from her go-round with the flu."

She'd had the flu?

"It's not that," Josh continued. "It's Daniel. His mother showed up at the clinic today. First of all, since you found him, I thought you might want to know before it gets all around town. And secondly, Charlie's had a hell of an afternoon. I don't know what happened between the two of you, but she's been moping around for the last week and a half. She's tired and it's been a rough few hours. She could use a friend today."

"I doubt she wants to see me." If she'd wanted moral support, she would have called. Wouldn't she?

"Well, do what you will with the information. I just wanted to let you know."

Clearly Josh didn't have a very high opinion of him, because he made an about-face and headed right back to his truck again.

Dave frowned. In addition to finding his way in his new, active role as parent, he'd spent a lot of time thinking about Charlie. Mostly about how he'd hurt her. Mostly about what she'd said to him after they'd made love.

She'd been right. Being with her had scared him and he'd resorted to his fallback position: getting out of the way.

Maybe it was too late for them, but Josh had come to him for a reason. Charlie needed him—or perhaps just needed someone. He knew she felt very alone in Jewell Cove. He realized she spent most of her life looking after other people, but who looked after Charlie? No one. Not a damned soul. From what he gathered, she'd been looking out for herself for a long time now. Maybe it was time that changed.

Maybe it was time for him to be honest with himself about his feelings. And honest with her.

Chapter Thirteen

Dave gripped the paper bag in one hand and wiped the other on his jeans.

Two police cars were still outside the clinic, along with an older-model sedan and another newer, flashier car. Maybe this was a bad idea. He kept thinking that but then he also kept thinking about what Josh said.

So he opened the clinic door and stepped inside.

Robin was still working at the desk and looked up. "Hi, Dave. Sorry, our walk-in's closed for today."

"Josh found me," he said in a low voice. "I came to see Charlie."

"Oh." Her cheeks colored a bit. "Let me just check with her."

He waited, his toe tapping nervously, until Robin came back. "Come on in," she invited. When she started to lead him down the hall, he stopped her. "It's okay. I know which one is her office."

"Right. Okay." Robin looked a little flustered and Dave figured she wasn't used to this much excitement at the office. At the end of the hall he gave Charlie's door a tap and poked his head inside.

"Hey," he said softly.

She looked up and his heart slammed against his ribs. She looked terrible and wonderful all at the same time. A few strands of hair were coming out of her bun, her eyes looked tired, her shoulders were slumped. In short, she looked done in. But she was still his beautiful Charlie.

His. From the moment he'd first held her in his arms, he'd thought of her as his. He wasn't sure why he'd fought it so hard. Now wasn't the time for that conversation, though. They could get into that later.

"You heard," she said wearily, leaning back in her chair and rubbing her temples.

"I heard. Are you okay?"

"Me?" Her brows lifted in surprise. "Of course I'm okay. But the girl in the next room is having a hell of a day." She tried a weak smile. "You might as well come in."

He stepped inside and lifted the bag of food. "I guessed you hadn't eaten yet, so I brought you dinner."

"Dave . . ."

"Don't." He lifted a hand. "Charlie, you've had a crazy day and you're exhausted. It's as simple as that."

She nodded, smiled wearily, then waggled her fingers. "Get it out then. I'm starving and that smells like Gus's handiwork."

It was. This close to Christmas Gus specialized in two things: oyster stew and roast turkey. Dave had opted for the turkey, thinking it would be better warmed up if she couldn't eat it now.

He presented two takeout containers, plastic forks and knives, napkins, salt and pepper packets, and a separate container with gravy. "Merry early Christmas," he murmured, handing her the gravy.

"To you too," she said quietly. She met his gaze. "Thank you for this, Dave. Really. It was very considerate."

"Can you tell me what happened? I mean, are you allowed?"

Charlie sprinkled pepper on her vegetables. "She wanted to make sure the baby was okay. I convinced her to turn herself in. She's just a young girl, Dave. Mixed up and afraid, who made a bad choice. She's not a bad kid." She paused, with her fork hovering over her potatoes. "I guess I still want to believe there's a happy ending in it for her."

Dave looked at her, felt a wave of love wash over him. God, she had such a generous and forgiving heart. He loved that about her. Hoped that her forgiveness extended to him too, because he really wanted to start over with her. Make things right.

Charlie looked up, met his gaze. "I want to help her, Dave. Whatever shape she wants her life to take, I'd like to help her get pointed in the right direction. We were right. She chose the manger because she wanted him to be found, and she stayed nearby until she saw us take him. She didn't just dump him without a thought. That's got to count for something."

"Phew." Dave shook his head. "It's still crazy to think about that night, isn't it? I wonder why she didn't just leave him at a hospital, or police station."

"I don't know. I suppose she might have been worried about being seen. I got the impression it wasn't really thought out." She cut into her turkey and took a bite. "Anyway," she finished, waving her fork in the air, "one good thing about it. The mystery of baby Daniel's mom is solved."

They ate in silence for a few moments until Dave couldn't take it anymore.

"What does this mean for Daniel?"

She shrugged. "I don't know. I'm reminding myself to be realistic. He was never mine to begin with. I always knew I'd have to give him up eventually. With the break in the investigation, I suppose things will move forward a little faster." Her lips quivered for a second. "At least we'll have Christmas. I doubt anything will happen before then."

She was hurting, and trying to cover. "You've been sick, Josh said."

"I didn't realize you and Josh were buddy buddy."

"We're not. He's worried about you. Seeing you today, so am I."

"I'm just tired. I had that nasty bug going around and so did everyone else in Jewell Cove, I think. We were putting in some long days. I'll be fine."

"I think, Charlene Yang, you tell everyone you're fine whether you are or not."

She stopped eating and stared at him.

"What do you mean by that?"

"I just mean that . . . well, I've been doing a lot of thinking. You tell people you're fine, you give of yourself, but you never really let anyone in. You don't want to be any trouble. And you don't want to give someone the power to really hurt you either. Because you've been disappointed a lot in your life. And it works but only a little because deep down you're lonely and you need someone to give all that love to. Being a doctor is perfect. You get to help people without becoming personally involved."

"Wow. That's some psychoanalysis."

"And that's exactly what I'd say if I wanted to avoid the issue and turn the tables. We're more alike than you think, Charlie."

"Except I did let someone in. You."

He hadn't expected her to admit it, and it took him by surprise.

"We don't have to talk about this now," he said. "On top of everything else."

"Or ever, right?" She picked up her fork again, and stabbed it into her mound of potatoes, her lips set in an angry line.

"I didn't come here to pile on, Charlie. Not after the day you've had."

"You pretty much said it all anyway," she reminded him, playing with the potatoes but not eating them.

"No, I didn't. I didn't say nearly enough. And I certainly didn't say the right things."

Her fork stopped moving. He might have imagined it, but he thought he saw her lower lip give another little quiver before she bit down on it.

"I went to see Nora," he explained. "And the whole time I was watching their family all together I was thinking about you, and the fun we had together, and how easy it is to talk to you, and how much I loved kissing you . . . and . . . and how much I missed you."

Her chin started quivering again.

"I was an idiot, Charlie. I let my fear of being tied down get in the way of what I really wanted. You. I told myself I didn't want to settle down, but the truth is I've moved around so much, I've never had much luck with romance that . . . well, I wasn't sure I was ready to put down roots. If I'd ever be ready." He swallowed. "I'm probably saying this all wrong . . ."

"You're doing okay."

She was looking at him with luminous eyes and he pushed forward. "I love you, Charlie."

❄   ❄   ❄

Charlie hadn't been expecting those words. Not today, not ever. And damn him for getting to her on a day she was emotionally vulnerable to start with. She blinked to clear away the moisture that had sprung to her eyes. "Don't say that," she whispered, her voice hoarse.

"Why?" he asked. He walked around her desk and turned her steno chair so it was facing him, then squatted down in front of her, just like she'd done with Michelle earlier. "Why don't you want me to say it? Because you don't want to hear it or because you want to and you're afraid?"

"It's been barely a month of you and me doing a dance and . . . whatever." She fumbled the words, words she'd dreamed of hearing and that now scared her to death. He was right. Because if he said them and didn't mean them, she was bound to get her heart broken. And if he did mean them . . .

If he did . . .

"Do you believe in fate, Charlie?"

She swallowed. Hard. "I don't know."

"I do." His fingers dug into her knees as he held on to her. "I think I landed here in Jewell Cove for a reason. I think I came here because I needed to. That night at the tree lighting something happened. I turned around with that baby in my arms and saw you and nothing has been the same since."

She heard the echoes in her head, echoes from her past. *"Make sure you keep up your marks, Charlene. Don't forget to wear your best dress, Charlene. This is important to the family, Charlene. Don't disappoint us, Charlene."*

She was no better than he was. She had dreams of a family of her own and it turned out she was too chicken to act on it when she had the chance. And now here was the man of her dreams standing in front of her telling her he loved her and she was backing away. What the hell was wrong with her?

He lifted his hand and touched her cheek. "A month isn't very long. But it was long enough for me to come to my senses. Long enough for me to recognize that I'd met someone who made me smile again, made me laugh, made me actually look forward to the future rather than just going from day to day. Do you know how rare that is?"

She put her hand over his and drew it away from her face, down into her lap. "Dave," she said quietly, "it was barely a week ago when you stood in your kitchen and told me flat out that you couldn't give me what I wanted. What changed? Why should I trust that?"

He got up from his squatted position but held onto her hand, gave it a tug until she was out of the chair, and reversed positions so that he was in the chair and he pulled her into his lap.

His arm was strong as it circled her, his face utterly open and sincere as he looked up at her. "Charlene."

She waited. He seemed to be gathering his words, and there was a sense that whatever he said next was going to be of utmost importance. Butterflies winged through her stomach and her fingers trembled. It terrified her how much she wanted to believe him.

And then there it was, a look in his eyes that was so beautiful that it felt like her heart was melting right there in her chest. It made her breath catch and a strange sort of excitement pulse through her veins. "David," she whispered, and reached out and placed her hand along the side of his face, feeling the stubble against her skin.

He turned his head slightly, kissed the curve of her palm.

"There are so many things I might have done differently," he said, his arms still tight around her hips. "I might have not gotten together with Janice. I might have put off having kids, or stayed in the Navy. I realize that right now, I'm exactly where I'm supposed to be. In Jewell Cove. With you. And that I wouldn't be here if any of those things hadn't happened. They all led me to you, Charlie. You are where I'm meant to be. You make my world make sense."

"You really mean that, don't you?"

"With my life. I don't need to count weeks or months to figure it out. And it won't be perfect all the time. I know that. I just know I want to try."

It won't be perfect all the time. She rolled those words around in her head a few times, mulling them over. She thought about Michelle in the next room, struggling so hard to make decisions, thought about Josh, who'd lost his wife overseas mere weeks before she was due to return home. She thought about Lizzie's mom, and how she'd had to be put in full-time care. Truth was, there was no such thing as perfect all the time, and perhaps that was Charlie's problem. She'd built up this imaginary dream life to be so perfect that it was an impossible, unattainable goal.

Instead she had a wonderful, slightly damaged, sexy, beautiful man holding her tight and asking her to give them a shot. And it occurred to her that perhaps she'd been demanding too much, because what he was offering was everything. Himself. All he asked in return was that she meet him halfway.

"You really mean that you love me?"

She relaxed into his arms, curling into his embrace so that her face was nestled in the curve of his neck. "Oh yes," he answered softly. "Charlie, there was a moment. I know you remember it. You have to. A moment when we were making love and our eyes met and it was like lightning."

She did remember. It had been a magical, soul-deep connection beyond anything she'd ever known. It had been the moment that had given her hope that the life she longed for might be within her grasp.

Now he was telling her it was. And she could either choose to believe him or walk away.

She thought of what Lizzie would say right now and she laughed a little, holding on to him a bit tighter. Lizzie would tell her to stop being a chicken and take a chance, because if she didn't, she'd always regret it.

"Is that a good laugh or a bad one? Cripes, woman. I spill my guts to you and you laugh?"

She pushed on his chest so that she was sitting up and could look him square in the face. "David Ricker, I am terrified of having my heart broken. But lucky for you I'm more afraid of what will become of me if I don't take a chance. So here it is. I fell in love with you too. Right about the time you turned around with a baby in your arms and told me we had a problem."

A smile bloomed on his face and he pulled her close, kissing her like she was a cool glass of water and he was a man dying of thirst. With a heart full of hope, she kissed him back, melting into him, loving the taste and feel of him until she realized someone was knocking on her office door.

Reluctantly she removed her lips from his and then felt heat rush to her face as she saw Josh standing in the doorway, his knuckles resting on the door frame and a goofy grin on his face.

"I hate to interrupt this reunion, but Michelle is getting ready to go now. She asked to see you first."

Charlie turned to Dave. "Do you want to meet her? She seemed very interested in knowing who found her baby."

"She brought us together, didn't she? Of course I'll meet her."

"I'll be right back."

Michelle agreed to meet Dave, and Charlie loved the way he smiled at the girl when she walked through the office door. He had a big heart too, whether he realized it or not.

"Thank you," Michelle said quietly. "For saving my baby."

"You're welcome," he answered, and he came forward and shook her hand. "Don't worry, okay? You've got Dr. Yang in your corner. And if I've learned anything, it's that when she's got your back, it's not the end. It's just the beginning. You're going to be just fine."

Michelle nodded, shouldering her backpack, and then she suddenly smiled. "Oh!" She let the pack slide to the floor and hurriedly undid the zipper. "I nearly forgot. I took this the night I left him in the manger. I didn't mean to steal it, I just wasn't sure . . ."

She stood up. It was the doll from the manger, still diapered and swaddled and wrapped in Dave's soft shirt.

Charlie started to laugh, and so did Dave. She put her arm around Michelle's shoulders. And in that moment, she knew that everything was going to work out exactly as it should. And it had nothing to do with facts or figures. It was all down to one simple thing: faith.

Chapter Fourteen

Light snow was falling on Christmas Eve. The tangle of lights Charlie had wrestled with the first day was twinkling from the shrubs throughout the churchyard. A floodlight lit up the nativity, and together Charlie and Dave went forward and placed the original Baby Jesus on the straw.

"Back where he belongs," Dave said quietly, holding Charlie's hand.

"It seems like so long ago I was sitting here talking to him like he was my best friend. So silly . . ."

Dave shrugged. "Who knows? Maybe he was listening."

Charlie laughed a little, leaning against Dave's arm. "That's even more embarrassing. I was telling him about this guy I could see from the window at Breeze's on my lunch hour. How I'd made up this fantasy boyfriend . . ."

"I hope the reality surpasses your imagination."

"Oh, definitely."

The parking lot was filling up and many of the towns-people walked to the church for the Christmas Eve service. It wasn't generally Charlie's speed, but lots of things were changing this year, and for the better. As she and Dave stepped inside the vestibule together, with Daniel cradled in Dave's strong arms, she felt more a part of the community than ever.

"Merry Christmas, Charlene," called Gloria Henderson, who was bustling her way toward the front of the church to take her place at the organ.

"Merry Christmas," she called back. The same thing happened a half dozen more times as they hung up their coats and took the baby out of his snowsuit. Robin showed up with her sister; Todd Smith was there in uniform, still on duty but stopping in to take in part of the annual tradition just the same. Josh and his extended family and lots of people she recognized from the businesses around town arrived, smiling and laughing and filled with Christmas spirit. She introduced Dave to several, and a warm glow filled her from head to toe as they finally made it to a pew near the back to enjoy the caroling and service.

A huge pine tree was at the front of the church, decorated in white lights and ornaments and exuding a festive piney smell throughout the sanctuary. But best of all were the candles, thick pillars of them, lit on every windowsill, the stained glass glowing in their light. Once the service was over, there was mingling again in the crowded entry, and a sense of peace and goodwill and happiness that Charlie wished she could bottle and carry with her forever. Meggie appropriated Daniel for a diaper change, and Charlie held on to Dave's hand feeling like everything was right in the world.

She looked at the door and saw Marissa Longfellow, and to her surprise, Michelle was with her, dressed in a new winter coat, black leggings and boots that came to just below her knees. She was quite pretty today, with her hair washed and falling easily over her shoulders, and a little hint of makeup. Charlie tugged on Dave's hand and led him to the entrance, where they stepped outside into the cool air peppered with fat, lazy snow-flakes.

"Michelle. You look wonderful." Charlie, who usually shied away from physical intimacy, gave the girl a quick hug. "I didn't expect to see you here."

Michelle smiled shyly. "Ms. Longfellow is my new Santa Claus. I have a court date after Christmas, but she convinced the judge to let me stay with her in the meantime. Extenuating circumstances, she said. And then we paid a visit to the secondhand store and got me some new clothes."

Marissa smiled. "Michelle wants to make a new start. It won't be a fast process or an easy one. She could use a helping hand, that's all."

"I agree."

"Me too," Dave echoed.

"I know that what I did was so wrong." She smiled sadly at all of them. "But I want to build a better life and I want a better life for him too. One that he'll find with a good family."

Charlie knew it had to be hard for Michelle to say. "That's very brave of you, sweetie."

"I hope one day I can be someone my son can be proud of. I'm thinking it might be like asking for a Christmas miracle, but who knows, right?"

"Stranger things have happened," Charlie confirmed, taking Dave's hand. "I happen to be a big believer in second chances."

"Me too," Dave confirmed, looking down into Charlie's eyes. For a long moment their gazes held, and Charlie felt like the luckiest woman in the world.

After they said their good-byes, they collected

Daniel and headed back to Charlie's for the night. She'd turned on her lights before leaving, and as they drove in the yard, cheery multicolored bulbs glowed on the new snow. She realized that she'd come to love this cottage. Come to love Jewell Cove, especially once she started to let people in. It was home. When Dave took the keys from her hand and opened her front door, her heart gave a little pang. She took a moment and made a wish. A wish that Dave would maybe want to make it his home too. When they stepped inside and shut the door, he pulled her close and kissed her: long, thorough, beautiful. She put her arms around his neck and squeezed. When he was here, it felt like a missing piece of the puzzle was finally in place.

She'd tucked Daniel into bed and poured them each a glass of wine as he built the fire, and she was ready to put on a Christmas movie when Dave took her hand.

"I have something for you."

He led her away from the entertainment center and to the front of the tree, where a few gifts already waited, tucked beneath the branches. Confused and a little excited, Charlie couldn't help the smile that curved her lips.

"What?" he asked. "You look like the cat that ate the canary."

"I'm just happy," she answered. "I've never spent Christmas with anyone like this. It's special."

"So are you. " He reached into the middle of the tree and took out a box, about four inches square. "I tucked this in here before we left. I thought about waiting for tomorrow, but I want you to have it tonight."

He held it out, and she took the red foil-wrapped box into her hands. It was light, and with shaky fingers she undid the ribbon and slid her fingernail beneath the tape holding the paper in place.

She lifted the lid and found an ornament inside—the same one she'd found at the bookstore at the Evergreen Festival, a perfectly round ball covered with paper quotes.

"Oh, Dave. It's lovely." She held it in her fingers. "It's the Shakespeare one, right?"

His gaze was intent on her as he gave a slight nod. "Yes."

It was very thoughtful, and she remembered him being a little longer in the store that day. "You said that they were changing the register tape, but you were buying this, weren't you?"

"I was."

"I love it." She was so perfectly happy at this moment, she was positive life couldn't get any better. But then she picked it up by the loop and went to hang it on the tree and a splash of green caught her eye. Bright green, like from a highlighter pen. She drew her hand back and turned the orb so that she could examine the strip of paper.

I would not wish any companion in the world but you.

A lump grew in her throat and the text blurred for a second. "Oh, Dave." She drew in an emotional breath. "What's it from?"

He put his arm around her waist and drew her close. "I looked it up. It's from *The Tempest*."

She took one step forward and hung it on a branch right in the middle of the tree. "I love you. You know that, right?"

"I do. So what do you say, Chuckles?"

"Say?"

He lifted her hand to his lips. She looked up at him, unsure of what he was asking, simply loving the sight of him there before her, knowing she loved him and was loved in return. Nothing could be sweeter.

"Companions. Partners. Lovers. I want it all. I want it all with you."

Okay, so she hadn't quite expected for her wish to be granted so quickly. But she was learning not to look a gift horse in the mouth. "I want that too."

"I'm on a month-to-month lease with Tom."

"And there's more than enough room for us here," she added, feeling ridiculously starry-eyed.

"We can always put on an addition later . . ."

"For the kids. Are you okay with that? I don't know what's going to happen with Daniel, but I want children, Dave. At least a couple."

He grinned at her. "I'm more than okay with that." He kissed the tip of her nose. "We're really going to do this."

"Yeah," she said. "We are."

He reached for her, curled a hand around her neck, and pulled her close for a long, searing kiss that left her breathless. Charlie let out a moan as he pulled her earlobe into his mouth, sending a dart of pure desire to her core. She reached for his dress shirt and started unbuttoning it, but his hands got in the way as he touched her breasts and pulled her against his hard body.

It only seemed to take seconds and they were stretched out on the rug in front of the fire. Without saying a word, they slowed their hands, took their time, savored each second. There was no urgency, just the sweet rush of anticipation. Charlie looked up at Dave and saw more than just a man. She saw her future.

"Merry Christmas, sweetheart," he said, and kissed her tenderly.

"You're my favorite Christmas gift," she decreed, and then the rest of the world disappeared. It was just the two of them, a sweet little cottage on the bay, and a dream for forever.

Christmas with the
Billionaire
Rancher

❄ ❄ ❄

by Mandy Baxter

ACKNOWLEDGMENTS

Thanks to my agent, Natanya Wheeler and everyone at NYLA and to my amazing editor, Monique Patterson. A huge thanks also goes to Alexandra Sehulster, the talented cover designers, copy editors, and marketing staff at St. Martin's Press! As always, any mistakes are my own. I can only imagine what I'd miss without the amazing support of SMP staff to keep me looking neat and tidy!

for the season: bright twinkling lights, garlands, and or-
nate Christmas trees scattered throughout. You'd think
tonight's dog-and-pony show was some sort of holiday
gala, not the somber "celebration of life" it had been
touted as. Nate gave the same mechanical canned response to each person who offered their condolences.
In the corner of the ballroom, wife number five dabbed
at her eyes with a Kleenex. He had to give it to Miranda,
her acting skills had gotten better since he saw her last.
Trolling for sympathy with her red, swollen eyes and
downturned mouth, the only people who paid her any
mind were the crowd of old hens near the buffet table
who gossiped with glee about Byron's child-bride widow
and the fact that she wasn't going to see a red cent of
his billions.

"How you holding up?" Nate's younger brother Travis held a plate piled with gourmet buffet food in one
hand. He stood six inches taller than Nate and his hours
spent conditioning showed in his bulk. He was one of
the largest goalkeepers in the NHL, as quick on his feet
as he was tough. One of the rock stars of pro hockey, he
looked the part with his shaggy hair and edgy designer
clothes. He had a reputation for being an irresponsible
party boy and notorious player, and while some of it was
true, Travis could be counted on when it mattered.

Nate was sick of everyone walking on eggshells
around him. As though his mental state simply couldn't
handle the blow of losing their dad. "I'm fine." It's not
like his dad had been blown to shreds by a mortar shell
or some shit. The man died of a heart attack. And everyone knew that he'd been exerting himself over Miranda
when the big one hit. "I just want this extravaganza to
be over so I can get the hell out of here."

Travis snorted. "This is only the beginning."

Wasn't that the fucking truth? Nate and his three

brothers were set to inherit Byron's kingdom. The oil magnate was worth billions. And as the oldest brother, Nate was in charge of the estate. "I don't want a dime of it." He brought the bottle of beer to his lips and drank deeply. "You can have my share."

"I don't want your share." Travis had more than enough of his own money. As the starting goalkeeper for the Dallas Stars, he was set. So was Travis's twin, Carter. Though they were identical in height and bulk, Carter was the epitome of the clean-cut, all-American athlete with his conservative dress and short-clipped hair. He'd just been traded to the Cowboys for a fat paycheck after they'd lost their star QB to the Seahawks when he went free agent.

"Fine, I'll give it to Noah." No doubt he'd be appreciative of a fatter inheritance check to supplement his salary as a county sheriff.

"What makes you think I want it?" Noah stepped up to him, arm outstretched, and handed over a fresh bottle of IPA. "Here. You look like you could use it."

No one could deny the Christensen brothers' parentage. They were all basically carbon copies of their dad. And while Noah was closer to Nate's height and not quite as bulky, they all shared the same towering frames and dark brown hair. Their hazel eyes were the only trait they'd inherited from their mother and Nate often wished that when he looked in the mirror, he didn't see so much of his dad staring back at him.

As a self-made man, Byron Christensen had adhered to the belief that it would build character in his sons to give them absolutely nothing. No financial support, no leg up with his extensive connections . . . And he hadn't stopped there. He'd been less generous with his affection. After their mom's death when they were only kids, they'd basically fended for themselves. And now that the old man was dead, he was giving them his fortune. They'd gone without it for so long, none of them was interested in it now.

Maybe they'd all built a little character after all.

"I'd bet his only concern was making sure *she* didn't get it." Travis jutted his chin to where Miranda sat.

"I'm sure she expects everyone to feel sorry for her," Noah said. "As though she deserves something for putting up with him. And—OMG—she still married him after he made her sign a prenup!"

Nate snorted at Noah's mocking tone. His dad had had the nerve to actually invite him to the wedding, as if Nate hadn't packed up his shit and run from that fucking bullshit as fast as his legs could carry him. In fact, he couldn't get far enough away from his dad and had already been on his way to basic when the invitations went out. Syria, Iraq, Afghanistan . . . Nate had traveled halfway around the goddamned world and it still hadn't been enough to wipe the memories of his father's betrayals from his mind.

"Nate . . . ?"

He shook himself from unpleasant memories. "What was that?" Carter had said something to him, but he wasn't tracking.

"I said, the girls are getting antsy and I should probably take them home."

"Oh, yeah. Sure. You don't need to stick around. Get out of here."

Carter's wife, Stephanie, had died of cancer last year. It tore Nate up to think of his brother trying to get over losing the love of his life—they'd been high school sweethearts—while juggling football and five-year old twins. *That* was a tragedy. The people at his father's *tribute* acted as though Byron kicking the bucket was some unthinkable, sudden catastrophe. Sixty-eight years old with a bad heart, an affinity for scotch and cigars, and a twenty-eight-year-old wife. Hell, it was a wonder he'd lasted this long.

"If you need anything, let me know."

Nate should have been the one offering Carter help, not the other way around. *Awesome.* He was the family fuck-up. The emotionally unstable war vet who hid out at his ranch so he wouldn't have to deal with real life. "I've got it under control," Nate said. He could assemble an AR-15 in less than ten minutes. Running an oil empire couldn't be much harder.

"All right. I'll call you tomorrow."

"Sounds good." Nate watched as Carter headed toward the buffet tables where his daughters, Jenny and Jane, were running in a circle with a few other kids.

"Gird your loins, brothers," Travis said out of the corner of his mouth. "The grieving widow is headed this way."

Great. If Nate's brothers didn't want his share of his dad's fortune, he bet he could convince Miranda to take it off his hands.

"Don't even think about it." Noah pinned Nate with an accusing stare.

"What? You don't want it. Carter and Travis don't want it. Why not give it to her? I'd say she earned it."

"She deserves shit," Noah said. "Besides, she's getting the house. And the cars."

"Maybe she needs some cash, too."

"Not a chance. She's a deceitful, lying money-grubber and nothing else. She'd party it away in a matter of weeks. Take the money, Nate. I'm not saying you have to be the CEO of Christensen Petroleum or some shit, but you deserve it more than she does. Hell, as much as any of us does."

Nate took a long pull from his bottle. "I don't need

it." He had all of about seven hundred bucks in his checking account right now. But he didn't want his life—or the people in it—to be defined by the numbers in his checkbook. Never had.

"Buy a few more cows. Hell, get a tractor. Make that sorry excuse of a ranch into something that might actually turn a profit."

"Wouldn't that violate dad's make-your-own-way policy?"

Noah cocked a brow and fixed Nate with a sad smile. "Doesn't matter now. The old man's gone."

❄   ❄   ❄

Chloe Benson had done some crazy things to get her hooks in a high roller's checkbook, but crashing a memorial service was a new low even for her. She didn't have time to debate the morality of getting in line for a handout when Byron Christensen's body hadn't been in the ground for even a week, though. This was her eleventh hour. And if she couldn't get her hands on some serious cash by Christmas Eve, she was as good as screwed.

Desperate times called for desperate measures.

She scanned the crowd in search of Nathan Christensen. According to the gossip mill, the oldest Christensen son was looking to off-load the substantial inheritance his father had left him. Speculation on the reasons why ranged from Nathan being mentally unstable to a falling out with his father years ago. Chloe didn't care why he didn't want the money. She simply wanted to be first in line when he started handing it out.

A small crowd gathered around a group of men and Chloe moved in. The Christensen brothers were infamous for being the black sheep of Dallas high society.

The rumor mill had speculated for years about why the brothers hadn't entered into the family business and why they never showed up at events, the country clubs, or any of the other places where the elite hung out to pat each other on the back. Two of the brothers were pro athletes, the other a sheriff a few counties over. As for Nathan, he was the blackest sheep of all. He'd run off and joined the Navy. Rumor had it that Byron hadn't even known when his son returned home. Talk about estranged . . .

Through the press of well-wishers and ass-kissers, Chloe caught sight of him. At least, she thought it was him. The picture of the brothers in the *Dallas Morning News* had obviously been several years old. The man she was now looking at resembled that guy. But he was older. Bigger. And projected a hardness that Chloe swore she could feel in the center of her chest. Probably a tough nut to crack. Fortunately for her, she wasn't one to back down from a challenge.

Chloe made her way toward the brothers, taking note of the fact that the accumulated net worth of the people here was enough to buy a country or two. Hell, with the politicians they all likely had in their pockets, it was safe to say they owned *this* country. Chloe had played to crowds like this for years. The rich and powerful loved to have their egos stroked. Unfortunately, she'd made the rounds and most of these people had already given her the cold shoulder—Byron included—which was why she had her sights set on Nathan Christensen. He didn't want his newly acquired wealth. She did. It was a win-win situation.

"I just loved him *so* much, you know?" Chloe stopped short of her goal. She recognized the woman fake-crying into a pile of tissues as Miranda Christensen, Byron's widow. Decked out in a sexy black dress, she looked better suited for a cocktail party than a memorial service.

"I gave him the best years of my life, Nate! How could he leave me *nothing*?"

Best years of her life? She was twenty-eight, for crying out loud. A year younger than Chloe. Nathan—*Nate*—listened to her rant with a stoic expression. With shuffling steps, Chloe sidled in closer and hid her curiosity behind the lip of her wineglass.

"He didn't leave you without anything, Miranda. You got the house, the cars, and I know for a fact you've got a bank account with plenty of cash in it."

"I'll have to sell it all," she sniffed. "Do you know how expensive it is to maintain a house that size? What was Byron thinking?"

Chloe was pretty sure he'd been thinking with what resided down south.

"Just consider my offer, okay, Nate? I loved Byron. And *I* was there for him at the end."

Oh, I bet you were. Chloe snorted a little too loudly. *Right underneath him.*

Miranda whipped around, her dark eyes glistening as she narrowed her gaze. The former social climber threw off enough shade to make Chloe wish she'd worn a sweater. Nate Christensen turned his head in the direction that Miranda directed her anger. Chloe froze and clutched the wineglass closer to her mouth to keep it from falling open. Up close, Nate Christensen was absolutely breathtaking.

Tall, and with a body packed with muscle that seriously stress-tested his dark gray dress shirt, he stood out among the crowd of leisurely wealthy. Dark brown hair brushed his brow in the front and the sides were buzzed short, giving him an edgy look. His nose looked as though it had been broken at one point, a tiny bump below the bridge that gave it away. Sharp cheekbones accentuated his full lips and strong jaw. But none of those godlike features held a candle to his eyes. The most beautiful shade of hazel she'd ever seen, and clear as a river in midsummer.

Chloe had never been the sort of woman to get weak in the knees over a good-looking guy, but holy crap. She wobbled on her stilettos as if the shock of his gorgeousness had temporarily disrupted her motor skills. Heat rose to Chloe's cheeks and the flush spread down her neck. Her heart rate kicked into gear and fluttered against her rib cage at the same time her stomach decided to crawl up her throat. Heat continued to swamp her as she studied him, her attraction almost embarrassing in its intensity. Guys like Nate Christensen hung out with supermodels. Willowy, bottle blond socialites. Starlets. Guys like that didn't date overworked charity administrators who didn't have the time for a walk let alone a personal trainer, and the hips and belly to prove it.

While Miranda and Nate continued their conversation in hushed tones, Chloe waited for an in. She usually had time to prepare, to research the fat cat she was about to butter up. Byron Christensen's death had been sudden, and the only information she had on his oldest son was that he'd been estranged from his dad for years. That and he had no interest in his family's wealth. Fine by her. She was more than willing to take some of that money off his hands. All she had to do was convince him that she deserved it.

"That money should be mine and you know it, Nate. Call me tomorrow and let's talk."

Chloe nearly choked on her chardonnay as Miranda brushed a hand along his arm and gave Nate a flirty smile in parting. *Really? At your husband's memorial service?* Byron Christensen's widow was *klassy* with a capital K. Nate watched her go, his expression an impassive mask that gave nothing away. He shifted his focus and that inscrutable hazel gaze locked with Chloe's. A shiver of anticipation traveled from her head to her toes as he studied her. Chloe had never felt more devoured by a simple glance and it wasn't altogether unpleasant. A renewed rush of heat spread from her abdomen, lower. She took a deep breath, held it in her lungs. And let it all go in a rush.

It was now or never. Time to make her move.

TWO

Nate turned toward the woman who'd been eavesdropping on his conversation with Miranda. He'd meant to intimidate her, to stare her down until she got the fucking message that he wasn't about to let some rich-bitch Dallas party girl spread any more gossip about him or his family. Whatever he felt about his dad or Miranda, it was *his* business and no one else's.

God, he was already so *sick* of this bullshit.

His gaze locked with hers and he prepared to give her his best fuck-off glare. Instead, Nate simply stared. His blood heated as he took her in. Pinup gorgeous with rich auburn hair, full lips, and a curvy figure that filled out her business-casual outfit in all the right ways. Her full breasts practically spilled from the open lapels of her shirt and the generous curve of her hips made Nate itch to reach out and grip them. He clamped his jaw down to keep it from hanging open as a rush of pure lust shot through his bloodstream. She hit every single one of his *yes please!* buttons and his dick perked up like a hound scenting fresh game. He didn't even know who she was and he wanted her. Their eyes locked and rather than look away, she met his gaze with a brazen challenge that fanned the flames of his mounting libido.

Nate forced himself to appear impassive when what he really wanted was to reach out and touch. A woman like that could bring a man to his knees and Nate was more than up to showing her what he could do for her from that exact position. Rather than tuck tail at his forced stoicism, she squared her shoulders and stepped up to him. Ballsy. And not at all what Nate expected.

"I'm sorry about your father," she said without preamble. "But between you and me, he could be a real ornery bastard."

Nate canted his head to one side as he regarded her, careful to keep his expression stern and emotionless. "So, you knew him?" He appreciated someone being straight up with him for a change.

"No," she replied in that same guileless tone. "We spoke a couple of times on the phone. Then again, I did tell his secretary that I was pregnant with his baby in order to get past the gatekeepers. It might have had something to do with why we got off on the wrong foot."

A smile tugged at Nate's lips but he didn't give in to his amusement. "Probably." In a sea of pretentious windbags and vapid, bottle blond daddy's girls, this one was a breath of fresh air. Her dark auburn hair was piled atop her head in a haphazard mess that made Nate wonder if she'd rolled out of bed and into her car. Freckles dotted her nose and dusted her cheeks, accentuating the deep emerald green of her eyes. Her full lips were glossy, but not painted on like most of the women here. She wasn't made up or overdone. It might have been the beer talking, but her fresh face and brash sincerity was exactly what Nate needed right now.

"I'm Chloe by the way." She held out her hand. "And you are the infamous Nathan Christensen."

His brow knitted. "Nate. I hadn't realized that my infamy elevated me to no-introduction-needed status."

Chloe smiled. An open, friendly expression that tugged at the center of Nate's chest. "Being a Christensen comes with its own brand of notoriety."

She had that pegged. Likewise, being a Christensen didn't always attract the sort of woman that Nate was interested in spending time with. He didn't have the time or the patience for Dallas high society. The women who fished that pond were as fake as their plastic surgery and wanted a man with a bulging wallet and one who wasn't carrying a closet's worth of emotional baggage.

"How so?" Her voice was naturally sensual, almost a purr and Nate couldn't help but wonder what it would sound like in the grips of passion. His heart raced just imagining it. He didn't want their conversation to end. Chloe was quick on her feet and her honesty was a fresh breath in the stale air.

She cocked her head to the side. "Oh, come on. Like you all don't know that you're the black sheep of this herd."

Nate smirked. "I'd say you're in the right company then."

Her eyes widened with feigned innocence. "What could possibly prompt you to think such a thing?"

Cheeky. Nate appreciated sarcasm. And in Chloe, it was goddamned attractive. His gaze swept her once again from head to toe with appreciation. Black heels, black pencil skirt that hugged her voluptuous curves in a way that was practically lewd. Crisp, pinstriped dress shirt with the top buttons left undone to tease him with the ample swell of her breasts. The heels brought her almost to his height and he liked that she wasn't another waifish socialite. His plan up until now had been to drink and continue to drink until he was so shitfaced that his brothers would have to carry him out of here. Nate had been so on edge for the past week that it was a wonder he hadn't gone off the deep end. He needed a release. Something to take the edge off. Maybe instead of using alcohol to numb the ache in his chest, he could fuck the emptiness out of his system.

"Why did you tell my dad's secretary you were pregnant with his baby?" It gave Nate a perverse sense of satisfaction to think of his dad's chains being rattled.

She gave him a sheepish grin that caused Nate's gut to clench. "I'd been trying to get ahold of him for weeks. His secretary shot me down every time I called, so I switched up my tactics." Her gaze turned devilish and a rush of liquid heat shot through Nate's veins. "She put me through without asking a single question."

His dad's reputation as a lecherous son of a bitch was pretty well-known. He liked his women young and tight. Arm candy he could drag all over town. That his secretary wouldn't bat a lash at the notion his dad had a mistress on the side left a sour taste in Nate's mouth. His dad had professed to Nate and his brothers that he'd been faithful to their mom until the day she died. In the back of his mind, however, Nate had always doubted the truth of it.

"So you weren't sleeping with him?"

Her insulted glare caused Nate's lips to twitch in an almost smile. "No way. I run a charity organization that provides sports programs for underprivileged and at-risk kids. A girl's gotta pay the bills and Byron seemed to have the cash to spare."

Nate snorted. His dad was a tightfisted son of a bitch. He didn't have to ask Chloe how the conversation went to know that he'd shot her down. "Somehow, I doubt you're here to thank us for Dad's generous donation."

Her mouth turned down in an almost pout that made her bottom lip deliciously full. "Not exactly."

Holy shit, did he want to bite that lip and then lick the sting away. "Maybe your tactics sucked."

Her mouth opened in shock but her eyes sparked with mischief. "Are you suggesting I rubbed your dad the wrong way?"

"I'm suggesting you need to learn more about your targets. Don't you know that the Christensens are notoriously disdainful of people looking for a handout?" Which was precisely why Nate was considering off-loading his inheritance. The last person he wanted a handout from was the one man who'd ruined his life.

❄   ❄   ❄

Her first assessment of Nate had been pretty spot-on. He was a tough nut to crack. His gaze had warmed from a cold, emotionless death glare to something altogether hotter, though. It sparked a warm glow in Chloe's stomach that steadily built to a slow burn. After talking to Nate, she realized that she was going to have to play this closer to the hip than she'd anticipated.

Notoriously disdainful of people looking for a handout. She didn't have much time to charm a sizeable donation from Nate, but it seemed she had no choice but to be patient. If she hit him up now, he might just tell her to fuck off—his earlier stare had certainly implied as much—and she couldn't risk letting him slip through her fingers.

"So you're saying I would have gotten farther with him if I'd actually been pregnant with his baby?"

Nate burst out into a round of cynical laughter. He

motioned for a cocktail waitress and scooped a flute of champagne off her tray and handed it to Chloe. "Probably." She took the glass from his outstretched hand and tried to keep her gaze from lingering on the muscles that flexed over his forearm. "Can you believe this spread?" He indicated the room at large with his bottle. "Any excuse for these people to get out and be *seen*."

Nate wasn't at all what she'd expected. He was like the anti–Byron Christensen. There wasn't a stuck-up bone in his body. "It's a little swankier than the memorial services I've been to," Chloe admitted. "I suppose his friends wanted to send him off in style."

"Hyenas." Nate took a long swig from the mouth of the bottle and Chloe's gaze wandered to his lips. Was it possible to be jealous of an inanimate object?

"They can't all be bad."

He cocked a brow. The expression faded into something akin to resignation. "Maybe." His gaze raked over her once again and Chloe felt her cheeks flush. "I'm reserving judgment until I get to know you better."

Two hours passed in the blink of an eye. Chloe had had enough champagne to know that one more would push her past tipsy, and it was time to head home and form a new game plan for how to handle Nate before she said something she might regret. Like how much she wanted to bite the delicious curve of his ass cheek for starters. The man was perfection. Every hard angle of his body begging for a closer inspection. Chloe wanted to bite him. Lick him. Taste that lovely junction between his hip and thigh right before she ventured lower.

Oookaaay. Time to go home. She couldn't curb the train of her erotic thoughts any longer and the future of her foundation depended on her keeping her damned panties on. She wanted a professional relationship with Nate Christensen. Nothing more. *Good god, his ass . . .*

"I think it's time for me to call it a night." Chloe placed the empty flute on a nearby table. "It was nice to meet you, Nate. And again, I'm sorry for your loss."

His brow furrowed as though he waged some internal battle. Chloe knew the feeling all too well. Before he could convince her to stay—and it wouldn't take more than a look—she turned and headed for the coat closet just outside the ballroom.

As Chloe searched through the rows of hangers for her jacket, she tried to slow her racing heart. Nate's gruff demeanor, no-nonsense attitude, and piercing hazel eyes stirred Chloe's lust to a fever pitch. How could she possibly charm him into parting with his money when she couldn't even look at him without being starstruck? He tied her into knots without even trying. Hell, if he asked her right now, she'd empty her own bank account and lay it all at his feet in tribute to his magnificence. *Way to melt into a useless heap at the first sight of a good-looking guy, Chloe.* Oh, hell. Who was she kidding? Nate Christensen left good-looking in his freaking wake!

The hairs on the back of Chloe's neck prickled as she sensed someone behind her. Her breaths came quick and shallow. She didn't have to turn around to know that Nate had followed her—and what he wanted. His gaze had practically set her on fire.

"Do you always run off in the middle of a conversation?" His deep voice rumbled close to her ear and Chloe shivered.

"I didn't know you had something more to say." Her own response was nothing more than a breathy whisper. Her pounding heart didn't allow for her to fill her lungs.

Nate's palms came to rest at her hips and the contact sent a jolt of electricity through Chloe's body that settled between her thighs. Her sex pulsed in time with her heart and her tongue darted out to lick her suddenly dry lips.

"I've got a lot more to say."

She swallowed. Hard. This was a bad idea, and yet, she couldn't help but ask, "Like what?"

"Like I want to fuck you."

A rush of wet heat spread between Chloe's thighs at Nate's brash words. Her head spun with his scent, his proximity, the sheer *size* of him that crowded her from behind. The length of his erection brushed her ass and Chloe hissed in a breath. "Are you sure that's not the IPA talking?"

"You and I both know we haven't had that much to drink."

True. If she had, Chloe could blame the epically bad decision she was about to make on the champagne. As it was, she had no one to blame but herself. His fingertips dug into her hips, a delicious amount of pressure that made Chloe bite back a moan. "Right here in the coat closet, huh? Wanna bend me over that chair in the corner and get right to it?"

"If you want." Nate's voice rippled over her skin as his mouth moved to her neck. He nipped at the skin and a thrill raced through her. God, the anticipation would give her an orgasm long before Nate was able to even get her clothes off. "I'll hike up your skirt right here and now if you want me to. But I'd rather take you upstairs."

Chloe couldn't help but grin. "Why's that?"

"Because I'm dying to get a glimpse of your pussy." Oh. *Wow.*

"Are you wet, Chloe?" He eased his erection against her ass again. A slow roll of his hips that made Chloe's breath hitch. Nate Christensen was a first-class dirty talker and he was talking her right into a wanton frenzy.

She didn't even have to guess. "Yes."

"Mmmm." His warm growl of approval made her wetter still. "My room's upstairs. All you have to say is yes, Chloe. Goddamn, I want to fuck you."

His mouth touched down on her throat, hot and wet. The scrape of his teeth on her sensitive skin coaxed goose bumps to the surface of Chloe's skin and she shuddered. If she gave in, if she said the word he wanted to hear, it might submarine her chances of saving her foundation. Problem was, only one word formed on her lips and she was powerless not to speak it. "Yes."

His hands moved up her torso and brushed the outer curves of Chloe's breasts. She sucked in another sharp breath as her nipples hardened to stiff peaks inside of her bra.

"Let's go. Now. Before I can't wait any longer and bend you over that chair anyway."

"Okay." Chloe tried to slow her racing pulse and frantic breaths. Already she felt naked, exposed to him and he'd barely touched her. If they didn't get upstairs, Nate wouldn't have the opportunity to bend her over that chair because Chloe was pretty sure she'd hike up her skirt and bend herself over it for him. "I'm ready."

THREE

Nate fumbled with the key card as he shoved it into the reader. Chloe's mouth was too sweet, her lips too soft for him to even consider breaking their kiss for as long as it would take to unlock the hotel room door. As he reached back to turn the doorknob, Chloe's fingers brushed against his fly and his cock throbbed through the layers of fabric that separated their skin.

"God I need to fuck." They stumbled through the door and it slammed closed behind them. Chloe sighed against his mouth and she gripped him harder through his slacks, cupping her palm around the length of his erection. He kicked off his ridiculous leather loafers and groped for the buttons on Chloe's shirt. "I can't get you naked fast enough."

Chloe's expression heated. *Goddamn.* There was nothing coy or shy about her. She was every bit as wound up as he was. When he unfastened the last button on her shirt, she tore it from her body and discarded it somewhere behind her. Nate buried his face between the swells of her breasts, biting, licking, kissing the tender flesh that spilled over the cups as he stripped off her bra. Chloe let out a low moan that vibrated down his spine and settled in his balls. She popped the button on his slacks and jerked down the zipper before sliding his pants and underwear down over his ass. With a firm grip she took his cock in her hand and squeezed. The delicious constriction caused his hips to buck, and she stroked from the engorged head to the base in a twisting caress that caused his stomach to clench.

He was ready to come right here and now and they'd barely gotten started.

"Do you have a condom?" Her voice was a breathy plea as she stroked him again with that same torturous precision.

"Wallet." He couldn't manage more than the one guttural word.

"Good. I would have hated to stop now."

Fucking hell. The heat between them built from a smolder to a roaring inferno. His mouth seized hers in a hungry kiss as he slipped her skirt down off her hips, leaving her clad in nothing more than her black stiletto heels and underwear. Nate shrugged out of his own shirt before he cupped his palm over the rounded curve of her ass, loving the sensation of the satiny fabric as his hand slid over it. He kicked off his slacks and underwear from around his ankles and Chloe shifted to step out of her skirt.

"Leave the heels on," he commanded against her mouth.

"Naughty," Chloe murmured in a teasing tone. "I like it."

"Get on the bed." Tremors shook Nate's body as he guided Chloe down onto mattress. She moved to push herself farther up on the bed but he stopped her. "No. Stay right on the edge."

Her green eyes darkened and her tongue lashed out at her bottom lip. He couldn't tear his eyes off her as he dug through his slacks for his wallet. With shaking fingers, he pulled out the condom from one of the pockets and tossed it onto the bed beside her. It took a sheer act of will not to roll the damned thing on, jerk her underwear aside, and bury himself to the base inside of her.

Chloe leaned back on her arms and spread her thighs. Nate scrubbed a hand over his mouth as he took in the sight of her pale skin, the curve of her hips, and the slight roundness of her belly, her breasts impossibly full and rosy nipples erect. She wasn't nervous or unsure or even a little shy. Her confidence turned him on more than anything. Wound him up so tight that his balls ached. She wanted this as much as he did. Maybe she needed it as badly as he did, too.

Nate leaned down and braced an arm on the bed beside her. Chloe's breath came in quick little pants of anticipation that sent his blood racing though his veins. He kept his eyes trained on her face as he reached down with his right hand and gently stroked between her thighs with the pads of his fingers. Her gaze went liquid and a barely visible tremor shook her. He stroked her again, this time circling the tiny bud of her clit that stood out against the satiny fabric of her underwear. Chloe's hips thrust toward him as a slow throaty moan escaped her parted lips.

She didn't look away as he continued to pet her. The intensity of her gaze, the dark sensuality of her flushed cheeks and full lips fueled his fire. She pushed herself up and reached out with one hand to stroke his cock. "God, Nate. You're so hard."

A wave of lust stole over him and punched straight into his gut. He took Chloe down to the bed and laid himself out on top of her, careful to shift the bulk of his weight off of her. His mouth seized hers again, slanting with a desperate ferocity as he thrust his tongue inside of her mouth. Her passion matched his and then some. Nate thrust into her hand, fucking her palm at the same time his tongue fucked her mouth. He gripped the lacy elastic band of her underwear and plunged his hand inside. A groan vibrated in his throat as he made contact with the slick heat of her pussy. Her lips were swollen, her clit hard and protruding from between them. Her arousal coated his fingers as he slid between the folds and what had started out as slow, easy caresses escalated into something purposeful and desperate.

Her quiet moans turned into loud mewling cries that echoed off the stark hotel room walls. She shifted, pulling her hips back but Nate refused to let her shy from his touch. He wanted her mindless and ready to beg if he asked her to. Hell, he'd beg her if she wanted him to.

"You're going to make me come, Nate." Chloe sucked in a sharp breath. Her thighs quivered around his hand. She was close.

"Not until I'm inside of you." Nate pushed himself up and tore into the foil packet. He rolled the condom onto his erection in a single stroke. He jerked Chloe's underwear off and scooped her leg up in the crook of his arm as he positioned himself at her opening. Her arm came up to encircle his neck and her fingernails scraped over the stubble of hair at the back of his neck. Her eyes held his and a tremor of fear rippled through him. He felt as though she could see right into his soul.

The darkness that he'd tried to bury threatened to surface and Nate pushed it back down. He needed to stay in the moment. To *feel*. To do whatever it took to keep that motherfucking endless void at bay. He eased the head of his cock into her pussy and Chloe's thighs fell open. He took a deep breath and thrust deep inside of her on a guttural exhale.

This was what he needed. Nate stilled as he adjusted to her tight hold that squeezed him like a fist. He pulled out slowly and thrust again, eliciting a gasp from Chloe. "God, I love that sound." He kept his mouth close to her ear as he repeated the motion. She writhed beneath him, her hips jerking up to meet his. He rolled his hips, seating himself as deep as he could go and she rewarded him for his effort with another sharp intake of breath. "How do you want it, Chloe? I want to hear you say it."

"Just like that," she said through pants of breath. "Fuck me hard, Nate. And don't stop until I come."

❄   ❄   ❄

When Chloe set out to win a chunk of Nate Christensen's newly acquired fortune, this wasn't how she'd planned the night to end. Not that she was complaining. It had been a long damned time since a man rocked her world. And right now the earth was positively quaking beneath her.

Nate fucked her as though he knew her inside and out. He wasn't about to pound into her like some groaning mass of man-flesh. He made sex an art form. A sensual dance that left Chloe breathless and trembling, drawing out her pleasure until she didn't think she could take another moment of his careful assault. She'd known he was intense, that something boiled under the surface of his unshakable façade. What would it be like to bring a man like that to the edge of his control? Lord, she wanted to find out.

Nate eased the leg he held in the cradle of his arm up higher, allowing him to penetrate her more deeply. She wrapped her free leg around his hip and dug her heel into the muscular globes of his ass as she angled her hips up to meet his. She couldn't remember the last time she'd felt so *good*.

"Your pussy is so tight, Chloe. So wet." Nate's voice strained with each word as he lowered his mouth to hers. He kissed her as deeply as he fucked her. With the same slow, deliberate motion. His free hand wandered up her torso, over the swell of her breast, and came to rest at her throat. Long fingers gripped her with enough purpose for her to recognize his barely restrained strength. His open mouth searched hers, his tongue danced with hers in a slippery tangle.

"Faster, Nate. Harder. Make me come."

He increased his pace, pounding into her with quick forceful rolls of his hips that caused Chloe's breath to catch. He kissed her as though he feasted on her mouth, reveled in the taste. And with every low grunt and slap of his skin against hers, her body heated to the point of combustion. Sex with a perfect stranger shouldn't have been so intimate. Lights on, eyes wide open and searching, inhibitions obliterated. She admired Nate's fearlessness. The unapologetic way that he took what he wanted.

Chloe's muscles contracted. Her core tightened as though her body folded in on itself. The pressure built inside of her and she arched her back, urging Nate deeper. "Come for me, Chloe." His command pushed her closer to the edge. "Come hard for me."

Her body responded to his gruff voice as though it had no other choice. Chloe's world shattered into myriad particles that swirled in a violent whirlwind. The orgasm swept her away on a tide of sensation and she cried out. Long, drawn-out sobs that grated in her throat. Nate's jaw squared as he clamped his teeth together. His grip tightened on her throat with just enough pressure to send another exhilarating rush through her bloodstream. He rode her with purpose, his brows drawing down sharply over his intense hazel eyes and he grunted over her like a mindless beast. She'd never seen anything so wild. Primal. Another wave of coiling pleasure rocked her and Chloe cried out again, "Don't stop. Oh god. Don't stop, Nate."

His wild thrusts became more disjointed. He threw his head back as he seated himself deep and nestled in tight against her thighs. Chloe felt the contractions of his orgasm against the sensitive inner walls of her pussy, a delicious thrum that sent a shudder of sensation through her. So intense.

Nate rode out his orgasm, his thrusts becoming slow and shallow. He braced his weight on an elbow but he didn't leave her body as he put his mouth close to Chloe's ear. "I'm going to fuck you until the sun rises." His hot breath coaxed goose bumps to the surface of her skin. "I need more."

There was a quiet desperation to his words that speared Chloe's chest. Maybe she'd underestimated the effect his father's death had on Nate. Maybe his unshakeable façade was just that. A mask he wore to protect himself. But from what?

She cupped the back of his neck and let her fingers caress the short stubble of his hair. He'd kept the military-style cut despite the fact he'd been discharged months ago. She liked that he grew it out on top, though. A sort of rebellious twist to a conservative haircut. For long moments they lay still, her legs wrapped around him, his cock still inside of her. He buried his face where her shoulder met her neck and inhaled deeply. "Sweet Jesus, you smell good," he said on an exhale.

"Are you sure that's not the liquor talking?" she said

with a nervous laugh. "After that workout I probably smell like a locker room."

"You smell like sex and honey," he growled into her ear. "And I'm not half as drunk as you think I am."

Her stomach did a little flip.

Nate pulled out and rolled to Chloe's side. It surprised her how she instantly missed his weight on top of her, the sensation of him filling her. They lay in silence as he played idly with her hair. Gone was the hardness, the impenetrable shell of Nate's stoic exterior. Pensive. Introspective. Chloe sensed that he was no longer there with her but millions of miles away in some other moment in time. He was no less intense; even the featherlight strokes of his fingertips carried a focus that was at the same time unsettling and strangely alluring.

"I really am sorry about your dad." Her voice was small, as though it couldn't push past the perimeter of their bodies.

"Mmm." The sound vibrated in Nate's chest. Though it was common knowledge that Nate and his father had been estranged, Chloe couldn't help but think his death had taken its toll. That despite Nate's hard-boiled exterior, he balanced on the edge of succumbing to the emotional fallout.

Silence descended once again and Nate's breathing became slow and even. Chloe lay on her back, staring up at the ceiling, his arm slung across her waist. She wanted to turn to look at him, but she worried that if he was asleep, she'd disturb him. Icy fingers of fear reached through Chloe's chest and squeezed her heart. She didn't know the first thing about Nate. There was no room for tender emotions and concern in a one-night stand.

With slow precision, his hand wandered from her belly, lower, eliciting chills that chased over Chloe's skin. He traced the juncture where her hip met her thigh and urged her legs to open. She drew in a sharp breath as his long fingers slid between her lips and slowly circled her clit. Again she was shocked that he knew her body better than she did as he rekindled her passion with easy, gentle strokes.

"Come for me again, Chloe," he whispered in her ear.

She arched into his touch as a moan gathered in her throat. The authoritative edge to his voice made her shudder with anticipation. Did anyone ever deny Nate Christensen?

FOUR

Nate woke with a start, the familiar nightmare jolting him into awareness. His breath sawed in and out of his chest. A sheen of sweat beaded his skin. The deafening thunder of mortar shells exploding pinged around inside of his brain, and he gave his head a violent shake as though it would dislodge the memory that would live with him until the day he died.

There was no fucking way he was going to get through the day. Meetings with his dad's lawyers and his board of directors and then a family meeting with his brothers so they could discuss Miranda and what in the hell they were going to do to keep her pestering ass off their backs. He'd be a basket case by dinner and everyone would see firsthand what Nate had known all along: that he wasn't even close to having his shit together and probably never would.

He needed a distraction from his own goddamned thoughts and memories. Something to take the edge off . . .

Nate reached for the piece of hotel notepad paper and

stared at the number scrawled across it. It had been a couple of days since his one-night stand with Chloe and he couldn't stop thinking about her. She'd left the next morning while he was still asleep, which usually sent a pretty clear message. But then he'd found her number scribbled on the notepad with her name below it.

Relationships weren't really Nate's thing. He used sex as a distraction. A form of self-therapy to keep him level. One-nighters and casual encounters with no strings attached got the job done. He hadn't even gotten Chloe's last name and that's how he liked it. Hell, he wouldn't have needed her first name to have fucked her that night. They'd had a good time, parted ways, and that should have been the end of it. Chloe was different, though. Her confidence, her brazen passion, and the fact that she was unashamed of wanting pleasure heated Nate's blood. He'd violate his one-time rule for her. He had to have her again.

Nate grabbed his cell from the bedside table and dialed her number.

"Thank you for calling the Youth Sports Foundation of Dallas. How may I direct your call?"

He pulled the phone away from his ear and compared the number to the one scribbled on the hotel notepad. "Is Chloe there?"

A pregnant pause answered. "Can I tell her who's calling?"

"Nate Christensen."

"Oh!" The receptionist's tone perked up instantly. "Just a moment please."

Her reaction was one of the reasons why he hated giving out his full name to people. He was immediately connected to his family's—well, his dad's—money and clout. Even in basic, they'd gone easy on him. Until Nate developed an attitude that gave the drill instructors no

choice but to go even harder on him. Some frilly top 40
hit played through the receiver as he waited.

"This is Chloe Benson."

Nate found himself smiling at her professional tone.
As though she didn't know who was on the other line
and the dirty things he'd whispered in her ear only a
couple of days ago. "I want to see you."

"I'm sorry, who is this?"

He heard the smile in her voice and it stirred something in his chest, not to mention his cock. "You know
who this is. I want to see you. Today."

"I don't know . . ." she said wistfully. "Usually when
a guy waits longer than a day to call me, I write him off.
I've got a pretty full schedule today."

"So do I," he said. "Doesn't mean I'm not willing to
move a few things around. I'll order room service."

"Oh, will you? You think that's enough to get me to
come over?"

"No," he said simply. "You'll do it because of the way
your body trembles when I make you come."

She let out a rush of breath and that whisper of sound
was enough to make Nate hard as stone.

"Eight o'clock." She cleared the breathiness from her
voice. "I have a late meeting tonight."

Before Nate could respond, she hung up. He tossed
his cell to the mattress beside him. He'd dreaded the trip
to Dallas. Didn't know how he'd get through the next
couple of weeks. But thanks to his feisty little eavesdrop-
per, there was a light at the end of his very bleak tunnel.

His? Not even close. But maybe he could make her
his for a few days at least.

A knock came at the door and Nate took stock of
what was going on down south before he made the decision to answer the door. He wasn't interested in dealing with company while his cock was flying at full mast.

He opened the door to find Carter waiting in the hallway, his shoulder propped against the wall. "Jesus, you're just now getting up?" Without waiting for an answer he plowed into the room leaving Nate to stare after him. "We're meeting with the lawyers in a half hour."

"I told you, you don't have to go. I can handle it." Christ, did everyone in the family think he was incompetent? "Where are the girls?"

"Babysitter. And I know I don't have to go. I want to go. If anything to convince you not to hand off the money you *deserve* to a deceitful viper who'll be moving on to her next seventy-year-old fat cat before the year is up."

Nate snorted. "If I'd wanted this life, I would have gotten my MBA."

"You wanted what we all wanted, to get the hell away from *him*. The business has nothing to do with it."

Nate didn't know the first thing about being an oil magnate. Their dad had coveted his company. Put it before his wife, his kids, *everything.* Byron hadn't wanted his sons to go into the family business. He'd wanted them to go out and make their own fortunes and to keep their hands off of his. "Honestly, I still can't believe he left us any of it."

Carter laughed. "Who the hell else was he going to give it to? Miranda?"

Nate shrugged. "I don't want this life. I like my house. Where I live and what I'm doing."

"You don't have to live the life to take the money," Carter said. "Why don't you wait to hear what the lawyers and the board of directors have to say before you start handing out checks?"

Nate stretched his neck from side to side. Eight o'clock was a long damned time away. He didn't know if he'd make it without blowing off some steam. "Yeah. All right." He could placate Carter for now. But his mind was made up. He doubted any of them would be able to change it.

"Good. Now get dressed. We're late."

❄   ❄   ❄

"You must have made an impression."

Chloe looked up to find her assistant Hailey smiling at her. "It took him two days to call. Somehow, I don't think that falls under making an impression."

"He called. It doesn't matter how long it took. You'll have a big fat check in your hands in no time."

Chloe doubted that. She'd showed up at Byron Christensen's ritzy memorial service in the hopes of beating the rush of people bound to show up at Nate's door with their hands out. She'd had a game plan: Find a way to introduce herself. Make a case for the foundation. And pray to god that Nate's generosity and compassion outweighed his father's. Instead, she'd fallen into bed with him.

"This is a disaster."

Hailey clucked her tongue at Chloe. "Rome wasn't built in a day."

"Was it built in a couple of weeks?"

How could Nate possibly take her seriously now that they'd slept together? How could she even broach the subject of the foundation with him? At best, she'd come off as a slimy opportunist. At worst, a high-priced hooker.

"You've already managed to secure a hundred thousand dollars, Chloe. That's not small potatoes."

"A hundred thousand might as well be a hundred bucks in comparison to what we need."

"This is a pessimism-free zone. Your rules, not mine. That sort of talk isn't allowed."

It was true that Chloe encouraged positivity at the office. They dealt with at-risk kids who grew up with next to nothing and a good attitude was essential for doing their jobs. It was tough to keep her head up though, especially when the future of the foundation was so bleak. She had a couple of weeks left to raise three million dollars in operating funds. It took a fortune to keep their heads above water, and they'd lost the support of several benefactors over the past year. The foundation was Chloe's baby. A chance for her to do some good in the world. Giving an opportunity to these kids, providing coaches, and facilities, and equipment—making their lives carefree if even for a moment—meant the world to her. She'd do anything to save the foundation.

Including sleeping with Nate Christensen? What a nightmare.

Only . . . it *wasn't*. Nate had been on her mind to the point of distraction since their night together. Her blood heated with the memories and chills broke out on her flesh every time she thought about the dirty things he'd whispered in her ear. His intensity drove her crazy and it made her wonder what it would take to break through his tough exterior and really get to know the man inside.

"Heeelllooo? Earth to Chloe . . . ?"

She shook herself from her reverie to find Hailey studying her with a knowing smirk.

"Whatcha thinkin' about?" Hailey asked in a sing-song voice.

"Nothing. Money. And whether or not a bank heist is an option."

"Oh, you're thinking about money all right. But more to the point, I think you're thinking about a certain new-moneyed Dallas hottie." Was it that obvious? Chloe swallowed down a groan. "And I bet he's thinking about you, too."

Chloe's cheeks flushed. "Why would you say that?"

"He was confused when I answered the phone," Hailey said. "Like he wasn't expecting to get a business. And he asked for Chloe. Not Miss Benson, not Chloe Benson. Hardly professional."

She hadn't given him her last name. God, she was an idiot. A horny, sex-starved fool. "We didn't get a chance to talk much." Oh, they talked all right. Just not about the foundation. "It was his dad's memorial service. I got cold feet mid-ambush."

"You're seeing him again, though. That's why he called, right?"

Somehow, Chloe doubted they'd be discussing business in his hotel room tonight. "Yeah, we're meeting at eight."

"So, put your people skills to work and talk that boy out of his millions!" Hailey exclaimed. "You can't give up now, Chloe. This foundation means so much to so many people. Just go for it."

That was the problem. She'd gone for it and then some. "In case I don't show up in the morning with a big fat check, can you make a few more cold calls today? I heard that the Blackwell Foundation might be looking to expand their charitable ventures."

"Will do." Hailey pulled out her tablet and scribbled something on the screen with the stylus. "I have a couple more leads I haven't explored yet, too. None of them are whales, but I bet I could shake them down for ten thousand apiece."

"Sure. That's a good idea."

"Hey," Hailey said at Chloe's downtrodden tone. "Every little bit helps."

"It does." She gave Hailey her best optimistic smile. "And I appreciate everything you're doing."

"You can thank me when we're back on our feet," Hailey said. "I expect a huge gala and a gold trophy."

"I don't know about the gala," Chloe said. "But you're *so* getting that trophy."

"With rhinestones," Hailey added. "Now, stop day-dreaming about Nate Christensen and get to work." She gave Chloe a wink in parting and closed the office door behind her.

Chloe slumped down in her chair and stared blindly at her computer screen. How could she possibly bring up the foundation with Nate now? Any attempt to plead her case for a sizeable donation would come across as sleazy. She'd never planned to sleep with him. She couldn't change what had happened, though, and it was going to happen again. Nate was a force of nature. She had no choice but to be caught up in the storm.

With any luck, Hailey would be able to secure some real, solid funding today and Chloe wouldn't have to worry about Nate's money and what it could do for her struggling foundation. She checked the clock on the bottom of her screen. In less than ten hours, she'd be back in his hotel room and too mindless to think straight. Chloe rolled her shoulders and opened the Excel file with her list of possible contributors. Without thinking, she picked a random name from her list, picked up the phone, and dialed.

"Hi, this is Chloe Benson from the Youth Sports Foundation of Dallas. Is Mr. St. Claire available this morning?"

Chloe waited as the receptionist put her on hold. *Think positive thoughts.* With any luck, this wouldn't be the bitch of a day she expected it to be, fraught with disappointment. Otherwise, she'd be begging Nate for a handout whether she wanted to or not.

FIVE

Ten minutes to eight and Nate was about to crawl out of his fucking skin. His day had been every bit as shitty as he'd anticipated with the lawyers, his dad's stuffy board of directors, and even his own damned brothers making their cases for why Nate needed to stick around and not renounce his inheritance.

Nate had been given controlling interest in Christensen Petroleum in his father's will. Talk about a kick in the nuts. His anxiety was beginning to crest—never a good sign—and if he had to sit in this goddamned closet of a room alone with his thoughts for another second, he was going to start smashing the furniture.

On the plus side, you now have the money to pay for the damages.

The soft knock at the door five minutes later became his lifeline. Knowing Chloe was on the other side of that door made him instantly hard. He rushed to the door and threw it wide. Before she could even say hello, he grabbed her by the wrist and hauled her against him, kissing her as though his life depended on it. His sanity sure as hell did. The door slammed closed behind them and Nate didn't waste any time. He gripped the hem of her skirt and jerked it up around her waist. On his way down, he shoved her underwear over her thighs and tossed them to the floor behind him. The buttons on her dress shirt posed a problem; he couldn't focus on undoing them while his mouth was busy devouring hers, but he eventually got them open and jerked the cup of her bra aside, covering the stiff peak of her breast with his lips as he nibbled at the hardened flesh.

Words had no place in their frenzy. Chloe tore at the button on his pants and shimmied them off, along with his underwear. Nate cupped her ass in his palms and lifted her up until she wrapped her legs around his waist. Their lips tangled in a slippery dance as they bounced down the narrow corridor from the door toward the bed, pausing only long enough for Nate to grab a condom off the dresser. Chloe slid down the length of his body and planted her feet on the floor, her emerald gaze sparking with passion as she watched Nate roll on the condom. He grabbed her around the neck and pulled her in for a ravenous kiss before hoisting her up again and bracing her body against the wall.

Her thighs glistened with arousal and Nate let out an impassioned growl as he entered her. She gasped at the intrusion, her gaze liquid as she kept it focused on his. He thrust hard and fast, pounding into her with every ounce of frustration that had built within him over the course of the day. Chloe's breath came in quick little pants but that wasn't good enough for Nate. He wanted to *hear* her. Wanted those sweet cries that he'd missed so much to echo off every wall.

"I want to hear you, Chloe." He thrust harder. Her nails dug into his shoulder as she whimpered. God, yes. That was it. "Again."

Her lips parted on a moan. God, she was so wet, so tight, so damned responsive. Nate's fingertips squeezed into the roundness of her ass that fit so well in his palms. Chloe's head rolled back on her shoulders. She arched into his hips, and his gaze was drawn to her full breasts that bounced with every deep thrust.

"Nate," she said on a sharp intake of breath. "Oh, god, Nate. I'm going to come."

He slowed his pace but continued to thrust deep. He didn't want to push her, but rather wanted her to drift gently off the edge. He knew it would make her orgasm more intense and that's what he needed from her, that intensity that matched his own. That unshakeable focus that kept them locked together in the moment.

"Faster, Nate. Harder. Please."

"No. Trust me, Chloe. I'm going to give you what you need."

Her moans bordered on desperate frustration, but Nate continued to pull out and drive home hard with slow precision. Her eyes grew wide as her pussy clenched around him. She cried out, deep, wracking sobs of pleasure that vibrated down Nate's spine and tightened his sac. Just a few more strokes and he'd be right there with her. Each contraction of her orgasm pulsed against his cock and when Chloe tilted her hips and tightened her thighs around him, it squeezed the head with the perfect amount of pressure. Nate cradled her ass in one hand and braced the other palm against the wall as he came, his hips jerking in time with every intense pulse of his cock. "Ah, fuck, Chloe!" he shouted. "You feel so good. God, that feels so good."

As the orgasm ebbed, Nate's thighs began to quake. He touched his forehead to Chloe's and let his eyes drift shut. A sense of peace crested over him, a calmness that he hadn't felt in a long goddamned time. She stroked the

back of his neck, the light scrape of her nails on his nape
coaxing chills to the surface of his skin. Nate's gut
twisted into a knot. He'd dragged her through the door
and fucked her without even a hello. His need for her
bordered on desperate and he didn't even really know
Chloe. All it took to lose himself to her was a couple of
sexual encounters and a single casual conversation.

Did Chloe help to fill the empty void that ached like
a sucking chest wound, or had he simply traded one dysfunction for another? It's not like he was in any sort of
mental or emotional condition to have a relationship with
anyone. So far, the extent of their time together had been
spent fucking. Not that he was complaining. Chloe was
amazing.

When Nate felt confident that he could take a step
without dropping the precious cargo in his arms, he
turned and carried Chloe to the bed. She wrapped her
arms around him, the soft caress of her breasts on his
chest a delicious torture that did nothing to cool Nate's
lust. He set her down on the mattress as though she
might break. Sort of laughable considering the fact he'd
nearly pounded her right through the drywall moments
ago. Chloe stared up at him, a wry smile playing on her
full lips. A rush of electric heat shot through him. He
wanted her again. Now. God, he was an asshole.

"I'll be right back." He placed a quick kiss to her forehead before hiking his pants up on his hips, and headed
to the bathroom to clean up.

Nate emerged in nothing but his boxer briefs. Chloe
had shed her skirt and wore only the white dress shirt.
She'd fastened the two middle buttons, leaving both the
swell of her breasts and her belly button exposed to his
gaze. The shirt flared out around her hips and painted
an erotic portrait that stalled his breath. Her auburn hair
framed her face in a tangle and when she looked up from

the room service menu and smiled, Nate's heart clenched in his chest.

Beautiful.

"I recall someone promising me room service if I showed up here tonight," Chloe remarked.

"I did," he said with a smile. "I guess it's time for me to pony up."

A shadow darkened her expression and he could have kicked himself for his choice of words. "Not that I have to pay you for anything. I mean . . ." *Way to stuff your foot in your mouth, asshole.*

"I know what you mean." Chloe's smile brightened and again that tightening of Nate's chest returned. "Are you hungry? I skipped lunch."

Unfortunately, he'd been wined and dined by a handful of his father's former minions who all had their heads up their asses. "I can eat." Nate never said no to food.

Chloe looked up at him from lowered lashes. "Worked up an appetite, huh?"

Hell, she tied him into knots. "I did," he replied. "And I plan on burning a hell of a lot more calories before the night is over."

❄   ❄   ❄

Chloe's cheeks flushed at the innuendo. The sight of Nate, wearing nothing more than his boxer briefs was enough to convince her that there were more important things in life than food. In any other circumstance, she would have been embarrassed at the way she'd thrown herself at him without even a "Hey, how are ya?" before she'd let him strip off her underwear and pound into her as though she'd die if he didn't take her right then and there.

He'd wanted her with the same mindless disregard, though. How could she feel embarrassed or ashamed when what had happened between them was mutual? Chloe wanted Nate. Couldn't get him out of her head. It didn't matter that she knew almost nothing about him. She wanted to live in the moment with him.

Nate settled down on the bed beside her and leaned over the room service menu. Every nerve ending in Chloe's body sparked with an awareness of him. His clean, masculine scent invaded her senses and the heat of his body infused her own skin with warmth. She thought back to their first night together and his breath hot in her ear as he'd said, "You smell like sex and honey." Chloe shuddered as a riot of butterflies swirled in her stomach.

"Are you cold?" Nate's arm came around her and he tucked her close to his body.

She was anything but cold. Her body was close to combustion. As they studied the menu in silence, she relaxed against him, loving the way his broad, muscular chest supported her. Nate's arm draped over her shoulder, his hand dangling over her breast. He idly caressed her, feather-light flicks of his fingertips that brushed her nipple through the crisp fabric of her shirt. Chloe sucked in a breath at the intensity of sensation and her pussy clenched as a rush of wetness spread between her bare thighs.

If he kept touching her like that, food was going to have to take a backseat to another hunger. A sigh slipped from between her lips and Nate changed up his tactics, plucking at the hardened peak through her shirt. Chloe's clit began to pulse in time with every gentle pull. *Dear god*. He made her absolutely *mindless*.

Her sighs transformed into shallow pants. The words on the menu became nothing more than jumbled symbols as she lost focus of everything but the tingle of sensation spreading through her body. Nate's free hand slid under her shirt and cupped her other breast. He took her in his palm, massaged her with slow pumps of his hand before he began to tease that nipple as well. Chloe's abdomen tightened and she squirmed on the mattress. She rubbed her legs together to find that her thighs were already slick and coated with her arousal.

She turned to face Nate to find him studying her with that same intensity that stole her breath. "I could watch you for hours," he said, his voice strained. "God, Chloe. The way you look when you feel good."

Her lips parted. She meant to respond to him, but all she could manage was a throaty moan. Nate shifted, rolling over her and coming to rest on his knees between her legs. He grabbed Chloe by the thighs and pulled her down until she was laid out on the bed. His gaze burned as he scooted down until his hips and legs dangled off the edge of the bed. Chloe's knees fell open and Nate's breath brushed her heated and sensitive skin.

"What about dinner?" Her voice went husky and thick.

"The only thing I'm hungry for right now is your pussy, Chloe."

Holy crap. The things he said to her. Chloe's stomach did a backflip, lodging itself in her throat before floating down on a cloud of sheer bliss. He dragged the flat of his tongue from her opening and ended on a flick at the tip of her clit. Her back bowed off the bed and her thighs quivered. "Nate!" His name left her lips in a breathy rush. "That feels so good."

He angled her hips up toward his mouth. The pressure of his fingertips indenting the flesh as he held onto her hips only pushed Chloe further toward the edge. He held her with purpose; every swirl, every pass of his tongue carefully orchestrated to give her the greatest amount of pleasure. Nate took her clit between his lips and sucked. Chloe's thighs tightened on either side of his head and she trembled. He reached to her thighs and spread them wide, holding her open to him. He refused to let her move, pinning her down with his mouth and his hands. Her breath came in wild pants as she tried to control her spiraling world. She knew that Nate didn't want her to be controlled or quiet. He wanted wild shouts and reckless abandon.

"Oh god." Chloe thrashed her head from side to side. She was helpless to do anything but feel and Nate brought her to the cusp of release with every slow, methodical pass of his tongue. "Ohgod ohgod ohgod . . ." A cry that was half pleasure, half frustration built in her chest. "I want to come, Nate. I need to. I want you inside of me."

"No." The word vibrated over her clit and she shuddered. "I want you to come on my tongue."

His words were the final push. Chloe toppled over the edge and Nate buried his face between her thighs, lapping unmercifully at her pussy as she came. He held her legs wide and every inch of her body quaked violently as wave after wave of intense sensation stole over her. Chloe cried out, deep sobs of pleasure that left her throat raw and dry. The orgasm seemed to go on forever, a violent storm of passion and sensation that left her weak and shaking.

Nate brought her down slowly, soft easy passes of his tongue that were goddamned luxurious. Chloe's body went boneless. She wouldn't have been able to move if she'd wanted to. "I think it's your turn," she murmured on a deep sigh. The thought of taking Nate into her mouth stirred her flagging desire.

He kissed the inside of her thigh, downward to her

knees. His kisses brushed the side of her knee and Chloe squirmed. "That tickles."

Nate smiled against her skin. "Oh yeah? Next time I might have to find where else you're ticklish."

"Nope. I said it's your turn." She wasn't about to *not* reciprocate. Not after he'd given her one of the best orgasms of her life.

"Later." He continued to kiss her. Warm, wet passes of his mouth.

She guided his head up to look at her. "Later?"

"Yep." A slow smile grew on his full lips, and Chloe's breath stalled as she realized she'd never seen him give a genuine, open smile before. Magnificent. "If I'm going to fuck you all night, I need to fuel up."

Dear lord. Nate Christensen was going to be the death of her.

SIX

"So, I'm assuming you don't live in Dallas."

Nate couldn't take his eyes off of her. He'd never met anyone like Chloe. His intensity had a tendency to scare people away. But she responded to it. Matched it, even.

"No. I live in Sanger. It's a couple of hours away."

"I've never been there, but I'm familiar. What does a newly moneyed billionaire do in a tiny town like Sanger?"

Nate took a bite of his cheeseburger and chewed. "Run cows," he responded before washing it all down with a swig of soda.

"Really?" Chloe smiled. Blinding and brilliant as the sun. "You're a cowboy?"

"Sort of," Nate said with a snort. "Trying anyway. My ranch isn't big. And I'm not a billionaire," he said as an afterthought.

"Okay, a multimillionaire?"

He pursed his lips. "I won't be that either, if I get my way."

Chloe's brows knitted. She swirled a fry around in her ketchup before popping it in her mouth. She'd devoured most of her BLT already. He wasn't the only one who'd needed to tank up. "Is it true that you joined the Navy to get away from your dad?"

Nate cocked a brow. "Doing your homework on me, Miss Benson?"

She averted her gaze and shrugged. "People talk."

"Only in certain circles."

"With my line of work, I have a tendency to butt into those circles."

Nate laughed. Chloe certainly wasn't the sort of woman who tiptoed into any situation. "Tell me about your work." He knew he shouldn't go there. It would be best to keep their relationship impersonal. Sex and nothing else. He wasn't interested in settling down and sooner or later, the high of being with Chloe would wear off and he'd move on. Curiosity won out over good sense, though. She intrigued him. How could he not want to know more about her?

"There's not much to tell." Chloe's demeanor changed. Her gaze wandered, no longer focused on him and she picked at her sandwich as though looking for a distraction. "I started working for the Make-A-Wish Foundation right out of college. It was great, but I wanted more control. The work was rewarding, but *hard*. So much sadness. I wanted to make kids' lives better, but I wanted to shift my focus to underprivileged and at-risk kids. Sports were always a really big part of my life growing up and I wanted to share that with kids who might not know how good it feels to be an athlete. So I rounded up a few donations and started my own organization. We've kept it local so far. It takes a lot of money to keep a charity afloat. I'd like to branch out eventually. Go national. Or global. This isn't about recognition for me. I just want to make the kids' lives better in any way that I can."

"Sounds like a sweet gig," Nate remarked. "Doing what you love."

She gave him a soft smile. "The foundation means everything to me."

They ate in silence for a few minutes. Nate was too wrapped up in his own head—to preoccupied with Chloe—to talk. Unlike Nate, her passions ranged far and wide. Her intensity in the bedroom didn't come from a need to quiet her mind and live strictly in the moment. She had a passion for life. For her job. And that fire translated into the way she kissed, touched, fucked. Nate envied that fire. On his best days all he felt was a gnawing desperation and numbness that he couldn't escape. He hadn't loved anything—or anyone—in a long damned time.

"How about you, Nate?" Chloe's soft voice pulled him from his thoughts. "What gets a soon-to-be nonbillionaire fired up?"

"You," he replied without guile.

Chloe's cheeks flushed. Damn, he loved the way she looked. "I'm serious."

"So am I."

"Did you love the Navy?"

Nate's gut knotted up. He'd started this. Drawn her into conversation to learn something about her. Now he was agitated that she wanted to know more about him? "I loved the challenge," he said after a while. "The excitement. And the thought that I was serving a greater good and protecting people. The SEALs were my family for six years."

Chloe studied him. Her green eyes were round and

wide. Her kind, caring expression damned near gutted him. "Why did you leave?"

Nate swallowed against the golf-ball-sized lump that rose in his throat. "I could have reenlisted," he said. "But I lost two team members and an asset during an extraction mission. Nothing was the same after that, so I got out."

"I'm so sorry, Nate." He didn't want her pity. Couldn't stand the compassion shining in her beautiful eyes.

"Don't be." He immediately regretted the harshness of his response. "It comes with the job."

The last time someone asked about his time with the SEALs, Nate had answered with a resounding, "Fuck off." Chloe wasn't just some curious asshole who thought the job was one big action movie. He sensed her sincerity. The lump in his throat grew bigger. *Goddamn it.*

"I can't imagine what it's like to lose someone in that situation. You prepare for it, sure. But when it happens, it still blindsides you."

Exactly. Jesus, she understood him like very few people did. "It does."

"I used to see it a lot. The families that came to Make-A-Wish—they were at the end of the line. They knew what to expect. They'd spent months, sometimes years preparing but when they lost their child, it was always a shock. It still hurt."

Nick rubbed at his sternum. The familiar anxiety slowly crept up on him, tightening his chest and constricting his airway. His ears rang and his heart pounded. If he didn't get some air, he was going to throw up. Or pass the hell out.

He shot up out of his chair with enough force to send it toppling to the floor behind him. He didn't look at Chloe—couldn't—as he rushed past her and threw open the sliding glass door that led to the balcony. He gripped the back of his neck and laced his fingers together as he took several deep, cleansing breaths. There wasn't enough fucking oxygen in the world to clear his head. His world was slowly unraveling.

"Nate?" Chloe's voice caressed his ears, so gentle it speared his heart.

"I need a second." What a way to make an impression.

"It's an anxiety attack. It'll pass."

"I know it will." Snapping at her wasn't going to help anything. She was trying to help, for shit's sake.

"Come inside. I'll help you take your mind off of it."

Nate let his head drop between his shoulders. She could see right through him, couldn't she? Two nights together and Chloe had his number. Knew why she was here and what he was using her for. Shame welled hot in Nate's throat. He was a son of a bitch for allowing this to happen in the first place. And he was a low-life bastard because he was going to go back in that room and fuck her again. Fuck her until his brain and body were too spent for anything else. In letting Chloe distract him from his past, Nate feared that he was developing a far more debilitating addiction. Because after tonight, he didn't think he'd be able to let her go.

❋   ❋   ❋

Chloe should have never broached the subject of his enlistment. She knew better than to open festering wounds. Had dealt with countless families who lived with grief, loss, and helplessness on a daily basis. The more they talked, the wilder Nate's expression had become. Like an animal caught in a snare with no other choice but to chew its own leg off or die. She'd pushed him too far.

She reached up and wrapped her fingers around his elbow. He wouldn't let her coax him to relax his grip. His hands were locked behind his neck, the knuckles turning white. Tense didn't begin to describe the way his muscles bunched at his back, fanning out from the solid wings at either side of his torso and tapering down to his narrow waist. He wouldn't budge and so Chloe changed her tactics, stepping behind him to lay her palms to the muscles she'd just been studying.

She'd ease his anxiety and tension whether he wanted her to or not. It was going to take more than a pit bull expression and a few barked words to scare her off.

Chloe reached out and gripped the mounds of muscle that rounded his shoulders. She massaged in slow circles with the pads of her thumbs, kneading every individual knot until she felt them loosen. Nate let out a slow breath and his hands relaxed their grip a fraction of an inch. Downward, she traced each vertebra until she got to the small of his back where it met the gentle swoop of his ass. So much power in his body. He exuded strength. The man could have been cut from marble.

Outward to his torso, Chloe focused her efforts on his laterals, pressing with the pad of her thumb and allowing her fingertips to splay out over his ribs. Nate's breathing grew deeper, more even, though he refused to release his grip on the back of his neck. For almost a half hour, Chloe continued. Over his shoulders, down his spine, up the sides of his torso, and then she started again. When he finally unlaced his fingers and let his arms drop, Chloe knew he'd finally calmed down.

She rose up on her tiptoes and spoke close to his ear, "Let's go inside, Nate."

Without a word he turned and followed her back into the room. She grabbed his hand and led him to the bed. "Lie down."

Again, as though he had no choice but to do as she said, he eased himself down onto the mattress. Chloe knelt down beside him and began to massage the solid muscles of his arms and across his chest. "It's okay to freak out, Nate." He let his eyes drift shut but she knew he was listening. "No one could go through that and just brush it off. You can't beat yourself up for it, either. It's okay to *feel*. And you don't ever have to be embarrassed about it. Especially with me."

His body relaxed into the mattress and Chloe soothed him with gentle touches and smooth passes of her palms, interspersed with harder concentrations of her thumbs and fingertips. His breathing grew more even and the deep furrow that marred his brow eased until he no longer appeared distressed. She thought that maybe Nate had fallen asleep until his hands reached out to grip her wrists.

Chloe paused and her heart began a wild rhythm in her chest.

Nate's eyes opened, the intense hazel depths boring straight through her. Her breath caught as he sat up. He released his hold on her wrists and unbuttoned her shirt before dragging it down her shoulders. Chloe shrugged it the rest of the way off and it fell to the floor with a rustle of fabric. Nate reached up and cupped her cheek as he brought her mouth slowly to his. The kiss was slow, sensual. A lazy caress that drew Chloe's stomach tight and caused her blood to race through her veins. When he pulled away, Nate simply stared for a long moment before pulling Chloe down beside him on the bed. He tucked her body against his and the heat from his chest nearly burned against her back. A long, exhausted sigh escaped from between his lips. Nate wrapped his arms around her, hugging Chloe tight to him as though he was afraid she might try to get away.

Long, quiet moments passed and Chloe listened to the sound of Nate's breathing as it transformed from short little clips to long, easy pulls of air. His arms relaxed around her as sleep overtook him. Chloe wished she could find the calm necessary to sleep but her heartbeat refused to slow as it pounded in her chest.

Her fingers drew a lazy pattern on the muscled length of his forearm as she stared off at some unknown point on the opposite wall. Whatever this was between her and Nate, she suspected that they'd just crossed into territory from which there was no return. And she wasn't entirely sure if it thrilled her, or scared her to death.

SEVEN

When Nate woke, Chloe's body was still tucked tight against him, her arms wound with his as she hugged him to her. It had been a long goddamned time since Nate had felt any kind of peace. Hell, he couldn't remember the last time he'd fallen asleep next to a woman without having exhausted himself first with sex. That's not to say she hadn't relaxed him. Her full-body massage had left him feeling downright boneless. After one motherfucker of a panic attack, he'd expected her to tuck tail and run. But Chloe was made of sterner stuff. She'd eased every ounce of tension, cleared his mind without the need to fuck those horrible thoughts out of his brain. Instead of tripping into a fitful sleep, he'd fallen on a cloud into a dreamless void.

The stillness and quiet of last night was worth more than tens of billions of dollars.

Nate smoothed the hair away from Chloe's face and kissed her temple. She stirred in his arms, a sleepy smile tugging at her lips. "What time is it?"

He leaned up on an elbow to check the digital clock. "Seven-thirty."

Chloe groaned. God, he loved that sound. Hell, she'd probably sound adorable grunting and wheezing after a twenty-mile run. There wasn't anything about her that Nate didn't like. They barely knew each other, but Nate found himself wanting to learn more about her. This wasn't about only sex anymore. Last night had proved that. The spark he felt for this woman went far beyond a simple physical attraction.

"I need to get ready for work." Her eyes were still closed and she didn't even try to get out of bed. "I have a meeting at nine with our board and—"

"Skip it," Nate said. The thought of her leaving for even a second made his stomach want to heave.

"I can't." Chloe turned in his embrace as her eyes slowly opened. The smile she gave him made the sun seem dull in comparison. "Good morning."

He lowered his mouth to hers for a quick kiss. "Good morning."

"I've already put this meeting off twice. No more skipping out for me. Plus, I promised Derrick that I'd take him out for lunch."

Nate played with the silky strands of her hair, loving the way it felt when it slipped through his fingers. "Derrick?" He couldn't do anything to keep the possessiveness from his tone. Who in the hell was Derrick?

Chloe bestowed him with a wry smile. "Jealous?"

The hairs at the back of Nate's neck prickled. Something was up. Her demeanor changed in an instant, her body no longer soft and pliant against his, but tense. It could have been work stress. Hell, for all he knew, that sense that she was keeping something from him was his own damned paranoia.

"Maybe."

She gave a nervous laugh which did nothing for the tension that pulled his muscles taut. "Derrick is one of the kids in our program. He's sort of my pet project. He's bounced around between too many foster homes to count and he works the system better than any kid I've ever seen. I try to keep an eye out for him because even soccer can't keep him completely out of trouble."

"Ah." Nate wondered at the relief that flooded his body. "Lucky kid. I bet you're good for him, though. You've done a pretty good job of keeping me in line so far." Chloe flushed and it made Nate want to say something else, something far dirtier to coax that color to her cheeks. "When will you be free?"

"Hmm. Probably after six or seven. What about you? Don't you have another full day of lawyers and yes-men kissing your newly moneyed ass?"

"Unfortunately." Nate was more than ready to have this business of his father's estate over and done with. Miranda was champing at the bit, more than ready to take ownership of the company's controlling stock and the money that had been Nate's share of his father's legacy.

"Nate, can I ask you something?"

Chloe faced him once again. She worried her bottom lip between her teeth. Was there anything she did that wasn't goddamned adorable? The uncertainty in her voice gave him pause, though.

"Sure. Ask away."

"Why do you want to get rid of this money so badly?" Her brows drew down over her brilliant eyes. "Did you ever consider that your father was trying to patch things up with his sons by leaving everything to you and your brothers?"

Nate had never really given it much thought. He'd

spent so many years being mad at his father that he'd never bothered with whether or not his father felt bad about what had happened between them. "I guess I figured that he was rubbing my nose in it. Like he knew I'd never make anything out of myself and so he had no choice but to leave it me. To save the family name or some shit."

Chloe reached up and cupped his cheek. Nate fought the urge to close his eyes and fall into that comfort she gave him without even trying. "No one is saying that you have to trade in your jeans for three-piece suits and move to Dallas. And I'm sure you don't have to quit running cows in exchange for long days at the office. I just think that if you sign your inheritance away, you'll regret it. Once it's done, you can't take it back, Nate."

"You sound like my brothers," he said with a snort.

Chloe smiled. "I'm sure they're all extremely intelligent and equally wise."

"What if I don't want to be Byron Christensen's son?" The familiar lump rose to Nate's throat and he swallowed it down.

"I hate to break it to you, Nate, but even if you give every dime of that money away, *nothing* is going to change the fact that you're his son."

"I didn't tell him when I came home." Admitting it to Chloe lifted a huge weight from his shoulders and at the same time, filled him with shame. "After I was discharged, I moved to Sanger. A couple of hours away, and he never knew it. I probably don't deserve that money. I wasn't any better of a son than he was a father."

"Nate." The sadness in Chloe's tone sliced through him. He wouldn't have been able to stand her pity, but this was something else. Empathy. "No one's perfect. That doesn't mean we're not deserving."

He didn't say another word. Couldn't. His own emotions would get the best of him if he opened his mouth. Instead, he lay his head back on the pillow and tucked her body into his. For long, quiet moments they lay in silence. When Nate could finally trust himself to speak, he said, "I'm headed home tomorrow. I want you to go with me."

❄   ❄   ❄

"I'm headed home tomorrow. I want you to go with me."

Chloe stared at her computer screen, the numbers on the spreadsheet nothing more than jumbled symbols. Nate's words had been running a loop through her head all day to the point of distraction. As well as the response she'd given him without an ounce of thought: "Yes."

What had she been thinking? What had started out as a ploy to convince him to help bail out her foundation turned into something that Chloe had no control over. And though she still needed his money like a drowning person needed a lifeline, her motive in convincing him to keep his inheritance was no longer selfish. She'd meant what she'd said: turning his back on his father's legacy would be a decision that would haunt him.

"Hey, you okay?" Hailey poked her head into Chloe's office and leaned against the doorjamb. "That was one bitch of a board meeting."

Understatement. The board meeting had been catastrophic. "Nothing like being told your number is up," Chloe replied. "I'd rather have all of my teeth pulled—without anesthesia—than tell these kids that their clubs and programs are going away. We've kept them motivated. Out of trouble. All of that is going to end. They're so used to disappointment. I never wanted to be just another person to let them down."

Hailey sighed. "You won't have to do any of this alone. I'm here 'til the bitter end."

Chloe gave her a rueful smile. "I'll give you a glowing recommendation wherever you apply. You'll find a job in no time."

"Oh, I know." Hailey brushed a hand down the length of her body. "All this and a killer set of grant facilitation skills . . . puhleaze."

Chloe snorted. She hoped she'd be able to find a job as easily. Otherwise she'd be living off of tap water and saltines. "I'm thinking about taking a few days off . . ." Thinking? She'd already told Nate she'd go home with him. "Would you mind holding down the fort until Monday?"

"I think I can manage this asylum without you," Hailey remarked. "So . . . whatcha doin'?"

"Nateaskedmetogohomewithhim," Chloe said on a whisper of breath.

"What was that?" Hailey leaned in, a wry smile tugging at her lips. "You sort of mumbled that last bit."

Chloe took a deep breath. "Nate asked me to go home with him."

"Get out!" Hailey exclaimed with wide eyes. "You're gonna kick it with the Billion Dollar Man? At *his* request? For five days? Chloe, this is freaking perfect!"

"No." Chloe held up her hand. "That ship has sailed, Hailey."

"Are you kidding me?" Hailey rolled her eyes. She stepped fully into Chloe's office and shut the door. "Okay, I can see how you didn't want to hit him up when you thought it was a one-night stand because you didn't want him to think you'd slept with him to get a fat donation in return. But this is different. He's into you, Chloe. Do you think he invites any random chick to his house?"

Chloe hadn't really considered it. Obviously something had changed between them last night. Her heart had ached for Nate. Seeing him in such distress and not knowing how to help him was the worst feeling in the world. He was such a strong man. So gruff and serious. Every smile he let slip was a treasure, every deep rumble of laughter a treat to Chloe's ears. His vulnerability had laid her low. Stabbed through her chest. She'd done the only thing she could when she'd reached out to caress the tension from his muscles. And she'd expected the subsequent massage to end up in another round of mind-blowing sex. Instead, he'd cradled her in his arms as though she was a breakable, precious thing that he couldn't bear to be parted from and fallen asleep beside her.

Chloe rubbed at her chest. God, just thinking about Nate made her *ache*.

"I don't know what this is or isn't between us. But until I do, I can't ruin it by making him think that I'm in it for the money."

Hailey pursed her lips. "You must be crazy about this guy, Chloe."

"Why do you say that?"

"Because I know how much you love this foundation and you're willing to sacrifice it for something that might crash and burn before it even gets off the ground."

Chloe stared at Hailey. A denial sat at the tip of her tongue but it refused to take form. Was she willing to sacrifice the foundation—something she'd poured her heart, soul, hell her *life* into—for five days with Nate that might end up being nothing more than a fling?

When she'd told Nate to keep the money and his

shares in Christensen Petroleum, it hadn't been the result of some selfish machination. In fact, the foundation and her own problems hadn't even entered her mind. She truly believed that Byron had meant for his sons to have a share in his wealth as a way to make amends. They'd all done well for themselves. Been the self-made men that their father had wanted them to be. And his legacy was their reward for venturing out and not relying on his name and wealth to get them ahead in the world.

"Hailey," Chloe said as a thought took form. "Do you have Travis Christensen's contact information?"

"I might," she responded slowly. "At the very least, I'll have his manager's information. What are you thinking?"

"I don't know yet," Chloe said. "I'm hoping it'll come to me."

Maybe she couldn't force herself to plead the foundation's case with Nate, but maybe she could manage to bend another Christensen's ear.

"I'll get it for you," Hailey said. "But in the meantime, your lunch dates are here."

"Dates?" Had Derrick brought a friend?

"Yep." Hailey flashed a conspiratorial smile as she headed out the door. "I'll tell them to come on back."

"Chloe! 'Sup?" Derrick strode through the door with a wide grin.

"Hey kiddo. Hailey said you brought a friend along."

"Hope it's okay if I tag along." Warmth suffused Chloe's skin at the sound of Nate's voice. He strode in behind Derrick and put his hand on the boy's shoulder. "I stopped by to see if I could take you to lunch and found out you already had a date."

"You didn't tell me you knew somebody so cool, Chloe," Derrick said with a wide grin.

Nate gave her a lopsided smile that nearly buckled her

knees. "I don't know about cool," he said. "Little man and I got to know each other while we were waiting in the lobby. Talked soccer," he added with a wink. "I have a feeling he's cooler than me."

"No way." Derrick practically bounced with enthusiasm. "Did you know Nate saw Leo Messi play? In person! How freaking awesome is that?"

Chloe's gaze locked with Nate's. "Definitely awesome."

Nate shrugged and gave her a sheepish half-grin that melted her heart. "A friendly. When I was overseas."

Derrick looked ready to burst out of his skin with excitement. "Can he come to lunch with us, Chloe?"

His hazel eyes flashed with heat. "I'm buying. It's the least I can do considering what you did for me last night."

Derrick looked from Chloe to Nate, a too-knowing grin spreading over his young face.

"Okay then." Time for a change of subject. She was sure her face had flushed to a deep rose. "I think we'd better take Nate up on his offer. Pizza?"

"Yeah!" Derrick exclaimed. "Want pizza, Nate?"

His gaze met Chloe's again. Intense and full of unspoken need. Need that echoed her own to a T. "Pizza sounds great."

"Great." Chloe's words came slowly. "Let's get going, boys. I'm starved."

She grabbed her purse and rounded the desk. Derrick took off at a tear down the hallway. Nate waited for Chloe in her office doorway and held out his hand. Chloe laced her fingers with his and he brought her knuckles to his mouth and kissed them.

"Hope this is okay," he murmured in a husky tone that sent a zing of electricity through Chloe's body. "I couldn't wait until tomorrow to see you."

It was better than okay. Chloe's stomach twisted into

a pretzel as she walked with him down the hall. "I'm glad," she replied. "I couldn't wait to see you, either."

He flashed a wide smile. "Perfect."

Perfect. Chloe couldn't agree more. In fact, she was beginning to think that this was too perfect. Too good to be true. She just hoped that by contacting Travis for help with the foundation, that she wasn't about to bring all of this perfection to an end.

EIGHT

"What's his name?"

Nate watched as Chloe nuzzled the little white-faced calf through the slats of the chute. Damned thing was already pushing a hundred and fifty pounds and would take all of his muscle to restrain. But Chloe treated it like it was a helpless newborn, tiny enough to carry around in her arms.

"He doesn't have a name," Nate replied. "He's a steer."

"He has to have a name." If Chloe had it her way, every last cow on the ranch would be wearing a name tag and a bow by the end of the week.

"His name's cheeseburger," Nate replied.

Chloe swatted at his shoulder before moving her hands to hover over the calf's ears. "Nate! He'll hear you!"

For the past few days, Nate had felt as though he were living another man's life. And that scared the shit out of him. With Chloe around, his mind was more than occupied. The familiar panic attacks made fewer and fewer appearances. His muscles had begun to loosen by small degrees and the tension that had strung his body taut for over a year was completely gone. He could almost picture a regular life in her presence. One where he smiled. Relaxed. Hell, laughed every once in a while.

He loved this sweet, caring side to her personality. She giggled as the calf nudged her face, his long tongue lapping out at her cheek. Seeing her like this made his heart feel as though it floated around in his chest. As though he could float away right along with it.

There was a flip side to her lightheartedness, though. A passionate intensity and a hunger that rivaled Nate's own. She wasn't ashamed to want him. To want satisfaction. He couldn't get enough of her fierce kisses, loud moans, and hoarse cries. The thought of her hands on him was enough to make him hard. Shit, he'd take her right here in the corral if she'd let him. Anywhere. Anytime. Nate couldn't imagine ever *not* wanting Chloe.

"Hand me that syringe, darlin'."

Chloe looked up and smiled. "Darlin', huh?"

Nate's breath stalled as though he'd been gut punched. The endearment had rolled of his tongue with ease. He hadn't even given it a second thought. He took the syringe from Chloe's outstretched hand and loaded it with the correct dosage of the vaccination. "Would you prefer I call you cheeseburger, too?"

Chloe soothed the calf with long strokes of her hand while Nate administered the vaccination. "I don't mind being called darlin'," she said without meeting his eyes. "But I think you'd better reconsider cheeseburger."

Nate sent the calf back out to the corral and urged the next one up into the chute. Chloe reached through the wood fence and stroked its red muzzle. The nervous animal calmed under her touch. Nate knew just how he felt.

"Have you thought any more about what we talked about the other day?"

Nate paused as he loaded the syringe and studied Chloe. "What do you mean?"

"About keeping the money," she replied.

"No." Nate tamped down his rising temper. Why did she insist on bringing the subject up again and again? What did it matter if he kept the money or not?

"Oh." Chloe scratched behind the calf's ear as Nate administered the vaccination. "Because I was thinking—"

"There's nothing to think about." The icy words left Nate's mouth before he could think better of it. "Stop trying to convince me to keep the money, Chloe. I'm getting rid of it. Why does it matter to you, anyway?"

She stopped petting the calf and straightened on the fence. Hurt cut through her expression as she hopped down to the ground below. Nate cursed under his breath. He hadn't meant to snap at her. But damn it, *why* did it matter to her? This was exactly one of the reasons Nate wanted that money gone. He didn't want to have to wonder if the people who wound up in his life were there for him or for the goddamned money in his bank account.

"It doesn't matter to me," she spat. Nate sensed the storm brewing but he did nothing to calm her. "In fact, piss it all away if that's what you want. I'm sure it would make your father proud."

"You know dick about my father, Chloe!" His own temper was a tempest. It wouldn't be long before it raged out of control. "So do me a favor and *don't* tell me what would or wouldn't make him proud."

He'd been through this before and the thought that Chloe might be another gold digger out to get her hands on his family's money caused an acidic burn to scald its way up his throat. He wanted her to want him for *him*, damn it. And the fact that she kept pressing the matter of money tore open wounds that Nate had spent years trying to heal. He couldn't stop his temper from rising. The subject of his father's money only served to remind him of why he left home in the first place. It was only money for shit's sake. And he knew from experience that money didn't magically make everything better. In Nate's case, money had been the source of *all* of his problems. He held on to his anger, irrational as it was. Because if he didn't the hurt would lay him low.

"Fine." Emotion glittered in her eyes as she said under her breath, "Stubborn ass."

"Stubborn ass?" Nate tossed the syringe down in the cardboard box with the vaccination vials and rounded the chute. Chloe took a tentative step back. "My father ruined our relationship. *Not me.* Everyone thinks I was running away when I joined the Navy, but that asshole *pushed me away.* He thought I was a coward for leaving because I couldn't face him after what he'd done to me. I left because I wanted nothing to do with him or our family name and I wanted to do something that would make me feel like I had some honor for a change. I saved lives, Chloe. I don't even remember how many. It's the ones I lost that I'll never forget. They're the ones that haunt me. Good men died unfairly. While he died, rich and comfortable and rutting over a woman he had no business being with."

"Nate." Tears pooled in Chloe's eyes and her chin quivered. Chloe didn't know his history with his father and how he'd betrayed him. How could she? Nate refused to let it soften him, though. He was pissed and wanted to stay that way. He didn't owe her an apology for anything. "I'm so sorry. I didn't mean—"

"I don't want to talk about it, Chloe. I just . . ." Nate snatched his hat off his head. He raked his fingers through his hair and let out a gust of breath. He'd let his temper get the best of him. Chloe hadn't deserved to be at the receiving end of it. "Forget it."

"I think that's a good idea." Without saying another word, Chloe turned and headed back toward the house.

Nate kicked at the ground, his fists clenched tight. *Son of a bitch.* He watched her march across the pasture, dust kicking up with every step, her arms swinging purposefully beside her. He hadn't meant to be so harsh with her. The expression on her face had grown more distressed with every forceful word. As though he'd had an out-of-body experience, his mouth continued to run while he watched from beside himself, helpless to stop the flow of his anger.

You dickhead. Way to fuck yourself over.

The echo of his front door slamming behind Chloe made its way across the pasture to the corral. The calves started at the sound and even Nate's heart skipped a beat. He walked slowly toward the house, giving himself some time to calm the fuck down before he talked to Chloe again. After a week of lawyers, advisors, his brothers, and Miranda all in his ear, the last thing he'd wanted was one more opinion on what he should do with his inheritance. The stress was starting to wear on him.

And instead of just telling Chloe that, he'd thrown a king-sized tantrum. Awesome.

❋   ❋   ❋

By the time Chloe hit the staircase, her temper had begun to ebb. She hadn't meant to push Nate's buttons—the situation had to have been stressing him out—but she wasn't going to give up trying to convince him to see her point of view.

Chloe wasn't stupid. She knew how her nagging must have come across. As though she were more interested in

Nate's money than Nate himself. Nothing could be further from the truth, though. If that had been the case, she would have asked him for the money to save her foundation before she'd even gotten her underwear back on that first night. It wouldn't matter to her if he had ten or ten billion dollars. She'd still want him. Still crave his touch. She'd still think about him every waking moment of every single day. Her gaze wandered over the dingy paint, rickety staircase, and creaking floorboards of Nate's house. It was run-down, sure. But it was a house she'd spend every day of the week in if he wanted her there.

His inheritance could offer him so much *more,* though.

She wanted that money, for *Nate.* He deserved every bit of ease it could offer him. He'd lived through enough. It was time for him to quit beating himself up and let life be good to him for a change. He could fix up his house, buy more cows if that's what made him happy. Travel. Nate was worried that his father's money would change him. Chloe simply wanted him to see it as the opportunity it could be.

"Chloe. Don't go." Nate's quiet voice rippled over her, a calm breeze in comparison to his earlier storm. "Please."

One little fight and he thought she was taking off? She paused midstep, her hand on the worn oak banister. "I'm not leaving. I thought we could use a time-out, that's all."

The stairs creaked under his weight as Nate made his way to where she'd stopped. Heat buffeted her back from his body and her eyes drifted shut as a shiver raced over her flesh. "I don't want a time-out." His voice slid over her in a dark caress. Even without touching her she felt him, and her body came alive as though it was trained to respond only to him. "I'm sorry I yelled at you."

"I'm sorry I butted into your life again." He reached out and wrapped his arm around her. His hand ventured under her T-shirt, splayed out over her belly. Chloe drew in a shuddering breath. "It's only because I care about you."

"You care about me?" He leaned over her and kissed her neck where it met her shoulder.

"I wouldn't be here if I didn't."

His hand ventured up past her torso and under her bra. He cupped her breast, kneading the flesh as he continued to kiss her neck. "I didn't like watching you walk away from me." Chloe's breath hitched as a rush of heat spread between her thighs. "Don't do it again."

Her head fell back on his shoulder and she gripped the banister for support. Nate's free hand loosened the button on her jeans and eased down the zipper before slipping into her underwear. His fingers slid over her clit and Chloe melted against him. Any words she'd thought to say evaporated under the heat of his touch.

Chloe recognized the moment for what it was: a distraction. When Nate couldn't deal with something, he used sex to run interference. The second he touched her, whispered low in her ear, or coaxed impassioned cries from her lips with his skillful fingers, she lost herself. Did that mean that Nate was her dysfunction? Or her addiction?

Probably both.

This time, Nate didn't seduce her with his words. The only sounds in the quiet house were that of their heavy breaths. Chloe stripped off her shirt and shucked her bra, wobbling on her feet as Nate circled her clit with the tip of his finger. She tried to spread her legs wider, but her pants restricted any movement. He increased the pressure, sliding through her lips as he continued to work the swollen knot of nerves at her core. Chloe's hips bucked and her thighs trembled under the onslaught. The restriction of her jeans tortured her. Without being able to open herself up to him, all Nate could manage were shallow flicks of his finger that teased but offered nothing in the way of release. He held her tight against him, one hand cupping her bare breast while the other cupped her pussy inside of her jeans.

If she didn't get her damned pants off, Chloe was going to go out of her mind. Just when she was about to beg him to do just that, Nate spun her around in his arms. His hazel eyes sparked with heat and the intensity of his gaze burned through her. A muscle at his jaw ticked and his nostrils flared before his mouth descended on hers in a scorching kiss.

His temper had been redirected into passion. Raw, visceral, completely untamed. His mouth slanted furiously over hers, and Nate took her bottom lip into his mouth, sucking greedily before he pulled away, letting his teeth scrape over the delicate skin. Chloe's arms flew around his neck as she kissed him back, her own passions mounting to a nearly uncontrollable level. They could've toppled down the stairs with one misstep, but her tongue plunged into Nate's mouth; she couldn't be bothered to worry about anything as trivial as a broken bone or two.

With a grunt, Nate shoved Chloe's pants down over her thighs. She toed off her shoes and shimmied out of them as best she could, unwilling to part their mouths while she kicked her jeans and underwear somewhere down the stairs. Nate broke their kiss and his breath heaved in his chest as he stripped his own shirt and tossed it down to join hers. He took her hips firmly in his grasp and spun her around. "Get on your hands and knees." The words were nothing more than a husky growl and another rush of wetness coated her thighs.

Chloe did as he told her. The carpeting that covered

the stairs wasn't exactly a cushion, but she didn't care. Nate spread her legs wide and tilted her hips so that her ass jutted up in the air. "Nate?" She turned to look over her shoulder and watched as he laid himself out on the stairs. "You're going to kill your back laying like that—Oh. *God*."

Nate's mouth sealed over her pussy in a wave of delicious heat that caused Chloe to shudder. He gripped her hips in his large hands, holding her right where he wanted her as he circled her clit with the tip of his tongue. Nate's hands ventured lower. Chloe gasped as he dragged the flat of his tongue over her lips. His fingers traced a path down the crease of her ass and lower still. He slid one finger through her slick arousal and guided his finger back up into the crease and the tight ring of nerves, circling the area while he sucked her clit into his mouth.

The sensation stole Chloe's breath. Virgin territory to be sure, no one but Nate had ever been bold enough to go there. She gripped the edge of the stair above her as she rocked on her knees, grinding her hips as she rode Nate's mouth. He let out a hungry groan and eased his finger past the tight barrier as he increased the pressure of his tongue and swirled it over her clit.

The orgasm took her without warning.

Chloe sobbed her pleasure, her hips jerking in time with each delicious throb of her pussy. Nate continued with his ministrations, long passes of his tongue and slow, gentle thrusts of his finger that drove her crazy with desire. The waves of pleasure seemed never ending, cresting and ebbing only to crest again. Her voice grew hoarse in her throat until she couldn't utter another sound if she'd wanted to. Chloe leaned her head on her arms and let out a slow breath. Her body was weak, shaky, and completely spent. And still, it wasn't enough.

NINE

Nate's breath puffed in his chest as though he'd run a marathon. His heart pounded, not from exertion but excitement, and his body hummed with the overwhelming physical need he had for Chloe.

Her honeyed taste lingered on his tongue as she leaned against the stairs, her own breath racing. The orgasm had rippled through her into him and Nate still felt the aftershocks in the satin-smooth skin of her thighs that caressed his cheeks. He pushed himself up to sit and shucked his pants whip-quick. He dug in his pocket for his wallet and before he sent it rolling down the stairs, snatched a condom from inside. With shaking hands, he rolled it onto his erect cock and let out a moan as his hand stroked down to the base. He was so damned wound up, it wouldn't take more than a few strokes to get him there. No woman had ever driven him as crazy as Chloe did. With every passing minute, he only wanted *more*.

Chloe let out a squeal of surprise as he reached

around and seized her by the waist, dragging her around until she was settled in his lap. He loved her lush curves and soft flesh. Loved that she wasn't some waifish stick that might break if he so much as jostled her. He lifted her up and settled her on his cock, leaning back on the narrow staircase so he could enjoy the view. *Fucking breathtaking.* Her cheeks were flushed and her nipples stood erect and rosy from the pale swells of her generous breasts. She reached out and gripped the banisters on either side of her as she began to ride him. Slow, easy strokes that ended on a flick of her hips that teased the head of his cock perfectly.

"Just like that, darlin'. Don't stop."

Her eyes became hooded as her head lolled back on her shoulders. Nate reached up and pinched her nipples, eliciting a gasp from Chloe that ended on a low, drawn-out moan. "Do that again, Nate."

Who was he to deny her? Nate rolled the stiff peaks and her pace increased. She used the banister for leverage, lifting her body up and off of him before plunging back down, taking him as deeply as she could. Ninety percent of Nate's pleasure came from watching her. He was fascinated with the dreamy expression on her face, the soft parting of her mouth, her hooded eyes and pink tongue that darted out to lick her lips. The soft sway of her breasts as she moved on top of him and the way they quivered when her breath left her chest in a shuddering rush. Every moan, every cry was music to his ears.

He'd never get enough of her. Would do anything to keep her. Hell, he might even . . . *love* her. Nate hadn't loved anything or anyone, aside from his brothers, in a long goddamned time. In a matter of days—little more than a week—she'd managed to work her way into that black pit in the center of his chest that he thought had died. Chloe had brought him back to life with her passion, fire, and compassion. He reached up and cupped her cheek, guided her gaze to his and held it.

"I want you looking at me when you come this time."

The play of her shapely body flexing and contracting as she moved fascinated Nate. Chloe took him deep and tilted her hips, sliding her hands farther up the banister as she ground her hips against his. What started out slow and measured increased into a wild frenzy. Nate's fist wound in the length of her auburn hair and he rose up to meet her, putting his mouth to hers. "Harder, Chloe. Fuck me harder."

She met the wild thrust of his hips and her mouth parted on a silent moan. He couldn't stand her silence and so Nate tilted his head to the swell of one breast and sucked her nipple into his mouth. "Nate. Oh, god, Nate. I'm coming!"

He pulled away and took in every detail of her beautiful face. Her inner walls squeezed him tight, pulsing around his cock until it pushed him over the edge. They came together, a harmony of sounds and sensations. He gripped her hips and thrust deep as wave after wave crested over him. Every ounce of worry and stress siphoned out of him, leaving nothing but calm, peaceful bliss. He wrapped his arms around Chloe and hugged her tight as he placed kisses on her shoulder, neck, and collarbone.

"You drive me crazy, Chloe," he said on an exhale. "I can't get enough."

He felt her smile against his skin. Her tongue flicked out at the sensitive skin at his neck and Nate shivered. "It's me who can't get enough. Every time you touch me, I lose my mind and can't think a rational thought to save my life. How's your back?"

Nate chuckled. "You haven't broken me yet. I wouldn't say no to a long, hot shower though."

Chloe sat up and studied him, a smile flirting with her lips. "What about the sweet little calves still waiting for their shots?"

Ah, shit. He still had five calves to vaccinate and his legs were about as reliable as cooked noodles. "I'll make you a deal. You start dinner, I'll finish up with the calves."

"And afterward?" Chloe asked archly.

"Afterward, I'm going to wash you from head to toe. Slowly."

Her smile was enough to stop Nate's heart. "That hardly seems fair."

"Oh, don't worry," he teased. "You'll be washing me when I'm finished. And I expect you to be thorough."

"Anything for my hardworking cowboy."

Nate's chest tightened to the point that he didn't trust himself to take a breath without choking on the intake. It wasn't just the sensual purr of her voice, but the possessiveness when she said "my" that caused his heart to pound. He wanted her to want him with the same inexplicable fervor. He wanted the thought of her leaving to make her break out into a cold sweat like it did him. But most of all, he wanted her to be satisfied with him if he chose nothing more than to live the life of a simple rancher.

"Good."

❋   ❋   ❋

Chloe watched out the kitchen window as Nate finished up with the calves. She could easily imagine a life with him here. Simple, and wonderful, and just the two of them. From where her purse hung on a hook in the mudroom, her cell phone rang. Chloe turned off the sink and dried her hands before rushing to the phone before the call went to voice mail. She didn't recognize the number but that wasn't uncommon since she used the phone for business calls. Her finger swiped across the screen and she answered, "This is Chloe Benson."

"Hi, Chloe. This is Travis Christensen. I got your number from your assistant. Is this a good time to call?"

Chloe's heart ricocheted up into her throat. She rushed to the kitchen and peered out the window to find Nate still dealing with the calves. "Um, yeah. It's fine. I didn't expect to hear from you so soon, Mr. Christensen."

"First things first," he said. "Call me Travis."

Talking to Nate's brother while he worked outside sent a wave of guilt washing over Chloe. She should have asked Nate before she'd sent Hailey after his brother. It somehow felt underhanded and sneaky now.

"Okay, Travis. So, I'm assuming that my assistant gave you the full-court press, otherwise you wouldn't be calling."

Travis chuckled. "She did. I gotta tell ya, she's quite the seller."

He sounded a lot like Nate but more at ease. Rather than talk shop, Chloe found herself wanting to use this opportunity to grill the younger Christensen about his brother. What was he like as a kid? Did he have many girlfriends? Was he always so serious, or had his time in the military made him that way? *Damn it.* This was such a wasted opportunity.

"This is our eleventh hour, Travis. We've got to go big or go home."

Nate looked up from pushing the last calf into the corral and smiled when his gaze met Chloe's. He waved before he started to box up the syringes and vaccines. Chloe waved back. *Crap.* She needed to wrap this convo up.

"Can't say I don't admire that go-to attitude. Why come to me, though?"

Chloe sensed that Hailey had given him the P.C. response to that question and that Travis wanted it straight. Something he had in common with his brother. "Honestly? Because I've reached the end of my rope and I know you've got more than enough money to help my foundation without even feeling a pinch."

"I doubt there's a soul in the state of Texas who doesn't know that," he remarked. "Okay, so why me and not my brothers?"

Hailey wasn't sure how much she should divulge. Too much and Travis might be suspicious of her. Too little and it would look like she hadn't done her homework. "Your youngest brother is a county sheriff. I'd feel like I was stealing from him. Your brother Carter has two kids and I know he recently lost his wife. I didn't want to pile anything more onto his plate."

"And my other brother . . . ?" Travis asked.

"Is planning to give his share of the inheritance away," Chloe responded. "To your father's widow if I'm not mistaken. I'm not interested in his share."

Travis snorted. "That's the rumor. How much do you need, Chloe, and when do you need it by?"

Chloe's heart soared. "Does this mean you're willing to back us?"

"This means I'm willing to consider it. You probably know better than anyone that it's not so easy to cut a check and call it a day. And regardless of the size of my inheritance, there are still loose ends that have to be tied up before I have access to any of those funds. Give me a dollar amount and a timeline and I'll see what I can do."

Travis obviously had a good head on his shoulders. The cut-and-dry personality must have been common to all of the Christensens. Chloe appreciated straightforwardness. "I need three million dollars," she said on a breath. "And if I can't secure those funds by Christmas Eve, my foundation will be closing its doors."

She was answered with silence and Chloe cringed. She wasn't asking for pocket change, and it wasn't like she'd given Travis a stellar time frame in which to scrape it together. She'd have been silent, too, in his position.

"I take it you don't need one lump sum. Just a commitment of funding?"

"Of course." According to their board, the foundation would be able to honor all of their present commitments and stay afloat for the next year if Chloe secured at least three million dollars in funding. "I'm not going to sugar-coat it, Travis. We need this money. Without it, we're done."

"I'm not saying yes or no," Travis replied. "But if you can give me a few days, I'll have an answer to you as soon as I can."

Chloe let out a sigh of relief. It was a stay of execution at least. "That's more than fair. Thank you."

"If you don't mind me asking, who else have you contacted? I might be able to throw a few names your way."

At his core, a nice guy. Like Nate. Whatever the Christensen brothers felt about their relationship with their father, they were better men because of it. "I've contacted everyone in the state who I thought could spare the money," Chloe replied. "Probably even some who couldn't."

"Even my father?" Travis asked.

"Yep. He shot me down before I even gave me a taste of my charming personality."

Travis snorted. "I'll be in touch soon, Chloe."

"Thank you, Travis. Really. Talk to you soon."

Nate walked through the door just as Chloe discon-
nected the call. "Talk to who soon?" he asked as he
crossed into the kitchen and leaned in for a quick kiss.

"Um, Hailey," Chloe replied. She set her phone down
on the counter and went back to tearing lettuce for the
salad. "The wheels keep turning even when I'm not in
the office."

"Everything okay?"

Nate went to the sink to wash his hands and Chloe
took a step to the side lest she get any of the guilt that felt
like it coated her body with an icky slime all over him.

"Yeah, just lining up a few things that I need to take
care of next week when I head back into the office."

Nate dried his hands and came up behind her. His
arms wound around her waist and he hugged her close
before planting a slow kiss to her neck. "I was thinking
about maybe getting a Christmas tree. This place isn't
exactly overflowing with holiday cheer. Wanna head out
to the lot downtown and buy one this evening?"

She needed to talk to him about Travis. She wasn't
doing anything underhanded or sneaky and she didn't
want Nate to think that she was. It was business, plain
and simple. "Sure. I want to talk to you about something
first, though. It's about the foundation."

He kissed her neck again. The wet heat of his mouth
soaked right through her until Chloe wondered how her
legs could still be holding her upright. Nate's effect on
her was instant and visceral. It didn't matter how much
time they spent together, it never subsided.

"Sure. I'm going to go change and then I'll start up
the barbeque." He kissed her again and murmured
against her skin, "We can talk over dinner. You wouldn't
believe how hungry I am."

Chloe's insides clenched at the seductive tenor of his
words. With each passing day she fell further under

Nate's spell. The past week had been a dream full of passion, peace, and a domestic bliss that caused her chest to ache with want. As Nate pulled away and headed for the stairs, Chloe wondered if she'd get everything she wanted or if she'd be forced to give up her dreams—the foundation—in order to keep the man she might just love.

TEN

Something niggled at the back of Nate's mind as he threw on a fresh pair of jeans and a clean T-shirt. He didn't want anything to cast a shadow on the past several days spent with Chloe but his stupid brain wouldn't quiet down. The same past doubts that had sparked their earlier argument gnawed at him. Was Chloe truly here for him, or something else? He wished he could tell his damned brain to shut the fuck up once and for all.

Nate didn't want Chloe there for any other reason but *him*. He'd only known her for a short while but it was enough to know that he didn't want whatever this was between them to end. In fact, the thought of her walking out on him after their fight had damned near thrown him into a panic attack. He couldn't continue to dwell on shit that wasn't going to do anything but fuck with his head. Instead, he let his stomach do the talking, and headed downstairs to fire up the grill.

"Just in time," Chloe remarked from the kitchen. "The steaks are seasoned and ready to go."

What would it be like to come home to her every single day? To know that Chloe was *his*. He took the plate from her outstretched hand. Her brow knitted as she studied him.

"You okay?"

He flashed a reassuring smile. "Yeah. Starving. I could eat an entire side of beef."

Chloe grinned. "Sorry, but a T-bone is going to have to do. I made salad and pasta, though. I think we might have half of a baguette somewhere around here, too."

We. Was it too soon for them to be a we? *Not at all.*

❋　　❋　　❋

"I'll keep the money, the shares in the company, all of it. If you want me to." Sometime while staring into the flames of the gas grill, Nate had come to a decision. He wanted Chloe. Not just for a night or a week or a couple of months. He wanted her for as long as he could have her. And if was important to her that he take that goddamned money of his father's, he'd do it. For her.

Chloe looked up from her plate, her jaw slack. "What are you talking about?"

"I'm saying that I won't sign my inheritance over to Miranda. If I have to, I'll live with it. If that's what you want me to do."

"This isn't about what I want you to do." Chloe set her fork down on her plate and fiddled with the stem of her wineglass. Her eyes met his, luminous gems that sparkled. "Nate, I just want you to be happy."

Nate swallowed down the emotion that threatened to cut off his airway. "You make me happy."

A slow, sweet smile spread across her face. "You make me happy, too. And you'd make me happy whether you had ten or ten million dollars."

He made her happy. Nate felt as though his chest

might burst. She wanted him and it wasn't because of the money.

"You were right earlier when you said that I didn't know anything about your relationship with your dad," Chloe continued. "It's not my decision to make for you. The only reason I wanted you to keep it in the first place was because of the good it could do for you. Your life could be easy if you wanted it to be. And I truly do believe that your inheritance is your father's apology to you and your brothers. I think it was his way of telling you that he cared about you. Loved you. I just don't want you to throw that away."

Maybe Chloe was right. Nate couldn't help but wonder if he'd been so insistent that he off-load his inheritance because he didn't want the headache, or because he wanted to spite his father. Sort of one last middle-finger to the old man for the way he'd betrayed him. The more Nate thought about it, the more childish it seemed. He wasn't spiting his father. He was spiting himself. Nate would be the only one hurt by giving it all away.

"I think I want to keep it. Maybe you can help me figure out what to do with it."

Chloe gave him a blinding smile. "I could probably do that."

"Now that that's settled, what did you want to talk to me about? The foundation, right?"

From the counter, Chloe's phone rang. Nate leaned back in his chair, reaching to the counter to retrieve it for her. He caught the number on the caller ID from the corner of his eye, and the chair came back down on its front legs with a snap as he lent his full attention to the screen. "Why is my brother calling you?"

Chloe's expression fell and her cheeks bloomed with color. "I can explain."

What in the hell was there to explain? Nate swiped

his finger across the screen and brought the phone up to his ear. "Travis?"

"Nate?" A pregnant pause filled the space between Nate and his brother. "Did I dial the wrong number?"

"Depends," he said. "Who are you trying to call?"

"Chloe Benson from the Youth Sports Foundation of Dallas."

Nate's heart sunk like a stone to the bottoms of his feet. "You dialed the right number."

Travis gave a nervous laugh. "She must've changed her mind about hitting you up for a big fat donation, huh? But dude, why are you answering her phone? Does a cool three million get you access to her iPhone or some shit?"

The hand clutching the phone went numb as Nate's grip tightened. His eyes met Chloe's and he knew everything he needed to by the guilt that pinched her usually soft expression. "Travis, can I call you back?"

Travis gave a nervous laugh. "Sure, but uh, could you have Chloe give me a call? My financial manager has a few questions that I need answered before I can green light this donation. She needs a commitment by Christmas, and it's going to be tough to finalize everything in time."

"Sure. Talk to you later." Nate ended the call and set the phone down on the table. Hurt and suspicion sliced through him and he tried to swallow it down, but his throat was already so goddamned clogged with betrayal that he couldn't get the knot in his throat to budge.

"Nate, before you jump to conclusions, you need to let me explain." Chloe's voice quavered. Her green eyes glistened with an emotion pretty damned close to fear and she pushed her chair slowly away from the table.

"Did you fuck my brother, too?" The words spilled out in an angry rush. Chloe's jaw dropped and Nate shot out of the chair. He braced his hands on the table and leaned over it, his entire body quaking with rage. "Answer me, Chloe! Is this some sort of fucking scam?"

❄   ❄   ❄

Nate's words knocked the air from Chloe's lungs. She'd planned to tell him that she'd contacted Travis. In fact, they'd been about to cover that very subject when her phone rang.

"Of course it's not a scam. And I didn't sleep with your brother! How could you even suggest that?" Nate cocked a brow and it was all Chloe could do not to throw her fork at him.

"You got me to keep the money and it didn't even take a full two weeks. When were you going to spring it on me? Tonight? Tomorrow? Were you going to use the foundation excuse on me, too? Beg for a donation and then take the money and run?"

Nate's eyes blazed with an angry fire that threw off enough heat to make Chloe sweat. "My foundation isn't an *excuse*!" Chloe railed. The weeks of stress and worry finally caught up to her and she cracked under the emotional strain. "Do you want to know the truth, Nate? I'm closing my doors if I can't come up with the operating funds by close of business Christmas Eve. And I'd do anything to save my foundation and the kids it helps. I went to your father's memorial service absolutely prepared to get down on my knees and beg you for that money."

Nate snorted. "You got down on your knees all right. You just forgot to ask for a check afterward."

Tears sprung to Chloe's eyes and she couldn't stop their ceaseless flow. "How could you say that?" Her voice was nothing more than a pained whisper.

"You know, at least Miranda was up-front about picking my pocket. She never pretended to be something she wasn't and didn't make up bullshit excuses for why she wanted the money."

"Piss off, Nate!"

"What about the kid? You pay him off, too? Pick him up on a playground somewhere and offer him twenty bucks if he could play his part and make you look good?"

"You're an asshole!" A sob lodged in Chloe's throat. "I never *once* asked you for money. After that first night together I decided that I was more interested in you than what you could do to help me."

"I'm supposed to believe that? You've spent the past ten days doing everything in your power to convince me to keep my inheritance. And you've already gone behind my back to wheel and deal with my brother. What else are you hiding, Chloe?"

"Not a damned thing. You know, Nate, for a second there I thought I was actually falling in love with you. But that could never happen. I could *never* love a man who'd suggest I'd give him a blowjob and expect a fucking paycheck in return! I don't care what you decide to do with your money. Have a nice life, Nate."

Tears streamed down Chloe's cheeks as she snatched her phone from the table and rushed past Nate. She paused only long enough to snatch her purse from the hook before she hurried out the back door. It slammed behind her as she fled across the old deck and down the rotting stairs toward the driveway where her car was parked. She didn't even care that she was leaving with only the clothes on her back. He could keep her suitcase and clothes for all she cared. It was worth replacing all of her makeup and toiletries if it meant she never had to look at his face ever again.

"Son of a bitch!" Chloe's fists came down on the

steering wheel. She reached down and turned the key, slamming the car into reverse the second the engine roared to life. Tears blurred her vision, but she didn't care as she sped down the narrow dirt lane that led away from Nate's house. No one had ever hurt her so badly. Cut her so deep. It was a wound that she feared might never heal.

And the worst part? She'd given him the weapon that he'd wielded against her.

The two-hour drive back to Dallas was torture. One hundred and twenty minutes of time alone with her thoughts. Chloe went over, and over, and over the events of the past several days. Wishing she'd done or said something differently. It wasn't like she'd scammed Nate or any of his brothers. And as far as dishonesty, her only mistake was not telling him before she had Hailey reach out to Travis.

Way to fuck yourself over, Chloe.

Her cell rang and Chloe's heart stuttered in her chest. For the barest of seconds, she dared to hope that it was Nate calling. That he'd apologize and beg her to come back. It would take more than an apology though, wouldn't it? No one had ever spoken such hurtful words to her. So it was a relief that Hailey's name popped up on the caller ID and not Nate's. At least, that's what she told herself.

"Hey, Hailey. I can't talk right now—"

"I hate to interrupt your wild sex romp of a week, but we have a problem."

Great. Her eyes drifted heavenward. *Pile it on, why don't you!* "What's the problem?"

"Oh, about three feet, ten inches, and sixty-five pounds of trouble," Hailey replied wryly. "He was picked up for shoplifting and he told the cops that his foster mom worked here."

Derrick. That little shit. "Can you drive him to his actual foster parents' house?"

"I tried," Hailey said in a near-whisper. "He told me he'd bolt if I took him back there."

"I'm on my way back to the city." She might as well deal with Derrick. What was one more disaster today? "Can you hang around for another half hour or so?"

"Sure. Why are you coming home early?"

Chloe didn't acknowledge the concern in Hailey's voice. If she did, she'd start bawling and wouldn't stop until she rolled into Dallas. "I need to get some work done and Nate's got ranch issues to deal with. No biggie."

"All right," Hailey said slowly. "I'll see you in a bit. Drive safe."

"Okay. Bye."

A fresh wave of tears threatened, but Chloe swallowed them down. After what had happened between her and Nate tonight, there was no way she could move forward with Travis. She'd have Hailey call him tomorrow and cancel. With Christmas a week away, the chances of finding another donor were slim. She thought about Derrick. That cute, freckled pain in the ass deserved every leg up in life that he could get. Without the sports programs the foundation offered, it would only give him—and so many at-risk kids—more free time. More opportunities to find trouble.

Her love life had crashed and burned in glorious fashion tonight. Chloe would be damned if she let her professional life follow the same path. Tonight she'd get Derrick situated. Tomorrow, she'd hit the pavement and she wasn't going to stop until she found someone—anyone—to help bail her foundation out. And then . . . ? Then, she'd try to do something about mending her shattered heart.

ELEVEN

"Jesus, Nate. Why in the hell didn't you tell me?"

Nate sat at the kitchen table, a bottle of beer clutched in his fist. Acid ate away at his stomach, burned a path up his throat. He'd really fucked up this time.

"Tell you what? That I hooked up with someone at Dad's memorial service and have been fucking her ever since?"

Travis cut him a look. "I probably wouldn't have put it that way, but yeah! You're not an island for shit's sake. It's like you forget that any of us are around. Did you ever consider calling? Coming out to visit? Hell, inviting us out here? We don't only have to talk when shit goes south, Nate."

He knew that. But he'd been through so much shit over the past few years that he couldn't ever seem to get out of his own headspace. Being with Chloe had finally started to coax him from that self-confinement. And instead of working through his anger like a goddamned adult, he'd lashed out at her yet again like a jaded kid.

Said horrible things to her. He'd never wanted to take anything back so fucking badly.

"You've gotta let it go, brother." Nate lifted his gaze to Travis's. You'd think he was the oldest brother, the way he treated him. "She's not Miranda."

Nate hung his head between his shoulders. He'd been too much of a chicken shit to tell Chloe that the real reason he'd enlisted—had to get the fuck away from his father—was because he'd caught him with Miranda bent over his desk one afternoon. His fucking fiancée and his own dad, going at it as though the world were about to end and the future of the human race depended on their procreation. God. Even now thinking about it made his stomach turn.

Nate snorted. "You don't know that."

"Yeah, I do. The first time I talked to her, I asked why she'd come to me. She said that she knew about Carter's situation and didn't want to pile anything more on his plate. That Noah should be allowed to enjoy having money for a change. And when I asked why she hadn't gone to you, she that you were signing your inheritance away and that she wasn't interested in a piece of that pie."

Another snort. "Doesn't mean anything."

"Listen to me, you pigheaded son of a bitch. If she'd been after you for your money, she would have asked you for it from the get-go. Believe me, she wasn't even a little shy about shaking me down. Did she ever once tell you that her foundation was in trouble?"

"No."

Travis gave him a pointed look. "Exactly. She wouldn't have hesitated to lay her sob story out for you if all she'd been after was a check. From what I can tell, the woman is a saint, Nate. I'm giving her the money she needs. And for what it's worth, everything she said to you was spot-on. Dad wanted us to have that money and the company. I absolutely think it was an apology. The man wasn't perfect. In fact, he was as far from perfect as anyone I've ever known. But everyone deserves a second chance, Nate. Even him. And especially *you*."

It was a nice sentiment. He doubted Chloe would ever give him the time of day, let alone a second chance after the things he'd said to her. It had been seven years since he and Miranda broke it off and he'd spent every day of it being a bitter, solemn, distrusting asshole. He'd finally found a woman who gave him the peace he craved and he'd driven her away. Nate didn't know how he'd get through another hour without Chloe. Days . . . weeks without her? *Impossible*.

"Nate? Did you hear me?"

His vision came back into focus as he shook himself from his thoughts. Travis was staring down at him, a furrow marring his brow. "What?"

"I said, if you give a dime of that money to Miranda, Noah, Carter, and I are going to beat the shit out of you. You hear me? Quit punishing yourself for things that weren't your fault to begin with and crawl out of the fucking hole you've been living in for the past year. This isn't about taking over Dad's legacy, Nate. It's about using the opportunity to leave one of your own."

"Yeah," Nate said. He peered down at his bottle. "Okay."

"And for the love of god, fix things with Chloe. I might not know anything about her, but she must be amazing. I've never seen you so wrecked. Make it right with her."

Nate didn't answer. Couldn't.

"I'll call you tomorrow," Travis said as he headed for the door. "You coming over for Christmas Eve dinner? Everyone else is."

"Yeah," Nate said without registering exactly what he was agreeing to. "See ya."

The door closed behind Travis and the silence of his house swallowed Nate whole. Chloe's absence gutted him, hollowed him out until he was nothing more than an empty shell. How could losing her scar him so deeply after knowing her for only a short time? Nate thought he'd felt all the pain there ever was to feel. Had experienced the gut-wrenching sorrow of loss. The anger of betrayal. The hollow ache of true heartbreak was a new and hellish torture, though. He hadn't felt half of this when he'd found Miranda and his dad together. Did that mean that what he felt for Chloe was so much more than what he'd felt for a woman he'd been ready to marry?

Was he in love with Chloe?

Goddamn it, *yes.*

Travis was right. For years, he'd beat himself up. Blamed himself for Miranda's cheating. Blamed his dad's money for taking her away from him. And when he'd enlisted, that guilt carried over into everything he'd done. He tried to control every out-of-control situation. And when the one mission he'd thought would go off without a hitch went south, he'd blamed himself for that as well. Took responsibility for every single life lost. It was time to let go of the guilt that was slowly eating him alive. It was time to start living his life on his terms.

First things first, he was going to make things right between him and Chloe. Even if she didn't want to see him, he'd make her hear him out. He refused to let her go, and he'd do anything to win her back.

Nate walked into the living room and grabbed his cell. He dialed and took a deep breath as he waited for her to answer. "Miranda, we need to talk."

❄   ❄   ❄

"You been cryin', Chloe? Your eyes are all red."

Chloe didn't even have the emotional fortitude to feel embarrassed about the fact that she looked like a train wreck. She deposited Derrick's duffle on the guest room floor, After a quick phone call to CPS, she and Derrick's case worker both decided that it might be best if Derrick stayed with Chloe for a few days. Which was totally fine by Chloe. She needed the distraction. If she was too busy keeping her pint-sized houseguest in line, she wouldn't have time to dwell on the fact that her heart was shattered into a million irreparable pieces.

"Allergies," she replied. "Okay, kiddo. I'm going to order a pizza and then *you* are going to do homework. Got it?"

Derrick huffed. "Whatev. I'd rather be playing ball."

"Think of it this way," Chloe said. "You do well in school, focus on soccer and *not shoplifting,* and maybe someday you'll get the chance to play on a college field. How does that sound?"

"Awesome," Derrick said. "MLS would be better, though."

"If we're going in that direction, Spanish Premier League would be better," Chloe teased. "Let's take it slow for now, okay? Because I'm telling you right now, kiddo. If you get into trouble one more time, you won't be able to participate in foundation-sponsored club ball. If that happens, you might as well forget about MLS. Got it?"

"I got it," Derrick said, his gaze downcast.

"All right. Get settled in. You can do your homework at the kitchen table."

Chloe left Derrick in the guest room and headed into the living room. Her legs gave out when she hit the couch and she slumped down onto the cushions. She'd never felt so damned raw and now she had to deal with the guilt of making promises to a ten-year-old boy that she knew she'd never be able to keep.

Volunteers were few and far between. The good ones were overworked and spread too thin. The purpose of the foundation had been to not only build the sports facilities but to pay full-time coaches. So many programs were pay-to-play. Club fees were outrageous and coaching fees were more than a lot of families could afford. Chloe had hoped to offer the same opportunities to kids who wouldn't get to play organized sports otherwise. Kids involved in sports were better students, more motivated, and stayed out of trouble. Now, all of her hard work was slowly swirling down the toilet. She hated to let people down. Tonight, she'd let Nate down. And next week, she'd be letting hundreds of kids and families down. *Awesome.*

Chloe ordered a pizza and got Derrick set up at the kitchen table. In addition to her last-ditch effort to find emergency investors, she'd be meeting with both social services and Derrick's foster parents tomorrow. She couldn't think much further into the future. If she did, she'd lose it for sure. Unemployment, job searches, failure, and heartache loomed over her like a noose that slowly choked her. Something had to give. If it didn't, Chloe was going to crack for sure.

Feet propped up on the coffee table and her laptop open and ready to go, Chloe hunkered down for a long night of research. She sent off several e-mails to former colleagues at Make-A-Wish. One of them might have a suggestion that she hadn't thought of yet. Her cell rang from beside her and Chloe checked the caller ID: Nate. With the speed of hummingbird wings, her heart took flight and Chloe's mouth went dry. She held the phone in her palm, her thumb hovering over the screen to accept the call. The hurtful words he'd said to her came crashing back and Chloe hit Ignore.

She couldn't open herself up to more hurt. Talking to Nate right now would only mess with her head and her heart. The voice mail alert went off and her fingers itched to play the message. *Don't do it, Chloe. The things he said to you can't be fixed with I'm sorry.* She was still too angry and hurt over the things he'd said to let him off the hook.

Yet, her finger slid across the screen. She brought the phone to her ear, fearful of what Nate would say and at the same, hopeful.

"Chloe." The sound of her name was a tortured groan at the back of his throat. He paused and let out a long breath. "God, Chloe. I'm so, *so* sorry. I was completely out of line. I know that an apology isn't going to erase the things I said. But I want to make it up to you. Want to prove to you that I'm not that asshole who said those horrible things. If I could take it all back, I would. Chloe . . ." His voice hitched. "I can't picture a tomorrow without you in it. We need to talk. There's a lot I haven't told you and I want a chance to explain. Please call me."

Chloe set her phone back down beside her. What else could he possibly have to say? Her heart softened as she thought about the way his voice broke with emotion. Maybe he truly regretted the things he'd said. Chloe knew that Nate wasn't exactly a serene pond. He was a volcano, ready to erupt with even the slightest disturbance.

No. She couldn't excuse his behavior. Couldn't let him think that it was okay to treat her that way. Was it fair to not give him a chance, though?

"Chloe, are you gonna marry Nate?"

"What?" She set her laptop aside and craned her neck toward the dining room. "No."

"Why not?"

She could think of a million reasons why not. The least of them being the fact that he hadn't asked her. Chloe was struck by how much had changed in just a few hours. She'd gone from daydreams of domestic bliss—maybe even marriage—to having her heart smashed under the assault of Nate's words.

"I don't think Nate wants to marry me." This totally wasn't the sort of conversation she wanted to be having with a ten-year-old. Hell, it wasn't a conversation she wanted to have at all!

"He does," Derrick said, matter of fact. "I could tell the other day at lunch. He looks at you like he wants to marry you."

Chloe choked on a half-sob, half-laugh. "I don't know about that, kiddo."

"You should marry him," Derrick continued on, lost in his own fantasy. "You guys could take me out for pizza and to soccer games. Do you think Nate would want to watch me play?"

Tears stung at Chloe's eyes. All Derrick needed was a stable home and someone who could give him attention and encouragement. It wouldn't take much to keep him from getting into trouble. And goddamn it, she was going to let him down. Let a bunch of kids just like him down. All because she hadn't been honest with Nate the first night they'd met. All because she hadn't been upfront with him when she'd made the decision to reach out to Travis.

"I think he'd love to watch you play," Chloe said through the thickness in her throat. "You're an excellent soccer player."

"Sometimes," Derrick said, his train of thought

already moving on to something else. "Coach says I need to kick with the top of my foot when I'm shooting, though."

"You'll get it," she said. "You just need to keep practicing."

"I will," he assured her. "I'm sorry I got into trouble today, Chloe. It won't happen again. I promise."

"I know," she said. Her chest ached with all of the crippling emotions she wished she didn't feel. Most of all, the want she felt for the only man who'd ever managed to lay claim to her heart and break it all in the same day.

TWELVE

"I've never seen a SEAL cower in the presence of an office building before."

Nate gave Travis the side-eye. It was true, Chloe's office had never looked more imposing, and his goddamned heart felt like it was going to burst out of his chest like one of those things in *Alien*. He hadn't heard a word from Chloe since he'd left the message on her voice mail five days ago. In fact, she'd washed her hands of the Christensens altogether, telling Travis that she didn't feel right accepting his donation after what had happened between her and Nate.

Fuck that. She might not have wanted to talk to him, but he refused to let her foundation close its doors. Like Travis said, it was time for Nate to think about the legacy he wanted to leave.

"You sure you don't want me to come in with you?" Travis teased.

"There's no use in both of us being thrown out. I'll be fine."

"Good luck, brother," Travis said. "Lunch later?"

"I have a pre–holiday break board meeting," Nate groused.

"Try not to sound so excited." Travis laughed. He put the Chevy in gear and waited for Nate to close the door.

"Yeah. That's easy for you to say. You don't have to sit through it."

"Damn straight. Good luck," Travis said as Nate shut the passenger door.

"Thanks." He was going to need it.

Nate drew in a deep breath and held it in his lungs. When they started to burn, he let the air out in a rush that made his brain buzz and his skin tingle. He pulled open the glass door and stepped up to the reception desk, piled high with banker's boxes and large manila envelopes. All he could see of the receptionist was the top of her blond head. "I'm here to see Chloe."

"Nate!"

A kid's voice called out from down the hallway and Nate turned to see Derrick rushing toward him. "Hey little man." Nate held out his fist and Derrick bumped it with his. "What's up?"

"Staying with Chloe," he said. "For a while, anyway."

Could that be why he hadn't heard from her? Nate could only hope that she'd ignored him not because she never wanted to see him again, but because she had her hands full. "Is Chloe here?"

"Yeah," Derrick said. "In her office."

Nate turned to the receptionist and she nodded. "Want me to buzz her?"

"No, that's all right." The last thing he needed was to give her the opportunity to throw him out before he could talk to her. "She's expecting me."

The receptionist gave him a suspicious glance but nodded slowly. "Okay, go ahead and go back."

"Do you think Chloe would let you get ice cream from the shop next door?" Nate asked Derrick.

"Sure. As long as I don't cross the street it's fine." He laughed. "Chloe acts like I can't take care of myself. I walked halfway across the city one time before anyone knew I was gone."

It was probably a good idea that Chloe keep a tight rein on the kid. Good lord. "Just for ice cream." Nate handed him a ten-dollar bill. "And then back here." The last thing he needed was for Chloe to find one more reason to hate him.

"Yes, sir," Derrick said with a crisp salute before he tore out of the office.

Nate headed down the hallway toward Chloe's office. *Dead man walking.* He knocked and her voice called from the other side of the door, "Come on in!"

He brought his palm up and laid it on the cool wood of the door and let his head hang between his shoulders. Anxiety crept up his spine, drawing his shoulders toward his ears. If she turned him away, it would ruin him. *She won't.* At least, he hoped.

Deep breaths. Nate pushed open the door and willed his thoughts and emotions to settle the fuck down. One look at Chloe and Nate was lost. Her hair was gathered up in a high, messy knot atop her head and she wore a pair of thick-framed glasses that gave her a decidedly naughty librarian look. Stress pulled at her expression and exhaustion weighed on her soft features, but damn. Nate didn't think she'd ever looked so beautiful.

"Hey."

Her brow furrowed and lips parted, soft and inviting. "Hey."

Nate had never felt so fucking awkward in his entire life. He would've rather stared down the barrel of a gun than meet the gaze of the woman sitting in front of him.

Words lodged in his throat. Stuck to his tongue and adhered themselves to the roof of his mouth. Maybe his actions would speak louder than words. He took the cashier's check he held in his hand and slid it across the desk toward her.

Chloe studied the check and her jaw took on a set that made Nate think his tactics were about to crash and burn. "What is this?" She waved the check at him. "You insinuate that I seduced you to get my hands on your money and then you drop a three-million-dollar check in front of me?"

Yup. Crash. And. Burn. *Fuck.*

The words Nate held back burst forth in a senseless rush. "Miranda was my fiancée." Chloe's expression softened somewhat and he continued on. "When she found out about my dad's philosophy—the whole 'be your own man' thing—our relationship got shaky. I stopped by the house one afternoon and I caught them together in his office. I enlisted the next day to get away from the both of them. That and the hurt and embarrassment. For the next six years, I blamed him for my life being shitty, for every bad thing that happened to me. I didn't want anything to do with him, Miranda, or that money that was so fucking much more important to her than I'd been. She chose my own father over me. For his *money.* So when Travis called that night, I freaked out."

Chloe's brow knitted but she no longer looked ready to chuck her stapler at him. "Nate." God, it cut through him whenever she said his name with tenderness. "I had no idea."

"The big, shameful family secret," he said on a sigh. "It doesn't excuse what I said to you or my behavior that night. I wanted you to know. That's all."

"And the check?" Chloe asked.

"You're a good person and you do good things for

people. I think you were right when you said that the money was my dad's way of apologizing. Travis says that I should use it to carve out my own name and my own legacy and that's what I'm doing. I don't want to see you have to shut down. I want to take care of this foundation." He brought his gaze to hers. "I want to take care of *you*. I love you, Chloe."

❄   ❄   ❄

He loves me. For days, she'd resisted the urge to pick up her phone and call him. To let him fill her mind and her heart with whatever excuse for his behavior that he wanted to give her. She never would have guessed the truth of it, though. Good lord. Miranda. Chloe had done extensive research on Byron Christensen when she'd courted him. Not even the best of the gossip mongers had known that the old man had run off with his son's fiancée. No wonder Nate had harbored so much resentment. Who wouldn't be emotionally scarred by that sort of betrayal?

Did that excuse the things he'd said to her though? Chloe didn't know if she could easily overcome the hurt that still speared through her chest every time she thought about it. Lying somewhere beneath her own pain though, was an indignation that sparked her temper. "She did that to you and you were going to give her everything? How could you have even considered the possibility?" His brow furrowed at her infuriated tone. "Seriously, Nate? That woman doesn't deserve a red cent of that money. Really, someone should kick her ass!"

A smile tugged at the corner of his mouth and Chloe's heart melted. A living work of art, there wasn't an inch of him that wasn't perfect. Not an inch of him she didn't ache to touch.

Nate came around to the side of the desk. Chloe sat

still as a statue, hands splayed out over the glossed chipboard surface. She didn't trust herself to move. Nate reached out and traced over the tops of her fingers. From the corner of her eye, she caught his lids droop. "Chloe." He said her name on a reverent sigh that sent her blood racing in her veins. "I miss you."

His touch tortured and excited her. She missed him, too. So much that she ached. He went to his knees beside her and Chloe turned her chair to face him as though she had no other choice but to respond to his gravitational pull. He reached out, threaded his fingers through the mass of her hair and brushed his thumb across her cheek.

"I'm fucked up, Chloe. I don't know how long it will be before I finally get a grip on the shit that messes with my head and screws with my emotions. I know I have a shitty temper. I'm not funny or easygoing. I'm trying to be better, though. I want to be better. For you. For us. I need you." His teeth clamped down into a grimace and his brow furrowed. "I can't get you out of my fucking head. I know it sounds crazy but I'm not going to deny it or play it down. I knew that first night we were together that I'd never get enough of you. I do love you, Chloe. I'll do whatever it takes to prove it to you."

Emotion clogged her throat. A flush rose to Chloe's cheeks and all of the breathable oxygen seemed to be sucked from the room. She leaned into Nate's touch. She couldn't help herself. The heat was a balm on her skin. With a trembling hand, she scooted the check over to him. "This will always be between us, Nate. I want you to have this money. Have wanted it for you all along. But after everything that's happened—everything I know now—you'll always wonder. I'll always wonder. And we'll grow to resent each other because of it."

"What are you talking about?"

"I don't want to be bought, Nate. And you don't want to be with someone who would allow herself to be."

"Now who's being stubborn?" A deep crease cut into his brow above the bridge of his nose. "You convinced me to keep this damned money, and now you're refusing to let me spend it the way that I want?"

"Can you really say that in the back of your mind you won't always wonder if I'm with you because of this check? Because I feel obligated somehow?"

"No," Nate said solemnly. "I *know* you, Chloe. I know you wouldn't put yourself in that position."

"You didn't think so the other night."

He let his hand drop from her face and pushed himself to stand. "You know why I freaked out the other night."

She didn't want to tear open wounds that were best left to scar. It wasn't fair to Nate or to her. Fear prompted her to do so. Chloe was afraid of the way he made her feel. The intensity of emotion he evoked in her. She was afraid that they'd never settle into a rhythm and their relationship would be spiked with highs and lows that would make them both miserable in the long run.

What scared her most was that despite all of her fears and doubts, Chloe wanted him more than she'd ever wanted anything in her entire life. The world melted away when Nate was near. She had so much on her plate right now. The foundation and now Derrick. Could she balance having Nate in her life and still maintain everything else?

"Derrick is staying with me," Chloe said. She didn't know why she blurted it out like that, maybe because she wanted to give Nate the opportunity to change his mind about wanting to be with her.

"I know," he said.

"How?"

"Saw the little man in the lobby. I sent him out for

ice cream. I love your big heart, Chloe. I love how much you care. Nothing you say is going to scare me off."

"I'm scared," Chloe whispered.

"I'm fucking terrified," Nate said. "The thought of not being with you *terrifies* me."

"I—I need some time." Chloe couldn't make a decision about what she wanted right now. There was too much going on. She needed to think everything through. Process what he'd said to her.

"I can give you that," Nate said. "I can give you *anything* you need."

Nate stood and headed for the door. Emotion tugged at Chloe's chest, as though Nate was about to take her heart out that door with him. "Nate, you should take the check. I meant what I said. Whatever happens, I don't want this money between us."

He turned around and strode to her desk. With his palms braced on the glossy surface, he leaned down to eye level. "You're keeping that money, Chloe. You can try and return it to me, but I'll just keep giving it back to you. And I think we both know I'm stubborn enough to do it."

His words coaxed a smile to her lips. "Nate." Tears sprung to her eyes and she couldn't speak louder than a whisper. "Thank you."

"I love you, Chloe," he said simply. "I'd do anything for you. *Anything.*" Nate turned and headed back to the door. He paused, hand gripping the knob. "We're having Christmas Eve dinner at Travis's house tonight. I want you and Derrick to come. Seven o'clock. Thirty-five twenty, Maple Creek Court." Without waiting for her to respond, he left.

Chloe picked up the check and smoothed her fingers over the crisp paper. Nate Christensen really was an extraordinary man and she'd be a fool to let him go.

THIRTEEN

"Behave yourself or I will have your butt, mister."

Derrick rolled his eyes as they walked under the portico to the looming front door of Travis Christensen's house. The kid had some serious 'tude, but Chloe planned to change that.

"You act like I'm not house-trained, Chloe. But *damn*, have you ever seen a house this big?"

"Language," Chloe warned.

"Yeah, okay. Think they have a butler?"

Chloe snorted. By the looks of the place, Travis probably ought to have one. Compared to Nate's run-down ranch house, this place was a palace. Chloe looked down at her black leggings and thigh-length sweater and felt suddenly underdressed. Maybe she should have reconsidered coming tonight. After all, she was sort of dropping in, despite Nate's invite. It's not like she'd told him she was coming.

"I have no idea," Chloe replied. "Just do me a favor. Say please and thank you and don't complain about the food."

"Please," Derrick said. "You should see the garbage my foster mom fed us for dinner. These guys could serve me a cow's butthole and I'd be happy about it."

"Oh my god, Derrick." Chloe resisted the urge to slap her palm against her forehead. "Language!"

"Oh, right." He gave her a sheepish grin. "Sorry."

He totally wasn't sorry.

Chloe reached out and rang the doorbell, fully expecting a butler to answer. The sound of male laughter filled her ears as the door swung wide. "Hey Chloe," Travis greeted with a knowing smile. "Glad you guys could make it."

Now it was Chloe's turn for a sheepish smile. "I hope this is okay that we're just dropping in. Nate invited us but—"

"I'm glad you're here," Travis said. "Nate's been a broody son of a bitch all night. Maybe this'll pull his mood out of the shitter." He winked at Derrick. Obviously, the Christensen brothers would do nothing to discourage Derrick's ornery streak. Boys will be boys, she supposed.

Travis ushered Derrick in ahead of Chloe and said, "The girls want to open presents after dinner. You game, little man?"

He turned and looked at Chloe with wide, expectant eyes. Her heart felt like it might burst in her chest. "Travis, you didn't—"

He answered her with a wink.

"You bet I'm game!" Derrick exclaimed. "Hey man, do you have a butler?"

The two walked farther ahead, Travis answering questions as fast as Derrick could lob them at him. She followed them through the foyer and into the vast living room. A giant Christmas tree decorated one corner of the room, the twinkling lights reflecting on the ceiling above. Two twin girls played near the tree, examining the colorfully wrapped boxes with gentle shakes. Travis led Derrick over and introduced him to the girls who waved sheepishly. They couldn't have been more than five or six, but Derrick took it in stride and joined them in their hunt for whose gifts were whose.

Chloe's gaze wandered to the opposite end of the living room. Grouped around a wet bar were Nate and the rest of his brothers. He looked up from the squat glass in his grip and a slow smile grew on his face as his eyes met hers.

"Thank god," Travis murmured at Chloe's side. "I was afraid he'd never snap out of it."

Chloe gave him a sideways glance and Travis nudged her. "Don't be shy. If you're going to be a part of this family, you'd better get used to hanging out with a bunch of boisterous jackasses."

She laughed. If the rest of Nate's brothers were as funny and easygoing as Travis, there was no doubt that she'd love them all. She loved their brother, after all.

Nate crossed the room toward her. The simple act held her rapt. She'd never seen a man walk with such predatory grace. Every move precisely placed. The individual muscles of his body rolled with every step and it took a conscious effort for Chloe to keep her mouth from hanging open on rusty hinges. Nate Christensen was *magnificent*.

He stopped mere inches from her. Chloe looked up to see into his face. His presence overwhelmed her and infused her with a delicious heat. How could she have ever thought she could stay away from him?

"Sorry I didn't call."

"Let's go out onto the patio and talk."

"Derrick—"

"Will be fine," Nate said. "Just for a minute. Please."

As though she had no control over her own body, Chloe let him lead her toward the paned French doors that led out to a wide covered patio. The nip of the December air soaked through her sweater but Chloe didn't know if it was the chill or the proximity of the man standing beside her that caused gooseflesh to rise on her skin.

"It's so pretty out here." White Christmas lights decorated the bushes and trees that dotted the yard while bright colored lights graced the hedges and the low stone wall that bordered the driveway.

"Travis did it for the girls," he said. "They love Christmas."

"You guys have each other's backs, don't you?"

"Always," Nate said. "But I didn't bring you out here to talk about my brothers."

Chloe turned to face him. Nate rattled her unlike any man ever had. His proximity intoxicated her until she swayed with drunken giddiness. "What did you bring me out here to talk about?"

❄   ❄   ❄

Nate stared down into Chloe's luminous green eyes. She thought a bunch of Christmas lights were pretty? Hell, all of the lights in the world didn't hold a candle to her beauty. "We didn't really get to finish our conversation today."

"We didn't?" she asked wryly. "I think you said more in those ten minutes than you've said since we met."

She joked to lighten the mood, but Nate wasn't interested in levity. Not when so much still hung in the balance. "I didn't say half of what I wanted to say."

"We don't have to do this tonight, Nate. It's Christmas Eve and everyone's inside waiting. I don't expect you to make a big scene for my benefit. I wouldn't be here tonight if I hadn't really listened to what you said today."

Nate wasn't good at apologies. He wasn't good at any of this emotional shit. He'd been dead since the day Miranda betrayed him and *finally* he felt like he was ready to join the land of the living. He was ready to quit wallowing in his own self-pity. He wanted to be happy. He wanted to heal from all of the tragedy that had weighed him down over the past few years.

"This isn't about making a scene. This is about making things right and starting fresh. I want you to know that I don't expect to pick right up where we left off," he said. Nate swallowed against the lump of emotion in his throat. The swell of hope that threatened to choke the air from his lungs. "I know that I need to earn your trust and respect back. That the things I said to you can't be fixed with a simple apology. I'm willing to take it slow, Chloe. I'm willing to do whatever it takes to win you back and to prove to you that I'll *never* disrespect you like that again."

She smiled up at him, the expression so soft that it melted Nate's heart. "Do you really think I could do what I do for a living and *not* believe in second chances, Nate?"

Relief washed over him. Nate lowered his mouth to Chloe's in a slow kiss. Her arms came around him as she rose on her toes and her body melted into his as though they were no longer two people, but a single form. They came slowly apart, their lips lingering. Nate murmured against her mouth, "I'll never give you a reason to have to give me a third chance."

"No one's perfect, Nate." She kissed him once, quickly. "I sure as hell don't expect you to be. Your love is all the reassurance I need."

"I do love you." He pulled away to gaze into her face, wanting her to see as well as hear his sincerity. "I didn't think I'd ever love anyone again, and you proved me wrong."

"I love you, too, Nate. I think I might've fallen in love with you that first night."

"In the coat closet?" he asked with a mischievous grin.

Chloe laughed. "Definitely in the coat closet."

From the window, Nate noticed Derrick waving them inside. "You've got a houseguest for a while, huh?"

"Yep. It might end up being permanent. Does that bother you?"

Nate grabbed Chloe's hand and twined his fingers with hers. "Absolutely not. I sort of like that little shit."

"Good." She squeezed his hand. "Because I sort of do, too."

When they didn't immediately go inside, Derrick threw open the door. "Hurry up, guys! Dinner's ready!" The kid looked ready to gnaw his own arm off. "You should see the spread, Chloe. So much better than a cow's asshole!"

Nate couldn't control his laughter and it spluttered from his lips.

"Language!" Chloe shouted, but the kid was already hightailing it for the dining room.

"So," Nate began as he pulled open the door for her. "Did you cash my check?"

"Are you kidding?" Chloe said with a laugh. "I deposited that bad boy fifteen minutes after you left."

"Good. I can't wait to see what you'll do with it."

"Oh, I have plans," she said archly. "First things first, I think we need a new name."

"Yeah? What were you thinking?"

They headed to the dining room where Nate's brothers

and the kids were settling down at the table. Chloe paused to look at him. "I want to call it the Nate Christensen Foundation."

Nate smoothed a thumb over her cheek. "I didn't give you that money for bragging rights, darlin'."

Her gaze went liquid and it stirred Nate's blood. Goddamn, he'd never met a more amazing woman. "I know that," she said, low. "Like you said, this money is about your legacy. I want this to be the start of it."

"You two ready to eat?" Carter asked as he got his girls situated and set up with plates. "Or would you rather stand at the head of the table and make goofy faces at each other all night? I mean, I'm okay with that; I'm sure we could all use the entertainment."

Nate threw his brother a look. "Hush." He placed a quick kiss at Chloe's temple. "I love you."

"It's a damned good thing, too," she replied. "Because you're never getting rid of me."

Nate led her to the table and pulled out a chair. Chloe took a seat next to Derrick and he eased her in toward the table. "Good. Because you're not getting rid of me, either."

Peace settled over Nate's heart and soul. He had everything he'd ever need right here in this room. And he was never letting any of it go. Finally, life was good.

Looking for more great reads about the Billionaire's Club?

Don't miss Mandy Baxter's

Tall, Dark, *Billionaire* Texan

Stories include:

The *Billionaire* Cowboy
The *Billion* Dollar Player
Rocked by the *Billionaire*
The *Billionaire* Sheriff

From St. Martin's Paperbacks